OBEDIENT
UNTO DEATH

Roger,
May you enjoy
your journey into
ancient Ephesus.
Blessings
Lisa

OBEDIENT
UNTO DEATH

LIISA EYERLY

ST JOSEPH, MISSOURI USA

Editor: Debra L. Butterfield
Cover Design: Tamara Clymer
Cover Image: ID 100619264 © Evgeny Ustyuzhanin | Dreamstime.com

Printed in the United States of America.

To my parents, who nurtured my love for the Lord.

ONE

The harbor lantern's flame flickered behind the two men blocking the entrance to the narrow alley. Black silhouettes of muscles and brawn quavered on the back street's crumbling brick wall like undulating cobras lured from the charmer's baskets at the market agora. The two men shifted uneasily. "If we catch her, she's mine," a deep voice boomed, echoing down the tunneled alleyway.

"Says you. I wouldn't mind a bit of fun." The men edged forward slowly. They paused, squinting into the gloom of the evening fog. A glint of metal flashed in one man's hand.

Halfway down the alley, Sabina squeezed, flattening her body into the concealing threshold of the abandoned boarded-up doorway. Her head turned a fraction. A jagged splinter of wood gouged her cheek. She blinked back tears, ignoring the sting. *Don't get caught.* Her father's threat resounded in her ears.

Her eyes riveted on the advancing men. It was too dark to tell if they were the imperial governor's watchmen or criminals fouling the streets of Ephesus. If caught, the result would be the same. She was a woman alone, and the last thing she could do was confess the truth.

A coarse laugh hurtled toward her down the constricted passage.

She clamped her mouth shut as the men bore down on her, the scuffle of hardened leather sandals approached. Her throat tightened.

She prayed the charcoal-gray mantle covering her tunic blended into the murky shadows of the shallow portal. It would not hide her for long. She was sure her clattering teeth resounded off the ancient walls. Sabina bit her lip. If she had any hope of escaping, she needed to run, now.

A chorus of snarls erupted a dozen feet from her, near a pile of putrid fish guts. She stifled a scream.

Her stomach had recoiled moments earlier when the moving mound of garbage exposed a trio of half-starved dogs, teeth bared, blocking her way. Scraping against the wall, she had sidled past, cooing words of friendship. Now hackles raised, the animals crouched aggressively, defending their supper from two new invaders.

"You've got us chasing a pack of mongrels," a raspy voice jeered. "I always knew you favored scabby bitches."

"Shut up."

One dog barked. The other two snarled, taking wary steps toward the men.

"You wanted her. The devil dog's all yours." The first man sniggered. "I'm out of here."

"I said, shut up." The crude banter continued as the men shoved and jostled each other.

Sabina's eyes locked on the backs of the men as they spun around. Her heart pounded in sync with their clomping retreat. The squawking of sea birds heading home late to their newly born chicks broke through her fear. Slowly, she peeled her fingers from the wall and prayed the men would not return. Please, God.

She stepped back, testing her wobbly legs. The evening mist rising from the Aegean Sea clung to her face and crept down her back, setting her teeth chattering again.

Her father would be furious with her. She would, of course, never tell him how close she came tonight to fulfilling his greatest fear. Death was preferable to losing his family honor and equestrian status, forfeiting his wealth, banishment, and humiliation—all risks if Sabina's illegal worship were made public. *You will drag our family to hell with your false God.* She had stormed out of the house

8

tonight, his warning reverberating in her ears. It did not matter who discovered her traitorous act. Two harbor rats would do just fine. Legs shaking, she turned and leaned her head against the wall. Well, she hadn't gotten caught—this time.

She didn't mistake the powerful Roman magistrate's admonition as concern for his only child. Sabina knew better. Since the death of her mother in childbirth twenty years ago, "the family" meant him, and "hell" was his assessment of his dead wife and eight-year-old daughter's bizarre new religion.

There would be no harmony in their home until she stopped worshipping Jesus, the Messiah. Was peace with her father possible? Was his approval worth giving up her faith? How many times had she asked herself that? Her fingernails bit into her palms. Knowing if her father forbade her, she would have no choice.

She shrunk from the doorway and drew the wool covering over her head, tucking the thick braid of russet hair securely out of sight.

Throaty growls reverberated along the stone walls, raising the hairs on her arms. Three pairs of yellow eyes lifted, glittered warily, fixed on her.

She backed away slowly. "Shhh, my guardian angel dogs. I'm not after your dinner." The dogs slunk back to the delicacy of their rotted fish.

She approached the back gate of a villa moments later. She fumbled for the latch, then pulled her hand back; she could turn around and go home. Family unity was still a choice. Somebody had scratched a crude fish symbol into the wood above her head. A sign of the Christ, a symbol of peace. Peace? She stifled a grim laugh and lifted the cold iron latch.

The villa stood prominently between two large harbor warehouses and across the cobblestone street from other villas fronting shops and businesses. No villa located within this square insula was as large or as opulent as the home of this successful silk trader and his wife, Portia, Sabina's closest friend. Sabina slipped through the opening, brushing aside the thin branches of a laurel tree. Ahead of her, a narrow rectangle of light silhouetted the back door of the villa's kitchen. She hurried past the emerging shoots in the kitchen garden and reached the door.

It sprang open. An older woman carrying a bucket collided with Sabina. "Eeeii!" The woman screamed; her eyes flared wide. The bucket crashed to the ground, and liquid splashed Sabina as the bucket rolled to a stop.

Sabina yelped and stumbled back, recognizing the kitchen servant. "Feya, it's me." Sabina dropped the head-covering onto her shoulders.

"I'm sorry. I'm jumpy as a grasshopper. What with Mistress Portia overseeing the feast for tonight's worship."

"It's a special celebration." Sabina shook water drops from her tunic. She bent and picked up the bucket and handed it to the trembling woman.

"I'm not complaining." Feya slumped, hugging the bucket to her chest. "I just got bad feelings coming on."

"We're all taking precautions." Sabina understood Feya's worry. Preoccupied with thoughts of the argument with her father, she had stormed from her house. Not taking her usual precautions, she could have led those men to Portia's back door, exposing Portia's family and the congregation she and her husband, Horace, hosted. *Don't get caught.* Her father's warning took on new gravity. If the authorities discovered this place of worship, they would arrest them.

She rarely allowed her emotions to distract her. She was usually logical, precise. Each time Sabina came for worship, she varied her route. Every member did—a reminder of the danger they courted. Yet Sabina came—tonight, and every time she had a chance.

"I know we're careful." Feya shook her head. "Apollos says God protects His faithful but…" The older woman raised her hand and made a pagan gesture to ward off evil spirits.

Sabina frowned. "Prayer is our power."

Feya pinched her lips together. "Then why didn't God save Procurius and his family? They were careful and were arrested last week and martyred. Even his children."

"We live in a world full of hate and sin. Christians aren't excluded. Surely, you feel God's comfort and strength when you pray?"

"I do. I'm solid as a rock in the Lord, and He is in me, but I'm telling you, Procurius is on my mind."

Procurius had been on Sabina's mind as well. "He lived miles away in Smyrna. The magistrates here in Ephesus are unaware of our meetings." Except for Sabina's father, who, for now, chose to look the other way. But disclosing a Roman magistrate knew of their Christian activities would not comfort the woman.

"I pray for the day when Christ returns. Apollos says it's soon. Not soon enough for me." Feya grumbled, raised her hand in the superstitious sign, looked at Sabina, and lowered her arm.

"I, too, look to the day we don't suffer for our beliefs. Until then, we pray for God's protection." She thought of the two men she had escaped from and said a silent prayer of thanks before stepping past Feya and into the villa's bustling kitchen.

The acrid smoke from the oven's fire struck her nostrils seconds before the earthy aroma of baking bread. The chaos of cooking preparations churned around her. She closed her mouth and inhaled, blinking away the sting of smoke. She focused on the tranquility of the enveloping heat as muscles relaxed. She exhaled her tension and fear of harbor watchmen. Not the peace of this world, but the peace and joy found in Jesus drew her here to worship, sing praises, and pray to her God.

"Bring the baskets. The bread's ready." Portia popped up from peeking into the oven. She pushed her bright red hair out of her face, her porcelain skin flushed from the heat of the flames. "Feya, have the mussels been steamed?"

"Yes, as you directed, an hour ago."

"Sabina." Portia flew toward her. The pale green silk of her floor-length tunic swirled, caressing her willowy figure. No one would guess she was twenty years Sabina's senior. "God's peace." Portia moved to greet her friend with a kiss, stopped, and frowned. "Your cheek is bleeding."

Feya spun around, lips pinched tight, expertly balancing two steaming loaves on a wooden paddle.

Sabina rubbed the jagged line of dried blood. "It's a scratch." She batted away Portia's concern.

Portia raised an eyebrow. "You're later than usual."

"I was held up." Sabina felt Feya's eyes watching her as the servant dumped the loaves into waiting baskets. "It's nothing to worry about." She wouldn't dampen the celebration the congregation had been planning for months. "I'm here now. What can I do to help?" Sabina grabbed a basket Feya had laden with hot bread and hoisted it onto her hip.

Portia lifted a second basket. "Follow me," she responded with an undercurrent of *You're not getting away that easy.*

Sabina trailed Portia down a short hallway and onto the covered colonnaded walkway bordering the villa's expansive interior garden. Palm trees bordered a large pond with a life-size bronze dolphin fountain in the middle. Crystal clear water gushed in a perfect arch from its blowhole. When visiting as a child with her mother, Sabina, had been mesmerized by the shimmering dolphin. Back then, their church family had consisted of a dozen people, and Sabina's mother, Korinna, and Portia became friends. When the emperor Nero began persecuting the followers of Christ, Korinna hid her faith to protect Sabina's father and his prominent government position. Portia guarded the secret for mother and daughter. Since Korinna's death, Christians had become more detestable and her father's political rivals more ruthless.

Sabina skipped aside, dodging a slave girl hurrying past juggling a large platter and two pitchers.

She spotted several plants she had cultivated and given to Portia. "Last fall's plants survived." A spindly grouping of pale green spikes would be a glorious border of purple hyacinth in another month. "This year, I will expand your herb garden. I just discovered some delicious Egyptian mint."

"Are you trying to avoid explaining what happened to your cheek?" Portia's eyebrow lifted in concern.

"I scratched it while evading a couple of harbor rats." Sabina smiled in a way she hoped reassured her friend.

Portia stopped and spun around. "Oh, Sabina, you take too many chances."

Sabina skipped around her. "I'm fine. They didn't see me. What about the mint plants?"

Portia shook her head. "I'll speak to my gardener."

Sabina followed Portia around a corner, through the atrium, and into a spacious dining room. Two slaves circled the large room. One lowered the chain of a hanging oil lamp while the other slave lit the wick, then hoisted it to join the other dozens of lamps casting glittering spheres of light into the dark corners.

A group of young mothers watched and laughed as four small children chased one another around the dining tables, their sandals slapping on the black and white mosaic floor.

A newly married young man lingered near the door. His wife, Iris, appeared several minutes later, arriving from a different direction. "God's peace to you, sisters in Christ," she greeted Sabina and Portia.

"God's peace." Sabina nodded and watched as families arrived at staggered intervals. Hopefully, they avoided the attention of curious neighbors or alert city officials. She recalled the slave's worries. Were their safeguards enough?

Eight low tables, each surrounded by six floor cushions, were arranged to view a small wooden altar at the far end of the room, the top adorned with a seven-branched silver candelabra and a linen cloth covering tonight's attraction.

The room hummed with conversation and relaxed laughter. Families arrived carrying bowls and covered platters and placed them on tables, then joined gatherings of friends.

"It appears everyone is coming tonight," Portia hefted her breadbasket.

"After months of waiting, our assembly is starved to hear the Isaiah scroll read." Sabina felt a shiver of excitement as she scanned the room. People crowded around the tables and overflowed, sitting along walls. Her fellow believers were eager to learn and grow in this new faith.

"'Man shall not live by bread alone, but by every word that proceeds from the mouth of God.'"

"A lot to consume. I heard it is twelve feet long."

"It is a lengthy book." Portia nodded. "God's words spoken to the prophet Isaiah over eight hundred years ago will come alive for us tonight."

Sabina pulled Portia aside, away from the noisy activity. "I pray God's wisdom will speak to me tonight. I need divine guidance." She shifted her basket from one hip to the other and pulled a small roll of papyrus from a pouch inside her tunic.

"You have heard from your merchant again."

"He is not my merchant..." The image of the stocky trader came to mind. Barely an inch taller than she, with bulging rocks for muscles from his years of sailing. "But yes, Marcus sent this."

The letter unsettled her, much like a newly hatched brood of pigeons. She couldn't help but think about the possibilities, joys, and complications. But unlike her loyal, dependable birds, humans were unpredictable.

"A love letter?" Portia's eyebrows raised.

Sabina's smile evaporated. "Marcus requested a private dinner." She unrolled the letter. She had been surprised by his communication. At twenty-eight, Sabina's marriage prospects had dwindled to zero. And her advanced age was not the only reason. "I have had no suitors since my husband's death eight years ago when everyone in Ephesus agreed I had caused Xeno's death on our wedding night."

"Not everyone...only the superstitious," Portia chided.

"Apparently, any potential suitors are superstitious. I dare not hope Marcus is different."

"Then you suspect a marriage proposal?"

"No. I've only met Marcus twice when Father invited him to his dinner parties." Sabina closed her eyes for a moment and smiled before answering. "I enjoyed myself more than I expected."

"More than your father's usual dinner parties?"

"I was intrigued by Marcus's company."

"Not attracted?"

Sabina shook her head. "Flattered. He sought me out and ignored the other guests. Even Felicia."

"Your beautiful fourteen-year-old neighbor?"

"She flirted with him mercilessly." Sabina's brows knit, remembering Felicia's coy smiles and timid touches. "A skill I will never master."

"A little seduction never hurts."

Sabina frowned.

"But it appears unnecessary here," Portia shrugged. "I believe you have a suitor."

"Perhaps not. Marcus returns home to Rome at the end of the week."

"I understand your determination to be out from under your father's guardianship. I advise prudence until you know more about him."

"I have a week. As far as I know, he wants our cook's recipe for boiled flamingo. He complimented my father on it multiple times." Was God only taunting her with a chance of a husband and home of her own? Sabina had never imagined a life alone at this age—hosting her father's social engagements, dutifully running his household. Women were supposed to be surrounded by their children and, at age twenty-eight, grandchildren. Examining her current life circumstances disoriented her. Where did a woman fit in when the purpose of her life appeared inaccessible?

Portia wagged her finger. "You are a widow, not a pariah. You have time." Portia had a gift of encouragement. Sabina usually relied on her advice. Not all marriages were a blessing.

"Do I? You were a grandmother at my age, independent, successful, and—"

"That's the same argument you gave me when you married Xeno." Portia held up her hand, cutting off any argument. "We each have a path to travel. Trust that God has a plan for your life and Marcus's."

"I know." Xeno had been a polite suitor, but fifty-eight years old, financially strapped, overweight, and afflicted with gout. He had offered to marry her for her dowry. The union had turned tragic when Xeno died the night of the wedding. Sabina, and her generous dowry, returned to her father's house, a widow, a virgin, and the populace believing she carried a curse.

"Does Marcus support your Christian faith?"

Sabina blinked rapidly. "We haven't had time to discuss that," she said defensively.

Portia frowned and leveled a steady gaze at Sabina. "You haven't had time?"

"Of course, I will…" Sabina looked away. Portia didn't understand. She hadn't experienced the isolation of an only child, the ostracism after a husband's suspicious death, or the following eight lonely years of widowhood. And yet, Sabina couldn't help wondering if veering off God's path and ignoring His plan for her had cost her a lifelong partner.

A scurrying child slipped and collided with Sabina and crashed to the floor. He screamed. Tears mixing with mucus ran down his face. Sabina plunked the basket down and bent over to help the child up.

Wiping his nose, he swatted her hand away and yelled louder.

Sabina grimaced at the slime smearing her hand. "Eeww," she said, wrinkling her nose. She stood up and stared into the eyes of the small boy's heavily pregnant teenage mother.

"I'm sorry." The young woman's expression tightened. She pressed her lips together. She picked up the crying toddler. His sobs quieted into hiccups as he dried his face, wiping his nose across her shoulder. "I know children can be a bother…when you don't have any yourself."

Sabina's tight smile absorbed the slight. "I love children." She clasped her hands together, trying to ignore the slick mucus on her palms. "I didn't mean…" Sabina's voice faded away as the young woman nodded skeptically and turned her back, but not before Sabina saw her rolling her eyes.

The mother waddled back to her group of friends, jostling her son on her hip. Their honored ranks closed around the brood of youngsters in the universal camaraderie of motherhood. As the young mother had pointed out, Sabina, an only child, had no experience with children. A familiar awkwardness swept over her.

"I offended her." Sabina rubbed her hands vigorously on the hem of her tunic. The mothers were giggling. She stopped and stared at her sticky fingers and picked up the basket, clenching the handle.

Portia reached out and gently released the basket from Sabina's grip. "I think she's over it. Young mothers are extra-sensitive about their firstborn. After her second baby, her attitude will change. Besides, she doesn't know you as well as I do."

"What does that mean?" Sabina narrowed her eyes.

"It means people can count on your honesty and straightforward advice and action. It's your gift and one of the many reasons I love you."

"My childhood nurse, Amisi, would call that tactless, opinionated, and inconsiderate."

"Opinionated, perhaps. Tactless, sometimes. But inconsiderate—never." Portia tipped her head toward the bevy of young mothers. "Your concern for her feelings when you did nothing wrong proves my point."

"Life would be easier if I weren't so...what, did you call me? Tactless." Sabina sighed.

"Direct." Portia's mouth curved in a sympathetic smile. "And conscientious and kind." Portia returned the breadbasket to Sabina and gave her arm a quick squeeze. "Come to my house tomorrow. We shall discuss what marriage advice we receive tonight from Benjamin's eight-hundred-year-old sage." Portia winked just as a young servant boy knocked a bowl of grapes off the table. "Oh dear, I should go and—"

"Be tactful, sensitive, considerate." Sabina smiled.

Portia laughed. "I acknowledge my gifts." She sauntered off, looking unruffled as always.

During Sabina's childhood, Portia had changed from a mentor into a friend. A friend Sabina hadn't listened to eight years ago when, wishing to escape from her father's control, Sabina had prayed but ignored Scripture's warning of marrying an unbeliever.

Now, eight years wiser, Sabina had promised herself she would listen to Portia's advice and diligently pray for God's guidance, precisely what she was doing tonight. Besides, Marcus was only nine years older than she, and his masculine physique and witty banter attracted her, as had his polite but firm rebuff of Felicia. No matter what Portia said, Sabina was running out of time.

She watched as laughing, close-knit families filled the tables in the dining room.

Marcus's letter could be her deliverance.

A dozen overflow worshippers reclined along the walls. She wound her way through a jostling of bodies, greeting friends she'd known all her life as well as the new believers she was getting to know. The church was growing. She counted nearly sixty people.

Sabina claimed an empty place at a back table.

The clanking of dishes almost obscured a rhythmic tapping nearby.

Benjamin, a quiet and reserved scribe, sat cross-legged on a floor cushion at the table across from her. His fingers danced on the tabletop.

Tap, tap, tap.

Sabina made her way to him and placed the basket of bread on his table. "God's peace to you, Benjamin. Shouldn't you be sitting in front by the altar?"

"I prefer here." The young man's drumming stopped. He grabbed his cup. His hands trembled.

"Excited?"

His brows knotted, and he dipped his head. "Yes, a little." He licked his lips and took a sip. "Mostly, I'm…nervous."

Sabina arched her brows. "It is a special night for you. Naturally, you would feel that way."

"There are so many people. It's tiring." His timid smile appeared forced.

"It will be over soon." She understood, too well, the discomfort of scrutiny, the emotional toll of duty. How many times had she retreated to the rooftop solitude of her father's pigeon loft? The birds' welcoming chortles were a respite, first for a lonely child and now a bewildered adult. "Try to relax and enjoy the evening." She bit her tongue, repeating Portia's advice to her. "We are all eager to hear the words of God read from your scroll."

"You are kind, but I only copied it." Benjamin smiled, his cheeks turning pink, his pride visible.

An older man with dark brown skin and tight curly black hair strode toward the table. "'For this reason, we also thank God without ceasing, because when you received the word of God which you heard from us, you welcomed it not as the word of men, but as it is in truth, the word of God, which also effectively works in you who believe.'"

"Brother Apollos," Benjamin said, standing and greeting the man with a kiss. "God's word to the Thessalonian believers."

"Benjamin, your memory of scripture is perfect as usual." Apollos turned to Sabina and clasped her hands. "Blessings, Sabina." He kissed her cheek, frowning at the scratch.

"I am well," she reassured as she clasped Bishop Apollos's hands. A rush of warmth flooded her at the return squeeze from the genial soul, whose trimmed black beard sprinkled with silver threads hid the burgeoning wrinkles of age.

Apollos's eyes lit up as he gestured toward Benjamin. "Sabina, are you looking forward to the scripture reading tonight as much as I am?"

"It is an amazing accomplishment for a scribe, so—" Sabina stopped before saying *young*. She did not know him well. Benjamin could not be much younger than she, though his thin frame, smooth olive skin, and shy demeanor projected the innocence of an adolescent.

"A scribe so talented." Apollos smoothed over the awkward hush. "We are blessed that such a gifted scholar chose to belong to our body of believers."

Benjamin's color deepened from pink to red before he dropped his head.

"Before I embarrass you more," Apollos squeezed Benjamin's shoulder, "I must prepare for our meal."

Apollos took his leave, and Benjamin sat on his cushion. When he looked up, his gaze passed over Sabina. His features tightened into a scowl.

Sabina turned in the direction of his gaze just as someone stepped on her sandal. "Ouch." She turned. "Magnus," she groaned as the heavy-set man shoved past her without apology. Uncharitable thoughts flew through her mind while rubbing her aching foot, *rude, ill-mannered, boorish.*

Magnus plunked his bulk down, half sitting on Benjamin and pinning him under a fleshy thigh. He reached for a wine cup, crushing Benjamin as he leaned forward. Magnus's elbow collided with Benjamin's throat, deadening Benjamin's yelp. Wine sloshed from the cup, splattering both men.

Magnus glared at Benjamin and then gazed into the empty cup, expecting more wine to appear magically. "You spilled my wine," Magnus thundered.

People nearby stared.

Benjamin's face flushed the same rose color as the wine. "That was my cup," Benjamin said with a note of defiance as he dabbed the speckles blooming red on his white tunic.

Magnus clambered onto his knees and reached for a pitcher across the table, elbowing Benjamin in the stomach.

"Magnus, stop it." Gallus, an Elder of the church, ordered from across the table. "Move." He pointed to Sabina's table as if directing a child.

"There's no room," Magnus said.

Sabina's jaw clenched. "I'll sit on the floor." Sabina grabbed her mantle from the neighboring table's cushion. "An empty seat." She brandished, controlling the urge to stomp on Magnus's foot herself.

Magnus grunted, shoving against Benjamin as Magnus heaved himself up.

Benjamin looked exhausted. His previously flushed cheeks glistened a chalky white. He rubbed his temples. "I'm so very sorry. I will move." His hands trembled; his pupils darkened, making him look even more vulnerable.

Sabina clenched her fists. Contention followed Magnus like skunk spray. "Don't apologize for Magnus. Tonight is your night. Stay there." Sabina plopped down against the wall.

Apollos clapped his hands, and the congregation quieted. "'We give thanks to the LORD, for he is good, and his love endures forever.'"

The members joined in chanting a psalm of thanksgiving. Baskets of bread, platters of mussels and fish, and bowls of olive oil passed from hand to hand down the tables. Slaves and servants circulated, passing out food to those seated along the walls and refilling pitchers of watered-down wine. Conversations muffled as mouths filled.

Sabina balanced a plate on her lap while relishing her last bite of tuna. She glanced at Benjamin. A glistening trickle of sweat snaked down his nose, beading on his upper lip. He swiped at it then dried his palms on his tunic.

He refused more wine and pushed his untouched food away. Nervous? Anxious? Ill?

The meal ended. Sabina joined the other worshipers as they pushed away empty dishes. Several women joined the household slaves scooping up and scraping greasy platters, stacking them before carting them to the kitchen. They returned, settling in and joining the rest of the congregation. The dining room transformed into a holy sanctuary.

Conversations fell silent, and mothers quieted their children. Heads turned toward the altar.

Sabina eyed the sacred text shimmering in the flickering oil light. Smoke from the altar's seven candles swirled around it as if alive.

Apollos unsheathed a knife and lifted the scroll. He sliced through the three wax seals guaranteeing the accuracy and authenticity of Benjamin's work. He smiled at Benjamin. "We thank you for the gift of God's message given to his people. Benjamin, believers will read your scroll tonight and a thousand nights hereafter."

Benjamin raised his head, this time acknowledging the praise with a feeble smile. His eyes glittered unnaturally bright. He swayed, and his smile tightened into a grimace. Was she the only one who noticed?

Apollos unrolled one side of the hefty manuscript. His finger moved down the scroll to his chosen verse. "The word of our Lord."

The congregation responded, attention fixed on their bishop. "'Man does not live by bread only, but by every word that proceeds out of the mouth of the LORD.'"

Sabina watched Benjamin. Creases of apprehension lined his face.

Apollos began reading.

"'All flesh is grass, and all its loveliness is as the flower of the field.'"

Benjamin dropped his napkin. He gasped and gripped the edge of the table, his fingers turning white. He groaned.

Sabina shot up. Something's wrong.

"'The grass withers, the flower fades: because the breath of the LORD blows upon it: surely the people are grass.'"

Benjamin doubled over.

"'The grass withers, the flower fades: but the word of our God shall stand forever.'"

He struck his head on the edge of the table. A wine pitcher toppled on its side, spilling its contents, and rolled toward the edge of the table. Apollos stopped reading.

"Benjamin!" Sabina raced over and dropped to her knees, grabbing at his arm.

Two men rushed to her side. Heads turned in her direction.

Benjamin vomited down the front of his tunic. His eyes rolled back as his body convulsed, jerking violently from her grasp.

Sabina fumbled for him. His robe flitted through her fingers as he slid to the floor. His weight fell against her and dropped her to her knees. She shielded his head as they tumbled to the floor. Somewhere in the back of her consciousness, more people were standing and moving toward her. She heard the scroll crash to the floor.

The empty wine pitcher reached the table's end, dropped, and shattered on the tiles—stinging shards sprayed Sabina's hands.

Spittle bubbled out onto Benjamin's chin. With one last spasm, Benjamin crumpled to Sabina's lap.

TWO

Sabina plucked feebly at Benjamin's robe. "Benjamin?" She stared blankly at the unresponsive man who had collapsed in her arms. Her mind swirled as if caught in an eddy, unable to land on a beneficial or constructive action.

Several people hurried over, concerned or curious. Magnus stood, his mouth gaping like a fish in the sand, pushed aside a woman next to him, and wormed his way back into the crowd.

"Coward," Sabina muttered exasperatedly. Her ire spurred her to action. She shifted Benjamin off her lap while juggling his sagging body to keep it from crashing to the floor.

"Let me through. Let me through." Apollos, arms flailing, pushed his way past the onlookers. People shuffled aside, making an opening. Two men followed on his heels.

"Move back, people. Give Benjamin space to breathe," said one of the men pushing the crowd back.

Gallus, the Elder, sitting across the table, hoisted himself up. He hobbled around the table, flapping his arms. "Move back! Benjamin's fainted. He needs air."

Murmured ripples of "fainted" spread Gallus's diagnosis to those outside the inner circle. Heads shook, brows furrowed, and necks craned before those in the front shuffled back a few steps.

Sabina nearly lost her balance as Apollos braced against her, dropping to his knees.

"Lift him upright, Sabina." Apollos tore open Benjamin's outer robe.

"I'm trying," she panted, tugging at poor Benjamin's arms as Apollos pulled the inert man's robe aside.

"I'll help." Gallus tottered over and painstakingly knelt beside Apollos.

Magnus's voice rumbled through the crowd. "He's drunk."

"No," Apollos barked, "Benjamin must have choked on something. Sabina, help me sit him up."

Sabina, Apollos, and Gallus hefted Benjamin's drooping body and propped him against the table.

The two nearby men shooed people back.

"Sabina, hold his neck steady," Apollos ordered. "Gallus, open his mouth."

Hurry. Sabina pinched her lips tight as she stiffened her grip. Leveraging all her weight, she pushed against Benjamin's shoulder. Their saving efforts were taking too long.

Apollos moved his finger in and around to dislodge whatever Benjamin had swallowed. Removing his finger, he shook his head. "Something must have gotten stuck farther down his throat."

"He's not breathing," Sabina said.

She heard a slight gasp, "Lord, help him." Louder mummers and shuffling from the people surrounding them broke through the drama engulfing her.

"Don't let the children see."

"Magnus saw him getting drunk."

"Did you hear him choking?"

"Turn him on his side," Gallus suggested. The two men close by struggled to help Sabina and Apollos rotate and hold the motionless body.

Gallus slapped Benjamin between the shoulder blades. Benjamin's head jerked forward with each smack. Several people looked away. After one thudding slap, a man fainted.

When nothing happened, Apollos took over, pushing against Benjamin's stomach. He pressed rapidly, then slowed, then stopped.

Tears glistened like silver drops in the somber black of his beard. "Gallus! Sabina! Help me," he begged.

Sabina felt a gentle pressure on her arm.

Portia knelt beside Benjamin. Her eyes avoided the body. She pressed her fingers against Benjamin's neck, staring at Sabina and away from Benjamin's face. "There's no pulse." Blood drained from her face. Portia put her hand on Apollos's shoulder. "Our Lord has taken him…" her voice broke. She rose and moved away from the body. "Taken him home. I'm sorry, I don't handle death well."

Sabina looked up. Even steadfast Portia shuddered at this reminder of our mortality.

"No." Apollos covered his face with his hands and muffled his sobs.

"Benjamin is dead," Gallus announced, his voice quivering.

The pronouncement broke the shocked congregation's spell—the knees of a man standing closest gave way. His wife caught him before he fell. They staggered away from the body. A woman gasped; another began to cry. People murmured and clasped their hands in prayer—a muted reprise of "choked" floated through the subdued assembly.

Sabina released her grip, and Benjamin's body sagged forward, slithering toward the floor. She reached out to stop it, but Portia's announcement had drained all energy from her. The table stopped the fall for one moment, leaving Benjamin propped up grotesquely against the edge of the low dining table before the final tumble to the floor.

A hollow, empty ache made Sabina feel ill. She had just witnessed a man dying—a young man whom she had spoken to minutes before. She wiped a tear hanging off the tip of her nose. What had happened?

Gallus struggled to stand. Sabina stood on trembling legs and offered her hand. She and Gallus stretched Benjamin's crumpled body flat on the floor.

Portia, subdued and pale, edged away from the corpse, trembling as if death might reach out and touch her.

Sabina's stomach began to settle. She surveyed the body, the table, the shattered wine pitcher. What had just happened? Obviously an accident or some mysterious illness. Any other conclusion was unthinkable.

People shuffled away from Benjamin's body— distancing themselves from Benjamin's mortality and, she suspected, their own. Some cried; a group of five people was on their knees, praying; others knelt alone, eyes closed, sobbing quietly; some sat silently in shock.

"Quiet. Benjamin isn't feeling well." A parent shuttled his children from the tragic scene.

Worshipers drifted from the room, leaving others to sort out the details of death and dying. "He looked fine when I saw him," one whispered.

"Was he eating fish stew? I had the fish stew. I don't feel well."

"A bit sudden for bad fish, don't you think?"

Whether an accident or illness, this death underscored her father's warning. They had argued over Procurius's execution in Smyrna. Her father had threatened to ban her worship before something happened to expose her association with the Christians in Ephesus. She had lashed back that nothing was going to happen.

A sour burning simmered in her stomach. There had to be an explanation for the unease that made her want to vomit right now—a simple reason why a man had died tonight.

Gallus wheezed and waved Sabina over. "Help me get Apollos to the bench."

Sabina stared into Benjamin's wide-open eyes, their once-warm luminous radiance, now sludge brown hollows in a muddy grave. She didn't know what had caused Benjamin's death. But one fact she knew for sure—he hadn't choked because he had not been eating. Life's harshness ended lives much younger than Benjamin's. However, hardship did not account for the circumstance of his skin's strange yellow pallor or the swift brutality of his death.

If Benjamin wasn't drunk, and he had not choked, what was left? Could he have eaten poison inadvertently? A poisonous plant? Deadly fish?

Sliding her arm under Apollos's quaking body, she helped Portia and Gallus lead him to a bench.

"I'm fine. Thank you." The ordinarily robust leader's voice broke, his swarthy skin now a faded gray.

"You're not fine. You're shaking uncontrollably." Portia gently pushed him to the bench.

Sabina bit back her words. She thought of Procurius and his children. None of them would be fine until they found out how and why Benjamin died. Until then, they were all vulnerable. No one could admit to what Benjamin was doing tonight without risking arrest. No one could explain his death without implicating themselves. The authorities would demand to know who was with him.

Don't get caught, Sabina.

She could not afford to leave it alone. Perhaps someone had seen something she had not. Magnus?

"Magnus accused Benjamin of being drunk. Did anyone recall his speech slurred or stumbling?" she asked.

"Benjamin was not drunk," Apollos said, his voice steady. "He choked, or perhaps his illness caused this collapse." He had quit crying, and his cheek color had darkened back to normal.

"Illness?" Hope flowed through her. Could the cause of Benjamin's death be so easily explained?

"He complained of headaches." Apollos rubbed his forehead as if suffering from the same disorder.

"Headaches?" Sabina's hope crashed.

"He had been losing weight." Apollos's eyes sparkled with fresh tears. "I lectured him about working too hard. Not eating properly and staying up late."

"He did not die from working too hard," Gallus said, his voice gruff with emotion. "And lack of sleep does not cause convulsions."

"Or drooling froths of bubbling saliva," a man listening in added.

"I know of a poisonous plant that can cause sickness and vomiting," Sabina said. "We could check."

"Check for what? He's already dead." Portia pursed her lips together to stop the trembling, then shook her head.

Gallus listened in. His subdued expression was turning somber. "It's the living who needs us now." He nodded at the grieving Apollos.

Sabina exhaled in frustrated understanding. Was Portia right?

There was nothing they could do to help Benjamin. But what if Gallus was right. What if it was the living who needed help? She could stay and comfort her friends, but one thought haunted her as she trudged back to the body. Benjamin may not be the only one in danger.

The pungent smell of vomit and excrement stung her nose and turned her stomach. She bunched her tunic up and away from the spilled wine and knelt. She gagged, then held her breath.

Like an imposter's death mask, a fierce grimace contorted Benjamin's face, impersonating the shy and affable young man. Did it signify pain? Shock? Fear? The last drool of foamy bubbles popped and disappeared. Tears rolled slowly down her cheek. She impatiently wiped them away. Tears couldn't bring him back.

His robe had twisted around his waist during the ineffective life-saving endeavors. She pulled and tugged it open. Gingerly she picked at his tunic and located the retching stain down the front. The pink phlegm proved Benjamin had drunk red wine. The prevalence of yellow and black bile confirmed there was not enough alcohol to cause him to pass out, collapse, or die. Magnus had been wrong.

Instead of gushing relief, the hollow in her gut began to ache again. She chewed on her thumbnail and scoured the vomit one more time for signs of solid residue.

She looked for evidence of swallowing a grain, meat, or a deadly flowering plant. Sabina spent many hours of her lonely childhood with the household servants and slaves. She developed a fondness for the mute slave who tended their gardens. He patiently demonstrated the pruning, watering, fertilizing of the different kinds of plants. She had nearly killed the man when he found her planting a slip of an unfamiliar tiny white flower in their garden. He ripped the plant out of the ground and made her wash her hands for what seemed like an hour. Only then did he calm down. He pantomimed a list of the poisonous plant's symptoms from throwing up to asphyxiation.

The gardener's crimson face and bulging eyes had increased her fascination for plants. But his graphic description of the suffering, should hemlock be mistaken for a common garden flower or worse an edible bush, gave her respect for nature's power. She cultivated only recognizable common flora. She left Amisi to grow exotic medicinal herbs.

Could someone from Portia's kitchen have made a fatal mistake? She readjusted Benjamin's tunic, re-examining the pink and yellow stomach contents. She found no sign he had recently eaten anything at the dinner, anything at all, including a poisonous plant. Steeling her nerves and holding her breath, she grabbed a dirty napkin from the table and opened Benjamin's mouth. Peering into the dark cavity, she saw nothing. She debated wiping the inside of his mouth but lost her nerve and dropped the napkin. Her father's voice flitted into her mind. *Romans are superior people because we rely on logic, evidence, science. When asking a logical question, we expect a logical answer. If not, either the question or the answer is in error.*

Sabina's brows drew together. If there was no evidence of an accident, then why was Benjamin dead?

She spit out a chewed bit of fingernail, pulled herself upright, and reviewed what she remembered. Where Benjamin was sitting, what he was drinking, the two adolescent boys sitting near him. Gallus sat across the table. She picked up the cup Magnus had commandeered and sniffed the inside. It smelled like wine.

She marched back to Portia, Apollos, Gallus, and the others deep in a discussion.

"We cannot allow the authorities to discover a dead body." Gallus's bushy eyebrows bobbed up and down. "Not at a Christian worship service."

Gallus also realized their danger.

"We need time to mourn. Benjamin's family needs to be…" Apollos shook his head.

"A body lays within our sanctuary. If word of this death leaks out, it endangers us all," Gallus said grimly.

"His family will have questions," Portia said.

"As will the authorities." Gallus's tone carried an urgency. "Our enemies accuse Christians of cannibalism as a part of our worship."

"Eating the body and drinking the blood of our dead," Portia said.

29

Apollos rose with determination from the bench. But his legs shook, and he dropped back on the bench. "Are you suggesting we run away? That we cover up Benjamin's death? Because we fear ignorant lies and slander?"

"No, because we fear the emperor, imprisonment, and death." Gallus's voice rose, taking on a stern admonition.

Many in the crowd murmured in agreement.

The teenage mother reached for her husband's hand. He drew his pregnant wife to him, then grabbed their toddler's hand and led his family out of the room. Two women collected their empty bowls from a table and followed them. The two young boys from the table had already gone home with their family.

Sabina shivered. It wasn't just Procurius from Smyrna. Last week, she had overheard an informant from Rome reporting to her father. A Christian had refused to honor Emperor Domitian as a god. The Christian's punishment in the arena had been recounted as mediocre entertainment. Was persecution against Christians increasing in Ephesus? Did her father know?

"You are right to care about our safety," Apollos said. "But Benjamin just died, and…we need the Lord's direction. We must take time to pray."

Gallus paced. "It is not just us. We have ties to other churches in the city." He persisted. "This incident endangers them as well."

Portia put her hand on Gallus's shoulder. "Apollos is right."

Apollos bowed his head, closed his eyes, and rocked back and forth as his lips moved in prayer, tears streaming down his cheeks. "Guide us as we submit to Your will, Lord."

Sabina, Portia, and the others folded hands and joined him in a calmness at odds with the danger Gallus predicted. Gallus joined in, his agitation lessening as the prayer continued.

"Amen," Apollos concluded and opened his eyes. "God will guide our decision."

"God is telling us to hurry," Gallus said with obvious impatience.

"Portia," Sabina turned to her friend, "if the authorities investigate, they will discover you are illegally harboring a Christian church. Your arrest and the confiscation of your home and business will follow."

Portia put her arm around Sabina's shoulder. "Thank you for your concern. However, we knew the risks when we offered our home."

"I trust our people," Apollos said. "I will instruct everyone to keep the news of Benjamin's death within these walls."

"We are too late." Gallus waved his arm at the emptying room. "Too many of our people have left. Some will not recognize the seriousness of this."

Sabina looked at the remaining members, silently counting twenty. Over forty had left. She understood human nature and the temptation to share tonight's dramatic events with trusted family and friends, a slip of the tongue, a child's tattling. Someone would discuss tonight's tragedy, in complete confidence, of course. Dire consequences would follow.

"We have perhaps a day or two to devise a plan, formulate a defense, invent a coverup," Gallus muttered, his tone bleak.

Apollos clapped his hands. "I need everyone's attention." Twenty sniffling people brushed aside tears and circled Apollos. "We have been diligently concealing our gatherings from the authorities. Our secrecy has been our protection. But this…" He glanced at Benjamin's body. "Is an unexpected complication. We will show Benjamin's body proper respect."

"And quietly return him to his family for burial," Portia nodded.

Gallus frowned. "We must find a way to do so without alerting the authorities."

"Then you have a serious problem." A rich, baritone voice reverberated from the dining room doorway.

Sabina's head snapped around to stare at a tall steel-gray-haired man wearing an official magistrate's toga fringed with a purple border. Four guards flanked him, sealing off the room's entrance. He didn't issue a command. He stared. All movement in the room ceased.

Sabina stopped breathing.

Unblinking, he scrutinized the congregation. His gaze swept past Sabina, then abruptly reversed and locked onto her.

She couldn't imagine his chiseled face getting more rigid. It did. His jaw muscles flexed. The intensity of his focus pulled her in like a

31

hooked fish. She stared straight into the ice-blue eyes of the Magistrate and Eirenarch of Ephesus, Guardian of the Peace. Quintus Catius Sabinus, her father. Her stomach lurched. She thought of Benjamin's vomit and tried to calm her roiling gut.

Then his gaze swept past. Sabina closed her eyes and exhaled deep breaths of air.

She was certain only she had noticed those agonizing seconds, then Portia's hand reached out to hers, and their fingers entwined. Portia squeezed her hand, acknowledging his identity. Portia and Apollos were the only Christians who knew about her father. The only people Sabina trusted not to expose their family relationship.

Her father's head turned to assess each face as if adding it to a mental sketchbook. She knew he would not forget any of their faces. People looked at the floor, the walls, anywhere to avoid his stare. His scan stopped at the body lying on the floor.

Sabina bit her bottom lip, stopping when the tang of blood hit her tongue. Her thoughts tumbled in confusion. Questions collided in her mind. Why was her father here? Had someone reported them? Why? How? It had been less than half an hour since Benjamin died. Not enough time to travel across town to report a death. Was he searching for her? None of this made sense.

Her father marched into the room with long, precise strides. His lifetime of military authority projected the image of a battle-hardened general, arrogant and dangerous. "Who is the leader of this rabble?"

The attending guards gripped their knife hilts. Sabina felt sweat running down her back.

Gallus shuffled forward to meet him. His earlier assertive voice was now unsure. "Lord Magistrate, the living God is our leader."

The magistrate struck Gallus hard across the face. The older man fell, blood running from his nose.

Sabina cringed. No one moved.

"Don't wordplay with me. I care nothing of your so-called God." His voice sizzled with anger. "I asked who is in charge?"

Apollos stood on unsteady legs and stepped between the two men.

"Magistrate, my name is Apollos. I will answer your questions." Apollos bent down and helped Gallus stand.

Gallus coughed, wiped his mouth with the back of his hand, and spit out blood.

Apollos steadied him. "We have broken no laws."

"It appears otherwise." Her father waved his hand at the altar, the candles, and the scroll. Someone had taken the time to re-roll and place it on the altar. "You meet in secret at night and flaunt the laws of your emperor. It is sedition, treason. How does this show him honor?"

Apollos swallowed and continued. "Our worship harms no one, Magistrate."

"A man lies dead on your floor." The magistrate's chilling glare contradicted his restrained and detached voice.

Sabina knew her father. His rigid bearing and his unwavering loyalty to Rome. She also knew he was livid. He had struck an old man. He didn't care about Gallus, but he had lost his temper. Throughout his life, logic and self-control ensured his survival. Showing emotion could lead to lethal consequences.

"Are you the priest of this illegal cult?" Her father's eyes narrowed.

"I shepherd this flock," Apollos said. "We have but one priest, Jesus the Messiah. I minister to the needs of these people. I teach the words of Jesus."

"Enough of your propaganda!" The magistrate's voice shook. He cracked his knuckles and turned his attention to Benjamin. He motioned his guards forward. "I will examine the body."

The worshipers jostled each other to clear a path.

A guard clouted one man not quick enough. He fell to his knees, moaning, and was kicked to the side by another guard. The magistrate followed in the wake of his guards.

"What is the dead man's name?"

"Benjamin ben Jonah."

"A Jew belongs to this…" The magistrate grimaced as if smelling excrement. He flicked his wrist toward the altar. "This cult of Christos?"

"We are beloved brothers in service to our Lord," Apollos answered.

"Your lord is Caesar." The magistrate's voice vibrated with menace. "Do not forget." A few people shuffled nervously.

The magistrate stopped inches from Benjamin's body. He lifted his toga away from the puddle of wine and reached over, pressing two fingers against Benjamin's neck. He stood and wiped his fingers on his tunic. "What happened? Where was he sitting? What did he eat? What was he drinking? Who was eating with him?"

"He sat there across the table from me." Gallus pointed. "He ate little, perhaps nothing. He drank the wine we all drank from the broken pitcher." Gallus pointed to the puddle of wine.

"Is anyone else feeling sick?"

A subdued "no" emanated from the remaining congregants, followed by a woman's sobbing.

"Where is his cup?"

Gallus reached for it. "That one is his."

A guard slapped Gallus's hand. Her father picked up a discarded cotton napkin from the table. He wrapped it around the outside without touching the cup and sniffed the contents, then dumped it upside down on the table, leaving a circle of moisture. He picked up a napkin from the table and wiped the inside of the cup. He smelled the napkin then dropped it on the floor.

He turned to the youngest guard. "Roll the body on its stomach, then back again. Slowly."

The youngest guard grabbed Benjamin's arm and flipped his body over. Benjamin's head thudded against the floor once and then back again. Sabina winced. Her father's attention did not waver. "Use a napkin and open his mouth. Swab the inside of his mouth."

The guards followed instructions.

"Show me the napkin." Her father examined the napkin, turning it and holding it up to the candlelight. He smelled it, then reached for a knife from the table. He bent over the body using the blade to prod and lift the folds of Benjamin's tunic, examining the vomit. Finished, he tossed the knife on the floor. Briefly, he gazed into Benjamin's sightless eyes, then straightened. Sabina imagined him mentally checking off his observations, the same inconsistencies, just as she had when she examined the body, looking for answers—looking for evidence.

"He vomited and choked," Apollos's chin trembled. "It was an accident. I tried…we tried to save him."

"An accident?" The magistrate's voice switched abruptly from credulous to ominous. "How stupid do you think I am?" Her father's fingers flexed as his glare bore into Apollos.

"Someone poisoned your Jew." His gaze swept across the room. "Apparently, one of his beloved brothers."

The crowd gasped in unison as if rehearsed.

Sabina closed her eyes and sagged against Portia. So the evidence was there. She didn't have the skills to recognize it. Still, she had known. She didn't know how, but she had. Was it the pain frozen on Benjamin's face? The unnatural color of his skin? The absurdity of a young man suddenly dying? A buzzing mosquito? The sting of death had made no sense. The others had rejected what was in front of them. Even she hadn't wanted to accept the logical conclusion—that a brother or sister in Christ could kill.

The magistrate pointed to two of the guards. "Take the body and wait outside." The guards hefted Benjamin's body between them. "For the love of Zeus, cover his face."

A few sighed when the guards pulled Benjamin's robe up, hiding his face. The people nearest closed their eyes or turned away. None seemed willing to look into the blank eyes of death.

Sabina did not turn aside. She took a shaky breath and crossed her arms. She would not ignore the truth again.

The guards twisted Benjamin sideways as they passed the magistrate. She saw a tiny flash of gold drop from Benjamin's robe. It landed soundlessly, its fall muted by the congregation's muffled sobs and mumbled prayers. She wondered what it was as she watched it roll under the table.

Prayers offered for Benjamin or us? Benjamin was beyond the reach of Roman justice, safe in the comforting arms of his Lord. She looked at her fellow worshippers, the innocent casualties of this tragic act. The guards left. Sabina shuffled her feet as if scraping off the stench of death and sending it with them.

The magistrate turned to Apollos. "Who killed him?"

"All here tonight are blameless," Apollos sputtered, staring at the now empty doorway. "We honor the commandment to love one another."

"Murder is a charming way to show love. Perhaps prison will correct your moral principles." The magistrate gestured to the remaining two guards. "Bind them all." The guards moved to encircle the congregation. A woman's scream turned into sobbing. She clung to her husband. A child cried. Portia's nails bit into Sabina's hand.

Sabina's body shook as a chilling cold settled in. She couldn't believe this was happening.

The magistrate turned and addressed Apollos. "Tonight, I seek one murderer. Tomorrow, if the perpetrator has not confessed, I will be forced to take action against this entire rebel assembly. Treason against our emperor is punishable by death."

"But we do not know," Gallus cried out, a smear of blood drying on his chin.

Portia squeezed Sabina's hand until tiny needles began to numb it. People began to murmur, the volume rising to a babble, punctuated by hysterical cries and wails.

"I poisoned Benjamin," Apollos blurted out.

"No!" Sabina screamed the word, but Apollos's confession had taken the air from her. Her scream came out a whisper. What was he saying? He tended and loved this small flock of believers. He sacrificed much to shepherd this congregation. His admission was unacceptable, aberrant, wrong.

"The others are innocent." Apollos stared at the magistrate. "You promised to free them."

All movements and voices stopped. In stunned silence, Sabina and the others stared from Apollos to her father. Muted questions filtered throughout the room. "What is he saying?" "What does he mean?"

The magistrate nodded grimly to Apollos. "Arrest the priest."

Apollos bowed his head as if they were in some perverse agreement. Sabina released Portia's hand and pushed past the man in front of them.

Portia reached out and gripped Sabina's forearm, drawing her back. Sabina pulled free. "Apollos—"

"He would never hurt Benjamin. I know." Portia shook her head and pointed to the wide-eyed stares of several children clutched tightly against their mothers. "He's setting them free," Portia whispered.

Gallus stumbled forward, his entire body trembling. He grabbed Apollos's shoulders and shook him. "What are you doing?"

A guard thrust Gallus away and bound Apollos's wrists.

Sabina's heart pounded violently as the guard conducted Apollos from the room. He had just admitted to the murder. His confession meant a death sentence. Sweat soaked the entire back of her tunic.

Her father narrowed his eyes at Sabina then turned to the huddled group. "I have no patience for the rest of you simpering fanatics." He waved toward the doorway. "Remove them from my sight."

Feet shuffled in confusion. Mothers hushed their whimpering children. Eyes darted between the magistrate and each other, their bewilderment visible in their expressions.

"Leave!" shouted the magistrate. People jumped. "Use a back door."

The guards herded the group toward the door.

Portia moved to the front of the group. "There is a kitchen door at the back of my house." She nervously signaled them to follow her into the atrium, encouraging everyone to hurry before the magistrate changed his mind and arrested them all.

Gallus stumbled. Sabina went to him and put her arm around his shoulders.

"Leave him," the magistrate ordered. A wave of defiance lit her eyes as she steadied the older man before stepping away. "You will stay." The magistrate pointed to Sabina.

Now Gallus reached out and squeezed her shoulder. The last guard shoved him in the back. Gallus tripped but caught himself before falling and threw a last worried glance at Sabina.

Sabina's heart pounded as they hurried past her, heads bowed, eyes downcast. The guards drove the quaking Christians from the room. Sabina stared at the floor, her mind reeling. She was left alone with her father.

"You will return to our house immediately," his voice stirred with irritation. He casually adjusted a fold in his toga.

She pushed down her cowardly wish to fly home like one of her obedient pigeons. Tears of frustration, tears held in check after Benjamin's murder, welled in her eyes. She blinked rapidly. She had to control her emotions if she was to get her father to listen to reason. Apollos was innocent.

Her father had no patience for her tears, not as a child and certainly not as an adult. Don't cry. She gritted her teeth, and sheer willpower slowed her tears. Sabina took several steadying breaths, wiped her eyes, and looked up, challenging his steely glare. "You arrested the wrong man," she said, embarrassed at the quiver in her voice.

His glare bore into her. She sucked in her breath and glared back, braving the cold crystal glare of his aqua eyes, a color nearly matching her own. But unlike his piercing hue of glacial ice, she was thankful her eyes cast a warmer shade of blue.

She blinked rapidly, startled by the drawn weariness she saw reflected in his face. She frowned. He looked his age. She was used to seeing his youthful vigor, his fit bearing disguising his fifty-five-year-old body within the persona of a man ten years younger. His façade had slipped. She coughed to hide her gasp. Her father was getting old.

At first glance, few would recognize her as his daughter. The ivory-colored marble of his patrician skin, now patterned in a web of fine lines, was the opposite of her darker olive complexion, inherited from her mother. Where her father's nose was narrowly sculpted, hers flared wide. His full lips were firm and indecipherable. Hers lush and expressive. But there existed similarities. They shared a sharply defined jawline and matching chiseled cheekbones, signs of an obstinate determination allowing neither one to give-in or show vulnerability. And both believed in justice, right and wrong. She was counting on his code of honor. "You know you're mistaken. You have no idea who killed Benjamin."

He whipped around. "And you do? Tell me which one of your beloved brethren is a murderer?"

"He could have eaten from a plant, oleander, before coming to the worship service. It's poisonous."

"You think he ate from a bush." He laughed and dismissed her with a flick of his wrist. "You know nothing. The sudden and violent death points to arsenic. If the man was walking and talking before he collapsed and died, he had to have drunk it, at or shortly before your worship service."

"Then he could have been poisoned before he arrived?"

"A significant amount of arsenic is needed to cause sudden death. It would shut down the body within an hour."

Benjamin was already seated when she arrived. Sabina calculated the time she had been there before Benjamin collapsed, at least half an hour. "It was improbable but not impossible someone had poisoned him before arriving, or it might not be murder." Her voice rang hollow and carried no conviction.

"Your life is in danger, yet you persist in arguing with me?" His jaw tightened, and his voice lowered to barely above a whisper. "You will leave this church. You will not return. Your game of allegiance to this Christos is over. And you will thank me if only your priest dies for your willful disregard of our emperor's edicts."

Sabina seethed. Inhaling deeply, she lifted her chin. They stood facing each other, unequal adversaries; both knew she had no say, no choice, no recourse. Years ago, Sabina and her father had reached an uneasy truce. He would allow Sabina to practice her faith, and in return, she would fulfill her obligations as a dutiful daughter and model widow. She promised to conceal her family ties from the church as much as possible and never publicize her faith. Until now, their pact had held.

"You are allowing the guilty person to go free?" Sabina asked.

"Why would an innocent man confess?"

"Because," she pointed her finger at him then rapidly drew it back, "you made your threat clear. If a murderer didn't materialize, you would have turned the entire congregation over to the governor."

"My threat?" His eyes glittered, but his tone remained chillingly level. "The only threat you should fear is our enemies discovering your religious fanaticism. They would descend like a wake of vultures to feed on our carcasses. Knowing this, you continue to disregard my warnings. You risk destroying everything. For what? This dead God of yours."

"He lives." She clenched her fists to keep them from shaking.

Her father's face slackened. He ran his fingers through his graying hair. "Go home and tend to your pigeons, Sabina. I am tired. For once, do not provoke me." He spun and stalked out of the room.

She wiped her cheek with the back of her hand. "A plague on you," she whispered under her breath. Her bottom lip quivered. "And on me." The rebellion surging in her drained away.

He was mistaken about Apollos, but she could not argue against a war commander's knowledge of death. Her father had orchestrated the death of thousands. His own battle scars proved he understood personal mortality. In civilian life, his talents had shifted from Rome's distant enemies to protecting the local citizenry from each other. Rome conquered, and the Empire had amassed wealth, influence, and power. Rome's inhabitants imitated their leaders, using any means necessary to accumulate power, including bribery, espionage, and murder. Her father no longer served Rome as an army commander, but his combat-honed experience and instincts survived.

He had concluded a murderer walked in their midst—he was probably right. But just as disturbing was why anyone would want to kill the shy, quiet scribe? Amidst tonight's shared fellowship, love, and joy lurked a mind filled with hate and murder.

An echo of hammering footsteps stopped outside the room. The drone of her father issuing orders snapped her out of her brooding. He controlled her future, but at least she had a future. It was Apollos who was facing death. Her father's guards carried Benjamin from this room. She remembered the item that had dropped from his robe.

Quickly she got down on her hands and knees and scoured the floor under the low table. Glinting next to a shard of the shattered wine pitcher, she found the small golden disc. A coin? Swiftly she reached out and scooped it into her palm. Scrambling to her feet, she glanced at it briefly, not recognizing the strange markings pressed into the metal.

Zarmig, her father's bodyguard, entered and signaled to her. Curling her fingers, she hid the gold piece in her fist as Zarmig escorted her home.

THREE

Sabina bolted upright in bed. Her teeth chattered as she groped for her blanket. It was wound tightly around one leg like a shroud. She tugged it free and pulled it over her shoulders. Her chill was at odds with the damp sleeping tunic and the sweat trickling between her breasts. Her nightmare had left her exhausted. Its vision still haunted her morning.

She bunched the blanket up under her nose as if warding off the nightmare's lingering stench of blood. She had struggled to wake, to flee the dream with blood spattering her face, the whistling leather whip slicing through layers of skin on Apollos's naked back. She had screamed, unable to move, to run to his defense. The iron spiked leather thongs tore into his quivering muscles again and again. She looked away only to witness Benjamin's rigid body on the ground at her feet. When she looked up, the soldier had transformed into her father. He wielded the lash, methodically counting the required thirty-nine strokes.

Shuddering and wide awake, she lifted her hand and touched her face, then looked at her fingertips, expecting to see the red smear of Apollos's blood that, only minutes before waking, she had wiped from her face. Her heart raced. She swallowed once, twice, trying to erase the tang of blood, trying not to think about Apollos's moans or her paralyzing fear of powerlessness. Closing her eyes, she lifted her arms, stretched, and

43

focused on a new day, banishing the dream from her mind. The chiming splash of water bubbling from the pool's fountain outside her door enveloped her. She opened her eyes and blinked at the sunlight. Normally, it was a glorious way to wake up and offer praise. Light streamed in through her slatted bedroom door, but it was too early in the spring for the morning rays to carry much warmth. Her brazier provided no comfort; its nighttime charcoal supply was spent. She shivered. Tingling bumps speckled her arms as last night's memories, like barbs, rose to the surface.

Her father's words shackled guilt to her every nerve, every muscle. *You will thank me if only your priest dies for your willful disregard of our emperor's edicts.* Would Apollos die because of her? Her father so much as admitted forcing Apollos's confession to safeguard her. And her father could not risk a prolonged investigation into the murder. Public testimony would bring attention to the church and implicate Sabina—and by association—her family. This he would never allow. Those thoughts of helplessness and her nightmare drained her. And there was nothing she could do. She flopped back on the bed. She would hide here all day.

The bedroom doors burst open. Amisi, her slave and childhood nurse, bustled in balancing a basket on her hip. She dropped the basket, turned around, and threw open the double doors, allowing fresh air and the crisp aroma of early spring to waft in from the garden courtyard outside. The branches on the apple tree were beginning to green with new buds. Soon the smell of blossoms would burst under the warming glow of longer days. "Time to get up. Much to do today."

Watching the fluttering vitality of the tiny elfish woman drained Sabina. She wanted to send Amisi away, slam the doors closed, sort out her fears for Apollos and the church members, her father's political rivals, and his order to abandon her faith. It was too overwhelming. "I didn't sleep well."

Amisi eyed the coverings from Sabina's bed twisted halfway on the floor, and her tunic, crumpled in a pile, on the rug. "I see." She frowned, whirled, and left the room.

Sighing in relief, Sabina pulled the blanket upon the bed, cuddling under it like a protective sanctuary.

Within minutes Amisi was back. She carried an earthenware bowl decorated with entwined snakes, a small jar, and a burning ember. Her voice shook with emotion. "You tempt the gods running around at night. It is dangerous. You have lured night demons into our house. They are searching for a corner to inhabit to occupy your dreams every night." She set the bowl on the floor, poured the contents of the jar into it, and lit the oil.

Amisi kept a shelf of herbs, oils, plant roots, crushed insects, dried animal entrails. Some smelled delightful, others made Sabina gag. Additional prized ingredients had no names, and their purposes were age-old secrets. This morning the cleansing smell of frankincense wafted from the bowl, supplanting the fresh scent of apple blossoms. Amisi fanned the smoke, sending it swirling throughout the room as she chanted in her native language, chasing away evil.

"I will speak to your father. If the wrong person sees you out unaccompanied, it will destroy your reputation. This Christ worship is scaring husbands away."

A *husband* reference again, lest Sabina forget the biggest failure of her life. It was an argument they had repeated many times and now bolstered by her father's decree to stay away from the church and its followers. She didn't have the energy to quarrel. She wrapped the blanket tighter around her. "I know you're worried, but—"

"A husband would put an end to this nonsense."

"Arrg," Sabina pulled the blanket over her head.

"You are too independent. You aren't a child anymore. Why can't you follow the rules and behave the way respectable widows do? Dependable and reliable is what a man wants in a wife."

"That isn't what you told me men want the night before my wedding." Her words were garbled from under the blanket.

Amisi picked up the bowl and moved it outside the door. Returning, she reprimanded, "You twist my words. Physical attraction requires no rules."

The memory of Sabina's wedding night was thankfully fading, even if the memory of her husband, Xeno, wasn't. She had thought his flushed face and labored breathing was due to excess celebrating. He had undeniably drunk too much. She had gone over the events of that horrible night a thousand times. Should she have noticed his faltering steps, his slurred speech as he climbed into their bed? Had she been too focused on the event to come and didn't notice what was happening before her eyes? He had rolled onto her panting. He'd kissed her, wheezed, and quit breathing. No one came when she screamed. She had pushed him off and ran to get help.

Sabina jerked the blanket down, ending the replay. "I'm thrice-cursed, Amisi. You said so yourself."

Amisi stood hands on hips. "I am working on that."

"Working on what, raising men from the dead? Two healthy men died, while betrothed to me, and then Xeno? Three."

Amisi let out a derisive snort. "You were six years old when Achilles died in his first battle. And they should not blame you for Tatius Quadratus's drowning. Shipwrecks are common enough. Two deaths could be explained, but three? Truly the stars are aligned against you."

"You're not making me feel better."

"And you are the only one who expects men to rise from the dead." The older woman smirked. "It is sorcery."

"One man. Jesus. It's not sorcery. His resurrection is God's miracle."

"Harrumph. Magic is more practical. I cannot perform miracles." Amisi bustled about the room muttering just loud enough for Sabina to hear.

Sabina tossed the covers aside and said from between chattering teeth as calmly as she could. "Can we not talk about this right now?"

Amisi snorted under her breath. "If you wanted to be married, you could try harder."

"Of course, I want to be—" She stopped. From the time she was born, she knew marriage and children were her goals in life. Three deaths had kept that achievement from her. How dare Amisi insinuate she wasn't trying.

"How many men have come? And you scare them away."

"They scare themselves away, thinking they'll be death number four."

"True, but if you were like your mother…"

"Beautiful?"

"You are beautiful. I was going to say reserved. You are too clever. You need to rely on your charm. Men notice your golden skin, full lips, high breasts, and perfect hips for childbearing. Any man would want you if you would just—"

"I know, quit talking."

"Don't be ridiculous." Amisi wagged her finger at Sabina. "Women must talk, flatter, and compliment. I only advised you not to argue. Men love women who agree with them. Tell them how wise or handsome they are. A little inventiveness goes a long way."

"Or your favorite, how rich they are."

"You make fun of me. But I am right. You are too honest, too obvious with men." Amisi sounded insulted, but Sabina knew her peevishness would pass.

"I am tired of the seduction game."

"Tired? You have never played it. That is your problem." Amisi threw her hands up. "And you had better start if you want to get married."

Of course, she did. Her conscience niggled at her. Didn't every woman?

Amisi handed her a small roll of papyrus. "The messenger said it was urgent."

Recognizing Portia's wax stamp, Sabina tore into the note.

My dearest sister, I prayed all night for your safety. I need your help.

"Why didn't you wake me? Or at least tell me right away."

"I just did. Your mysterious visitor said she would wait until you are dressed." Amisi peered at the note, scrunching her face as Sabina was reading.

"It's Latin." Sabina threw the note on the bed. She rushed to her clothing trunk and turned around. Amisi stood with her arms folded and lips pressed tightly shut. "I'm sorry, Amisi." Her nurse had a remarkable memory for recipes and spells, but she could read only a few Greek words. "I need to see Portia immediately."

47

She pulled out several tunics and threw them back. She sighed and gave up looking through the chest. Amisi hadn't moved. "Show Portia in." Sabina braced to follow the request with a strict order, but Amisi snorted and strutted from the bedroom.

Sabina sat and waited on the edge of the bed.

Urgent? A call for help? Sabina had trusted her father to release the other members of the congregation unharmed. She had fallen asleep praying for Apollos. She had not worried about the safety of her friends. Had something happened to them?

Amisi opened the door and followed Portia in. Portia ran to Sabina. The two friends embraced, exchanging kisses.

"Sit down." Sabina pointed to an ornately carved ebony stool. Portia, pale with dark circles under her eyes, sat. Sabina perched on the edge of her bed. "You may prepare breakfast for us, Amisi."

"I did not sleep last night. I can't eat anything." Portia wrung her hands.

"Then a tea of hyssop leaves with mint and honey. Amisi's draughts are magical at calming nerves."

Amisi gave a smug placated smile and bustled from the room.

"What has happened to our brothers and sisters?" Sabina asked.

"Nothing bad that I have heard. It is Apollos we are afraid for," Portia's voice shook.

"I had a terrible dream about him last night."

"We have searched for him," Portia's voice cracked. "A trusted brother has checked the prisons. Apollos is nowhere. Everyone is frantic. And Benjamin's body has disappeared."

"I returned home last night. I don't know where they are."

"I recognized your father."

Sabina nodded. "Did anyone else?"

"No, and I will not reveal that your father arrested Apollos." Portia grabbed Sabina's hands and clutched them tightly. "You can help us find him. Apollos did not kill Benjamin."

"I know. But you don't know what you're asking me to do. I can't go knocking on prison doors, asking to speak to a confessed murderer, or worse, a Christian bishop."

"Ask your father where he took Apollos so we can minister to him. He will need food and blankets. It's a small request."

"I am the last person to whom my father would reveal that information. He's forbidden my involvement. He threatened me if I went near the church again."

"He has always distrusted your faith." Portia shook her head.

"It's different now. It's not just me. If my father's political rivals found out, they would destroy him."

Portia's lips quivered as she nodded. "I understand."

"I wish that I…but when the wheels of Roman judgment are moving, one person cannot stop them." Sabina pulled her hands from Portia's.

"God can."

"I agree. Apollos's fate is in God's hands, not mine."

"Pray, Sabina. Perhaps your hands are God's tools." Portia stood. "We can't give up. Apollos has sacrificed much for us."

"I will pray." Apollos, the man who had stepped into the life of an inconsolable eight-year-old after her mother's death and demonstrated the inexhaustible love of God when nothing made sense in her world. A man who had guided her spiritual growth and validated her priceless worth and value as a child of God. A man who was the opposite of her father.

Amisi entered with a quick knock, brandishing a tray with two cups of tea and a wax tablet.

Portia waved her away. "I must help with the search."

"I can't." Guilt tightened Sabina's chest. "I'm sorry. I have no choice." The two women kissed. Sabina tasted the salt of Portia's dried tears.

"Sabina, when God asks us to do the impossible, He supplies the battle plan."

"One without risk?"

"All faith is a risk." Portia hugged Sabina. "But I do not want to lose another dear friend. I know my way out."

Amisi watched Portia leave and set the tray on the bedside table. "Good, good. You were right to send her away."

The burden Portia placed on her lightened. "Were you eavesdropping?" Sabina picked up the note.

Amisi shrugged. "That Christ woman? She wants to cause trouble." Amisi stood hands on hips, staring at her.

Sabina understood Amisi's fear even as she chafed under her consistent nagging and worry. Amisi's protective instincts had begun when Sabina's mother began taking Sabina to worship and grew as Sabina's commitment to her faith grew. Until last night nothing perilous had occurred.

Sabina crumpled Portia's note into a ball and looked over at the brazier, its coals a dead gray. She tossed the crinkled papyrus onto the tray.

"Your father told me you were not to leave the house today. He should have said no visitors as well," Amisi mumbled under her breath. "What did you do?" She picked up the discarded tunic and tossed it in the basket.

"Nothing. A man died last night."

"Men die all the time." Amisi eyed Sabina intently. "What does that have to do with you?"

"He was poisoned at my church."

Amisi lifted the wrinkled cloak off the floor and shook it out. Benjamin's small gold disk clattered onto the floor. She bent to retrieve it as it rolled toward the bed.

Sabina threw off her blanket and sprang out of bed, catching her foot in the covers. She landed hard on her knees. "Ouch." She reached out and grabbed the disk off the floor.

Amisi stopped and frowned. "Dead men bring trouble. I will make you a protector charm."

"I don't need a charm." Sabina rose with a groan and placed the disk next to Portia's note. "I wasn't the one poisoned."

"The charm protects from the ghost of the dead man." Amisi tossed the mantle in the basket with last night's tunic. She lifted the lid of the clothing chest, shuffled through the top layer of garments, and pulled out a rust-colored woolen tunic. "I finished the embroidery on your new tunic." She ran her fingers over the border of stitched ivy.

Sabina sighed. She knew the disagreement over charms and spells would never be resolved. "The emerald leaves are beautiful." Sabina allowed the slave to help her out of her cotton night tunic.

Amisi's charms began the day Sabina was born, the same day Amisi was added to the household inventory of magistrate Quintus Catius Sabinus. Sabina, the squalling firstborn of Catius and his young wife, Korinna, needed a wet nurse. Amisi was purchased, a thirteen-year-old slave, devastated by the death of her own newborn. Amisi had wrapped her dead child's threaded bracelet around Sabina's tiny arm. And although Korinna forbade pagan magic, she had told Sabina this one time she hadn't the heart to forbid Amisi's gift. Over the years, Korinna had three more children, all stillborn. According to Amisi, her mother died from three heartbreaks. According to the midwife, Korinna had bled to death during her last delivery.

There had been many charms since Sabina's mother's death. Spells cast into necklaces and bracelets and sewn into Sabina's clothing; to prevent illness, to protect her from demons, to increase her beauty, but not so much beauty that the gods would be jealous, to bless her with fertility and healthy children, to bring her a husband, many, many charms for a husband. Sabina sighed. Well, that hadn't worked quite right.

Amisi looked at the gold disk and the crumpled papyrus on the table. The crease between her eyes deepened. "I think a powerful charm," Amisi smoothed the rust tunic, running her hands down it, then held it up.

"My bishop is to be executed for the murder. He needs a miracle," Sabina protested, "not a goddess's magic spell."

"You disrespect Isis," Amisi wagged her finger at Sabina. "One day, the goddess will not smile on you. I thank the gods you have me."

"I thank my God for you every day," Sabina said, meaning every word. Her relationship with her slave was complicated. Amisi had stepped in when Sabina's mother had died. Amisi had not filled the role of a mother, but Sabina knew Amisi's admonishments were made out of love. A love Sabina returned. Amisi's devotion to her mistress, a woman she had raised, was unquestionable.

"The gods have decided," Amisi babbled to herself as she helped Sabina into her tunic. Sabina automatically lifted her arms while Amisi pulled the tunic down, attached the shoulder clips, and adjusted the folds of the finely woven wool. "There, now my mistress's secret will be safe—" Amisi stopped abruptly. "Now you will be safe…and beautiful." She knelt down and yanked the bottom of the fabric to even it. "The color brings out the flames of the sun in your hair."

"What secret?"

"Sit down." Amisi half pushed, half shoved her down on a stool.

"Your mistress? My mother?"

"You are my mistress." Amisi snatched up a comb from the bedside table. "I will fix your hair now."

"I don't have a secret. What did you mean?" Sabina spun on the stool to face Amisi. "You know my bishop? Apollos?"

"I know many men named Apollos." Amisi's eyes darted everywhere before settling on the door out to the garden.

"Amisi, if there is something Apollos did, a secret that could help him. I could tell Father, and Apollos could—"

"Oh, no, no!" Amisi turned pale, her eyes wide. She waved the comb in the air. "Your father cannot know." She dropped the comb.

"What can't Father know? Why is my mother's secret safe if Apollos is dead?"

Amisi knelt to pick up the comb and fumbled with it, dropping it twice more. When she stood up, her color was back. "You never listen to me. One time I babble nonsense, and you pay attention. There is nothing to know." Amisi pinched her lips shut. "I forget."

"If there is nothing, how could you forget?" She grabbed Amisi's hands, holding them in hers. "Apollos is going to die."

"This dead Apollos has nothing to do with you." Amisi pulled her hands from Sabina and crossed her arms under her breasts.

"He's not dead yet."

"You said he would die soon."

"And you said he knows a secret about my mother."

"I swore an oath." Amisi shook her head, turned Sabina around by the shoulders, and began combing her hair.

"But—"

"The gods have spoken. This way is best."

52

Sabina wanted to shake the information out of her, but if she decided Apollos's dying would benefit Sabina, nothing would change her mind. "Not best for Apollos," Sabina mumbled. Amisi knew Apollos. How? Amisi was not a Christian and had never mentioned Apollos's name before. Sabina cherished every fading childhood memory of her mother. Her recollections were based on stories asked for and repeated by Amisi, Zarmig, and anyone who would put up with her pleas. And the few she recalled with clarity had transformed her mother into a saint. A mother dedicated to her only child, loving and loyal. Not a woman who kept secrets from her husband. Not a woman who would confide in another man and then require an oath of silence from Amisi. Questions swirled through her head.

Amisi vigorously tackled the knots from last night's sleep, tugging as if she could straighten Sabina's thick natural curls by pulling hard enough.

"Ouch." Sabina turned and took the comb away. "Enough!"

To Amisi, Apollos was already dead. To Sabina, he was very much alive and holding a secret involving her mother. A secret her father did not know, which was impossible because her father knew everything involving his family.

Whatever the truth, it would soon be lost to this world with Apollos's execution.

Could she speak to her father? Did she dare? She pondered arguments to convince her father to tell her where Apollos was. She mentally rehearsed each one through to its ultimate failure. But to fail, she first had to try.

She opened her jewelry box and handed Amisi two silver hairpins. "No braiding…something simple. I need time to plan for dinner." Did her mother trust Apollos? With what? Apollos could answer her questions. But no one knew where he was. That wasn't true. Her father knew. "Did Father go to his office today?" "Sabina asked, surprising herself with her question.

"He left early this morning. He canceled all meetings with his clients," Amisi said, then lowered the tunic. She narrowed her eyes, staring hard at Sabina. "What are you planning?"

"Nothing! Why are you looking at me like that?"

"Because I see that light in your eye. Like a fox stalking a squirrel, you will follow it off a cliff. Forget this dead man."

"I saw him die."

"No, no, no! Last night did not happen." Amisi waggled her head. "You were not there. You saw no one die. It is a bad omen. You stay safe in the house with me."

"Father has already ordered me to stay away from the church," Sabina said.

"Then, listen. He knows best for you." Amisi nodded as if her statement was a fact that solved all of Sabina's worries.

Worries. She thought of the church, her second home, and the friends she had grown up with, people she loved and depended on, who were now relying on her.

"You have worries enough for today. You have many duties. The mistress of the house has no time for dead men." Amisi pinned the final loop of hair with the second silver pin. "Done. You must plan for tonight and tomorrow's dinners. I will help. Your father has invited a special guest."

"Who?"

"He did not say, but it is a woman." Amisi rolled her eyes. "Maybe not so special. But dinner must be prepared."

Amisi reached for the tray and the wax tablet and handed them to Sabina. "Here is today's list of tasks and the names of the slaves to be punished. Your father didn't have time."

Sabina moistened her lips, picked up the accompanying stylus, skipped over the names, and continued down the extensive list of duties. They would devour her day. And Amisi would be by her side the entire time. Something she was rapidly deciding needed to change.

With a dismissive glance at Amisi, she said, "It's too bad I have so much to do. Do you remember the merchant, Marcus, who dined with Father last week?"

Amisi stopped picking up clothing and straightened up. "The merchant from Rome? A bit short, but he could pose as Hercules with those muscles."

Sabina smiled. Amisi had noticed Marcus's physique. "Yes, and rich."

"How could I forget him. You and he argued all night. And he left," Amisi emphasized by jamming the tunic down into the basket.

"Yes, well. He has requested to see me again."

Amisi's eyebrow shot up. "Your father said nothing to me."

Sabina rummaged in the basket and pulled out her cloak and retrieved Marcus's note. She handed it to Amisi and pointed. "That's where he is lodging. I thought I'd invite him to dinner tomorrow night."

Amisi's eyes lit up, and then she shook her head. "Your father's guest comes tomorrow night. But Tuesday night, I will help the cook plan your dinner."

"I want this to be perfect. I should choose the vegetables myself. You complained about the vegetables chosen by the cook at the last dinner, rotten spots." She chewed on the end of the bone stylus then looked back to Amisi. "I don't have time to do everything."

Amisi snatched the stylus from her. "The punishments can wait." She placed the tablet on top of Sabina's soiled clothing and picked up the basket. "I heard a large catch of eel was coming in tomorrow. Perhaps your merchant would enjoy steamed eel." Amisi hummed as she carried the dirty clothing away.

"Perhaps he would," Sabina said.

Sabina did not go anywhere without her mantle, a long-established habit peppered with a fair amount of practicality, and Amisi had taken Sabina's to clean. She would have to borrow her old threadbare cloak, the one she had given Amisi, after outgrowing it years ago. The length fit the slave's diminutive figure perfectly but barely reached Sabina's knees.

She snapped up the shopping basket, almost forgetting it on the way out the door. She descended the steep and narrow street leading down the hill from their house and looked west toward the frenzied haggling of the market agora and the fish market. She turned east. With a shudder of trepidation, she strode toward the State Agora, the headquarters of Rome's officials and city government.

The walk to her father's office would take twenty minutes.

FOUR

Portia said Apollos was not being held at one of the public prisons. Sabina assumed all captives were imprisoned in the public jails of Ephesus.

Her father's magisterial duties included the capture and return of runaway slaves and escaped criminals. However, her father answered only to the Roman governor and not the city council, a position that allowed him an unprecedented level of autonomy. She would need a miracle to find Apollos in the third-largest city in the Empire with nearly one hundred and fifty thousand people and expanding daily. A miracle, or her father's cooperation.

Over and over, she had heard the sermons on fulfilling God's purpose for her life. Was finding Apollos and provoking her father's wrath God's will? Or was she once again taking matters into her own hands as she had with her marriage to Xeno? Was she making another mistake? One her father wouldn't forgive.

She turned at an intersection and caught a glimpse of the harbor. The ships from this distance looked like toys. She imagined the merchants bartering in Greek yet speaking in a continuous undercurrent of their native tongues, transplanted from around the conquered Roman world, Coptic, Hebrew, Celtic, Hispanic, Ge'ez, Berber, Arabic.

Five steps further, and the harbor disappeared, her view obstructed by four-story insulas rising beside her. These over-crowded family apartments filled entire city blocks, creating shady canyons to walk through early in the morning and stifling furnaces later in the day.

Her father had risen, over the twenty years since the death of her mother, to the position of eirenarch, the magistrate in charge of public peace. It was a never-ending job, with no local Roman legion, keeping crime at bay. His position allowed him considerable latitude, but Benjamin's murder would prove a delicate dance if he were to shield Sabina from official interrogations and protect himself.

If Apollos, a Christian murderer, were to disappear, who would complain? Not the worshippers from the illegal assembly where the murder had been committed. Apollos had no immediate family. Her father could report the murder solved and the perpetrator dead.

No one could trace her involvement back to the church. Her guilt flared; Apollos and her nightmare flashed through her mind. Was the threat already eliminated?

With the early morning gust came the scent of freshly baked bread. Sabina took a deep breath and gagged. Warned by the stench, she jumped aside, barely avoiding the bucket of last night's sewage tossed out onto the street.

At the bottom of the hill, she turned east and melded into the crowds coursing their way to and from the State Agora along Curetes Street. As the capital city of Asia and home to the Roman governor, the State Agora hosted a sprawling complex encompassing hundreds of magisterial and judicial offices. She walked under the colonnaded walkways, with clusters of harried magistrates and their attending clients, aediles, lawyers, temple priests, council members, and visiting dignitaries scurrying like mice down the wide paved street.

Her father's office sat tucked among the dozens of minor bureaucratic offices housing the public servants charged with managing the city's public water systems, sewage, roads, and religious holidays, amenities a modern city provided.

Her father had been offered a prestigious office directly off the Agora, more prominent, more visible, and worthy of his service. He had refused. His job required dealings with the anonymous members of society: runaway slaves, criminal informants, and spies, constantly spies, secretly slipping in and out to report on the latest conspiracies and twisted alliances of the illustrious and not so outstanding citizens of Ephesus.

She stopped at the door to her father's obscure office and whispered a quick prayer. She had no idea how to find out where Apollos was being held when her father's genius was extracting information, not divulging it.

The longer she stood at the door, the more vivid her failure loomed. Sabina groaned. She dropped her shoulders. Her exhilaration at starting out and the shiver of excitement had turned into an itchy sheen of sweat under her tunic. Her father would scoff at her request and then dismiss her.

Or just dismiss her.

She took a deep breath, raised her hand to knock. She heard footsteps approaching on the other side of the door. The door swept open.

Zarmig stared at her, his eyebrows rising. "Sabina?" He blocked the opening and did not move. "Why aren't you home?" He didn't need to add, as your father ordered. His unwavering stare made the statement.

"I came to see my father." Her voice quivered, but she stared him in the eyes, daring him to refuse her.

Her father's scowling bodyguard could intimidate nearly anyone if he wanted to. At forty-six years old, Zarmig's daily workouts had sculpted a body envied by any man ten years his junior. His coal-black hair flowed thick, its silver threads routinely dyed. "I would not advise it."

She heard an unfamiliar male voice, strident and coming from her father's office. Sabina frowned and stretched her neck to look around the tall bodyguard and across the anteroom at the closed door.

"He is busy." Zarmig moved over to obscure her view. He appeared uninterested in the drama taking place behind the heavy wooden door of her father's office. Zarmig stepped back and began to close the door.

"I will wait." She stepped forward, her body pushing through and stopping him from shutting the door.

59

Zarmig shrugged his shoulders and stepped aside. "It's your time to waste."

She slipped inside. A loud bang, as if something had been thrown, or slammed down, reverberated through the door, across the room. The muffled words increased in volume. Her curiosity peaked. She wanted to see the idiot who dared argue with her father.

Zarmig went back and sat in a chair behind the one table in the room. Sabina sat across from him on a bench. She stared at the bare wall. The workspace mimicked her father's personality, stark, unadorned, and efficient.

The words vibrating through the door were inaudible. The rising pitch of the one-sided dispute grew louder. Sabina's face turned pink, embarrassed for the simpleton who dared raise his voice to her father. She could think of no one reckless enough to lock wills with him or to intentionally antagonize him. Well, maybe one person. She folded her hands demurely in her lap and waited.

Sabina watched Zarmig, who appeared unconcerned over the calamity about to explode. He concentrated on the ledger spread over the table before him, tapping his pen and pursing his lips without once looking toward the closed office door. But she noted the bodyguard sat positioned with his right ear turned toward the conversation, the disfigurement of his left ear, the ear that had been cut off, stayed hidden beneath his shoulder-length black hair.

Abruptly the yelling in her father's office stopped. The silence jarred her nerves—no surge of muffled arguing, no movement, no scuffling, nothing. Her curiosity, always her liability, nearly propelled her out of her seat. She glanced at Zarmig dipping his pen in the inkpot, scratching out his figures, seemingly oblivious to the change in the air—the still after the roar. Did she detect a slight tilt of his head? Yes, Zarmig watched her from the corner of his eye.

The door to her father's office swung open, banging against the wall. Sabina jumped. She could see the back of the idiot, soon to lose his liberty.

"I demand the truth," the man's voice sounded from the doorway of the office. His words stirred the air; his robe swirled around his body.

Bracing her elbows on her knees, Sabina leaned toward the office door, anticipating her father bursting from his office to arrest the man for his disrespect. She waited. Nothing happened. Her father did not appear. Nor did he order Zarmig to detain the red-faced, heavily breathing man. Sabrina was intrigued.

Her curiosity turned to the man. Who is he? From her angle, she noticed his prominent nose. It dominated the sharp cheekbones as if announcing, I a nose, comically hooked, define this man. Then he turned. And she knew she had been tricked. Like a street thief diverting attention with a ploy, the obvious had distracted her from the truth. His steely gray eyes and proud posture, his self-assurance, intelligence, and bold superiority were the reality.

Sabina could not tell the man's age. Sweat dripped from his curly black hair, stylishly cut. Not old. He gripped his floor-length robe. His long fingers were tanned, the strong sinews built up over years of work. Not young either. The expensive linen robe fashioned itself around him, vertical stripes of tan, black and red, worn as if to accentuate his tall, gangly frame purposely, but the assured smoothness of his movements proved he had long ago come to terms with his body. And this certainty communicated an imposing control.

She recognized the arrogance. She looked toward her father's office. She had lived with it her entire life.

The man did not look at her; his hot gaze continued to glare at the open office door, jaw muscles taut, his mouth a grim line, firing distrust, anger, defiance. "I will not be made a fool of, Magistrate." He spat the title as if issuing a challenge.

"A man is being interrogated," her father said.

"I will confront his murderer. It is my right." A threat? A mandate? That reversed her initial opinion of him. Maybe not such an intelligent man.

Sabina stood up, partly to get out of the man's way, mostly to relieve the tension stiffening her body. Her movement startled him. He glanced toward her with barely a flicker of eye movement before his attention riveted back to her father.

"I will be back tomorrow for Benjamin's body. There are preparations to be made. And you will tell me how and why Benjamin died."

Sabina winced. The man slipped farther down the intelligence scale with every demand he uttered, *You will, I am, I will.*

"Just because we are Jews, do not think you can sweep his death away." He spun around, the back of his robe billowing as he strode from the room. A whispering odor of expensive cedar perfume lingered after him.

Zarmig looked up from his ledgers and frowned.

Benjamin? Who was this man? His arrogant demands indicated he did not have confidence in her father. Why hadn't her father told him he had a confession? Was her father reassessing the murder and Apollos's arrest? She could only hope.

Sabina could see into her father's office. He stood by his table with his back to her. He hadn't seen her. Perhaps this wasn't the best time to ask her questions. She could leave. Her heart raced.

Her father turned around. Too late.

"Zarmig," her father's voice boomed. Sabina jumped again. He glared at his bodyguard, his face as cold as carved marble. It did not change when he saw Sabina. "What god released this hive of wasps on me today? Are you not here to protect me from these…" he waved his hand at Sabina as if shooing her from the room, "insidious pests?"

"You need to warn me when you are taking a day off." The bodyguard responded without looking up from his figures.

"And you need to warn me when you confuse your mouth with your butt." Her father growled at Zarmig under his breath and slammed the door shut.

Sabina stared at the closed door. Her courage wilted. She looked to the ceiling to keep the tears pooling in her eyes from spilling. Almost every time she gathered the courage to speak to her father, he managed to put her on the defensive. Sabina slumped down on the bench.

Self-pity churned in her stomach, solidifying into hurt, then resentment. The same reoccurring emotions she had felt as a child after her mother died. The same reaction that irritated her father. He labeled her emotions a female failing. She felt isolated from him, as if stuck on the opposite side of an endless chasm, neither one able to throw the rope across that would begin their bridge. She wondered if she ever made the connection, what would he do? Throw her rope back? Her resentment did not rise to anger but simmered into a stubborn yearning. She wasn't his slave or his bodyguard. Too many times in her life, he had closed the door and walked away from her. Sabina sucked in her breath and stood. She wouldn't walk away and let him, once again, toss her rope aside.

Zarmig looked up, patiently blotted the ink for drying. He shook his head. His frown deepened into unspoken and unambiguous counsel. *Don't.*

Before her father freed Zarmig, he had served as her father's army aide-de-camp. Captured during the Armenian rebellion in 62, twelve-year-old Zarmig's mission to steal siege plans from her father's tent ended in failure. Her father spared Zarmig's life and took him as his slave. Over the years, both men's trust and respect grew into loyalty. Zarmig enjoyed a candor that her father permitted no one else. Zarmig kept nothing from her father.

Acquaintances knew him as her father's freedman, bodyguard, and secretary. But if you belonged to one of her father's inner circles, you knew Zarmig as his master spy and confidant. Sabina knew him as the sympathetic friend to a lonely girl. He had taught her how to dislocate an elbow, break a finger, or knee a man in the groin should the need arise. She bit her bottom lip, remembering his instructions as clear as when he first taught them to her fifteen years ago. *Never rush into an enemy camp. Wisely choose your time and place.* The click of his tongue emphasized this wasn't the time or the place.

She took a deep breath and walked into her father's office.

"How did I know you weren't going away?" He sat at his table, arranging a pile of notices. He did not lookup.

She asked the first question that came to her mind. "Why didn't you tell that man Benjamin died from poisoning?"

"He will find out soon enough." Her father looked up from the notices. "Stay out of this. It is not your concern."

If she earned two minutes with her father, she had just wasted them; asking about a man who her father stated correctly was none of her concern.

"Am I to endure another interrogation? That spectacle was your fault." Her father gestured toward the door, the dust still flying in the air where the tall man had stormed out.

"Me? I have never seen that man before," Sabina answered.

"Do not be flippant with me. Your trouble invariably lands at my door. He is a relative. The brother of your dead Christian."

"Benjamin?"

"Is there more than one body?"

"No!"

"I thank the gods for one small favor. I do not know who is testing my self-restraint more, you, your priest, or this obstinate Jew."

"He is not a priest." Sabina stopped. How could she describe to her father a religion without priests presiding over animal sacrifices, or telling fortunes, or leading frenzied festival processions? He had no grasp of Apollos as a shepherd ministering to the needs of the believers, a teacher, and a spiritual leader. She pursed her lips together.

"The man berated me for calling him a Christian. As if I can keep all you agitators apart." Her father yelled at Zarmig. "The Jew, what is his name?"

"Yechiel." Zarmig entered the office and placed a wax tablet on her father's table. "He signed his name for permission to obtain the body. He said he's an architect and married."

Her father looked at the record quickly. He grunted in disdain. "I am becoming as soft as a rotten eel. If one of my men had dared the impertinence of this…this architect," he spat the last word, "I would have had him flogged to within an inch of his life."

"But you didn't," Sabina said.

"I do not need two dead Jews. One body can be covered, dealt with, explained away. But this Yechiel may make me change my mind."

"How did he know to come here?" Sabina asked.

"Apparently, someone from your church informed the family." Zarmig took the tablet her father handed to him.

Portia was the only church member who knew her father. Benjamin died at her home. She would have told his family. Oh, Portia, why didn't you ask me first?

"When I agreed to let you continue in this Christian cult, you promised you would remain anonymous," her father challenged. "Apparently, I now have throngs showing up, as if I have advertised with the Christian sign of a fish on my door."

"Yechiel is one man." Why did he have to provoke her with his sarcasm? "He doesn't know me or that I'm a Christian." Sabina felt the heat of an argument rising in her. She knew if she took his bait, this discussion would be over. Was that his strategy? "You knew Benjamin's family would come for his body."

Zarmig stepped forward. "Better Yechiel came directly to you for answers," Zarmig said. "Rather than voice his complaints in the forum for all to hear or bring his questions about a suspicious death to the new governor."

"He is demanding to question your priest," her father said.

"You told him Apollos confessed to the murder?" Sabina asked.

Her father grunted. "I've told him nothing, and he is not the type of man to accept my explanation. He insists on questioning the priest to find out how and why his brother died."

Sabina saw her father's dilemma. "Apollos will have no answers."

"Only if he is innocent," her father said. "Apollos declares he is not."

"You know he did not poison Benjamin," Sabina flared up.

"I know someone killed his brother. We will give Yechiel his justice," her father said.

"Are you sure you can convince Yechiel that Apollos is guilty?" Sabina asked.

"That could be a problem," Zarmig said. "If Apollos cannot satisfy Yechiel and he believes our arrest is a cover-up, he could appeal to the governor to investigate."

"I am tempted to let him. And be rid of these fanatical Christians." Her father clenched both fists.

"Apollos didn't kill Benjamin, but he might know who did," Sabina said.

"He disclosed nothing more after his confession," Zarmig said.

"Did you question the person who told you Benjamin had been murdered at the church?" Sabina asked.

Her father looked at her as if she were a toddler. "I had never heard of this Benjamin until I saw his body."

"But you came...to examine the body..." Sabina stammered; her confusion returned. How had her father shown up within minutes of Benjamin's death?

"The man died while I was en route to the church," her father said. "Of course, I would examine an unexpected body. Poisoning was a disturbing conclusion."

"If you didn't know about the murder...why were you there?"

"A street beggar stopped me in our courtyard yesterday," Zarmig interjected. "He asked for directions to the office of magistrate Flavius Fortunus."

Sabina blanched. "Flavius?" Her father's enemy had just been elected to the magisterial head of religious worship and festivals. Flavius Fortunus's duties included carrying out the edicts of Emperor Domitian. Edicts that mandated arresting anyone not making the required sacrifices to the official sanctioned gods of Rome.

"The beggar's letter gave Flavius Fortunus directions to a Christian meeting near the harbor," Zarmig said.

"Last night's worship?" Sabina's jaw quivered. "If Flavius Fortunus knew..." she stammered, unable to go on.

"I gave the boy a copper coin and told him I'd deliver the message personally," Zarmig said.

Her father rifled through his pile of notices and pulled out a small square of papyrus. "Imagine my surprise when I read directions to a house I have had under surveillance for years."

"Worshipping right under our noses. We were stunned," Zarmig said.

"I don't appreciate your sarcasm." She chewed at her lower lip.

"I assure you we took it extremely seriously," her father said.

"Who reported us?"

"Well, it sure wasn't the street beggar," her father said. "I don't know if Benjamin's murder is connected. But the coincidence is suspicious."

"We don't know who sent the note. But whoever notified Flavius wanted your worship stopped permanently," Zarmig said. "Is someone mad at your God?"

Sabina brushed the suggestion aside, puffing in exasperation. "If someone from the congregation poisoned Benjamin, why would they report it to the authorities? That makes no sense."

"Unfortunately, we don't know that the note writer will not try to alert Magistrate Flavius Fortunus again," Zarmig said. "And we can't forget the brother."

"The two incidents may not be related," her father said. "Either way, you will go home and stay away from that church and anyone connected to it. We shall deal with Yechiel when he picks up the body. The symptoms of arsenic are not obvious, but the vomit and the blood mixed with his—" Her father stopped. "It ran down his legs. He will know the death wasn't natural."

"And if Yechiel threatens to bring Benjamin's death before the city tribunal or the governor?" Zarmig said.

"Find out more about this Yechiel. What kind of relationship did he share with his brother? What would be the benefit of bringing this to the governor? Find something we can use against him should we need to silence him," her father ordered.

"He appeared brash but not stupid. Not many people want to be the focus of an imperial court trial if it can be resolved another way," Zarmig pointed out. "Especially if you are a Jew."

Her father breathed deeply and placed both hands on the table and stood up. "I will give Yechiel his resolution tomorrow. With Apollos dead, Yechiel will have to rely on my word and Apollos's written confession for the murder."

"You will sacrifice Apollos for our security?" Sabina shook her head. "He may know who sent the note. At least speak to him."

"Go home, Sabina. Your priest confessed."

"To a murder he didn't commit." She saw any chance of finding Apollos fading away.

"You have no proof. Your priest has offered no defense, and I don't have time to risk further inquiries. Would your beloved Christians allow me into their confidence to investigate? Open their private lives to a Roman magistrate?"

"No," Sabina said.

"You see the logic of your priest's confession. He knew it was the only way to keep your members from public interrogation and an official murder investigation." Her father placed the note on the top of the pile and slid the notices to the side of his table. He rubbed his neck. "It is not yet noon, and I am in need of the baths and a massage."

"The church members would talk to me," Sabina said.

Her father's face turned red. "Have you not heard a word I've said? You will never speak to those people again." He spit on the floor.

"I could look for proof." She pushed. What did she just offer to do? She had come to find Apollos so Portia and the others in the congregation could minister to him. She wanted to speak to him. That was all.

"You have persisted in your mother's foolishness long enough." Her father frowned and folded his arms. "I have shown great leniency over the years, yet you blatantly make yourself a target. You are ignoring the genuine threats of Flavius Fortunus. Now, your carelessness has ensnared our family in a web of murder. You disregard your loyalty as my daughter, and I refuse to let this madness continue. I forbid you from entering that church again."

She stared at him, her words lost in a shock of panic. She had seen the wisdom in staying away from the church for a short time, not forever. "You can't do that. You can't dictate my choices." Her voice quavered but did not break. "You swore you would allow me to worship my God…Mother's God. You made an oath."

Her father gritted his teeth, his face turning mottled as he answered in a barely controlled growl. "Your foolish actions force me to dishonor that vow. I have cursed your mother's spirit for demanding that pox-ridden oath on her deathbed. I have honored my word until now, and I am no longer bound."

"You would risk it?" Sabina's eyes flew wide in shock. Her father did not tolerate superstitious beliefs ruling his life, but all Romans acknowledged and feared the terrifying penalties exacted from broken oaths, especially a promise sworn to a dying loved one.

"Because of you, your mother's ghost will haunt me." He scowled, resignation in his voice.

She shuddered in disbelief at the meaning of her father breaking his oath and antagonizing the Furies. For the first time since the shock of Benjamin's death, Sabina comprehended the danger arrayed against them. Like a gladiator fighting multiple opponents, her father had chosen to defend against the immediate hazards of their flesh and blood enemies. He accepted a spirit being who would torment him eternally in the underworld. The weight of her father's choice and their vulnerability crushed her. Sabina shook, quivering with anger, frustration, and guilt. Apollos would die to keep her safe.

She wished, with all her heart, that her father's concern was for her safety. But she could not discount the danger lurking for him as well. "And when Yechiel finds out Apollos is not the murderer?"

"Once Apollos is dead, Yechiel will have no reason or opportunity to question his confession," her father said, his voice hard.

"Then two ghosts will haunt you. The innocent death of Apollos will be on you as well." Sabina breathed deeply and glared at her father.

"By the gods, woman, you battle me even when I am protecting you from your own idiocy." Her father stood up and slammed his fists against his desk.

Zarmig stepped beside Sabina. "In my limited interactions with Yechiel, he does not appear to be a man who accepts whatever fabrication he is told."

Sabina grabbed at the straw of hope Zarmig held out. "What if he demands justice for his brother's death from the governor?" She had no idea what Yechiel would demand or not, but her hurt like yeast expanded and rose to challenge her father.

"And we can't forget the note writer," Zarmig said, his expression neutral. "He remains a risk."

Sabina glanced at Zarmig. Was he on her side? She swallowed and, with more confidence than she had felt since entering the office, added, "If Yechiel desires the truth, and finds out the real murderer is free and unpunished, your vulnerability will not end. You need to find out who poisoned Benjamin."

"You haven't heard a thing I've said." Her father's voice raised again. He sat down, shaking his head. "It is impossible without additional inquiries." Sabina imagined walking around the table and kneeling beside him. Instead, she stood, spine straight but unable to keep the suppliant note from her voice. "I can ask questions."

"She harangues you with the wiles of a woman," Zarmig said coolly.

Sabina jerked like a puppet at the word *woman*. Her role was rigidly defined and strictly enforced. Women did not ask questions.

Growing up, she had taken advantage of her father's negligence and lived outside of society's restraints and boundaries. Zarmig had reminded her she had just crossed even her father's lax boundaries. Her shoulders slumped, she stepped away from Zarmig.

"However, she makes an intriguing point," Zarmig continued. "No one would expect inquiries from a woman. She could surreptitiously ask questions. Flavius Fortunus would never suspect."

Sabina didn't know if her father's face or hers displayed the most incredulity.

"Are you encouraging this farce?" Her father's gaze narrowed, his jaw flexed.

"I can attest to the effectiveness of feminine guiles." Zarmig smiled as if recalling a specific instance. "In fact…" He grimaced, his brow puckering.

"Stop your lunacy," her father bellowed, his hands pounded the table.

"I am only reminding you of your battle tactic." Zarmig held up his hands as if surrendering. "Better to have eyes on the enemy than to be blind and ambushed. Someone sent that message to Flavius Fortunus. If the murder is connected, we should find out."

"She cannot infiltrate—" her father said.

"I don't have to." Sabina caught Zarmig's eye briefly. Hope sprouted like water soaking a parched vine.

"Her membership in this superstitious faith is advantageous to us," Zarmig said, appealing to her father's logic and his Achilles heel.

"Advantageous?" Her father scoffed. "We might as well throw ourselves to the lions."

Her father threw out the barb, but he did not order her from the room. He did not say no.

"I can inquire." Sabina stopped and pressed her lips together. What was she proposing? She had come to find Apollos for Portia and the others. She had hoped to speak to him and ask about her mother—not to probe into the lives of her fellow believers. To worm her way into their confidences and betray one of them to her father. What was she doing?

"You give yourself too much credit," her father said with a derisive smirk.

She bristled. Her whole life, she had sought his approval or at least his attention and had found one way: head-on defiance. "Someone from the church may know who wrote the note."

"This discussion is ridiculous." Her father's vehemence slacked. "Would Apollos have confessed if he knew who the murderer was?"

"Someone else may know. Once Apollos is dead, your options are limited," Sabina said.

Her father picked up a pen and then set it down. "I find your motivation baffling. Have you considered how this action could destroy your reputation should your involvement leak out? Eliminating your dwindling opportunities for another marriage."

Of course, she hadn't weighed the consequences. This hadn't been her plan. She had no plan. She looked over at Zarmig. "I will be discreet."

Her father stood and then sat. His characteristic calm obviously in tumult. "Very well, talk to Apollos," his voice level as if daring her. "I will hold Yechiel at bay."

"For a week," Sabina said.

"A day," her father replied.

"There is no time for…" she stammered.

"May I suggest four days," Zarmig interjected. "A compromise."

71

Her father's brows drew together. "If Apollos loves his friends as much as he says, at the end of four days, if nothing has been found, he will die a martyr. Isn't that what you Christians long for?" her father derided.

Sabina didn't move. "And if Apollos isn't the murderer, I can return to the church?"

"Only if the murderer is found and this threat eliminated. If not, you will dutifully return home under my rules."

She met his stare. The challenge was evident to them both. She would run his household, host his dinner parties, and socialize within his social class. Christians excluded. "When can I speak to Apollos?"

He fingered a pen lying on his desk, dropped it, and began cracking one knuckle at a time.

She watched, knowing he wanted to deny her, waiting until his pragmatism won out.

"Be here tomorrow afternoon after the offices have closed." He said. Picking up his pen and choosing a papyrus sheet from the stack, he started to work.

"But tomorrow afternoon—" Sabina felt a firm grip on her arm.

Zarmig whispered in her ear, "He agreed to your terms." He steered her by the elbow and escorted her from the office, closing the door behind them. "Don't give him an excuse to change his mind."

FIVE

Sabina stopped outside the door. What had she just agreed to do? She closed her eyes and took several deep breathes. "All I wanted was to find out where Apollos is being held."

"You succeeded," Zarmig said.

Her spontaneous visit had swerved onto a road she wasn't prepared to take. Find clues to Benjamin's killer? Free Apollos? And if she couldn't? Had she completely shifted the responsibility for Apollos's death to herself? Had she just agreed to renounce—not her faith, her father could never stop that, but he could prevent her from fellowship with the church. He could prohibit her from leaving the house, and she had assented to it. She had willingly walked into this. No, she had jumped without looking or thinking. She slumped against the wall for support, closed her eyes, and began to shake.

"I see you understand the magnitude of your request," Zarmig said, moving in and putting his hand on her shoulder. "Do you need to sit?"

She opened her eyes and let Zarmig lead her to a bench.

"I can't find a murderer," she said, shaking her head.

"Nor will you. You are to question Apollos, that is all."

"Yes," she whispered, not able to confess the information she initially wanted from Apollos. Whatever Amisi's secret was, it would end all possibility of freeing Apollos.

73

"And tomorrow, you will. You will find out what Apollos knows and inform your father. If the priest implicates someone else in the church, you will be in a position to confirm his information."

"So I am being used as your spy?" Sabina blinked at him, letting the word *spy* roll off her tongue. To worm her way into the confidences and betray a fellow believer. Not a believer, a murderer.

"Apollos trusts you. A few questions and your involvement will be over. I would not have proposed this action if I did not believe you were capable of recognizing dangers and avoiding them."

"Apollos is not dangerous."

"The letter writer is. We will continue our search. Hopefully, we will intercept him before he knows we are hunting for him...or her."

"And the murder?" Sabina asked.

"That guilt rests on Apollos. Your father would not have agreed to this extreme measure were you not at risk," Zarmig said.

"Father is not concerned about my safety." She sounded petulant. All she had to do now was cross her arms and stomp her foot. It wasn't a feeling she admired but one she often regressed to around her father. Her confidence and self-control abandoned her, and she fought to govern the feelings of a confused and lonely eight-year-old, desperately missing the love of her mother and confused by her father's remoteness.

"He is worried." Zarmig sat on the edge of the table, facing her. "You have forced him to maneuver a dangerous set of events. He must remain vigilant until Apollos is..."

"Is executed? That is his solution to save himself?" She leaned forward, her head hanging. She chewed on her lower lip. Rationally, she knew her father couldn't release a confessed murderer.

What would she ask? She knew Apollos would not change his plea. He understood as well as her father. A prolonged investigation endangered his Christian flock.

Where would she begin? She knew little of Benjamin. He was a Jewish scribe who had joined the congregation almost two years ago. He had chosen their small group of believers over the larger fellowship founded by the apostle Paul and comprised mostly of Jewish believers. Was there a dark secret to be uncovered there? There was Magnus, but she had heard nothing to warrant his murdering Benjamin. The more she thought of the scribe, the more bewildering his murder became.

She knew so few facts, and irritation at her father's bullheadedness made logical thinking difficult. She pushed up from the bench, gritting her teeth. "Why can't Father see executing Apollos will solve nothing? You said yourself, Yechiel is not going to give up until he learns the truth."

"Your father is bound by certain duties. You are not. He has allowed you time to exonerate your priest."

"Only four days." Sabina flung her arms in the air, then took a breath and tamped down her natural tendency toward theatrics. "It is impossible."

"You are not solving the murder. One day is more than enough time to ask Apollos a few questions. To find out what he knows."

"I want to see Benjamin's body."

Zarmig's eyebrow rose. "The body is not here. And you would find nothing helpful. The signs aren't as obvious as other poisons, but your father is certain arsenic caused the death. There is nothing to look at."

"Nothing?"

"Yechiel insisted I return Benjamin's belongings to him." Zarmig rolled his eyes. "My mistake."

"Why?"

"When I handed the items to Yechiel, he erupted. He threw one against the wall, insisting it did not belong to Benjamin. He accused us of desecrating Benjamin's body and vowed he would not leave until he spoke to your father."

"What item?"

"A small silver votive statuette of the goddess, nothing special. We found it in a pouch sewn into his coat." He shrugged. "Along with one denarius, four stylus tips, and a small sharpening knife. Yechiel took them."

"You found nothing else?" Sabina remembered the strange gold coin resting on her bedroom table.

Zarmig squinted, eyeing her closely. "That is what Yechiel asked. Twice."

A twinge of guilt pricked her conscience. She wondered if Yechiel had known Benjamin carried the coin. Was its disappearance significant? Did it have something to do with Benjamin's death? She pushed the guilty twinges away. "Where is the votive?"

"After his fit, Yechiel took the goddess with him. He wrapped it in a cloth. He wouldn't touch it."

"It is forbidden to possess a pagan idol." Sabina sighed and bit her lower lip. She had little to go on. Perhaps the votive bore some significance to Benjamin's death. "I need to go back to the church."

"Curiosity without caution is a deadly combination. I repeat, you are not to expose a murderer. That is my job." His black brows drew together in an expression akin to worry.

"It is not just curiosity. Perhaps Portia can explain the votive. As a deaconess, she has been chosen by the congregation to lead the ministry and counsel the women of the flock. She knows what goes on in her home and much of what occurs between church members. It could provide insight for questioning Apollos."

Zarmig stood up and grasped her hands between his. "While persuading your father on this course of action, it served no purpose to point out the dangers to you. But I would be negligent if I did not mention overcoming the guilt of murder is not easy. If this killer has silenced their conscience, they will kill again. Do not take chances." His gruff tone could not hide his concern.

"I will be careful." Sabina pursed her lips tightly together. It took severe concentration to mask the smile of affection tugging at her mouth, which would only elicit another Zarmig lecture on the seriousness of her assignment.

"I trust you to observe the lessons I've taught you."

"Of course, I will." She remembered doubting Yechiel's intelligence when he repeated *I will* with the same bravado. She groped anxiously within the hidden pocket for the small knife Zarmig had given her many years ago. Then she remembered she had worn Amisi's mantle today. When she returned home, she would make sure she took the knife with her everywhere.

"Be smart, Sabina. Be very smart. You are a woman and easily eliminated." Zarmig waved her from the room. As she shut the door, she thought she heard him mumble, "Your father will not forgive me if something happens to you."

Sabina paused, then shook her head and put up the cloak hood. That couldn't be.

Sabina retraced her steps home, composing questions for Portia. When had Benjamin arrived at the worship service? Had she noticed anything suspicious near his table or near his wine cup? Had she seen Benjamin with a votive of Artemis? What was the relationship between Benjamin and Magnus? She had separate questions tomorrow for Apollos.

Her probable failure and its consequences weighed on her. With so little to go on, Zarmig was right; she couldn't squander her time. Benjamin's murder made no sense, and for all the confidence she had displayed before her father, she had no idea how to find a killer.

Her father's mule-headed stubbornness saddled her with an impossible timeline, only four days. She would focus on what she could do and be thankful she would be able to get Apollos's information about her mother. She prayed that by tomorrow, the prison guards would leave him fit to answer.

Amisi's voice chattered in her head and almost made her turn back. Instead, she plowed forward, misbehaving, risking her reputation as a respectable and well-behaved widow and eliminating her prospects for a suitable marriage in a desperate mission to find Apollos.

She came to the intersection to go home. She should retrieve her mantle and her knife. It would also be fastest to ride in her litter to Portia's. But she didn't need a gossipy escort reporting on her every move. She didn't turn up the hill. She stayed on the main street, joining the flow of pedestrians.

She passed by the gate, announcing the market agora. A wig maker in a stall just inside the market entrance, called to her in a sharp tongue, flourishing a tied truss of long honey blond human hair. Sabina continued toward the harbor, threading her way in and out of the bustling haggle of voices and overflowing merchant carts entering the vast market square, and the shoppers exiting with bags full of verdant green asparagus bunches, clumps of earthy smelling radishes and onions and freshly picked dandelions for eating and medicine. Sabina swerved from the path of a slave awkwardly juggling eggs, a rope, a bottle of wine, and a pair of leather sandals.

She bumped into a man and stumbled to catch her balance. She stopped gawking and paid attention to her own path down the Marble Road.

Away from the riot of the market, she reviewed the little she knew about Benjamin. Could she, in four days, obtain his life's information? Doubtful. They had met less than two years before when Benjamin became a member of their religious community. He had immediately joined in, helping wherever needed, even in the kitchen with the slaves and women. She remembered a shy man who would smile when greeted, but spoke little in larger groups.

She had heard Benjamin had continued to attend his synagogue and practiced many of the Jewish traditions. Fewer Jews joined the Christian faith now, unlike forty years ago when Sabina's mother and grandparents had been baptized by the apostle Paul. Paul, a Jew, preached to an assembly of mostly Jews. Paul believed in Jesus as the promised Jewish Messiah. Sabina's Gentile family represented a minority in the church.

The church grew and embraced many diverse cultures. Some practices brought to the church by new converts sparked disputes within the congregation. The bishops and elders often met to decide if these practices conflicted with the teachings of Jesus or not. She had not heard of Benjamin embroiled in any of these deliberations. Did someone resent him for his Jewish observance? Enough to kill him?

What about Benjamin's votive? A false idol to both the Christian and the Jewish faiths. Was that a reason to poison him?

Hopefully, Portia would have some insight to point Sabina toward some answers or instructive questions. Portia's house hosted worship and meals, instruction sessions for new believers, and meetings between the deacons, elders, and bishops. Portia, a deaconess, joined the deacons in distributing food to the poor and the widows of the church. She knew the members and their problems, in some cases, better than Apollos. And she had worked alongside Benjamin at her home.

The theater cupped the hillside like a giant open clamshell. Its twenty-four thousand seats strung in rows, like so many pearls, gracing the rising breast of the hill. The gulls dipped and soared overhead, their shrieks reverberating off the empty theater stage. The volume and number of gulls increased as she neared the harbor. The throngs of people thinned. She turned left on Harbor Street, thankful to avoid the normal jostling of sailors, merchants, and frantic warehouse slaves. She could almost walk in a straight line, no longer needing to weave in and out amongst the crowds. The competing aromas from several food carts and the rumble of shopkeepers shuttering the storefronts that lined the harbor colonnade signaled the afternoon meal and naptime.

As she walked, she reconstructed the events of the meal from the previous night. She had been speaking to Benjamin as the room filled with worshipers. Apollos had joined them. She tried to think of anything that appeared out of the ordinary between the two men. Anything that signaled Apollos and Benjamin had had a disagreement or an altercation. Benjamin had been nervous until Apollos spoke to him. Their discussion seemed to calm him, not increase his agitation. Benjamin had barely eaten. Had it been nerves or the poison? She reconstructed the timeline, the end of the meal and the start of worship, Benjamin's tussle with Magnus. She had attributed it to Magnus's standard rudeness and lack of manners. Or perhaps just tired people unleashing short-tempers at the end of a demanding day. But Magnus's bullying took on an ominous meaning in light of Benjamin's death.

She had observed Benjamin perspiring. Was sweating a sign of arsenic poisoning? She would ask Zarmig. Benjamin's retching, followed by convulsions and choking. She corrected herself, not choking—dying. How fast did arsenic attack the body? Her father said Benjamin had been poisoned at the meal. How much would he have had to consume to die? She added the questions to her mental list.

Benjamin's death had shocked her. She tried to remember the reactions of other members: Apollos running to help, Gallus kneeling beside her, fear permeating the faces of those watching. Everyone had acted precisely as if Benjamin had accidentally choked, everyone except Magnus. She wondered again what had caused their dispute? Why hadn't Magnus come to Benjamin's aid instead of watching Benjamin choke to death? And why did Magnus vanish from the scene?

The cooling breeze from earlier had died down, barely rippling the water's surface. Two ships sailed in the harbor. One's sails unfurled in slow motion as if yawning and languidly stretching, waking from a restful night's sleep. The other arriving, its crew bowing and rising, partnered in a well-rehearsed dance, with ropes and oars. A balmy Sunday afternoon. She exited Harbor Road onto a street between two of hundreds of columns lining the road to the waterfront. At the first corner, she turned toward Portia's warehouse and home.

Sabina's anticipation grew as she planned the questions to ask her friend. Perhaps finding Benjamin's murderer wouldn't be so difficult after all. The midday break would allow the women a leisurely chance to compare what they knew and strategize the next steps.

The doors and windows of Portia's successful import and export business were closed. With no early morning worship service and the worshipers in hiding, Portia would have cloistered herself, keeping her doors locked and her household safe.

She knocked on the door, expecting to hear the peep window sliding open as the door attendant checked her identity. No one answered. A good sign? Portia knew to stay out of the public eye. But Sabina needed to talk to her. She knocked again, louder. She jumped in surprise when the door swung open immediately. The excited chatter of commerce greeted her from inside Portia's front storerooms.

"Sabina," the door attendant bowed to her. "I apologize; I did not hear your knock. A caravan arrived this morning, and we descended into chaos." His wide grin welcomed her. "Please come in."

Sabina stepped inside and stopped. The shelves and hanging rods, empty last night, were now full of shimmering merchandise. The large storeroom at the front of Portia's house brimmed with activity. She counted at least thirty people holding up rainbows of glistening material. One woman scrutinized a piece of golden silk, matching the color of her eyes; two men clenched and tugged at opposite ends of one length of pale saffron fabric. People were wrapping and arranging lengths around their shoulders and midriffs—silk-starved people gorging at Portia's import buffet.

Not in hiding, not cloistered for safety, Portia wore a shimmering robe of multi-hued pink silk adorned with silver embroidery. She dipped in and out among her customers like a butterfly. She stopped next to a bearded man scrutinizing a length of turquoise blue silk. Sabina could hear the lively banter as Portia skillfully manipulated the smooth fabric, sliding it through her fingers, making it ripple and shimmer as if it were the waters of the Nile pooling into the man's hands. The man grinned and wrapped it around his arm for purchase.

Sabina waved when the lively conversation slowed, and Portia excused herself from a woman tugging at her sleeve and rushed toward Sabina.

Portia pulled Sabina down the entry hall and into a semi-private corner in the atrium. More customers had gathered ahead in her office, settling accounts with her accountant nephew.

"You changed your mind?" She gripped Sabina's hand tightly. "Did you find Apollos? Has he been harmed?" She looked deeply into Sabina's eyes with desperation matching Sabina's own.

"He's not dead." Sabina shook her head slowly—*yet.*

"Our brothers and sisters in Christ have been praying non-stop. Your father made a mistake. Benjamin couldn't have been murdered."

"It was not a mistake. Someone put arsenic in his food, or most likely his wine."

"Arsenic," Portia rolled the word slowly off her tongue as if it were a foreign language. She shook her head. "We were at worship. How could a stranger gain access to Benjamin's wine?"

"A stranger? You saw someone you didn't know?" An impossible hope flared within Sabina. A simple identification of someone who didn't belong here could clear Apollos.

"Well, no." Portia stammered. "I meant it couldn't be one of us."

"I don't want to believe one of our congregation is a murderer, but…" Portia bowed her head, and a tear fell, clinging to her chin. She swiped it away. "Oh Sabina, I am afraid for Apollos, for all of us."

"Then why, when you know you are not safe, do you open your home with your husband away…" Sabina trailed off, sweeping her hands toward the bustling market in front of her.

"I have a business to run. The caravan arrived this morning, a month late."

"Horace has returned home?"

"He is delayed in Parthia," Portia's voice trembled. "He sent the caravan ahead."

"Is there trouble?" Sabina took her friend's hand.

Portia closed her eyes and took a deep breath. "Trade is synonymous with problems. But I pray for him every day. It is what I can do. And it would look suspicious had I not opened." She gently squeezed Sabina's hand. "Promise me you will help Apollos. He has been a counselor and a friend to so many of us."

Promise? A shiver of unfamiliar emotion ran down Sabina's back. She had brazenly told her father she would find the murderer. But her bravado had been mostly pretense, and he knew it. He expected her to fail. Her father had practically guaranteed failure when he granted Apollos only a four-day reprieve. She had not given him the satisfaction of backing down. But what she had not admitted to herself until now was she, too, expected to fail.

Shivers of anxiety spiked the hairs along her neck and arms. She didn't like the panic that could follow. Her father did not care if she couldn't save Apollos, but Portia did. She believed in Sabina. If she promised Portia, she would be obligated beyond a mere attempt for her personal interests. This promise would not be a reckless bluff. "I'm not sure what I can do."

"I will help you in whatever way I can. No one else has your father's ear. He will listen to you."

"Listen to me?" Sabina laughed cynically. "My father is the problem.

Someone must be punished. If not, the authorities will search for the killer. The church and its members would be interrogated and exposed. Apollos confessed to make sure that didn't happen."

"He will die to protect us. We can't let that happen," Portia said.

"I pray for a miracle, but—"

"You are not alone. God guides and protects you in this undertaking." Portia reached out and held Sabina's hands in hers. Tears again flowed.

Sabina's heart sank. She felt none of her earlier boldness. Only a sinking hollowness throughout her body. "I will try." She remembered the reason she had gotten herself in this situation. If uncovering facts to a present-day murder appeared impossible, what could she hope to discover about a death that occurred twenty-one years ago? "Portia, do you remember the day my mother died?"

"Of course." Portia squeezed her hands. "I will never forget it."

"Did she ever share anything with you…a secret, something she asked you not to tell my father?"

"We were friends, but she did not confide anything of that nature. Why do you ask?"

"I believe my mother trusted Apollos with a secret the night she died."

"Do you think that is why your father arrested Apollos? I know your father distrusts, hates, everything associated with our faith."

"He does. But my father suddenly taking revenge on Apollos after twenty years, makes no sense. He didn't appear to recognize Apollos and made no reference to a connection between Mother and Apollos."

"Would he remember someone who had been at her bedside the night she died?" Portia asked.

"Perhaps when she realized she was dying, she summoned her bishop one last time."

"There is no reason for Apollos to have been there. He wasn't a bishop," Portia said.

"But I saw him."

"We had no bishop then. It was years later that Apollos was called to the ministry. It must have been Erasmus. He was an elder."

"I have forgotten nothing of that night. Erasmus was an older man even back then. Apollos and my mother were young."

"You were grieving."

"I would not have mistaken him."

"Then Korinna kept something from her husband…or kept her relationship with Apollos a secret."

Portia's words stunned her. The blood drained from her face. The allegation, spoken aloud by Portia, took an ugly shape in Sabina's mind. She searched Amisi's denials and forgetfulness for a suggestive meaning. Had her mother shared a bed with Apollos? "My mother would never be unfaithful."

"Nor would Apollos," Portia said. "Sabina! I do not believe your mother and Apollos were lovers. That is not what I meant."

Sabina recalled the attention Apollos gave to her after the death of her mother. Was there a hidden motive besides compassion? Did Apollos act out of guilt? Did guilt point an accusing finger at her mother? She could not believe that. Did this revelation open a new chapter of her mother's life? Or her death?

"I will find out where Apollos is tomorrow." She had new questions for him. Sabina wrenched her thoughts away from horrible words like *infidelity, betrayal, affair.*

"Then God has already provided a miracle." Portia raised a hand to her heart. "I knew you would find him. Tomorrow we will provide for his needs."

"Portia, I need to go alone." Sabina held up her hand to stop Portia's rebuttal. She spotted a small group of working-class men who looked uncomfortably out of place amid the bustle of wealthy merchants. They sat huddled together, on a bench, beside the atrium pool. "What are they doing here?"

"It is a small private showing. I invited my elite clients to be the first to—"

"Not your customers, I mean Gallus and the others. …It is unsafe for Christians." Their homespun woolen tunics and worn sandals stood out next to the exotic textiles and richly dyed tunics of Portia's elite patrons.

84

"They are desperately worried about Apollos and waiting for news," Portia said. "Where else would they go?"

The men spoke in low voices and turned their faces toward her. Faces Sabina knew well. "Anywhere but here. It puts them and you at risk."

Portia pulled her by the hand, leading her farther away from the haggling of the business transactions in the front storeroom of the house. "You are their hope."

Had others in the congregation put their hopes in her? False hopes. Sabina threw back her head and groaned. Looking forward, she inhaled a long-drawn-out breath. "I didn't know Benjamin well. I will need your help. Who might have wanted him dead?"

Portia shook her head. She stared thoughtfully at Sabina. "No one. I know this sounds naïve, but Benjamin was truly a saint."

"Saints on the outside are not always saints on the inside."

"If you had known Benjamin better, you would not say that. His devotion to Christ even inspired Apollos. His work as a scribe enabled him to live and breathe the words of the Jewish scripture and lent insight into the letters and books written by the Apostles. He and Apollos often studied God's words together; they were friends. I believe Apollos is why he joined our congregation."

"There has to be something Benjamin did besides worship and study," Sabina prodded.

"Gallus had nominated him to work as a deacon to help our poor and aid Apollos in serving the members of the church."

"He is young for the responsibilities of a deacon." Sabina frowned.

"Yes, Magnus pointed that out. They were both nominated, but only one deacon would be chosen. He argued he was older than Benjamin."

"By a year or two," Sabina noted.

"Many believed age was Magnus's sole qualification. He spread rumors about Benjamin, but no one paid any attention to them." Portia clucked dismissively. "We attributed the rumors to the pressure placed on Magnus by his father to hold an office in the church. Magnus treated the appointment like a contest."

"And Magnus intended to win?"

"He resorted to the behavior we expect from him. You can ask Magnus yourself."

"Magnus is here?" Sabina's glance swept over the atrium.

"He talked to Gallus a little while ago. I think Magnus was attempting to make a good impression. But when he started gossiping, Gallus lectured him and sent him away."

"What did he say about Benjamin?"

"You couldn't take the stories seriously." The man caressing the blue swath waved Portia over; she waved back and turned to Sabina. "I have to go. I am sorry, my customers have been anticipating this caravan and are anxious to make purchases. We will talk later."

"I'd like to talk to Magnus."

Portia embraced Sabina, kissing her on each cheek, holding her a second longer than necessary. "May God go with you," she whispered the blessing. She released Sabina and hurried toward the man tramping toward them. "Aristarchus, let me show you a length I know your wife will…"

Sabina surveyed the customers milling about the store and atrium. No Magnus. She approached the small group sitting with Gallus around the shallow atrium pool. They spoke in whispers. Each man's eyes were sleepless, hollowed circles. Gallus's split lip remained puffy and swollen from her father's blow last night.

Sabina shared her news that Apollos was alive but skirted their questions about her detention last night. "I am fine. The guards released me soon after you left." Sabina repeated her father's warning, "You should not be here. You put yourselves and the others in danger."

"We will risk our lives to help Apollos," Gallus said.

"You cannot help him if you get arrested," Sabina said.

"There must be something we can do." Gallus wrung his hands.

"Can you think of anyone," besides Magnus, "or anything that would make Benjamin a target of murder?" Sabina asked.

The men muttered, reasserting Portia's incredulity that anyone would have a reason to kill Benjamin.

"If you think of anything from last night that seemed unusual, even if it doesn't seem important, tell Portia," Sabina prodded. "She said

Magnus is here. Do you know where?"

"I don't. And you should stay away from him. He stomped away in a surly mood." Gallus nodded, his bushy eyebrows rising and falling, accentuating each word.

She left them bemoaning the evils of the Roman magistrate that arrested their beloved bishop, the virtues of Benjamin, and with incredulity, the murderer within their ranks.

She had not seen Magnus pass by her when she had entered the front of the store. She checked there anyway. She did not see him mixing with the customers among the dwindling piles of silks.

She expanded her search, looking into the communal rooms opening off the atrium. She paused at a doorway, tapping down the dread that flooded her when she scanned the dining room where Benjamin had died. She pressed her lips tightly together and tipped her head back to keep her tears from falling.

Portia had rearranged the room. Three reclining dining couches were arranged in a *U* around one remaining table. The other tables were gone. Whether by accident or design, the sole table sat in the center of the room, covering the spot where Benjamin had died. The altar, its candles, and the scrolls had disappeared, as had Magnus. She backed out and continued looking. A small library. A waiting room. She discretely knocked and peeked into two guest bedrooms, both empty. Magnus must have slipped away while she and Portia had shared their news.

Discouraged, she decided she would ask Gallus about Magnus's gossip. She walked back to the atrium. The men were gone. A surge of relief swept through her, glad they had listened to her warning, but now she had no one to question.

She could not dismiss Magnus's gossip as ridiculous until she knew what he had said. Portia asserted no one paid any attention to the rumors. Perhaps someone had paid serious attention. Serious enough to want Benjamin dead? She would have to wait for Portia's business to conclude to find out. She plopped down on the bench Gallus had occupied.

She glanced into Portia's office and at the lengthy line of customers waiting their turn to make their purchases. A copper and ivory inlaid chest glinted, its lid propped open, as Portia's nephew deposited a customer's money. A swirling copper chain decorated the legs of the chest and ingeniously secured it to a metal bar anchored into the office's mosaic floor.

The office served as a transition room from the storefront and large public atrium at the front of the house to the family's private living area and gardens at the back of the house. Matching arches opened on opposite sides of the atrium, and from where Sabina sat, she could look through the office into the garden beyond. A beautifully symmetrical arrangement of trees and bushes edged a life-size marble fountain of a lion.

The garden's calming design and tranquil space were lost on Sabina. Instead of relaxing in the bubbling melody of the water chiming through the office, she stood up and paced. She sighed in frustration as three more women joined the end of the growing line. She counted the minutes of Apollos's life ticking away while she lingered, counting the garden statuary.

She had just decided to interrupt Portia when she glimpsed a swirling flash of red, black, and tan stripes stirring behind the fountain.

SIX

Her feet did not move. Instead, her nostrils twitched as she remembered Amisi gripping her ten-year-old nose and lecturing, "You keep your nose glued to your own face. You are always sniffing around matters that are not your business, and one day," Amisi pinched harder, "you're going to get your nose bit off. And no man wants to marry a woman without a nose."

Sabina wrinkled her nose and had just convinced herself it could not be the man from her father's office when she saw Magnus. He strolled along the garden walkway, heading toward the back of the house. The man in the tan, black, and red-striped robe disappeared into the shrubbery, only ten feet behind Magnus.

Zarmig's voice replaced Amisi's. *Coincidences are never coincidences.* If Yechiel wanted answers for his brother's murder, it would make sense he would come here to the murder scene. He must have come directly from her father's office.

Offering apologies, she slipped through the line of people waiting to pay for their purchases and exited the office. The arch led onto a covered portico encircling the garden. The tiled walkway was unoccupied. She turned in the direction she had seen Magnus walking. Without stopping, she quickly peeked into an open doorway leading off the portico: a bedroom. The next two doors were closed. Magnus

89

couldn't have entered that quickly. She hurried forward, glancing into the family's private dining room, two more closed doors, on her right a hallway branched off, leading toward the slaves' quarters, kitchen, and back door. The walkway continued around the garden. Sabina stopped. She deliberated over the opposite directions Magnus could have gone.

Two serving girls hurried out of the kitchen hallway, balancing trays piled high with sweet dates and fruit. They giggled as they passed, accustomed to guests and customers frequenting this area of the house. Sabina had used the latrine located down the hall by the kitchens.

She turned toward the kitchen. No sounds filtered down the hallway ahead of her. She slowed, muffling her footsteps. Her ears strained, listening. Nothing. Magnus and his stalker had disappeared.

She passed the closed latrine door. Then paused and tiptoed back. She stared at it. She could wait to see if anyone came out. Or she could knock; she raised her hand to pound on the door, just as a high-pitched squeal burst from inside, jolting her. She lowered her hand and pressed her ear against the door, hoping no one opened it. Silence. She tested the door latch. It lifted easily. She pushed the door open a sliver and pressed one eye against the crack. A clay oil lamp flickered in its niche, dimly lighting the small enclosure. Magnus was pressed against the wall; a knife blade glinted at his throat.

Horrified, Sabina watched as the pressure from the knife lifted Magnus up on his toes. The man holding the knife had his back to her, but she didn't need to see his face. Yechiel's tall, slender figure filled out under the flowing striped robe.

Yechiel loomed over the bulkier man. Whether Magnus had been caught unaware or froze in fear, Yechiel's tall frame and lean muscles had prevailed. His forearm crushed Magnus against the wall, the edge of the knife dangerously close to a pulsating artery.

"My brother, what do you know of his death?" Yechiel's arrogant and demanding voice increased the threat.

Sabina's mind raced through possible actions. She could run for help, but it would take only one second to end Magnus's life. If she left him, there would be no chance to intervene. The knife glinted in the lamplight. Her resolve faltered. She searched, stumbling through her memory for a strategy. A better time? A better place?

Sabina held her breath and opened the door.

Yechiel turned toward her. His brief glance puzzled. As if wondering why she looked familiar. "Leave us, woman. You have no business here." He returned his focus to the artery pulsing in Magnus's neck.

"Sabina, don't go," Magnus croaked. Yechiel pressed the knife deeper into the skin. A thin red line sprang up under the blade. Magnus yelped but said no more.

"You won't get your information if you slit his throat." Sabina stood in the doorway. How dangerous was Yechiel? Until that moment, she had not thought of the risk to herself. He could easily overpower her and slit her throat. Had it only been a few hours ago when she had assured Zarmig she had learned his lessons of cunning and caution? She would have to review her tactics—if she survived.

Yechiel glanced at her again, and a sizeable frown creased his forehead. "Sabina." He rolled the name around his tongue, obviously unfamiliar to him. "I will not kill this fat toad…yet. It will depend on why he murdered my brother."

"I didn't," Magnus croaked.

"When I came in, I heard you accuse Benjamin of offending your God. I heard you confess to the old man."

"Confess?" Magnus's voice squeaked.

"The old man said your ambition harmed an innocent man. He scolded your jealousy. Do you deny it?"

"No…yes. Gallus meant it harmed my relationship, my communion with Benjamin…not that I killed him."

"Benjamin gave his life for your prophet Jesus. Yet you denounce him. Why?" Yechiel's voice shook with emotion. He rotated the blade, sticking the tip into Magnus's fleshy neck folds.

Magnus whimpered.

Sabina saw the trickle of blood running down Magnus's neck. She stepped into the small chamber, halting four feet from Yechiel…one lunge away. "I, too, am here to find the truth about Benjamin."

Yechiel looked at her and scoffed, "I remember you...you were in the magistrate's office. Are the officials so desperate to hide the truth that they send a woman to spy on me?"

Sabina bit back a retort. Making this man angrier would solve nothing. "I am not following you. I am here to get answers."

"From this fat toad?" Yechiel pressed his forearm harder against Magnus's chest. "I heard him confess. He murdered an innocent man."

Magnus's eyes widened in terror, locking on Yechiel. "Benjamin was not innocent." Magnus's chin quivered.

The knife shifted.

"Magnus," Sabina warned. "You're not helping your cause." Did Magnus have a cause? She understood why Yechiel wanted answers. Magnus's actions made him an obvious suspect. A man bearing a grudge and sitting in proximity to Benjamin's wine cup. She, too, had questions for Magnus, and she wanted him alive to answer them.

Tears sprang into Magnus's eyes, but he continued. "Benjamin was always trying to impress. Praying, more than anyone else; fasting; he helped with the meals for the poor; he taught the orphans. Just because he could read and write didn't make him better than the rest of us."

"Magnus, you aren't making sense," Sabina said.

"I think he is making perfect sense. Go on." Yechiel prodded with the blade.

"I can't think with a knife at my throat." Magnus's eyes pleaded with Sabina.

Yechiel lowered the knife but didn't step away from Magnus.

"Just like Apollos taught last week about hypocrites." Magnus panted and slid as far away from Yechiel as the small chamber allowed. "Benjamin acted perfect, but like the whitewashed tombs Apollos preaches about, Benjamin hid secrets."

"Secrets?" Sabina asked, thinking of Benjamin's gold coin and the votive of Artemis.

Magnus glared at Yechiel. "He had women." He touched the line of clotting blood on his neck and looked away.

"Women?" Sabina and Yechiel asked in unison.

Yechiel raised the knife again.

"Gallus didn't believe me. But I saw them together. The woman Marcella, I followed them to her house."

"That is proof of nothing," Yechiel growled.

"Magnus, Benjamin could barely speak without blushing whenever I greeted him." If Yechiel weren't prepared to slit Magnus's throat in front of her, Sabina would have laughed.

"Then why did her husband and Benjamin get into a fight last night before worship started?" Magnus asked.

"Last night?" Sabina asked. "I saw no fight."

"Marcella's husband burst in before most people had arrived. He grabbed her and started dragging her out of the room. Benjamin tried to stop him, and he knocked Benjamin to the floor. He stood over him, yelling at him to stay away from his wife."

"You didn't arrive until after I did," Sabina said.

"Ask the slave who told me. He saw it all." Magnus tilted his chin away from the blade.

"Marcella is a new believer," Sabina said. "She is going to be baptized soon, but I have never met her husband." She remembered how tense Benjamin had been the night they talked. She assumed his nervous behavior was excitement over the scroll. If Benjamin had been attacked, he had reason to act distressed.

"The slave said Marcella's husband's name is Davos, a silversmith." Magnus was warming up to his subject. "They live just off the metalsmith's guild street. I told Apollos about Benjamin going home with her. I warned him Benjamin couldn't be trusted. If there are two chickens in the nest, there are eggs hidden in the grass." He glanced defiantly at Yechiel.

"Two women?" Sabina asked.

"Give me names, Toad." Yechiel again pressed toward Magnus.

"I don't gossip."

"You won't live long enough to." Yechiel grabbed Magnus, slamming his back into the wall. His forearm pressed into Magnus's neck, cutting off his breath. When he removed his arm, a choking Magnus croaked.

"Livia, a widow."

"I don't know a Livia." Sabina narrowed her eyes in suspicion. She needed the information Yechiel's intimidation extracted from Magnus. She hoped that information was all Yechiel wanted, not revenge.

Without taking his eyes from Yechiel, Magnus choked out. "She's not one of us. She just comes for the meals. I warned Benjamin to stay away from her. I am sure he took advantage of her. Then he comes and shares in Christ's sacred meal with us, his infidelity unconfessed. And God struck him dead."

Yechiel smashed his fist into Magnus's face. Magnus's head hit the wall, and he crumpled to the floor. Yechiel turned and pushed past Sabina, nearly knocking her down.

She looked down at Magnus. His eyelids fluttered. She should help him. But what could she do? Nothing. And right now, she had questions for Yechiel, pressing questions. She would send someone to check on Magnus, after she talked to Yechiel.

She hurried out into the hallway and paused, looking right toward the kitchens, then left to the garden. Yechiel had disappeared again. Debating, she turned left, scurrying back the way she had come, hoping she wouldn't lose him in the crowd of customers.

The two servant girls ran down the portico toward her. "Guards are searching the house."

Sabina stopped them. "Whose guards?"

"We don't know. They told Mistress Portia they were under the orders of the city council. They said they were looking for evidence of a murder. Our mistress has hidden all our Christian books. They can't arrest her." The girls held onto each other's hands tightly.

Sabina looked across the garden and saw her father's young guard from last night. He was shuffling through papers in Portia's office. Why had her father sent his guards? Her brow creased in confusion until the magistrate of religious matters, Flavius Fortunus, the chief adversary her father had warned her about, strode up to the guard and gestured an order. Her father had not sent the young guard; he belonged to

Flavius Fortunus. A spy? Sabina blanched. "I have to get out of here. I cannot be found in this house."

"The kitchen." One of the girls pointed back down the hallway.

Sabina turned around and ran. The door hinges creaked loudly in protest as she entered the kitchen. The oven that had welcomed her last night, with its radiating warmth, stood cold. A sweeping glance into an open closet revealed a jumbled pile of onions, pink turnips, and purple carrots. No place to hide.

The door leading outside swung on its hinges, the latch left undone. Sabina raced through, closing it silently behind her. She found herself in the familiar narrow back alley of the house. The gate she had entered through last night lay a few feet away. She heard the screech of the kitchen door opening from the hallway.

It would take the guards a minute to realize the kitchen hid no one. She ran the short distance to the gate and yanked the handle. It jammed. She slammed her hand against the handle attempting to jostle it loose until she realized it wasn't stuck. Her only way out was locked. She froze, trapped between the house and the thick stone wall. Her head snapped as she stared from the locked gate to its sentinel laurel tree. Its top branches towered over the wall, but a few lower limbs were within her reach. If she could climb, she might be able to get to the top of the wall.

She could hear the guards' voices questioning the kitchen girls. But the words sounded muffled as if echoing from the far end of the hallway. Sabina lifted her mantle and knotted it around her waist. She gripped a low branch of the laurel tree. Leveraging her toes against the solid trunk, she pulled herself to the lowest branch and hung by her armpits. The limb bowed, but she held on and reached for the next limb. Her mantle slipped loose, its tie catching in the crook of the trunk and a bough. She kicked the fabric free, and the mantle dropped to the ground. She reached for the next branch. It snapped off in her hand, and she slithered down the trunk. She heard fabric tearing. Her hands grasped and stripped leaves from the branches. Her fingernails dug into one limb and held on. She stopped, dangling several feet from the ground.

The outside kitchen door banged open, then closed.

She hung, suspended in pure terror, unable to turn and confront her captors.

Her legs were grabbed. She screamed as she was lifted into the tree. "Climb," she heard Magnus's choked voice order.

Without thought, she did. Clutching one limb, then the next, until a final heave hoisted her to the top of the wall, where she perched precariously. Glancing down through the leafy branches, she saw Magnus with his shoulder braced against the trunk.

She leaned over and offered him her hand, just as two guards rushed through the kitchen door. Magnus spun around to face the intruders. Sabina lost her balance and fell backward off the wall. Her back smacked hard on the dirt-packed street outside. She lay, her breath knocked from her, unable to move, unable to escape. She closed her eyes and imagined dying of suffocation. Her lungs refused to fill.

A deep, low-pitched voice sounded as if it came from on top of her. "By the gods, what bucket of lard do we have hiding out here with the garbage?"

She needed to hide. She needed to move. But first, she needed to breathe.

"I wasn't hiding. I was dumping water from the kitchen," Magnus said, his voice croaked.

"I don't see no bucket in your hand," the baritone said. "I heard a scream. Were you squealing like a girl?"

"Hey, what's this by the gate?" the other man said.

"Someone lost a piece of their clothing. Is there a poxy girl out here with you?"

"I'm helping with the midday meal," Magnus said. "Ask the slaves."

"That's not what I asked." A thunderous whack was followed by a thud, then silence. "Leave him; we weren't ordered to arrest kitchen scum."

"Do you think someone is on the other side of the wall?" the baritone said.

Sabina's heart nearly stopped. She didn't dare draw a breath, even if she could have.

Someone rattled the gate latch. "Gate's locked."

"We can break the lock," the other guard said.

"Easier to climb the wall for a look." Sabina felt as if she would pass out. She needed air.

"You climb the wall then."

"When did you get to be captain? You climb the wall." The baritone's voice was getting louder.

Her chest cavity relaxed, and tiny puffs of air began to enter her lungs. She slowly rolled over.

"Piss on your mother." Two solid thuds followed, and Magnus groaned.

The kitchen door slammed shut, followed by the echo of receding footsteps, then silence. "Thank you, Magnus," Sabina mouthed, slowly rising. She braced her palm against the wall and half pulled, half pushed herself from kneeling to standing almost erect. She rested her back against the wall and sucked in a small but glorious breath of air. She exhaled. Several shallow inhales returned her breathing to normal. She ran her hands up her arm; nothing appeared broken, only bruised. She shuffled down the side street, bent over, and walked like an old woman. It was as fast as her lungs allowed. Her entire body shook.

When she reached the corner, she could stand up. She watched as a tan, black, and red-striped robe disappeared in the distance.

SEVEN

"Ayee, there you are." Amisi accosted Sabina as she attempted to slip quietly into the house.

Sabina flinched. "Amisi, you frightened me."

"Frightened you! You don't tell me where you are going. I have been fearful of every sort of harm imaginable. All day, you have been gone."

"Before you start your lecture. I had Father's permission to be out."

Amisi eyed her suspiciously, then her shoulders slumped. "And he knows someone is out there murdering Christians. You are not safe. Look at you. You have blood on your hands; your hair is tangled."

Sabina examined her hands. She had not escaped the fall without bruises and an aching wrist. She had worried about Portia and Magnus on the walk home and hadn't noticed her lacerated palms. "I am fine." Thanks to Magnus. "I need to wash and change my clothes. I lost your mantle." She shrugged her shoulders out of her tunic and groaned, surprised by the stiffness of her joints. "I will make sure my father buys you a new one."

"I do not care about the mantle." Amisi pursed her lips and watched in consternation.

"I know. Thank you for worrying about me." Sabina tentatively passed her the garment. She closed her eyes, ignoring the frown she sensed Amisi focusing on her. "I'm hungry. I missed lunch."

"I will bring some goat cheese and apricots." Amisi bent and picked up the soiled robe. On her way out the door, she quipped, "I was told Marcus likes an obedient woman."

Sabina watched the door close behind Amisi. "Then he's chosen the wrong woman," she mumbled under her breath.

She took out her pen and inkpot. Send one missive to Portia, asking about Flavius Fortunus's search and Portia's and Magnus's safety. She chose her words carefully. Her wrist throbbed as she wrote. Her hand shook. And another letter to her father to alert him to Flavius's spy planted inside her father's personal guard.

Amisi returned carrying a tray with apricots, cheese, an egg, and a cup of wine.

Sabina sealed the notes with her wax stamp. "Find a house slave to deliver this note to Father and this other to Portia."

Amisi set the tray on the small crowded table, pushing the inkpot aside.

"Direct the slave to deliver the note into Portia's hands alone." She thought of the note meant for Flavius Fortunus that Zarmig had intercepted. If it had been delivered to her father's enemy, she'd be in shackles right now. That thought had steadied her shaking hand while writing.

She handed Amisi the sealed notes. Amisi scowled, but for once, did not hammer her with questions before flouncing out the door.

Sabina yawned and collapsed back on her pillow. She should eat before she searched for Silversmith's Street and interviewed Marcella.

She stared at the food. Her leaden limbs refused to respond as if locked in a dream, desperate to move but unable to. Fatigue took over. She closed her eyes, just for a minute.

The staccato hoot of an owl woke her. The cheese square had softened into a round blob. She didn't know how long she had slept or what time it was. Moonlight shimmered through her open door, carrying the shrill chirp of the garden's crickets.

She groaned. She had slept through precious daylight hours instead of staying awake, instead of resuming her search, instead of exonerating Apollos. She pushed the guilt away. Her remorse would not find the murderer, and even she wasn't reckless enough to risk getting lost in the dark city streets lit only by moonlight.

She swung her legs off the bed and sat up, noticing a note on her bedside table. She first thought it was Portia's note from this morning, but this did not bear her seal. And Sabina had destroyed that one before she had left the house. Amisi must have delivered this to her while she slept.

Sabina opened and read the note.

All is well. Flavius Fortunus's wife happens to be one of my best customers. She's not happy.

No names, no Christian sign of the fish. No identification.

Her empty stomach growled. She wondered when Apollos had last eaten. She pushed that thought aside. She devoured the small tray of cheese, scooping large bites of the soft cheese with the apricot halves. She slowed down and savored the watery wine. She would know soon.

While she had slept, Amisi had laid out a bedtime tunic. Sabina changed into her nightclothes.

Awakened by the chilly morning air, Sabina's mind instantly returned to the love connection between Benjamin and Marcella. Magnus had observed Benjamin following Marcella into her house. Marcella was old enough to be his mother. Sabina guessed at least forty-five years old. It seemed implausible, but after Sabina's three tragic engagements, she was no expert on someone else's love life. She knew several older women who were rumored to have young lovers.

And it was the only clue she had.

Had something gone wrong between them? Perhaps Benjamin planned to leave her for a younger woman? Livia? Did Marcella poison him out of jealousy? When love rules, reason is brought to its knees.

She wanted to rush through dressing and eating and get to Marcella's immediately. Amisi had other plans. She insisted on washing, perfuming, and styling Sabina's hair. She pulled out several tunics, requiring Sabina to decide, then insisted on choosing jewelry and dyed kid slippers that matched. She continued to hover while Sabina ate breakfast. Had her father sent Amisi to report on Sabina's movements? It was a possibility. Amisi may also have her own concerns to keep Sabina out of trouble.

"Your father's guest is arriving tonight, and we are eating fresh oysters. Octavia praised my selection last time."

"Octavia?"

"You met her. Your father invited her to dinner last month."

"I'm surprised he has asked her again. She is older. Almost his age?"

"She made your father laugh. A rare sound."

Her father could decide to remarry. After all these years, it seemed implausible. But she would then no longer be the mistress of her father's house. She would be fed, clothed, and housed depending on the whims of his new wife. She should be counting her current position as a blessing.

"I have been asking around about your merchant."

"He's not my...never mind." She had long ago learned not to question Amisi's sources. The gossip web between the city's slaves and servants rivaled any imperial spy organization. "Asking about what?"

"He is not married."

"I knew that from our dinner conversations."

"Did he tell you his family is demanding he finds a wife? He is almost forty and has no heirs."

"I've only spoken to him twice."

"I think he is testing you to see if you would be a good wife."

"Aren't you worried about my curse?"

"A man wants to marry you. My magic must be stronger." She nodded with certainty. "Now we have a chance, a chance for everything we've longed for, a home of our own and children. You must stop your Christ worship immediately. Even my spells cannot undo that damage."

"Father has probably told him already."

"Your father tells no one that shameful fact."

Not wanting another squabble with her slave, Sabina waited until Amisi left to supervise the laundry in another part of the house, then slipped into her robe and stole out of the house.

She found Davos's workshop and a storefront on a quiet avenue, a block off the bustling main street that housed the large retail shops of the silversmith's guild. Davos's storefront was narrow, with a door and one small display window. A sign nearly as large as the window. Under the words *Davos – Silversmith*, a painting of Artemis, the patron goddess of Ephesus, leaped out in red, yellow, and orange, advertising his trade and specialty. Davos belonged to the guild that made silver votives, the statues of the goddess Artemis, tourists and worshipers purchased as souvenirs or presented as offerings with their prayer requests at her temple.

Sabina peeked through the open display window into a small showroom, hoping to see Marcella. No one tended the shop. The highly polished counters were bare, the wares stored out of sight. Valuable merchandise displayed unguarded invited even the most pious of thieves. The silver votives and charms were sacred—stealing them was not.

Peering through the shop window, she saw an open doorway across the room. She could hear a muffled tapping or hammering resonating from inside the house. A rope hung inside the window attached to a tiny brass bell. Sabina jiggled the cord. She steeled herself and prepared to meet the man who had threatened Benjamin only hours before he died.

Instead, a lovely young woman entered the shop. She clutched a broom and wiped a smudge of dirt from her face. Upon seeing Sabina, she brightened. "I will be with you in a moment. Let me rinse my face."

"I am here for Marcella. Is she home?"

"Oh." Her smile faded in disappointment at losing a potential customer. "My mother is here, but she is with someone. Would you like to come back later?"

"I can wait."

"Very good. Please come around to the door." The young woman pointed to the front entrance. She ushered Sabina into a hallway with a narrow alcove just wide enough to hold a bench. "You may sit if you'd like while I get my mother."

Sabina sat staring into the family altar mounted across the hall from her. Small bits of food lay inside the cupboard-like shrine, gifts dedicated to the Lares, the household gods. Sabina recalled Marcella's husband was not a Christian. Nor had she seen Marcella's daughter at the church.

The hammering pulsated with a dull thud through the wall behind her. The vibration jarred her sore shoulders. She leaned forward, away from the wall. She assumed the noise emanated from Davos's workshop, conveniently located down the hall from the storefront.

Past the workshop and further down the hallway, the murmur of conversation drifted from inside the home. Sabina recognized the playful lilt of Marcella's voice but couldn't discern the words.

Sabina had worked beside Marcella. They had distributed food to the widows of the church. Marcella laughed and often joked when they were together. Sabina envied Marcella's gift of patience with the sick and elderly. Sabina pictured the attractive middle-aged matron, with her thick black hair arranged in ornate silver clasps, displaying her husband's handiwork, no doubt. Was she Benjamin's love interest? Or only *one* of his love interests?

She searched her memory for instances of Benjamin and Marcella together. She recalled Marcella chatting with groups of women and Benjamin sitting with the men. Men and women mixed during worship, often started out sharing a table with family and friends, and remaining together. Had Marcella joined such a group? She couldn't remember. Of course, there were other opportunities for the two to get together.

Marcella had joined the congregation a little over a year ago and seemed curious and eager to learn about the new religion. Apollos met with new converts regularly to teach the beliefs of those who worshiped Christ. Benjamin also studied with Apollos. Was that the link? Had Benjamin and Marcella learned of Christianity together and fallen in love?

Perhaps Magnus told the truth?

Sabina calculated; Marcella would soon confirm her vow of faith and be baptized. She would join in the fellowship of those in Christ.

A loud masculine voice startled her out of her musings. She recognized the voice. It sprang from the same direction as Marcella's.

Sabina looked around. Marcella's daughter hadn't returned. She stood up. Why was he here? She wasn't the only one who wanted to corroborate Magnus's accusations.

She sat down. Then stood up again and crept down the hall, following the sound of the conversation. She peeked around the corner. She recognized the back of Yechiel and watched a smiling Marcella exchanging banter with him. Sabina frowned and took a squeaky step backward toward the hall bench.

Marcella turned toward the sound. "Sabina?"

Yechiel turned around and glared.

Sabina stepped forward. "I am so sorry to intrude. Your daughter showed me in and…" She could think of no good excuse to give for interrupting them or eavesdropping on their private conversation. She blushed and avoided Yechiel's eyes.

"A surprise, but you are welcome, of course." Marcella gestured for her to join them. Sabina bent forward, and the women shared the kiss of peace before sitting next to Yechiel. Marcella's eyes asked the questions she was too polite to verbalize. "May I offer you some honey wine?"

"That would be wonderful, thank you."

"Davonia." The missing daughter appeared from another room. "Please bring a pitcher of wine and cups."

Davonia nodded, curiously glancing back at the two visitors.

"Why are you here?" Yechiel hissed under his breath. "Leave." His glare made her catch her breath.

"Do you two know each other?" Marcella asked again, a note of confusion in her voice.

"Yes," said Sabina.

"No. Yechiel raised his hands, his fingertips rested under his chin as if praying. He did not look at her. "No," he repeated as if coming to a decision.

"We met yesterday," Sabina said.

Yechiel cocked an eyebrow and glared at her, but he did not argue.

Marcella's daughter delivered a tray loaded with cups and a pitcher. She set it on the table.

"You may go," she dismissed the girl. When Marcella stretched out her arms to pour the wine, the sleeves of her robe pulled back, revealing purple bruises on her forearms. She casually pulled her sleeves down and handed each a cup of honeyed wine.

"I had hoped to find you home." Sabina turned to Marcella.

"Ahhh," Marcella's eyes lit with comprehension. "You are here to see if I am safe after the other night."

Sabina did not correct her misunderstanding. "And I hope to get information about that night at the church."

"I cannot help you. I stopped at Portia's for a short time." Marcella sipped her wine. "Davos, my husband, warned me about the danger. I should have listened to him. If he had not rescued me, I would be in prison, like the others. As you can see, I am unharmed."

Magnus had not described her exit from the church as a rescue. "Only Apollos was arrested. The others were released unharmed," Sabina added, giving her father credit.

"Are you sure...I thought. Of course, I am thankful, but Davos said everyone had been arrested." She looked confused, then shook her head. "Why only Apollos?"

"They took the bishop because of Benjamin," Yechiel said.

"Benjamin?" Marcella's gaze swept from Sabina to Yechiel.

"Did you speak to Benjamin that night?" Yechiel asked.

Marcella's eyebrows drew together. "Briefly, as I said. I left almost as soon as I arrived."

"Your husband argued with Benjamin. Do you know why?" Sabina asked.

Marcella clutched her cup and frowned at Sabina. "Yechiel asked the same question. Why?"

"Marcella, Benjamin is dead," Sabina said.

Marcella dropped her glass. Shards sprayed across the floor. Her face blanched white. "You are here to accuse..."

"We're accusing no one," Sabina said, certain Marcella's shock wasn't an act, but noticing no concern for Benjamin.

"Davos did not hurt him. They had an argument." Marcella's voice strained in protest. "Davos got angry. He pushed Benjamin, but Benjamin got up and walked away."

"He didn't die from the fall. Someone poisoned him," Yechiel said.

"Poisoned?" Her face went still, as if a veil fell over it, wiping away her earlier surprise and justification. "I can't help you. I did not know. You need to go." Marcella stood and stepped toward the hallway.

Sabina and Yechiel remained seated. Both ignored Marcella's request.

"I have to clean up this mess. My daughter…" Marcella closed her eyes and inhaled deeply. Then exhaled, opened her eyes, and sat down. "Who poisoned him? How?"

"The authorities have a suspect," Yechiel said.

"Apollos," Sabina said.

Marcella's eyes grew wide. She shook her head. "That is absurd; he is the bishop."

"Marcella, if you could answer a few questions," Sabina said. "To help us understand what might have led to Benjamin's death. You spoke to him that night."

"I'm sure many people spoke to him. I barely had time to…I don't understand why that is important."

"Did Benjamin say anything unusual?" Sabina asked. "Do you know of anyone wanting to harm him?

"Besides, my husband, you mean?" The color in her face and her composure returned. "No."

"How well did you know my brother?" Yechiel questioned.

"He was the person who told me about Jesus the Christ. He brought me into the church. Benjamin felt a special burden to help the poor, the widows, and the orphans of the church. He said Christ taught us to love the poor. Who spoke of such strange ideas? I had never heard of a God who loves all."

"What did your husband and Benjamin argue about?" Yechiel asked.

"Just a misunderstanding." Marcella's shoulders raised and stiffened.

"About what?" Yechiel pressed.

Marcella sat, emotions playing over her face. After several minutes of silence, she said, "I betrayed my husband. Davos got angry. That is his way, but then he forgets the reason he lost his temper. He is over it." She rubbed her arms.

"If Davos thought you were leaving him for Benjamin, perhaps he wouldn't forget so easily," Sabina said.

Marcella blinked, staring at Sabina, a blank expression on her face. Sabina wondered if Marcella had heard her.

Suddenly, Marcella's eyes flashed wide open. She slapped a hand over her mouth, and a minor hiccup escaped. Marcella's shoulders shook as she uncovered her mouth. A crooked smile played on her lips. "You are here because Benjamin and I were lovers?"

"You admitted as much."

Marcella pursed her lips and crossed her arms. "You're accusing me of adultery?"

"You said you betrayed your husband," Sabina said.

"Not by sleeping with another man. I'm not sure if that is an insult or a compliment." Her eyes gleamed. "I shall choose to be flattered you thought me attractive enough to entice the lust of a man half my age."

"But Magnus told us—"

"A lie. The fat toad tricks the gullible," Yechiel said.

"If it is a lie, why are you here?" Sabina spun on him. "I'm not the only gullible one."

"I came to collect Benjamin's belongings," Yechiel answered smoothly. If he had the slightest twitch to his mouth, she would have thought he was laughing at her.

"His what?" Sabina asked.

"Yechiel came to collect his brother's possessions," Marcella explained. "Benjamin lived here."

Sabina's face turned red. She refused to look at Yechiel, and his I-told-you-so smirk. When Magnus mentioned Marcella's name, Yechiel would have known she was Benjamin's landlady. "That is why Magnus followed Benjamin to your house," she said, attempting to hide her defensiveness.

Marcella continued, seemingly unaware of Sabina's discomfort. "Benjamin rents…rented a room above Davos's workshop. That is all."

"Marcella, I apologize." Again, Sabina sensed Yechiel enjoyed her confusion. If a man can snigger with his lips pressed together and with no sounds coming from his mouth, then Yechiel was doing it.

"You obviously didn't know Benjamin well," Marcella said.

"Obviously," Yechiel said.

Sabina forced herself to remain calm and to quit interpreting the deepening creases in his dimples as a direct taunt.

"My daughter, Davonia, would flirt with Benjamin when he tried to tell her about Jesus. She teased him outrageously. His face would turn as red as a pomegranate, and then he would scamper to his room. Even Livia...you know her from the church?"

"Magnus mentioned Livia," Sabina remembered the name of the second woman Magnus connected to Benjamin.

Marcella continued. "Even Livia's relentless and pathetic attempts at seduction could not distract Benjamin from his work and his calling."

Magnus's gossip about Marcella had been baseless. Could she believe Marcella's story implicating Livia? "You said your husband and Benjamin fought over a misunderstanding," Sabina said.

"You can hardly call it a fight. Davos knew I wanted to be baptized. He became livid and blamed Benjamin. Benjamin shared the love of the Christians and their God with me. He became upset that night when I told him my decision not to get baptized. I was leaving the church."

"You are not getting baptized?" Sabina's voice rose in surprise.

"I cannot endanger the life Davos has worked so hard to build for us. He has had remarkable success lately and will soon be able to buy his admission into the highest level of the silversmith's guild. He has worked years to build his reputation as a master smith. My baptism would destroy that."

"You don't believe in the one living God?" Sabina asked.

"What I believe doesn't matter. I have insulted the goddess and the guild that serves her," Marcella said. "We depend on the tourists buying our votives to offer at Artemis's temple to accompany their requests for her assistance and favors."

"It is blasphemy for a Jew or a Christian to own an idol of the goddess." Yet Benjamin took that risk. Did Benjamin pray for a favor from Artemis? Yechiel had taken the Artemis votive found on Benjamin's body. She needed to see that votive.

"You see my dilemma." Marcella stopped and faced her. "Even if I don't believe in Artemis's power, Davos does…so do the people who buy his votives. I would be branded as an atheist if I failed to sacrifice to the goddess. In turn, the temple priests would refuse to bless Davos's statues and amulets, a grave rebuke publicizing to all Ephesus that Davos's work is not acceptable to Artemis. Without a blessing, the pilgrims can't trust the influence and power of Davos's merchandise. It is the goddess who provides for us, whether I believe in her or not."

"Davos would be banned from the silversmith guild?" Yechiel asked.

"He would be expelled and unable to work as a silversmith."

"That night, Davos blamed Benjamin for your conversion to Christianity?" Yechiel asked.

"No. I promised Davos three nights before that I would leave the church. He had no reason to hurt Benjamin." But Marcella's voice had lost its earlier conviction.

"If you had already decided this, why did you return to the church that night?"

"I had not planned to go. Davos and I argued. He told me he planned to evict Benjamin from our house. I wanted to warn Benjamin. I hadn't told him I had stopped worshipping Christ. Davos followed me. He thought I had lied to him when I told him I promised to leave the church. He became angry. Benjamin stepped in. Davos pushed him. It was all a terrible mistake. I should never have given Benjamin—" She stopped abruptly. "It doesn't matter now."

"Given him—"

A door down the hall opened and slammed shut. Footsteps advanced toward them. "Marcella." A man's deep voice bellowed down the hall.

"Davos!" Marcella stood up. "It would be best if he didn't see you here." She put her finger to her lips and pointed Yechiel toward an archway located on the back wall. "Benjamin's room is upstairs. You can gather his belongings, then leave through the outside stairway. Hurry."

Yechiel stood and strode toward the archway. Because she wasn't sure what else to do, Sabina followed.

She heard Marcella scurrying toward the entry hall. "I am coming, Davos."

Sabina trailed Yechiel up a set of narrow wooden stairs leading to the second story of the house. She grabbed the railing. It shook precariously. She immediately let go before she lost her balance. She noted the stairs rose toward the front of the home. Benjamin's room must be located above the storefront and Davos's workshop.

Marcella caught up with them before they reached the top stair. She pushed past Sabina. "Nothing serious. A missing leather apron." When they reached the top, she moved in front of Yechiel. "This way." Marcella turned down a dark, narrow hallway and nodded to a door at the end. "I am sorry about what occurred between Davos and Benjamin. But there is nothing more I can tell you. Davos will not allow Benjamin's name to be mentioned."

"He has not forgotten his anger?" Yechiel asked.

Marcella became defensive. "It is not just Benjamin. It is the church. That includes you, Sabina. If he knew you were a believer in Christ, he would be furious that I talked to you." She rubbed her forearms. Portia's words flashed through Sabina's mind. *Not every marriage is a blessing.*

"What have we done to draw his wrath?" Sabina started to rub her own arms then dropped them to her side, relieved they had avoided a confrontation with Davos. Would this have been her life had Xeno lived? Would his expectations for a wife have restricted her faith? Would Marcus force her to choose between her husband and her God? She did not know, and that was a terrible thought.

"Davos felt he was tricked, first by Benjamin and then by me. Davos is not an overly contemplative man. If I publicly performed my veneration to Artemis, he did not care what other gods I worshipped. He considered Benjamin harmless, a member of a secret club in which Davos had no interest. He said I could waste my time however I chose."

Marcella tripped on an uneven floorboard, catching herself. "Be careful." She continued walking down the hall—the dull thud of hammering echoed from below. "The trouble started when I told Davos

I would no longer worship the goddess. I told him the worshipers of Christ allowed no other gods. Life became difficult. He laughed at me and said only idiots believed in only one God. Look at the world, the trees, the rivers, the volcanoes, the seasons, the sun, the stars, and he went on and on to make his point. How could one God rule over the entire world? Even Zeus does not claim dominion of everything. Davos allowed me the freedom to worship any and all gods." Marcella gestured, unaware her sleeve had risen, displaying the ugly bruises, the newer ones layered on old injuries. "In my woman's stupidity, I picked the only one that would ruin our lives."

"There are many ways our faith threatens old ways of life." She and Marcella shared this struggle. "Our God promises to provide for us. You can trust in Him," Sabina said, remembering her doubts after Xeno's death. Her emptiness. She questioned God's providence, much like Marcella was now.

"I do not have that much faith. I do not want to live under Christ's care, begging for food. Davos laughed when Benjamin compared Christ to a priceless pearl. I laughed too. Davos was right; I am a foolish woman. Benjamin lived in poverty; he owned nothing. I refuse to live like that."

"Not all are called to serve God in the same way. Benjamin chose that sacrifice." Sabina tried to imagine the congregation without Portia's wealth and hospitality. "Portia's gifts benefit the believers in Christ as much as Benjamin's."

"He worked and gave everything away." Marcella shook her head, frowning in disapproval.

"Not everything," Sabina murmured under her breath. A valuable gold coin lay on her bedside table.

They reached the closed door at the end of the hallway. A curl of smoke spiraled up through the hallway floorboards from the forge below. Sabina coughed. The steady dull thud of the hammer had resumed.

"Benjamin is dead and Apollos in jail. Did they choose that? I confess I do not understand this God. Benjamin was the kindest, most gentle man I have ever met. His witnessing faith brought me to Christ.

What kind of a God punishes so devoted a believer? Such a good man." Marcella lifted the latch and pushed the door open. She gestured for them to go ahead. "This is Benjamin's room."

Yechiel stepped through the door, ducking his head. Light from the doorway and open window illuminated the small cell with its sloped roof. He halted abruptly.

Sabina bumped into him from behind, then scooted around him, and she, too, stopped. They both stared.

EIGHT

Marcella pushed Sabina aside and scurried around Yechiel. "What is the…by the holy Oracle!" She bent over, frantically grasping at loose straw scattered around the floor, torn out of a shredded bed pallet, now lying in a limp heap. Under a broken table, water pooled from a shattered pitcher, its pottery shards strewn like tiny islands.

Yechiel pushed Sabina aside. He reached out; his fingers traced a fist-sized hole in the plaster wall beside her head. He stepped over a heap of splintered kindling, once a small stool. "When did this happen?" he asked.

"I don't know." Marcella's voice trembled. "Davos will be furious; I should have watched over the house more closely." She knelt and pushed soggy wet straw into a pile in a corner.

Yechiel walked around the room, his head brushing against the low ceiling, and stepped over a toppled bedside table, the only item in the room not broken. He kicked straw from his path and paused and picked up a piece of a broken washbowl; water dripped from his fingers. He dropped it onto the floor next to the cracked pitcher. "Benjamin lived here?" He dried his hands on his tunic without any expression.

Marcella stood up, her posture stiffening. "He had a solid roof over his head." She fixed Yechiel with a stare.

Yechiel cleared his throat and looked away.

If Yechiel had not known Benjamin lived like this, how close was Yechiel to his brother? Sabina lifted a blanket crumpled on the floor. Light filtered through its threadbare weave. She wondered at Yechiel's expensive robe and refined appearance. More questions came to her mind. Did Yechiel know Benjamin lived in poverty? Sabina dropped the blanket. "Can you tell if anything is missing?"

"Missing? He owned nothing. Why would thieves break in here?" Marcella kicked at the loose straw.

"There are costly silver statues downstairs, yet thieves come here? It makes no sense," Sabina said.

"He was a scribe. His writing instruments were valuable," Yechiel said as he picked up a cracked clay lamp. Its oil was floating atop the water.

"I did not come up here," Marcella said. "But I never saw him carry tools back and forth. I am sure he kept them at the scriptorium. He went to work early and came back late. I really only saw him at Portia's." Marcella's hands massaged her bruised arms. She stopped when she noticed Sabina's concerned frown.

Sabina stooped to pick up a torn scrap of parchment; water, gray with washed-out ink, dripped from it. "This is a terrible room for writing." She pointed to the small window—the only source of light and fresh air to combat the invading smoke from the hallway.

She picked up another bit. "It's been burnt." Black ash crumbled from its soaked edges. She laid both pieces on the floor and gently lifted another segment from the puddle of water and laid them next to each other to dry. "There is writing on these, but the water has blurred and faded the ink. I can't read it…something *of the eyes*. List, lost, last of the eyes. I think it says *lust of the eyes*."

"It sounds like a love letter," Marcella said.

Yechiel turned in disgust. "Love and lust could be a poem about our depraved emperor. We have no way to tell," he scoffed, his foot stepping on a soggy pile of ash.

Sabina continued to sift through the broken debris and scattered straw. She picked up more burnt fragments. "This piece didn't get wet. I can read the script." Sabina held the scrap on her palm for them to see as she read, "*how can he love*. And this piece says *the spirit of truth*. This had words on it as well," she pointed to a faded gray splotch, but it had faded in the water.

Yechiel shuffled a few dry pieces with his toe. Flakes of ash fluttered up like black flies. As if speaking to himself, Yechiel added, "Why would thieves take the time to burn a piece of writing?"

"Perhaps they retaliated in rage when they didn't find valuables," Sabina said.

"Davos threatened Benjamin the night he died," Yechiel turned, his eyes locked onto Marcella.

"Davos has a temper; I admitted that, but he would not destroy his own property. He protects what is his." She raised her voice.

"Yet you went to warn Benjamin," he said.

Marcella responded defensively. "Only to alert him that my husband intended to throw him out of our house. Davos is innocent."

Sabina wanted to trust Marcella's assertion, but she did not believe Davos was as guiltless as Marcella claimed. Apparently, Yechiel didn't either.

"And to warn Benjamin to stay away from Davos?" Yechiel pressed.

"I readily answered your questions." Marcella's chin jutted out. "Now, you point a finger of guilt at my husband and me."

"We are not accusing either of you." Sabina thought of Marcella's bruises. Could the votive, which should not have been in Benjamin's possession, be a clue? What did she really know of Marcella? Was there something she didn't want them to find out about her husband or perhaps herself?

"There is a street entrance, down the hall, and you can leave through that door." Marcella pointed to a second door at the end of the hall. "It is the stairway the tenants use."

Sabina gathered the scraps she had found, gently lifting the damp parchment off the floor. "I think I have salvaged all I can." She dumped her collection of scraps in the bottom half of the broken water pitcher. "May I take these?"

"Take all of his garbage. It is less for me to clean," Marcella said.

Yechiel stared at the thin blanket, the torn pallet, and the broken furniture. He turned and walked out the door.

"Perhaps you should report this theft to a magistrate," Sabina suggested as Marcella ushered her through the door.

"What theft?" Marcella asked, shutting the door and bolting it behind them as if locking the door erased Benjamin and his connection to her family.

When they reached the street level, Sabina kept her eyes on Yechiel, expecting him to vanish, but he remained.

He stared at her intently. "Why were you in the magistrate's office yesterday?"

Not expecting the question, Sabina bit her bottom lip, unsure of how much she dared reveal to this man? She believed his goal was only to find his brother's murderer, not to betray Christians. But she didn't know.

By now, Yechiel knew her involvement with the church and Apollos. That knowledge, paired with her connection to her father, would give Yechiel dangerous power over her family. Could she hand Yechiel proof of her father's treason, putting his family first and betraying his sworn duty to Rome to protect his daughter? Not yet. "The magistrate possesses information I seek about Benjamin's murder."

"You are Christian?" Yechiel asked.

"Yes, like Benjamin."

"This bishop the magistrate arrested. Do you agree with Marcella that he is innocent?"

"I do."

"Then we have nothing more to discuss. My brother joined your sect, and now he is dead. I will find out why your bishop murdered him, and he will be punished." His voice was low, without passion. But his eyes glowed with all the fury his voice hid. His anger spilled over to Benjamin's new faith and its adherents.

Sabina stepped back. "Punishment or revenge?"

"Justice is not revenge."

"Justice does not seek the death of the innocent. The magistrate made a mistake."

"You have proof?"

"Isn't that why we are here? Someone killed Benjamin. It wasn't Apollos. Don't you want the actual murderer punished?"

"You are a woman." Yechiel's gaze traveled down her length and back to her face. She watched as he tallied her feminine failings. She braced for the expected patronizing assessment. "Marcella and the fat toad spoke of another woman."

"Livia." She nodded, surprised at his response.

"She is another of the toad's lies."

"Truths are often hidden under the lies," she said. Perhaps Magnus revealing Livia's name was an attempt to deflect suspicion away from his involvement in Benjamin's death. And Marcella had added credibility to Magnus's attempt. Or perhaps Livia had something to hide.

"You can find this Livia?" Yechiel broke into her thoughts.

"I can," said Sabina, not at all sure she could.

"Good, you can tell me what you find."

She wasn't sure she had heard him correctly. "You want my help?"

He grunted, not a yes or a no.

"And you will show me Benjamin's votive."

His eyes narrowed. "What do you know of this idol?"

"Only that Benjamin carried one. And Davos makes votives."

"The votive does not involve you."

"I see. I tell you what I find, and you share nothing." Sabina crossed her arms, steadying the contents in the broken pitcher.

"I will find the murderer with your help from inside this church."

Sabina stared. "Great plan."

"Yes—"

"No, we share information equally or not at all."

"But you are a—"

"A woman, I know."

"I was about to say, a Gentile. It is forbidden to associate with—"

She turned to leave. "Good luck finding Livia." She walked twenty paces before he responded.

"Stop."

She looked back over her shoulder. "You agree to share what you find?"

He glared at her, silent, at first, then said, "I will show you the votive."

Sabina thought of the gold coin. She had not brought it with her. In fairness, she needed to show it to Yechiel. "If we cooperate, you will get your justice faster. I will search for Livia, and where will you go?"

"I am not accustomed to questions from a—"

"Gentile, I know."

"No. A woman. Even my wife does not ask questions of my whereabouts."

"Thankfully, I am not your wife." He definitely, didn't deserve to hear about the coin—yet.

"I plan to visit the scriptorium," he said and stalked away.

"Where Benjamin worked?" she turned and followed him.

He did not stop or turn around. "You are not coming." Yechiel said, his tone adamant.

"I should talk to his employer, as well."

"Valerius, the owner, is a Christian. He would recognize you," Yechiel spun around and growled.

Sabina crossed her arms and faced him. She wanted to snap at him *you can't tell me what to do.* But she knew that would sound petulant. "I have never met the man. He must belong to another Christian congregation."

"We cannot both ask questions without causing suspicion or worse…silence if Benjamin's fellow scribes believe they are suspects."

"Are they suspects?" Sabina raised her eyebrow. He had not mentioned any suspicions to her.

"I won't know until I talk to them…question them by myself."

"What about the parchment sample?"

"We don't know that it came from the scriptorium."

Sabina looked at him incredulously. "We don't know that it didn't."

"I will hire the owner to write a letter for me. It's a legitimate reason to be there and an excuse to question Benjamin's co-workers and Valerius. Perhaps they know of grudges or jealousies between Benjamin and this Apollos."

"I have a legitimate reason. Apollos, my friend, is going to die because you are investigating the wrong man."

"Apollos sits in jail accused by the magistrate. I don't want you with me." Yechiel's jaw flexed.

She stepped back despite herself. "I need proof if he is to be released from jail. And two assessments are better than one. I can observe, quiet as an eel lurking beneath a rock."

"Quiet? You don't know the meaning of the word."

"Then I will go alone," she said with false assurance. She felt anything but self-confident after considering the violent person who destroyed Benjamin's room.

His mouth settled into a resolute scowl. He spat what sounded to her like a foreign curse. "If you come, you will be silent. You will not ask questions. None. You will be there as my..."

"Sister," she suggested.

"Yes, it is obvious that we are related." His sarcasm eviscerated her proposal.

She looked at his tall whip-thin body. At his long sinewy fingers and sharp facial features, in marked contrast to her rounded curves and short stubby fingers. They were opposites.

"You will be my slave."

"Your what?" Sabina stiffened.

"Would you prefer playing my mistress?" He raised an eyebrow.

"I shall borrow a tunic from a house slave," she said stiffly.

Yechiel gave her directions to a street corner. Later in the afternoon, around the tenth hour, they would meet and travel to the scriptorium together.

NINE

Sabina, I have no idea where Livia lives." Portia refolded lengths of shimmering silks thrown into crumpled piles left by the rummaging of yesterday's customers. "Or what she has to do with Apollos." She rubbed the back of her neck. "Join me in the garden. I need a respite after the pandemonium of yesterday."

"And Flavius's search of your home?" Sabina thought of her father's fellow magistrate and enemy.

"Flavius found nothing, of course, but it heightened our worries for Apollos. Thankfully, you had already left," Portia said.

She would not divert Portia with the details of her *escape* yesterday. "Yes, extremely fortunate," Sabina said.

Portia led Sabina through the atrium and into the same private garden where Sabina, only yesterday, had followed Magnus and Yechiel.

"Flavius knew about Benjamin's death," Portia said. "News travels fast. Especially confidential news."

"A guard, disloyal to my father, informed Flavius."

"A Flavius spy within your father's personal guard? Interesting."

"I have sent word to my father. He probably already knew."

"I played up that a guest had been drinking too much and choked at my dinner party. I had no idea what happened to him after that. Flavius suspected something but couldn't prove anything without a body. He railed against his young informant."

"He expected to arrest a traitor, not a drunkard," Sabina said.

"He did not say what he was searching for, but we suspect he hoped to find signs of Christian worship."

"You take a great risk."

"Flavius will not zealously barge in here again soon. He spent a large portion of time later in the day, placating some of my most influential and irate customers. But as much as I enjoyed watching him fawning and apologizing, I'm not convinced his apologies were in earnest or that he was giving up."

Portia strolled past the stone lion fountain. The spray cooled the air in a private arbor surrounded by sculpted shrubbery. A couch covered in pale peach pillows was tucked into the verdant sanctuary. Portia reclined and patted the seat next to her. Sabina sat. A small table held a bowl of fruit, a carafe, and a goblet. "I will call for another cup. It is a new wine from Gaul, excellent." Portia signaled a slave.

"I do not have much time. Father is allowing me to visit Apollos this afternoon."

"Oh, Sabina." Portia reached out and hugged her. "I knew you could find him. Feya is cooking today. She will spare some food from the orphans for you to bring him."

"I won't visit until late. Save the food for the orphans. I will bring food to Apollos."

"Now, you will find proof of his innocence." Portia held out a bowl of pomegranate seeds to Sabina. "He must know something we can present to acquit him."

Sabina took a handful. "That is why I am here. Magnus mentioned Benjamin was involved with a widow named Livia."

Portia scrunched up her face. "And you believed him?"

Sabina shrugged. "I didn't know Benjamin well. He has been with us…what, two years?" Sabina sucked at the red tips of her fingers.

"Benjamin gave up much to follow Christ's teachings. He was mesmerized by the debates in his synagogue, arguing the meaning of Jesus's miracles and the healings by our disciples."

A young girl returned with a wine cup. Portia poured the two cups full. She handed one to Sabina.

"When Benjamin first professed belief the dead Rabbi Jesus was the prophesied Jewish Messiah, his family became irritated. When his father and the local rabbi were unable to convince him to abandon his belief that Jesus called all people into a relationship with God, inviting pagan Gentiles to join the chosen people of God, his family distanced themselves. When he insisted Jesus was raised to life from the dead…"

"They disowned him?"

"I know his mother secretly kept in touch. I sent word of his death. Benjamin said his family prayed for him."

"Prayed he would come to his senses." Sabina understood the internal conflict Benjamin must have struggled with. How traumatic it would be to reject the security of your traditions and the stability of your family. Until now, no one had asked her to make that sacrifice.

"After what he gave up to follow the teachings of Christ, it makes no sense he would throw it away and have an affair," Portia said. "Ridiculous."

"Marcella also mentioned Livia's name," Sabina defended her questioning. "I don't know who Livia is."

"Livia just started attending our worship."

"Which explains why I haven't seen her at church." Sabina sipped her wine.

"She ate here…the night Benjamin died." Portia tilted her head.

"Her relationship with Benjamin is curious. I need to find her. Magnus also insinuated Benjamin and Marcella were…together."

"Ha, what a baboon Magnus is."

"We spoke to Marcella."

"We? You have been busy," Portia said.

"Benjamin's brother, Yechiel, is searching for the killer also."

"Then Benjamin's family did not abandon him. Feya works with the widows. Now that I think about it, she may have mentioned something to me about Livia and Benjamin."

Sabina lifted her eyebrows. She set her cup on the mosaic table.

"Don't give me that look. I'm a busy shopkeeper; I hear all kinds of gossip to which I pay no attention." Her long, ringed fingers popped a glistening ruby red seed into her mouth. "Go ask. Feya's in the kitchen. But before you go. What has transpired with Marcus? Another love letter?"

"No, I have not spoken to Marcus."

"Then you haven't discussed your faith?"

"I will. It's not something you just blurt out. Marcus, I'm a Christian and a criminal. You can arrest me."

"Hmm." Portia's raised eyebrow said it all.

"Marcus is everything Xeno was not—handsome, intelligent, funny. I'm not sure why he wants to see me again."

"Because you are beautiful, intelligent, and witty."

"And belligerent and awkward."

"You are afraid he will reject you?"

"No…yes. I have agreed to dinner tomorrow night. I want to know if there's a possible future with him before I end any chance of one by confessing. I need to find Livia, and I have to stop at the fish market."

"Then go find Feya. She's cooking lunch." Portia dismissed her with a wave.

Sabina stood, passing halfway through the garden before she yelled back to Portia. "Thank you."

Sabina saw Feya's short, stout figure filling a pot from a lead water spigot protruding from the kitchen wall. The same lead pipe branched off, supplying water to the gushing fountains and baths of the villa. The three long whiskers sprouting from a brown mole on her chin, weren't visible until Sabina stood face to face.

"Sabina!" Feya put the pot down and kissed her soundly on each cheek.

"The peace of our Lord be with you," Sabina managed to say before the heat of Feya's fleshy arms wrapped her tightly, pulling her into her bosom.

Feya loosened her grip, held her at arm's length and examined her, up and down, then pulled her back into a loving embrace again before finally releasing her. "It is such a relief to see you…we prayed after the magistrate ordered us to leave you that night." Feya's lips quivered, and

126

Sabina heard the unspoken words of worry and apology underneath. "Portia reported you were safe, but—"

"There is nothing you could have done. And you see, I am fine."

"You weren't hurt?" Sabina knew Feya's underlying question was rooted in unbelief. How are you here today after being detained by the Roman guards?

A reasonable question. One Sabina couldn't answer and at the same time hide her relationship to the magistrate and his complicity in letting them all go free.

"I'm fine. The magistrate asked a few questions and released me shortly after you." She changed the subject abruptly. "Feya, what do you know about Livia and Benjamin?"

Feya shook her head disapprovingly as she balanced the pot upon her hip. "Have you been listening to Magnus's tales?"

"Not exactly." Sabina grabbed one end of the pot, and together they carried it and set it on top of the oven.

Feya returned to a table of three other women rinsing, chopping, and cooking in preparation for the evening meal. She picked up a knife. "I thought you were more sensible than that, Sabina." She clucked her tongue. "Livia would appear at our meals occasionally, accepting the food and disappearing as soon as she had eaten."

"We were friendly to her," said one woman chopping onions.

"Livia reacted…how do I say this nicely…offended by our overtures," Feya said. "Eventually, most of us gave up trying to welcome her and let her eat in her corner in peace.

"Then one day, I saw Benjamin sitting by her. She had him pegged to his bench, talking non-stop as if a dam had burst, and all her words came gushing out at once. Later, Benjamin came up and asked if I knew Livia was a widow? Well, no. How would I know when she never said so much as a 'good day' to any of us? The next thing I know, Livia's showing up at church. I think she was studying to join the church."

"Have you seen her lately?" Sabina asked.

"I haven't seen her since the night Benjamin died." Feya shook her head.

"Have any of you seen her?" Sabina asked. "Or know where she lives?"

The women shared their accumulated bits and pieces of collected gossip and guesses, but no one knew any useful facts about Livia's family, where she came from, or where she lived.

One woman recalled overhearing a bit of conversation between Livia and Benjamin. "I couldn't hear it all. Livia talked, and Benjamin nodded. She talked, bragged about her dead husband and how much money he had. She said he had a house bigger than any other house on the Street of the Bakers. I wouldn't give it any credence. She was trying to impress Benjamin."

"Did Livia lie a lot?" Sabina asked.

"I don't know anything about her, but you don't wolf down food, as if you are starving, if you live in the biggest house on the street," Feya waved her knife, emphasizing her point.

Had Livia been bragging? Lying? A woman overheard the name of a street in passing. It wasn't much help, but she would try to find Livia's house with no other clues to follow.

Sabina made her way back to Harbor Street. Some windows and shops along the arcade were opening again. As she walked, she sorted through the facts and unknowns of Benjamin's short life.

Marcella dismissed Benjamin as her lover. Still, her husband had warned Benjamin to stay away from her. Could Benjamin have been killed for sharing his faith with Marcella? Yechiel had dismissed the burnt love letter found in Benjamin's room, but destroying it made little sense unless it had some importance. Had Benjamin hidden something valuable there? Did the thief find it? Or not? With a sense of guilt, she remembered the gold coin she had taken.

As much as Yechiel asserted Benjamin's celibacy, what did Yechiel really know about his brother? Benjamin appeared devoted to his calling as a scribe. Being a scribe did not prohibit the lusts of the flesh. He was a man, after all. Magnus had also suggested an affair between Benjamin and Marcella. According to Magnus, Livia and Benjamin were connected. Had Magnus intentionally misdirected them?

Increasing her pace, Sabina wiped a rivulet of sweat from her brow. The cooling breeze from the sea lessened as she left the harbor district. Only one person could answer her questions, Livia—if she could find her.

She turned left toward the stadium on the north edge of town. The city nestled between two hills, and the land flattened as it neared the Cayster River bordering its northwest side. This area would flood when heavy rains and melting snow from the mountains to the east made their way down the river, overflowing the sewers and side streets. Today the sun-baked thoroughfare she walked swirled only with dust.

She entered an older neighborhood. The homes and insulas long past their prime had not enjoyed the recent decades of prosperity that flourished in Ephesus, first under Nero, and now with Domitian's frenzied empire building. The insulas she passed were missing large sections of plaster, exposing the brick beneath.

Sabina felt the press of people packed into small spaces. People crowded into narrow shopfronts, selling an uninspiring selection of goods and poor-quality items. She passed a woman selling two coarse homespun woolen shifts. Sabina scratched involuntarily and thought of the slippery weightlessness of Portia's silk floating through her fingers.

The farther she walked, the more cobbled the grand old houses became. Boarded-up windows, additional doorways, and altered staircases divided homes into smaller and smaller apartments—a common practice of landlords in this crowded city. A shop or room housing one family could be twice as profitable partitioned and rented out to an additional family or several more. After renovations, family members would take turns sleeping, their living space too small for the entire household to lie down at the same time.

Sabina easily located the most distinguished home on the Street of the Bakers, a name as old as the antiquated buildings, for she saw no bakeries on the Street of the Bakers.

If this was her home, Livia's house had remained true to its classical Greek design and space. The family did not share their sidewalls, doors, or stairways with shops or rented out insulas. It stood, a solitary bastion among its dilapidated neighbors. Its plaster, intact but stained with age, clad what had once been an impressive house.

The afternoon sun hung high in the midday sky. Ornately carved marble pillars flanked the door. Benches lined up left and right on opposite sides of a shaded alcove, waiting for clients to arrive and present their bequests, complaints, and business proposals to the home's patron. Or not. She looked closer at the benches covered in a thick, undisturbed coating of dust.

Sabina knocked on the large door. A spindly older man wearing a slave tunic answered the door. He glanced behind Sabina, conveying his expectation of seeing the mandatory escort that accompanied any respectable female visitor. Seeing none, he glared at her, spit on her sandals, and began closing the door in her face.

Sabina breathed deeply, her nostrils flaring at the insult. She anticipated a disapproving reaction, but the look of pure loathing on the face of the man caught her unprepared. She pushed, stopping the door from shutting.

He shoved back.

"I am here to speak to Livia." At least she would state her business if forced to stand outside like a common plebian. She wedged her shoulder against the door, causing a standoff. The door began to give way as the man tired.

He stopped pushing but didn't move aside.

She watched through the crack as his mouth puckered. "What is your business with Livia?"

"Is this her home?"

He snorted and rolled his eyes. "Wait there."

Sabina shoved against the door and swept past him into the entry hall. His face contorted in a display of distaste as he closed the door. He couldn't force her to leave. "I will inform my mistress."

She waited for a considerable period. Petty revenge, or was Livia unwilling to meet her? She started to think he wasn't coming back when he returned. He led her down a hall, a silent hallway. His mouth pinched into a knot.

With a loud snort, he ushered her into a lavish room, then bowed to his mistress as he exited, backing out.

A boney, middle-aged woman sat enthroned on an elaborately carved ebony chair. Her black tunic and robe, years out of date, hung from the rigidly upright figure. Her blond wig tipped slightly off-center. Sabina didn't know what she had expected Livia to look like, but this woman wasn't it. No one had mentioned her age, and Sabina hadn't thought to ask.

Her glance darted quickly around, searching for another person in the room. There was no one else. She tried to imagine this woman chatting excitedly to Benjamin, or for that matter, getting excited. She couldn't.

She waited respectfully for the older woman to speak. Her thoughts skittered from one improbability to another, trying to fathom a relationship between this matron and Benjamin. She could imagine her surly and silent in her widow's garb. She had pointed elbows and hollowed cheekbones, making her look starved as Feya had described. But still?

The woman tipped her head back and picked her brown teeth with a cracked and yellowed thumbnail. She flicked a piece of food onto the floor and scrutinized Sabina for several uncomfortable minutes before declaring in a reedy, high-pitched voice. "Mano informs me you are a friend of Livia's."

A friend of Livia's? A wave of relief washed through Sabina. She was not Livia. But if she wasn't Livia, who was she, and why had Sabina been allowed into the house? "Is Livia here?" She wondered if the slave had made a mistake.

"As simple and unsophisticated as my daughter-in-law is, she does occasionally surprise me. You are a surprise."

"Livia is your daughter-in-law?"

"Yes, she managed to manipulate my son into marrying her. That was my first surprise. You are not dressed like a prostitute."

Sabina blinked. "Excuse me?" Surely, she hadn't heard the woman correctly.

"I said you don't look like a whore. I have seen whores accosting and propositioning decent men in the streets. Your dress is costly. A gift from a patron?"

Sabina's eyes blazed from embarrassment and outrage. "I am not a… prostitute." She was of the ruling class and sympathized with the abuse her inferiors suffered. Still, she experienced a spark of this degradation for the first time, enflaming her emotions and churning her stomach. "How dare—"

"If you say so. Yet you are Livia's friend?"

"I have never met Livia…and I am not a—" Sabina stuttered.

"Hah! I knew Livia lied. She told me she had a friend." The woman snorted the same exaggerated snort as her slave. "Livia patronizes the lowest rungs of society. Since our son died, it has fallen on me to curb her indecent behavior." She sighed. "It has been a futile effort, but I continue for the sake of my son. I see you have bettered your own position. You speak Greek quite well."

Sabina switched to Latin. "I came to see Livia." She attempted to control her anger, but her emotions burst out in her labored breathing and the stilted rigidity of her voice.

"Impressive." The older woman's eyes glinted like a crocodile. "I am sure a night with someone of your talent is worth the price of a glass of good wine. You must learn to walk with more grace, however. You sounded like an elephant clomping down the hall."

"Is Livia home?" Sabina repeated, feeling the flush of her face warming.

"I haven't seen her in two days. She will return…eventually. Mano, I am bored." The woman snorted, flicking her finger at Sabina. "Remove her, and don't disturb me again."

The door slave had appeared unnoticed, and Sabina soon found herself standing outside the door, seething and grinding her teeth. "A glass of good wine." She fumed. But worse than the insults, she had learned nothing about Livia and had no clue where to find her. So much for being an investigator. She had not even asked the woman's name.

TEN

The cool of the morning had diminished into a pleasant afternoon. Sabina could wait on the street, hoping Livia returned home before dark. But she didn't have the luxury of that much time. Neither did Apollos.

She let out a sigh and stopped for a moment to plan. The meeting with Yechiel at the scriptorium wasn't until later. She needed to change her clothing. The cook's tunic should fit since Amisi's would be too small. She determined the quickest way home and set off in the opposite direction from which she arrived.

That had been a wasted trip. Sabina hoped they would have better luck at the scriptorium. At least Benjamin's employer and co-workers should be there for them to question—for Yechiel to question. She recalled her agreement to be as silent as an eel.

The crowds had thinned. At this time of day, men were at the public baths. The food vendors and merchants had shuttered their stalls. She moved quickly through the streets.

In the center of a small public piazza, a group of young children splashed in the fountain. A boy, about eight or nine years old, cupped water as it gushed from the protruding lips of a marble fish. He flung it into the air, showering the heads of his squealing playmates. Sabina stepped around their game, avoiding all but a few splashes.

"Sabina."

She stopped and turned around. A girl, not much older than the children, sat on a stone bench opposite the fountain. Sabina didn't recognize her, but the girl waved to her.

"Sabina? You are Sabina?"

Sabina walked to the bench. "Yes." The girl, bone-thin, smiled up at her. Her brown hair needed to be washed but had been carefully braided and wrapped in an adult woman's hairstyle. She wore a dingy gray tunic that had faded long ago from black.

"I recognize you from the church," the girl said.

Sabina looked around, anxious to see if anyone heard her. "Church?" She whispered.

"Benjamin's church."

"You knew Benjamin?" Sabina asked.

The girl's eyes filled with tears.

"You are Livia." Sabina guessed.

The girl nodded.

"May I sit?"

Livia nodded again, and tears streamed down her face. "Benjamin's dead, isn't he?"

"Yes. He was your friend?"

"He loved me. We were going to get married."

Sabina kept her face from showing her surprise.

Livia fingered the rough wool of her tunic. "When my mourning period ended."

"Portia told me your husband died. When?"

She looked up at Sabina, a teardrop clinging to the end of her raised chin, pride brimming from the set of her mouth. "Almost two years ago."

"Two years! How old are you?"

Livia sat up straight, her back rigid and her lips clamped shut, her pride turning to iron.

Sabina regretted the question the second she uttered it. She could see the stubborn girl Feya had described, sullenly sitting by herself in the corner. "I'm sorry. I should know better. I am a widow, and I get asked the same question, but it's because I'm old and haven't remarried."

Livia's spine relaxed. "You're not that old."

"Will you forgive me?"

Livia shrugged her shoulders. "My parents said I was too young to get married. They made me wait three weeks until I turned twelve. We had been married two months when Theo died," Livia said with a catch in her voice.

Sabina felt a jolt of pity she knew Livia wouldn't appreciate. "My marriage lasted one day," Sabina shared.

Livia's mouth dropped open. "Really? Only one day?" The natural curiosity of a young girl taking over. "What happened?"

"His name was Xeno. Our wedding guests had just ushered him into our bedroom. He removed his clothes, crawled up on the bed, and collapsed. The doctor said too much excitement for his heart or…"

Livia frowned, not hiding her skeptical expression. "Or someone cursed him."

"That was the consensus of the doctor, the guests, and Xeno's children. They returned my dowry and sent me back to my father's house."

"Wise of them." Livia nodded with great sympathy showing on her face. "Did he die flailing in pain? Theo writhed in pain." She grimaced and mimicked a suffering man.

"No writhing, only a whimper."

"Was Xeno handsome? My Theo was the most handsome man ever. I could marry an old man, but I couldn't bear to marry an ugly one."

"You would think Xeno old, but fifty-three is too young to die." Xeno's extended belly and gout-swollen joints, symptoms of life's excesses, flashed across Sabina's mind. His ruddy splotched face and bulbous nose hid a once vigorous and handsome man.

Livia stared intently, waiting for Sabina's answer.

"No, he was not ugly," Sabina responded.

"Thank the gods. I mean God…the one God. And you loved Xeno with all your heart. Your life has no meaning now that he is gone," Livia said in a dreamy voice.

"He and my father arranged the marriage. I agreed."

"Then you hated him," Livia scowled her tone, switching to the theatrical.

"No, I liked him. I wanted to be married…" Sabina wasn't sure she wanted to elaborate on the heartbreaks of her life, which would only encourage Livia's sense of the dramatic.

The girl stared at her wide-eyed and waited.

She would make it short. "I had been betrothed twice before Xeno. Achilles and I were betrothed shortly after I was born. I was six years old when he died in battle. He was eighteen. My second arranged marriage was Tatius Quadratus. He drowned when I was twelve."

"Oh, how romantic. Your Xeno must have been very brave to marry you, knowing he would die. Now, you will never marry. And live to old age resentful and cursing your misery."

Sabina didn't know whether to laugh or cry. "It's not complete misery." Resentful? Livia's embellishment veered uncomfortably close to the truth. "Tell me about you and Theo."

Livia settled in as if preparing for an epic tale. "Theo's first trading voyage as captain was to Corinth. His father had drowned the year before, like your lover Tatius."

Sabina coughed and motioned for Livia to continue.

"Theo got off his ship, saw me, and fell in love. He said I saved him from a childhood betrothal and a bloodless witch." Livia giggled.

Sabina wondered if Livia meant Theo's betrothed or his mother. "It sounds romantic," Sabina remembered Theo's mother's accusation of manipulation and thought it might have been Theo who did the manipulating.

"My father cried when I told him I would be living in Ephesus, but my mother shut him up. She saw how handsome Theo looked standing on his ship."

And how rich he must have looked on his ship. "I am sure your mother was overjoyed."

"I loved him with all my heart. Sailing back to Ephesus, he stepped on a stupid iron nail. We ignored it once his foot stopped bleeding.

We had other things to think about," Livia wiggled her eyebrows and laughed when Sabina blushed.

After Sabina's two betrothals and her tragic marriage at twenty years old, no one appeared willing to risk Sabina's marriage bed. Eight years older, Sabina no longer anticipated the physical delight Livia had shared with her young husband. She preferred not to dwell on it.

Perhaps sensing Sabina's discomfort, Livia's mood and the topic shifted. She smiled at Sabina, a knowing, grown-up smile. No longer the smitten, love-struck bride. "Theo died on his twentieth birthday."

"And you fell under the care of Theo's mother." Sabina looked at the tunic, barely covering Livia's half-starved body, her toes hanging out of shabby sandals she had outgrown months ago.

"I hate her," Livia said. "Benjamin told me to hate is a sin, but I don't care. I would do anything to get away from her."

Sabina shivered at Livia's vehemence. Could this young girl, this young woman, have caused Benjamin's death? Did *anything* include murder? The tragic events dictating Livia's life were not her fault. A picture of Livia's mother-in-law jumped to mind. People who feel trapped are often driven to desperate actions. But murder? If Livia saw marrying Benjamin as her only way out, how would she have reacted if he had spurned her?

"Livia, do you know how Benjamin died?"

Livia's eyes widened. "I saw him choking. I got scared and ran away." Her pale skin got even paler. Sabina watched her reaction. Fearful innocence? Or anxious guilt?

"He choked because someone poisoned him. Do you know anyone who would want to hurt him?" Sabina asked.

"Why are you asking me?" Livia fidgeted and started gnawing on a fingernail.

"If you were going to be married, Benjamin must have confided in you. Did he mention people he didn't like?"

"I don't like Magnus. He's fat and ugly, and he lied when he said Benjamin loved Marcella."

"I wouldn't listen to Magnus," Sabina said.

"Benjamin smiled at me every week when I came to eat at the church." She twirled the loose hair around her finger, looking even younger, if not innocent. "I could tell he was falling in love with me. Anyway, Marcella already has a husband."

"Did he talk about a disagreement or an argument with anyone?"

"Well, he argued with Marcella's husband. I'm hungry."

"So am I." Sabina wasn't surprised at the change of topic. Sabina saw the girl's bones pressing against her skin. Not an unusual sight for the impoverished living on the streets of Ephesus, but Livia's family possessed property, at least one ship, and money.

"There's a popina on the next block," Livia said, pointing down a dark and narrow street.

Sabina hesitated; popinas were not establishments upper-class women frequented. Respectable women didn't eat and drink in public, subjecting themselves to vulgar slaves, freedmen, foreigners, and compromising situations. She remembered Livia's mother-in-law's lurid insinuations. A jolt of anger heated her cheeks. "Lead the way."

Livia's sullen wariness wore off. Her chatter picked up the closer they got to the food.

They arrived at a small counter set back a foot or two from the street. Two pots set into the concrete counter held soup of some kind and porridge.

Sabina ordered barley bread, a slice of cheese, and one of the pork sausages hanging from a long string draped behind the counter.

Livia's eyes widened when she stared at the picture menu painted on a board over the counter. "So many choices." She ordered the cabbage stew, changed her mind to baked parsnips, then ended with the same meal as Sabina.

Sabina took a handful of coins from a small purse. Benjamin's gold coin glinted against the silver and copper in her palm. She chose two brass sestertii and began returning the extra money.

Livia reached out and grabbed her hand. She plucked the gold coin from Sabina's palm. "I have one like this. Did Benjamin give it to you?"

"You have a coin like this?" She nearly dropped the coins in surprise.

"Benjamin asked me to keep it for him. He said I was a special child of God." Livia smiled conspiratorially and whispered, "He trusted me with lots of secrets."

Sabina started to ask more about the coin when their food arrived. They stood at the counter and ate. Livia devoured her sausage rapidly, then piled the cheese on the hunk of bread and gnawed at it with vigor. Sabina worried she would choke.

Livia finished and began licking her fingers, lingering on her thumb.

Sabina had not taken Livia's declaration of marriage to Benjamin seriously, but if he had given her the coin, there was more than simple friendship. Dozens of questions were swirling through Sabina's mind. Instead, she asked, "Another sausage?"

Livia nodded. Sabina ordered and included another cup of honey wine for herself.

Her meal finished, Livia wiped the sausage grease daintily from her lips with her tunic sleeve. "Thank you very much. I truly enjoyed our meal together."

"I did too." Sabina smiled at the woman in a child's body. "Livia, you said Benjamin shared secrets?"

Livia tensed and narrowed her eyes. "I can't tell anyone. I promised."

"Benjamin's dead. I don't think he would mind if you told me."

Livia stared hard at Sabina. She started nibbling on the tip of a thumb. "You have to promise not to tell anyone. Promise with the kiss of death; your lips sealed to your grave." Livia bent forward and kissed Sabina's lips.

Sabina pinched her lips together to keep from smiling, "My lips are sealed." She responded to the vow she had playfully recited as a child.

"Benjamin took me to visit the man he was going to work for." Livia sucked her thumb farther in her mouth, then pulled it out abruptly and folded her hand into a tight fist.

"At the scriptorium?"

"The scriptorium's not a secret." Livia giggled and shook her head. "Benjamin was hired to be a scribe, a secretary, for that old apostle… the one who's sick."

"John?"

Livia nodded.

"Did Benjamin tell anyone else?"

Livia lifted her chin and rolled her eyes at Sabina. "Uhh…it's a secret."

Sabina nodded over the rim of her wine cup. She did not need to ask why Benjamin kept his new job assignment a secret. She knew the church had given John up for dead, an old man banished for his outspoken beliefs, to the island of Patmos by Domitian. Miraculously John had returned to them. But Domitian, their egomaniacal emperor who calls himself a god, could always change his mind. The bishops of the churches were taking no chances. They kept John and his location hidden, ministered and tended to by the faithful throughout the empire who prayed for his recovery.

"Benjamin took me to meet John after I told him only ghosts come back from the dead."

"You were arguing about Jesus's resurrection?" Sabina asked.

"Benjamin said after Jesus died…John saw him alive. Jesus talked to him, and they ate meals together, fish." Livia stopped talking and looked guardedly at Sabina. "I think John saw a ghost?"

Sabina guessed Livia expected her to agree. "Ghosts don't eat." Sabina pointed out.

"You believe Jesus is alive? You believe John?" Livia rolled her eyes.

"It isn't just John. Paul, a friend of John, wrote about thousands of witnesses who shared Jesus's life during the forty days after his resurrection. Paul lived in Ephesus. I have read his letters."

"Well, anyone can write anything they want."

"True, but you cannot sing with a joy you do not feel," Sabina said. "I was little when a man and his wife moved to Ephesus from Jerusalem. They were old, crippled. The woman's body bent over with pain. But she sang like an angel. I sat on my mother's lap with her arms wrapped around me so tight I could hardly breathe." Sabina closed her eyes and repeated the song.

"Therefore my heart is glad, and my glory rejoices;
My flesh also will rest in hope.

For You will not leave my soul in Sheol,
Nor will You allow Your Holy One to see corruption.
You will show me the path of life.

"They were followers of Jesus. They ate with him, walked with him, learned from him; before his crucifixion…and after. My mother's tears soaked the top of my head. Yes, I believe John."

Livia heaved a loud sigh. "I don't think I do. It would be easier to believe in Jesus if he came back from the dead as a ghost because everyone knows ghosts are real. John said a spirit talked to him when he wrote his letter. I believed that."

"What letter?"

"John asked Benjamin to read a letter John had written. John said the Spirit of the Lord spoke through him, and the Spirit's word was on his tongue."

"We believe the Spirit of God lives in us. His Spirit reveals truths to us through his prophets of long ago and now through His apostle John."

"That's what the letter said. *The Spirit testifies because the Spirit is the truth.*"

"Christians believe God loves His people and teaches them through His Spirit," Sabina said.

"You aren't very smart." Livia shook her head. "Gods don't love us. We have to go to them and give them offerings and promise to do things so they don't get mad at us." Livia pointed to a bowl filled with tiny pinkish fruit. "Are those cherries? I've never tasted a cherry."

"Those don't look ripe."

Livia stared longingly at the bowl. "I don't trust anything. Look what the gods did to Theo."

Sabina signaled the server and pointed to the bowl. "We'll take a few of those. Everyone trusts something, money, government, maybe themselves."

"I trust in the Oracles and fortune-tellers." The server grabbed a handful of the fruit and dropped the pile in front of them on the counter. Livia clapped her hands together. "When Benjamin started getting sick, I told him he had to bring gifts to Jesus, or Jesus wouldn't heal him. I think Jesus didn't help him because Jesus is dead. That's what I think."

Perhaps Benjamin did listen to you. Sabina pictured Benjamin's two-inch silver goddess.

Livia grabbed a handful and bit into one of the hard fruits. Her lips pinched into a tight knot. "Eeew." She spat it on the ground.

"In another month, they'll be so sweet the juice will drip like honey from your tongue. When did Benjamin get sick?"

"He started getting headaches when I started coming to the church."

"You met Benjamin when you came to the church meals?"

"He wasn't there at first. Then one day, he showed up reading and praying for us poor orphans." Livia giggled. "I didn't tell him I wasn't an orphan."

"You were hungry?"

Livia nodded. "Benjamin liked me. Just like Theo, we fell in love."

"And he asked you to marry him?"

"He wanted desperately to ask me, but he couldn't. First, he needed money. Wives are expensive. He had to wait until he started working for John. Then he'd get rich because John is famous."

After Marcella's interview, Sabina was sure Benjamin had no ambition to become rich or famous. His livelihood, like John's, would depend on the charity of faithful believers. And Christian fame tended to lead to death.

"I had to keep our meetings a secret because Theo's mother wouldn't want me going to the church. She has a lot of rules. Don't touch this. Don't walk there. Don't wake her up. Don't talk loudly. Then she yells at me because she can't hear me. I try, but I can't remember all her rules, and sometimes she changes them, and when you break a rule, you don't eat. That's one of her rules. I have another secret. You don't have to promise the kiss of death, but you can't tell anyone." Livia whispered into her ear. "I'm going home to Corinth."

Sabina remembered Livia's mother-in-law saying Livia gave her few surprises. But this young widow continually surprised her. "Back to Corinth! Is Theo's mother paying for your passage?"

Livia shook her head. "The passage on a ship costs a lot." She smiled broadly; her eyes sparkled. "She doesn't know I'm saving money." She laughed and unrolled a thin, dirty piece of cloth she had tied somewhere inside her threadbare tunic. She proudly displayed six small copper coins.

"Oh," Sabina forced a smile at the meager savings.

"I know it's not enough. But if I keep begging—" Livia stopped abruptly. Her face lost its animation, and she pushed the remaining cherries away. "Benjamin didn't want me begging. He said he would tell Theo's mother. I told him not to. He wouldn't listen. Now he's dead, and he can't tell my secret."

Sabina remembered the kiss of death. This time she didn't smile.

ELEVEN

When she and Yechiel had left the ruin of Benjamin's room, the sun had blazed straight overhead, providing a hint of the coming warmth of summer. Precious time had elapsed, securing directions from Portia to the Street of the Bakers. Sabina had providentially found Livia, or rather Livia had found her. Now, with barely enough time to rendezvous with Yechiel, she scuttled into her bedroom. She quietly fastened the doors to avoid alerting Amisi.

Her fingers ruffled through the woven hairstyle Amisi had fashioned atop Sabina's head that morning. Loosened hairpins fell, scattering on the floor, freeing a single thick plait that plopped down her back. She removed her earrings and brass studded sheepskin slippers, replacing them with a pair of old leather sandals and the cook's tunic. Minutes evaporated like sand running through the narrow passage of an hourglass as she transformed into her role as Yechiel's slave.

She embarked on meeting Yechiel.

She forced herself to slow down. Shuffling with eyes downcast, she practiced the humble demeanor of a slave, immersing herself in the invisibility and irrelevance of a non-person. It wasn't totally foreign to her. As a forgotten only child, she had often felt irrelevant after the death of her mother. She shambled to the meeting location and concentrated on looking down and stepping into the street when encountering her superiors on the sidewalk.

Unlike the logical grids of Roman colonial cities, Ephesus sprawled out then folded back on itself in a web of curving back alleys and shrouded neighborhoods. The city, hundreds of years older than its current overlords, had grown according to geography, not geometry. And like the Street of the Bakers, Sabina had never visited the neighborhood of Benjamin's work establishment.

She passed several grand homes, fronted by prosperous shops. She peeked in a crowded wine shop, advertising a new vintage from Campania. Her transformation from a wealthy patrician to slave had taken less time than expected, and she was earlier than the agreed-upon meeting time with Yechiel. She went inside and browsed.

The volcano Vesuvius had destroyed Pompeii seventeen years ago. The ash and pumice that rained for two days also buried the fertile vineyards on the mountainside and in the valley. The coveted Italian wine from the surviving wineries around Naples brought a premium and was difficult to acquire. She jiggled her coin purse, then remembered she had dumped her coins out. The limp leather pouch she had secured to her belt weighed far less with its new contents: one bronze sestertius and the surviving parchment fragments salvaged from the confusion in Benjamin's room. With regret, she left the shop. She would remember the location for a future visit.

She wondered at the wealthy neighborhood of Benjamin's workplace compared to the deprivation of his living conditions. Benjamin undoubtedly had benefited from the prosperity of his employer. She recalled the shock she felt when she entered Benjamin's room. Even the destruction of the space could not hide the poverty, the sparse furnishings, and the threadbare blanket.

It was a lifestyle Sabina could not imagine choosing. Nor could she imagine Yechiel making that choice. She remembered the smooth tight weave of his expensive tunic and expertly woven robe. Yechiel obviously appreciated comfort and quality.

She reached the corner Yechiel had designated. She spotted him a block ahead of her, also ahead of time. Then he disappeared. Was she at the wrong location? She reviewed his directions. No, she was correct. She looked down each of the other three intersecting streets, no Yechiel, perhaps someone who looked like him.

Sabina's patience turned to irritation as time passed, and she held her tongue in check while enduring numerous indecent comments. Just as Yechiel turned the corner, a leering man pinched her hip. She erupted. "May your head boil in horse urine."

The man raised a hand to strike her.

Yechiel grabbed the man's sleeve. "Do not touch my slave," he warned. One look at Yechiel and the man disappeared. Yechiel turned to her. "Your sharp tongue loosens quickly."

"And you prefer slow-witted women?"

"My wife, Eunice, matches you in cleverness and intellect. But hers is a quiet intelligence with gentle persuasion. Something I am sure your husband would much appreciate."

"I am widowed." Sabina bristled at providing him another excuse to deride her. Her second-class status.

"Ahh, that partially explains your unrestricted wanderings. And your patron has no control over you?"

"My father has encouraged this investigation." Sabina felt a bit guilty at stretching the truth.

Yechiel's face lit in surprise. "What gives him such faith in your capabilities?"

Sabina's laugh sounded cynical. "It's not my capabilities he needs. It's my connections to the…" She stopped abruptly. She had almost said *church members*. "He doesn't need my advice." This situation was getting complicated. She couldn't continue hiding the relationship between the investigating magistrate and his daughter.

"Sabina?" A voice broke from the crowd, and a stocky well-dressed man elbowed his way toward them.

"Marcus!" Sabina looked down at her clothing. She struggled to find a justification for her current dress. Nothing came to mind. Instead, her words tumbled out, "What are you doing here?" Her embarrassment carried with it a tone of accusation she hadn't intended.

Marcus looked sharply at Yechiel. She saw his confusion. "I am meeting a customer. I hope Amisi is not shirking her companion duties." Marcus's point was obvious. Scorching heat rose from her chest to her face. "A woman of status and class does not go out in public unchaperoned, or worse." She followed his eyes as he surveyed her from the bottom of Amisi's too-small sandals to her uncovered hair and simple braid. She blinked rapidly and opened her mouth to explain. When nothing came out, she snapped it shut.

Yechiel took a step. "I am late for my appointment." He began walking down the street. "You should stay."

Sabina looked at Marcus. Her father's question flashed through her mind. *Have you considered the consequences of your actions?* Sabina looked feebly from Marcus to Yechiel's rapidly retreating figure. "I don't want to interrupt your business," she stammered.

"I would consider it my honor and pleasure to escort you safely back home." Marcus bowed and offered his hand.

She watched as Yechiel had reached the corner of the next block. Would he find a clue to save Apollos? Would he tell her if he did? I should take Marcus's hand. I should go home.

She stepped toward Marcus and shook her head. "Thank you, but I can get safely home."

Marcus's eyebrows drew together until they touched.

"Will I see you at dinner," she said, her eyes darting between Marcus and Yechiel, "tomorrow night?"

Marcus dropped his hand. His shoulders slumped as if trying to make sense of her refusal for his help. "It should be an interesting evening."

Yechiel turned the corner and disappeared.

With one last glance at Marcus, she said, "I'm sorry. I have to go." She took several steps and shouted over her shoulder. "Don't worry. He's a married man."

She whirled around and pelted after Yechiel, afraid he would enter the scriptorium without her.

The troubling image of Marcus standing alone, his brows puckered, and mouth pinched, jabbed at her with each running slap of her sandal. It wasn't until she turned the corner and caught up with Yechiel that she realized her parting comment to Marcus hadn't helped her cause one bit. When had getting married dropped in her priorities?

Unlike the poorer shops, taverns, and craftsman booths pushed onto dirt-packed side roads, the business of Benjamin's boss, Valerius Gratus, dominated a prosperous marble-paved street only three blocks from the central market agora. Its location was ideal.

As they neared the business, two men exited the building. Each bore a bag slung over his shoulder. Several rolls of papyrus stuck out the top, and the men carried a wooden box tucked under their arm. Yechiel had told her Benjamin's fellow scribes worked in the market and state agoras, out of stalls and shops owned by Valerius. Valerius appeared to possess a healthy slice of the professional letter writing, will drafting, and business contracts in Ephesus.

At the door to the scriptorium, she bent over, taking shallow breathes and pinching a twinge in her side.

"That is one way to keep you quiet."

She hadn't had a chance to tell him about Livia. And after that comment, her news could wait. She straightened and focused on slowing her panting.

Yechiel gripped the scriptorium's door knocker, a brass feathered quill attached to the back end of the duck. The duck served as an inkpot and brass knocker. Below it, a small brass plaque embedded in the door advertised, *Valerius Gratus – Book Seller*.

At another time, she would have smiled at the clever humor.

Yechiel rapped once. When no one answered, he knocked again and waited. He impatiently grabbed the duck for the third time, just as the door opened and the knocker slipped out of his grasp.

"Illustrious sir, I apologize for your wait." The door slave flicked a crumb from the corner of his mouth and bowed solicitously.

Yechiel watched the slave lower his eyelids to surreptitiously assess Yechiel's clothing. Sabina recited the litany of social class requirements she knew the slave itemized: tunic, fine white linen, no band of office;

boots, soft dyed leather; rings, none. The science of discerning the prominence of his master's visitor alerted a well-trained slave to the amount of fawning and flattery due to each customer.

"I am here to see the proprietor, Valerius Gratus," Yechiel said.

"Of course. I shall see if my master is available. Please follow me." The slave preceded Yechiel down an entryway hall and into a small waiting room. Sabina trailed. "While you wait, his personal secretary, Rufus, would be happy to review your business."

Apparently, Yechiel hadn't passed the slave's status inspection.

"I don't discuss business with secretaries."

"No, no, my mistake. If you will, please be seated here. I will see if my master is available. What may I inform my master you are interested in?"

"I don't discuss my business with slaves either."

The slave frowned. "Of course not. Your name, perhaps?"

"Yechiel ben Jonah."

"I shall inform my master." The slave bowed and left.

Sabina looked out of the waiting room. Unlike the silversmith, the operating scriptorium was not located at the front of the building. The family living quarters appeared to occupy the first floor. There were no other offices or scribes in sight. Wall murals included scenes of the Olympian gods with scrolls cradled in their hands, reading Homer's stories and poems about themselves, no doubt.

Were it not for the door plaque and the floor mosaics of unfurling scrolls, she would have thought she stood in a Roman senator's home, where crass commerce and the offensive work of *earning a living* never sullied one's reputation. Labor fell to the lower classes and the slaves.

Sabina surveyed the atrium connected to the waiting room. She noted three public rooms opening off from it, their waiting room, a combination office and library, and a dining room, all typical Greek accoutrements, but a mirror sister atrium linked to the first through an arched breezeway exhibited stunning innovation.

A young woman sat in the second secluded atrium, weaving on a loom set among potted lemon trees. A small boy splashed his feet and threw pebbles at a squawking duck fluttering around in the pool under the open roof. The impluvium pool brimmed with collected rainwater.

Barely visible through an elegant archway in the office, she saw a large peristyle garden like Portia's, surrounded on all four sides by a covered walkway, and above it, a second-story portico bordered the peristyle on three sides. Sabina's opinion of the wealth of Benjamin's employer increased.

"I must remember this ingenious layout when I design my next villa," Yechiel said as if taking mental notes of the home's architectural layout.

They turned toward the sound of reverberating footsteps that came from a recessed and undetected stairway to the left of the entry hall. From the sound of footfalls, the stairs led to the upper level. Two men emerged from between two palm trees painted on the wall. The familiar slave trailed a tall man robed in a costly tunic and meticulously groomed but for his ink-stained fingers marking him as a man of letters.

He approached, his lips set in a practiced smile. He bowed to Yechiel. "Valerius Gratus, proprietor. Pistus informed me you have business of a private nature." The slave bowed in acknowledgment behind Valerius. "I am most happy to accommodate you. However, I must declare that my slaves and employees are chosen for their reliability and confidentiality. My secretary would have been more than capable of meeting all your needs." Neither slave nor Valerius glanced at Sabina.

"I am here because your personal services were recommended," Yechiel said.

"I understand. Satisfied customers abound in our illustrious city. I can assure you we can supply whatever you require. You appear to be a man of elevated tastes, perhaps a copy of Plato's *Allegory of the Cave*, resurging in popularity this year. A newly favored poet of our emperor has written a sequel to Virgil's poem *Aeneid.* I have scrolls of both here in my library. If you desire a work I do not currently own, I have connections throughout Ephesus, and if need be, the libraries of Rome and Alexandria, to find whatever your taste requires." His fixed smile widened. "And who recommended us?"

"Benjamin ben Jonah."

"Benjamin." Valerius's smile disappeared. "Perhaps you have not heard of his recent death, only two days ago." Sabina noted the surprise and sadness behind Valerius's statement.

"Benjamin was my brother. Our family is in mourning."

"Your brother?" Valerius glared at his slave. "I was unaware. Pistus did not mention…well, no matter. So much talent is gone. I offer my condolences to your family."

"I will relay that to my mother. Did you see him daily, at work?"

"Of course, every day. I agreed to his request to come in late on Sunday mornings. Even with this time off, he surpassed the workload of everyone else."

"That was generous of you," Yechiel said.

"Had Benjamin's dedication to his work decreased, he'd have been back to seven days a week, like the rest us. But I can attest his productivity never wavered, and he never complained. For an illness to overtake him so quickly, it's a shock." Valerius pursed his lips tightly together, then spoke. "I do not wish to be impolite, but do you know if it was contagious? Many others work here. Perhaps I should take precautions."

"I do not believe it was infectious," Yechiel said.

"I will, of course, contribute to his funeral expenses."

"That is not necessary. But thank you," Yechiel said.

"As you wish."

"Benjamin promised to draft a private letter for me, and now…" Yechiel raised his shoulders in a shrug, letting Valerius assume what he would.

"I see, a delicate matter." Valerius tented his fingers, placing them under his chin. "You do not write?"

"My Greek and Hebrew are adequate, but the letter needs to be written in Latin. I understood, from Benjamin, you are a business of impeccable quality and discretion."

"We are the most trustworthy and respected scribal service in all the Empire if I might be so bold. We often serve our illustrious magistrates at times when their personal scribes are unable to perform their duties. Last year we wrote a public decree and a private correspondence for our Roman governor. Of course, I am not at liberty to reveal the nature of the business, but rest assured, even our highest officials trust our discretion. All at a compensatory fee rate, of course."

"Of course."

The men conversed, and Sabina listened and observed as if she were nothing more than one of the potted lemon trees.

"You may choose your writing material or trust my apprentices to choose the material that best meets your needs. We have a variety of parchment and papyrus. My scribes work with the best inks and tools possible, and—"

"I would very much like to see where Benjamin worked."

Valerius stroked his chin as if he caressed a beard that no longer adorned his face. "It is an unusual request."

"I wish to share some memorable details with our mother, provide her with good memories of Benjamin's last days, to ease her grieving. To sit in his chair, perhaps to better understand what he had devoted his life to. If that's not a problem?"

"I realize the shock of this tragedy must be difficult for your family. If you could come back tomorrow, I will arrange a full tour of our scriptorium."

"Tomorrow then. And my letter?"

"I will draft it personally."

TWELVE

The meeting at the scriptorium had been short. Sabina had extra time but not enough to go home and get back to her father's office for her discussion with Apollos.

When they left the scriptorium, Yechiel departed to collect Benjamin's body. If their joint investigation continued, she had several confessions to make—the first admission, revealing her relationship to her father, the investigating magistrate. And the second, the reason he had allowed her involvement in this murder. It would be tricky convincing Yechiel that her motives, though aligned with her father's, were entirely trustworthy.

That would take skillful persuasion and a plan. She would wait to strategize until after speaking to Apollos. Hopefully, by then, she would have information to prove Apollos's innocence. And when she revealed her family ties to Yechiel, it wouldn't matter who her father was or why she hadn't told Yechiel from the first. When to enlighten him about the gold coin in her possession would depend on how he reacted to the first news.

She had wandered back to the wine shop and sampled the new wine. The robust wine smothered her tongue, rich, earthy, and undiluted. Delicious. She would be back. She stopped by a street vendor selling loaves of bread. She hadn't eaten since lunch with Livia. She purchased a thick slab of the barley bread and doused it with olive oil. Amisi will have delivered a food basket to her father's office. Sabina would bring it when she visited Apollos.

She attempted to skirt a tight knot of men, but not before they jostled her off the sidewalk and into the path of a cart. She jumped aside and bumped into another man who struck her with the back of his hand. Tired of playing the subservient slave, ducking and dodging her superiors on the street, she decided to arrive at her father's office early. She'd wait there until meeting Apollos.

Sabina skirted the central courtyard to her father's office. Her footsteps echoed eerily down the deserted colonnade, bouncing off the columns as if reverberating off tombstones in the graveyards at the entrance to the city. The surrounding offices were nearly as empty as the courtyard they encircled. Two lamplit gray windows stood out among the dark expanse of shuttered workspaces, signaling slaves laboring late after their masters had left. These magistrates, having finished their customary social bathing routine, would be home dressing now for dinner with family and friends or to spy on enemies under the pretext of social entertaining.

She turned the corner and stopped in a short side hall where her father's office neighbors were simply empty storage rooms, discreetly located with an optimal vantage point to monitor the clientele coming and going to other magistrates' offices.

Occasionally a useful bit of information drifted in and out of this administrative center. Zarmig's interception of the note exposing the time and location of the fateful church meeting was one fortuitous piece of business. An interception, Sabina had no doubt, was divinely arranged.

Although she thought cynically, affairs of any importance were conducted at a magistrates' home in the morning before parading out with their retinue of staff and clients to this work site where laborious paperwork got filed. The privileged conferences resumed around this time of day, during afternoon exercise and bathing engagements. The confidential, no paperwork, *quid pro quo* transactions occurred at night in private homes, during exclusive amusements and dinners. Sabina had organized many such calculated evenings for her father.

She left the hall and spied Yechiel striding across the courtyard from the opposite direction. She froze mid-thought. He should not be here. Not at her father's office. Not with her. She would slink away before being seen. Yechiel changed course and barreled straight toward her. She jerked her head around, looking for an escape route. None. With her nerves on high alert, she walked to meet him.

They arrived at her father's office simultaneously.

"Why are you here?" he demanded.

"Why are you here?" she evaded his question.

His eyes narrowed. "I was detained in collecting Benjamin's body. What business do you have with the magistrate?"

Yechiel reached for the door latch. Sabina put her hand on his arm, stopping him. "I need to tell you something…before we go in." He jerked his arm out from under hers.

Annoyed, she ignored his reaction. "You should know the magistrate is my father."

Yechiel spun, his robe billowing out. He stalked toward the courtyard.

Sabina followed him, hurrying to catch up and explaining as she ran along beside him. "I didn't tell you earlier because I didn't know if I could trust you."

After ten feet, he stopped abruptly. For a long minute, Yechiel said nothing. "Trust me? It appears you and your father are who cannot be trusted." He clenched his teeth as if to bar errant words from escaping. His jaw flexed.

"That's not true. Because I am a Christian he couldn't announce—"

"Your father has no interest in finding who murdered my brother. He is protecting your church."

"He is not protecting the church." She huffed louder than she had intended. Her eyes widened in indignation. Her adamant denial did not include that he was protecting her. "I would not be here if he did not want to find who poisoned Benjamin."

Yechiel turned to leave then and spun around, his voice raised. "My brother's murder is such a high priority that he assigns his daughter. Am I to be impressed?"

"No, but—"

"You are here because either I am a fool or your father is."

"My father is not stupid."

"Then I am."

"My father understands that one informer on the inside of the church is more valuable than an army of strangers investigating. You and he are outsiders. And our people are good at keeping secrets. Our lives depend on it."

"You're also good at lying." Yechiel bared his teeth in a menacing scowl.

"I didn't lie to you. I am taking as much of a chance in trusting you as you are me."

Zarmig abruptly opened the door. He called to them. "I do not advise arguing in public. We are not the only ears trafficking in scandalous gossip." He gestured them inside. Sabina noticed a large basket on the floor near Zarmig's desk.

Zarmig turned to Yechiel. "You have come for your brother's body?"

"Apparently, I have additional business to discuss with Magistrate Sabinus," Yechiel said between clenched teeth and glaring at Sabina.

"Magistrate Sabinus is a busy man." Zarmig shook his head.

"We could see him together," Sabina said.

Zarmig looked from Sabina to Yechiel and frowned. "Together?"

Sabina nodded.

Zarmig pointed to the looming open door of the inner office. "Don't waste his time."

Sabina's father guardedly eyed his two visitors as they approached, side by side.

Sabina saw the questions and the follow-up calculations as his eyes flickered over her and then Yechiel.

She spoke before her father arrived at a conclusion that would stop her from visiting Apollos and send her home permanently. "We have agreed to work together."

Yechiel's head snapped around to look at her. He covered his mouth and coughed but did not contradict her.

Her father's usual detached and indifferent comportment slipped. Sabina noticed the tiny fraction his chin lifted, marking his surprise. "You are a Jew…and male. This is not ideal."

"I couldn't agree more." Yechiel's face hid little of his disgust in the situation. "I have turned this wineskin inside out, and I see no other way."

"He is in the same predicament. He needs access to the Christians," Zarmig belched.

"My daughter's reputation is—"

"I believe having a male chaperone is safer than being alone," Zarmig pointed out.

Sabina tensed. Her stomach roiled. Now would be the time to back out. To say she couldn't risk it. Amisi's voice sounded. *If you wanted to be married.* Her nervousness wasn't concern or worry. She shivered with excitement.

"How do you know he can be trusted?" Her father scowled at Zarmig. "Why are you so invested in her investigation?"

Zarmig shrugged. "Securing our reputations, not to mention saving our lives, appears a good enough reason."

Yechiel shuffled from foot to foot. For the first time, appearing uncomfortable. "My wife believes finding my brother's killer is a good enough reason."

Her father pursed his lips together. "Well, if we have your wife's permission, I believe it is all settled."

Sabina knew her father resorted to sarcasm when he had no other argument. "Our best chance to find Benjamin's murderer is to work together." She held her breath, allowing Yechiel one last chance to disagree.

Her father's eyes glittered as they looked from her to Yechiel. "She is difficult to work with."

"I couldn't agree more," Yechiel said, his voice taking on more fervor than Sabina felt was necessary.

She exhaled. It was hardly a pact, but at least Yechiel appeared willing to bear this fool's errand out.

"And as usual, I will suffer the wrath of Amisi for the willful contempt of your proper role. Which, by the way, you look ridiculous." Her father's hand flicked from her slave tunic to her dusty sandals to her loose braid. Yechiel looked at her and cocked his eyebrow, then turned to her father. "You have arrested a man for the crime."

"He has signed his confession," her father said. "It would save us all trouble if Apollos were to die today."

"I wish to speak to him before that?" Yechiel asked.

Sabina opened her mouth to protest, but her father held up his hand. "I have given my word and will endure this farce for three more days. The priest has been informed if no evidence is found to exonerate him, his execution will proceed at the end of the three days. In return for his written confession, I promised a swift execution."

"A confession to protect the members of the church?" Yechiel asked. "And a swift execution to protect your daughter from questions regarding her involvement." Sabina felt a cold chill run through her. Yechiel had grasped the entire situation in the few minutes since entering the office. "I do not want a convenient scapegoat for Rome. I want the murderer found," Yechiel said.

"Then you have three days to prove the priest is…or is not the killer." Her father held up a piece of papyrus. "With his confession, the investigation is officially over."

"This is Rome's justice?" Yechiel said.

"This is Rome's efficiency," her father said.

"You promised to hand over my brother's body."

"Zarmig will show you where to retrieve the body."

"I will speak to this priest," Yechiel said.

"You demand," her father growled.

Yechiel said nothing as the two men glared each other down.

"He can come with me when I speak to Apollos," Sabina said. "Yechiel will see for himself Apollos is innocent. Zarmig can bring him to retrieve Benjamin's body after."

Zarmig held the door open for Yechiel.

"I will speak to Sabina alone," her father said.

Yechiel tensed. He didn't move except to look from Zarmig to Sabina and, lastly, to her father. With an almost imperceptible shrug, he turned and left the office.

"Your collaboration with Yechiel makes us vulnerable. Do not trust him. Zarmig could find little about him."

"His family?" Sabina asked.

"A large extended network of relatives, respected and prosperous within the Jewish community and in Ephesus. But private," said Zarmig. "Too private."

"Unlike the refugees fleeing here after Jerusalem's destruction, their family has lived in Ephesus for generations. They have had years to conceal any criminalities," her father said.

"What about his employer. Yechiel is an architect."

"Apparently a much sought out talent," Zarmig said.

"Again, beyond the obvious facts, we found nothing to give us leverage to keep him quiet," her father said. "You must be careful about what you reveal."

"Did you find anything helpful about Benjamin?" Sabina asked.

"The family is fiercely loyal," Zarmig said. "I had to cast my net well beyond the customary relatives to uncover any gossip. Where would we be without nosy neighbors? Two years ago, Benjamin's family threw him out of the family nest."

"That doesn't sound like a loyal family to me," Sabina observed.

"Apparently, Benjamin had been warned to recant and turn from his sacrilegious Christian wandering," her father snorted as if to agree with Benjamin's family. "He refused to disavow the Christian Messiah."

"According to our cooperative neighbor," Zarmig continued, "Benjamin grew passionate about sharing this sacrilege with his family. When his father and the local rabbi were unable to convince him to abandon his beliefs, the family tie frayed. The neighbor assured me his family had no choice but to distance themselves and pray Benjamin's reason would return. The neighbor expressed her dismay at his terrible death."

"How kind of her," Sabina said. "I observed Benjamin's convulsions and his dying. How fast does poison attack the body?"

"Rapidly after consumption of a fatal dose of arsenic," her father answered. "The sudden and violent reaction would indicate he swallowed the arsenic within one hour of his death."

"Probably mixed in his wine. Straightforward and disguises the taste," Zarmig said.

"That places the killer in the church that night," she mused.

As she and Zarmig turned to leave, her father added, "It points the finger of guilt at your priest."

"And sixty others with no apparent motives," she said dishearteningly. "Thank you for the information, sir." Sabina closed her eyes for a moment. No matter how self-serving her father's actions, his Roman ideal of right and wrong followed a close second—if the guilty person could be identified, the guilty person would be punished.

"Does Apollos also know of our relationship?"

"I don't know." Did Apollos recognize her father? Did her father remember a younger Apollos at his wife's deathbed?

"Find out."

She followed Zarmig out of the office. Yechiel paced. He stopped and spun around to face them. The man was strung tight as a bow.

"Follow me," Zarmig said, then pointed to the basket in the corner by his worktable. "Amisi delivered that earlier today. She said by your orders." Sabina peeked inside the basket. The smell of the soup filled her nostrils. She hefted it onto one arm then transferred the unexpected weight between her arms.

A shiver of excitement and nervousness went up Sabina's spine. She would soon be talking to Apollos. Her mission to acquire information leading to Benjamin's killer, once thought to be an impossible task, now appeared accomplished. Well, almost accomplished. She didn't take the time to congratulate herself but moved on to her next hurdle. How to breach the subject of her mother's secret? The questions she had to ask Apollos about the night her mother died must be carefully worded in case Zarmig should overhear, yet she could not be too discreet or confusing. Her time with Apollos would be short. Her head began to pound. How would she get answers?

They walked east across the courtyard, away from the public office buildings. They turned abruptly and entered a narrow alley used by slaves. A space so utilitarian as to be imperceptible to Ephesus's illustrious citizens conducting the grand business of city and empire. *Like a grape hiding in a vineyard,* she could hear her father say, *invisible.* She pulled her elbows in to keep them from scraping the walls forming this passageway between insulas. The deepening shadows absorbed the warmth of the day's fading light. Zarmig carried no torch. She stumbled numerous times, unable to see the partially paved and uneven graveled surface. The alleyway opened into the amber glow of a wider street. They crossed the intersection and plunged into an even narrower gap, between a block of one and two-story insulas built along the slopes of Mt Pion. The rise was noticeable. She began to pant.

She did not recognize where they were going. This wasn't one of the city prisons, at least not a prison many people knew about.

She stopped briefly and put the basket down. The basket handles marked the palms of her hands. She flexed her cramping knuckles and picked up the basket.

"Give me that." Zarmig turned and took the basket. Church members often ministered to prisoners, especially those who had no family or friends to bring them food. Sabina often helped distribute the bread and cooked porridge. Today she delivered a heavier load of bread, cheese, wine, dates, and her cook's thick lamb stew wrapped inside the basket.

Exiting onto a deserted street, they walked beside a vine-covered, stone wall for sixty feet and stopped. Obscured by vegetation, and tucked back in an alcove, stood a door anchored with thick iron hinges and strapped with iron bands. Zarmig knocked, and a small panel in the door slid aside. Sabina saw no one, but the door opened immediately. They followed Zarmig into a narrow entrance hall. The smoke from the lamps smelled of cheap oil. A guard stationed inside the door saluted Zarmig.

"We are here to see the prisoner brought in last night."

Another salute, and they were led into a small office space where two guards playing at dice jumped to attention immediately, knocking over a stool.

"I will get a lamp," the first guard said, scowling at the dice players.

They followed the bouncing sphere of the guard's lamp, its flicker illuminating the blackness at the end of a short hall.

"Leave the light and return to your post," Zarmig instructed. The guard placed the small oil lamp on a ledge fashioned into the wall. A large key hung on a hook outside a scarred wooden door with the same iron banding and a sturdy iron lock. Her father was taking no chances. No one would access this cell or the prisoner within.

Zarmig handed the basket back to Sabina, retrieved the key, and unlocked the cell door. The stink of excrement permeated the musty dead air that flowed into the corridor. Sabina's eyes watered. She pulled her mantle hood forward to cover her nose and mouth. Zarmig led the way, holding the lamp.

"Apollos!" Sabina dropped the basket, and the hood fell to her shoulders. She hurriedly knelt beside him as he attempted to rise out of the filthy straw strewn on the stone floor. The chains shackling his ankles clinked together. He sat up, a small groan escaping as his movements were jerked to a stop by the short chain attaching his leg irons to the wall. He blinked rapidly in the dim lamplight casting shadows around the stone walls. The dark hollows under his eyes, the bruises, and dried blood on his bare arms and face told their own story.

THIRTEEN

Sabina glared at Zarmig. He stood impassively inside the door and stared at a spider working its way down the wall. Yechiel entered the cell behind Sabina. He stopped next to Zarmig and stared silently at Apollos.

Apollos reached out a hand toward Sabina. "Sabina, I have prayed day and night you would be safe." She clasped his hands between hers. "I was frightened."

"Frightened for me? You are the one who is hurt." She pointed to the ring of crusted blood banding his ankles above the iron shackles.

"Worse is the chill. Satan attacks my very bones; they ache with the cold of the floor. I am surprised the evil beast considers me worthy of his attention." Sabina could not believe she saw him smile. He looked at Zarmig and then back to Sabina. His smile disappeared. Deep furrows creased his forehead; his fingers tightened on her hers. "Are you being arrested?"

"No, I am not a prisoner." Apollos did not appear to realize her connection to her father. Her mother had kept her Christian activities and friends at a safe distance from her husband. She debated confessing her father's position and protection to ease Apollos's worry. But her father had warned her any information linking her father to the church endangered them all.

Flavius Fortunus and her father had a bitter history. Flavius would use this opportunity to incriminate her father, making Apollos a disposable pawn in the political maneuvering between city magistrates. If Flavius suspected Apollos held incriminating evidence against her father, Apollos's torture was guaranteed.

"I am here because I don't believe your confession. No one does."

"I do," Yechiel said.

Apollos's face registered resignation. "The magistrate has promised a swift beheading. No arena spectacle." Apollos coughed. "Our dear apostle Paul learned through affliction to trust God in all circumstances. If Paul suffered, who am I to escape torment. My life and death are God's to command."

Zarmig's deep laugh was followed by a belch.

Her father's words flooded back to her. *Isn't martyrdom what you Christians desire?* "I'm here to prove your innocence. Find who had a reason to harm Benjamin."

"Only a mad person would hurt him. I know no mad people."

"Then you can share what you know about the night of his murder."

"Benjamin was the gentlest man I have known. I counted him among my most trustworthy friends. I miss..." He shivered, choking back a sob, and then began to cry.

Sabina took a napkin from the basket and offered it to the weeping man. He bowed his head and wiped at the tears marking a path through the grime and dirt embedded on his face. His shivering continued.

"I brought food." Sabina began removing the items listing them as she emptied the basket. "Cheese, wine, dates." The smell of lamb stew mingled with the stale stench of sweat and urine. "We can talk after you eat."

Yechiel stepped around to face Apollos. "Or while he eats. Our time is limited." His voice held no compassion.

"He will eat first." She handed Apollos a date. "This rude man is Yechiel, Benjamin's brother."

"Yechiel? You are the architect. Benjamin told me you were the most talented member of his family, yes." Apollos sniffed and wiped his nose with the back of his hand. "He was extremely proud of you."

"If you cared for my brother, then tell me how and why you poisoned him." Yechiel's tone showed no patience for Apollos's hunger or his condition.

"He's not the murderer!" Sabina's eyes flashed as she raised her voice.

"It is fine, Sabina. Thank you for defending me," Apollos said in a weak voice.

"He confessed. Who else would have killed my brother?" Yechiel raised his voice above Sabina's.

"He can't answer any of your questions if he collapses from hunger," Sabina said.

"I am not planning to stay here all night," Zarmig said. Producing a thin wooden pick, he began cleaning his teeth.

"I will answer and eat." Apollos groaned as he reached for the date Sabina held out. "I have been struggling with that question since the magistrate established poison as the cause of death. It made no sense then, and after contemplating, even less sense now."

"Chew," Sabina placed another date into his hand.

"It is much easier to think when a grumbling stomach is not swallowing your thoughts." Apollos bowed his head and closed his eyes. "Thanks be to God, the provider of all gifts, the good and the difficult. Amen." He looked up and placed a date into his mouth and chewed slowly. He wiped a stray tear away and put the second date in his mouth.

Yechiel paced two steps one way, then back.

"I worried about Benjamin." Apollos spat a pit out on the floor and reached for another date. "He had lost weight. He complained of headaches. I told him he worked too hard. Day and night at the scriptorium, and when he wasn't writing, he helped the deacons feed the street orphans."

"That is how he met Livia," Sabina said.

"Yes, he also tended to the sick, another endless job. I had hoped once he finished his training at the scriptorium and began working for—" Apollos stopped.

"Working for...whom?" Sabina prompted, remembering her promise to Livia. Surely Apollos already knew. She handed him the uncorked wineskin. He drank. She tore a chunk of bread from the loaf.

Apollos washed a large bite of the bread down with a swallow of the wine. He sighed. "With Benjamin dead, does it matter who knows? John's scribe, Prochorus, is ill. He has barely been able to work since returning with John from Patmos. We do not believe he will recover."

"Who is this John?" Yechiel asked.

"He is an apostle. The last living apostle," Sabina said, with a breath of awe in her voice. "Chosen by Jesus the Christ, and granted the authority to speak on God's behalf. He teaches the messages of Jesus, our Scriptures."

"In two more days, we had arranged for Benjamin to start as John's scribe," Apollos said.

"I find that a disturbing coincidence," Yechiel said.

"That is hardly a reason to murder him. And we kept it confidential. Only a few select people knew." Apollos closed his eyes. He leaned his head against the wall, exhausted.

"A secret?" said Yechiel, his eyebrows rising in disbelief.

"Livia knew," Sabina said. "Benjamin took her to visit John. He told her he would be working as John's scribe."

"Well, not so private then," Apollos sighed, his eyes fluttered open. "His work would have eventually been known. It is all of our jobs to spread Christ's message throughout the provinces."

"Rome would consider that sedition...the spreading of a resistance movement," Yechiel said. "Would they want John dead?"

"Eat," Sabina prompted, taking the wine bottle and handing him more bread spread with goat cheese. "The emperor already banished John, but he survived."

"Rome is one reason we kept Benjamin's appointment secret," Apollos said. "The churches in Ephesus have assembled a substantial library. Our most valuable books are the Gospels telling of Jesus's life, His miracles, and His mission to reunite us with God. We have also preserved the letters written by the apostles."

"Written by John?" Yechiel asked.

"Yes, John's letters and any surviving writings from the other twelve apostles, and Paul. We have only their writings and the testimonies of their disciples left to direct the church," Apollos said.

"And my brother's involvement?"

"The Ephesian churches possess the apostle Paul's original letters, written to Bishop Timothy, and the gospel written by John. Their letters are getting worn out and fragile. Believers around the empire are desperate to hear these words from Jesus to His church."

"How does this concern my brother?" Yechiel's tone was thick with impatience.

"He was copying them. A lifetime of work lay ahead. Like the Jewish prophets in the past, the foundation of our faith is the witness of God's chosen emissaries. Jesus selected His apostles. Our faith stands or falls on preserving their eyewitness accounts of Jesus. Losing your brother's skill and training is a tragedy."

"Perhaps that's why he was killed. To stop the spread of your message," Yechiel said.

"If that was the motive, their plan failed." Apollos's chains rattled as he attempted to stretch his legs. "Benjamin is not our only scribe. The Scripture he copied has been preached for decades. We have had many scribes over the years. Hundreds of copies of our sacred Scripture exist. But accurate transcription takes time. Like you, we believe our written Scripture is God communicating with His people. Killing one man, or thousands, would not stop God's message."

Yechiel guffawed. "Your vision is of thousands following a dead Messiah?"

"No, thousands will not follow a dead messiah," said Apollos. "Twelve men would not follow a dead messiah. But millions will worship a living Messiah."

"Your dreams will die, old man. Just like all the false prophets who have claimed to be the savior and messiah of Israel."

"You are correct; false prophets die. Unfortunately, their spurious messages continue to deceive and damn the lost. The true Word of God brings life. Benjamin believed in the work he carried out."

"How did he accomplish this if this work is illegal?" Yechiel asked.

Apollos shifted, then bit his lower lip as the shackle dug into his ankle, tearing a scab. A trickle of red oozed out. "The owner of the scriptorium is a Christian. He cannot confess his faith openly."

Sabina looked pleadingly at Zarmig, who ignored her, and calmly scraped the dirt from under his fingernails with his knife-tip.

She scooped up a cup of the stew and held it out to Apollos. He took a sip and began coughing. He set it down. "His death has come at a terrible time," Apollos said.

"I agree." Yechiel glared at Apollos.

"I'm sorry. I did not mean there was a good time," Apollos stammered. "It is just that our bishop, Timothy, is away, and I am under arrest while a murderous wolf stalks our sheep."

"Sheep?" asked Yechiel, a bewildered expression on his face.

"Our congregation," Sabina said. "Our shepherds are absent."

"This bishop, did he know my brother?" Yechiel asked.

"Timothy knew John required a new scribe and would have told him of Benjamin's skill. Timothy is beyond suspicion. He is the oldest bishop in Asia, a disciple of Paul, chosen by Jesus himself."

"That means nothing to me." Yechiel's foot nudged the chain snaking between Apollos's ankles. "He is beyond suspicion, like you?"

Sabina gritted her teeth and began to rise to Apollos's defense.

Apollos put a staying hand on her wrist. "He has been in Philadelphia for over a week, meeting with a council of bishops. They are drafting a statement of belief combating the gnostic heresy that is deceiving some within our churches."

"We stray from our purpose," Yechiel said. "Would these Gnostics have reason to kill my brother?"

"As I said before, I can't imagine any reason to murder him. None." Apollos shook his head. "Timothy and John fight against the gnostic distortions, the mixing of Jesus's messages with Greek philosophies. The Gnostics claim a secret knowledge only a chosen few are worthy to receive."

"The opposite of Christ preaching His saving message for all," Sabina said.

"It is a battle of words and ideas that poison the mind, not the body," Apollos said.

"If Rome wanted John dead, and he's in Philadelphia, would my brother, as his new scribe, have become their target instead?" Yechiel asked.

"John did not go," Apollos said. "Not for lack of determination. He resolved to add his authority to the document affirming Jesus's teachings. But the deprivation of his recent banishment left him too weak to travel. The council will compose their statement without him. John wrote his own letter."

"A letter my brother transcribed?" Yechiel asked.

"Benjamin had no part in it. John completed his letter and sent copies to the bishops before his scribe became incapacitated. John's poor Prochorus contracted a case of loose bowels caused by a severe reaction to—"

"By the depths of Sheol! If this John has nothing to do with the murder, why are you wasting time describing squirting bowels? Or do you seek to distract me from your involvement?" Yechiel accused.

"There is no deception here. I loved him as a brother," said Apollos.

"He was my brother, and he is dead, and you have confessed. Excuse me if I doubt you," Yechiel growled, his suspicion obvious.

Zarmig threw his toothpick away and pushed off the wall. He turned their way, a look of impatience clouding his face. But worse, they had learned nothing helpful.

Sabina abruptly changed the course of the inquiry. "Magnus told us about a relationship between Livia and Benjamin."

"Pay no attention to his prattling. His family pressures him to live up to his father's and grandfather's prominence in the church. When he can't measure up, he tears others down. He viewed Benjamin as a rival," Apollos said.

"Which makes him a suspect," Yechiel added.

"I admit he carried a grudge against Benjamin. But it is Magnus's pride and arrogance that will disqualify him from the duties of a deacon. Not Benjamin. He is learning, as we all are, to follow the humble example of our Lord Jesus. For Magnus, this process is challenging. But that is far from murder."

171

"He sat beside Benjamin the night he died," Sabina pointed out. "He had the opportunity to administer the poison."

"Magnus had many opportunities. They worked side-by-side every week," Apollos said.

"Did they both know Livia?" Sabina asked.

"Yes. Benjamin found out she was not an orphan but a widow. Although she roamed the streets like a homeless child, he shared his fears for her safety with me. I am sure Magnus sympathized."

"Having met Livia, I share your fear," Sabina said. "She pleaded with Benjamin not to interfere on her behalf with her family."

"He decided he had no choice," Apollos said. "He never got the opportunity."

Yechiel stiffened. "Could she have poisoned him?"

"She is a simple child. She spoke to Benjamin the night he died," Apollos said. "I witnessed nothing suspicious or unfriendly."

"Not exactly a child," Sabina recalled a woman's passion Apollos was unaware of or dismissing. "There is also Marcella's husband, Davos. The two quarreled over Marcella."

"I witnessed their dispute from across the dining room," Apollos said. "It was over before I could intervene. Marcella had just approached Benjamin when her husband arrived. Davos gestured aggressively toward Benjamin. I heard Davos yell before he pushed Benjamin, who appeared unhurt after they left."

"What did he yell?"

"It was absurd. He called Benjamin a thief. Then Davos dragged poor Marcella out the door. It was a strange altercation and ended quickly."

"Did he think Benjamin had stolen his wife?" Sabina asked.

"I believe we put that theory in the dung heap." Yechiel glared at her.

"We visited Marcella," Sabina said. "Benjamin's room had been vandalized. I found the remains of a letter or small book." She pulled out the burnt parchment pieces and handed one to Apollos.

"Do you know of anything my brother kept that was of value?" Yechiel asked. "Anything worth stealing?"

Apollos fingered the piece of the parchment and shook his head.

"He lived a frugal life. After being asked to move from your family's home, he owned little, and what he earned, he used to buy food or medicine for others. I am surprised he had parchment of this quality."

Sabina glared at Yechiel. "You kicked him out of his home, and you blame us? We welcomed him into our family of brothers and sisters."

"When he chose to obey your false Messiah, he did not choose to die." Yechiel clenched his fists. "Your idolatrous faith took him from our family and his Jewish faith."

"His Christian family did not kill him," Sabina said.

"That remains to be proven," Yechiel challenged.

Apollos picked up the stew and slurped loudly. He set it down. "You said his room was destroyed."

"As if someone was searching for something," Sabina said.

"Searching? What was stolen?" Apollos asked.

"We don't know," Yechiel said.

Sabina spread the remaining parchment fragments on the floor before Apollos. "Spilled water faded away most of the writing. When I arrived home, I tried piecing them together. Almost the whole letter had been burnt to ash. These pieces survived." The puzzle on the floor consisted mostly of gaps. "The majority of the pieces have a letter or two but no discernable words."

Apollos squinted. "I cannot see. It is too dark."

"Zarmig, your lamp?" Sabina asked. "Please."

Zarmig brought the small oil lamp to her, and she placed it on the floor next to the parchment. He scanned the scraps of wreckage and went back to cleaning his nails.

Apollos gently picked up a piece and squinted. "It is Greek, faded, and difficult to read...*how can he love,* and these words appear to be *lust of the eyes.*"

"Does it mean anything to you?" Sabina asked.

"The Greeks are famous for their romantic poetry," Apollos said.

Sabina nodded. "That was Marcella's guess."

Yechiel's eyes narrowed. "We waste time. A story or a poem in a scribe's room would not be unusual."

Sabina picked up another piece that blurred with a swirl of ink. I thought this could be *is a liar.*"

"A confession, perhaps. If you could find a bit more of something, we recognize..." Apollos stared at the fragments.

"Between the water, the lamp oil, and the fire, these were the only legible pieces." Sabina sighed, her disappointment evident as she gathered her fragile pile. "If it is a love letter, Benjamin could have written it to Livia."

"Or bought a cheap Greek poem at a market stall," Yechiel countered.

"I doubt the manuscript was valuable," Apollos said. "Whatever the reason for Benjamin's murder, money appears the least likely."

Sabina picked up the scraps and tucked them into her bag. "Money isn't the only source of value."

"Finding out where the parchment came from may help," Apollos suggested. "It appears to be of good quality, but I am a poor judge of such things. You should show it to Valerius, Benjamin's employer."

"We are visiting the scriptorium tomorrow," Sabina said.

"Excellent. Valerius is a faithful brother in Christ. Tell him I sent you. He will help."

"At this point, I do not trust the help of Christians," Yechiel said.

"Have you other clues?" Apollos asked.

She wanted to show Apollos the gold coin, but she had not yet told Yechiel she had taken it. She dreaded another rebuke, such as when she told him who her father was. Instead, she said, "Benjamin owned a silver votive of Artemis."

She felt more than saw Yechiel stiffen and waited for his angry denial. He said nothing.

Apollos sat up, rubbing his ankles again. "You found this idol in his room?" he asked skeptically.

"The authorities found it on his body when they examined him. Do you know why Benjamin would have a pagan votive?" Sabina asked.

"I can't imagine any reason."

Yechiel added. "Davos makes votives of the goddess Artemis."

"An interesting coincidence. Was it valuable?"

"I will soon find out," Yechiel said.

"We will be asking Marcella and her husband more questions," Sabina clarified.

"Good plan." Zarmig cut her off. "We are finished here." He sheathed his knife.

"No." Sabina shot up. She needed more time. She hadn't asked Apollos about the night her mother died. Why had he attended the birth? Why couldn't she ask her father? Sabina looked at Zarmig, who was observing her with acute impatience. Zarmig, her father's second set of eyes and ears. "Could you leave us alone for one minute? I need to ask Apollos…"

"Ask him what?" Zarmig said.

Sabina stared at Apollos, the question about his relationship with her mother and his involvement the night of her death burning her tongue. Did she dare be direct and candid? "The night my mother died…were you…"

She looked over at Zarmig. Her best approach was cryptic and secretive. "You knew my mother before she died?" She lowered her voice to barely a whisper.

"Of course," Apollos looked puzzled. "I loved your mother. We all did."

"The night of her death, I saw you."

Apollos blanched even whiter than he had been. He stammered, "I attended your…"

Zarmig came near and retrieved the lamp. He turned his undamaged ear toward them.

Apollos's gaze darted to Zarmig, the consequences of an admission starkly displayed by his quivering lips. Sabina squeezed Apollos's arm, silencing him. Apollos looked at her in bewilderment.

She didn't know the reason Amisi feared her father finding out or the reason her mother had sworn Amisi to silence. She could not risk Zarmig hearing his answer. She looked at Apollos, the man who had given her the love and acceptance she had not received from her father. A man she had loved and respected for over twenty years. She looked into his eyes. Did she want to hear his answer?

175

"I was going to ask if there is anything more you can think of to help us or to help yourself."

Apollos slumped back against the wall. Exhaustion taking over. "Benjamin followed the one true God. That is enough to cost any Christian their life."

"Enough guessing," Zarmig said.

Sabina and Apollos exchanged kisses on each cheek. Sabina's lips a gentle caress over the older man's bruises. "I will bring healing salve when I come again." Sabina took Apollos's cold hands between hers.

On the way out the door, Zarmig said under his breath. "Salve will not cure a headless man."

"Sabina, you must be careful. Whoever poisoned Benjamin may kill again," Apollos said.

FOURTEEN

Yechiel and Sabina had agreed to a simple plan. In the fourth hour, they would meet at the corner one block away from Davos's shop. They arrived within minutes of each other. What to do next was not so simple.

"I am sure Marcella would talk to us again," Sabina said. "We just have to show her Benjamin's votive."

"She has nothing more to tell us. We need to confront Davos."

"Once Davos knows what we are searching for, we will never find out—"

"Find out what? We don't know what to ask or for what we are looking. Davos has a temper. I can provoke him into revealing his reason for fighting with Benjamin," Yechiel argued.

"Or provoke him into a rage, where he throws us from his shop. That's a terrible idea."

Sabina and Yechiel continued to argue the merits of their opposing strategies as they approached the shop. They stopped at the corner across the street from the shop and glared at each other. Just then, a short, stout man with bulging arms exited the shop and walked away in the opposite direction of their street corner.

"If we wait here until we agree, we'll be here until next year," Sabina said.

"If Davos just left, then our only option is to question Marcella," Yechiel said.

Sabina smiled. She had won out of default, but still, she had won. They crossed the street and knocked on the shop door. Marcella's daughter, Davonia, answered.

"I remember you. Sabina, correct?" Davonia turned to Yechiel with a radiant smile. "And I am sorry, but I have forgotten your name."

"Yechiel."

"My mother isn't here today. I am so sad about Benjamin. She told me you were his friends." Yechiel and Sabina looked at each other and silently agreed to the third line of questioning.

"You knew Benjamin?" Sabina asked.

"Not well. I tried to get him to talk to me, but the more I tried, the more embarrassed he would get. I must admit it became a bit of a game for me. Oh, but I wasn't mean," the girl hurriedly explained, flipping her long braid behind her back.

"Davonia, we aren't here to see your mother. We are trying to find a special votive," Sabina said.

"You have chosen the best artisan in the city. You will find no votives more special than my father's." Davonia's arms opened wide, welcoming them inside. "If you present one of his votives at the temple, Artemis will be so pleased that my father guarantees she will give you whatever you ask. Artemis loves his artistry over all the other silversmiths in Ephesus." The sales pitch rolled off the girl's tongue. Her beauty only added to her intelligence and vibrant personality. Davos was lucky to have her marketing his merchandise.

"We are anxious to view his work," Yechiel said.

Davonia beamed. "This way." She ushered them to a shop counter. "Our selection is not as large as some of our competitors, but only because my father takes the time to fashion each piece out of the purest silver," she said proudly and pulled out a tray from under the counter.

Sabina stared at the rows of miniature goddesses varying in size from an inch to six inches long.

"Notice the garland of the zodiac around her neck." Davonia lifted one of the six-inch statues. "This one is especially powerful. My father takes it to be blessed by a special priest at the temple." She put the larger votive back on its tray and picked up a smaller three-inch votive. She pointed to the midriff of the goddess. "You will notice all of my father's creations feature Artemis's ornamental fertility bulbs, guaranteeing unlimited virility." Davonia fluttered her eyelashes at Yechiel and smiled. She put the smaller votive back and picked up the larger one again. "Her favors grow in proportion to the size of your gift. However, I understand if your funds are limited, we have smaller votives and medallions that still meet her expectations of adoration."

Yechiel picked up the smaller votive. He turned it over in his hand several times.

Sabina had no idea what he was looking for until Yechiel reached into his robe and pulled out a small votive. "I would like to buy a votive like this." He handed Benjamin's two-inch statue to Davonia.

Even standing on the other side of Yechiel, Sabina could see the difference in Benjamin's statue compared to the shiny goddesses lined up on the counter. Benjamin's votive lacked any delicate details. The head had no facial features, the edges of her crown were rough and unpolished, and the bulbs on her midriff were barely discernable lumps—crude workmanship.

Davonia turned the votive over in her hands, looking at it briefly, before handing it back to Yechiel. "Even without seeing my father's mark," she pointed to the bare bottom of the statue, "I knew my father didn't make this." She pointed to an identical size votive with finely crafted details, smooth edges, and a gleaming finish. "I don't mean to be rude, but you can see for yourself, ours is far superior. I wouldn't risk offending the goddess with this cheap trinket."

"This belonged to Benjamin. We would like to know who made it," Yechiel said.

Davonia lost her smile and, with a glint of suspicion, frowned at him. "Why would Benjamin, a Christ worshipper, have this? My father warned us that Christians denigrate the goddess and draw her wrath upon us all." Davonia was scrutinizing Sabina. "Are you Christians?"

"I am not," Yechiel answered. "I want nothing to do with those atheists who deny the gods."

Davonia relaxed. "Artemis is more powerful than Benjamin's God anyway. My father would be furious if I…never mind." She put on her salesgirl smile again.

"Perhaps you could come back later. My father just left, but I am sure he would make you a replica of this one. Or show you a piece especially blessed by the temple priests. He keeps his exceptional pieces locked in his workshop." Her voice rose in the sing-song enticement of an experienced sales clerk saving the best for last.

"We are short on time. Could you show us?" Sabina asked.

"I'm sorry. My father's workshop is locked. No one is allowed in. Metalsmithing is dangerous work," she explained. "He should be returning any minute." Unwilling to lose a sale, she pulled out another tray of pendants and bracelets cast with variations of the goddess. "Perhaps you are an animal lover. This bracelet has Artemis surrounded by her wild animals. Tourists love these miniature temples. Are you pregnant?" Davonia asked Sabina. "We have fertility pendants that can be worn around the neck."

"Pregnant? Oh, no, not pregnant."

"Ah, then wanting to become pregnant, I thought so." Davonia smiled and winked knowingly at them both. Sabina flushed as much as she imagined Benjamin did when confronted by this self-assured young woman. "This is the perfect votive for conceiving a baby." She picked up a medium-size Artemis, her breasts and hips fashioned larger than the other statues. "I can personally attest to over seventeen women who offered this as a gift at the temple with their prayer petitions, and within six months, they looked as if they had swallowed an Egyptian watermelon."

"I will keep that in mind…for the future," said Sabina.

Davonia's lips pursed, and her mouth bowed into a troubled pout. Using a cautionary tone, she said, "I would not risk petitioning the goddess with an inferior gift. You do not want to insult her. She could make you miscarry or infertile. I personally know of six women who—"

"I see nothing here that meets our needs," Yechiel interrupted. "You said your father stores more merchandise in his workshop at the back of the house?" He tapped Sabina's foot.

Sabina sent him a glare and stepped away from him.

"No," Davonia said. "His workshop is just on the other side of the entry hall. If you wait, he would be happy to show you more of his art."

When Davonia bent to return one of the trays, Yechiel moved in and elbowed Sabina.

Sabina turned full force on him, "What are you—" then stopped when she saw him nodding furtively to the door across the entry hall.

"May I have another look at that tray?" Yechiel asked Davonia. "Perhaps I missed a piece after all." He smiled a dazzling smile, his tone light and charming, so unlike the Yechiel of Sabina's experience that she stared in stunned silence.

Davonia's face lit with her own surprise at his change of mind. She pulled out the tray she had just put away.

"I am so sorry to impose, but may I use your latrine?" Sabina asked, roused from her stupor. "Do you have a latrine?"

"Oh yes," Davonia said proudly. "We are the only house in this insula that has one. Everyone else dumps their pots in the street or the collection barrel at the end of the block. I would show you to the back of the house, but I cannot leave the store unattended."

Not all the old backstreets of Ephesus had the modern pipes and sewers of the newer insulas and buildings. Sometimes progress was slow.

"If you give me directions, I'm sure I can find it. After all, I have been here before visiting your mother." The small twinge of guilt Sabina felt at manipulating the young woman stopped the second she envisioned Apollos's head rolling off the block. Davonia gave a short list of directions.

Yechiel scrutinized the displayed handiwork, engaging Davonia with questions and comments. His interest moved from one piece to another, and then another. Sabina withdrew into the entry hall.

Three doors led off the entry hall. She had exited the shop door, the entrance to the home was to her left, and the door she now scrutinized was located across the empty hallway. Sabina crossed the hall and jiggled the workshop door latch. Locked. Of course, Davonia had said it would be. Did Yechiel expect her to break into Davos's forbidden domain? Sabina hadn't seen any household slaves lurking about yesterday. She looked warily around. She was alone. Examining the lock, she found it cheap and insubstantial. The security device could easily be broken with one solid strike against the door. Apparently, Davos didn't worry about a member of his family vandalizing it to gain access. The lock could also be picked.

Sabina instantly felt her hairpins poking into the back of her scalp. She had not picked a lock since her teenage years. Zarmig had bribed her into *borrowing* a book from her tutor's private collection. A collection kept under lock and key, a rusty old lock, and a key he kept on a chain around his neck. A key she didn't need, after Zarmig's detailed, lock-picking instructions.

But even if she still retained her dubious skill, this time there were consequences, unlike the excitement of sneaking around her dozing old tutor. Here the danger of a slave, or even Davonia, discovering her and yelling "thief" had disastrous repercussions.

A short distance across the hall, she could hear Yechiel's banter and Davonia's salesgirl laugh. Would they hear her tampering with the lock? No, because she wasn't going to do it. Breaking into the workshop was reckless. She let out a pent-up breath, one she hadn't realized she had been holding. She needed to use the latrine.

She turned toward the atrium and recited the directions Davonia had given her, glanced back, and from the fringe of her vision, she saw a key. It hung on a nail above the door. Apparently, the family's fear of Davos's temper kept intruders out. She looked from the lock to the key. She wasn't family.

The key hung out of reach of a shorter person but dangled just above Sabina's fingertips. A few strategic jumps dislodged the key from the nail. It fell, clinking on the tile floor. To Sabina, it sounded like a gong vibrating throughout the house. She froze, her heart pounding. No one came bursting down the hall or out of the store. She grabbed the key, and before she could change her mind, she quickly let herself into the workshop.

She shut the door silently behind her and leaned her back against it. She took several deep, calming breathes and listened. No sounds came from the hallway; no sounds came from inside the workshop. She looked around. A current of tension charged through her body.

Nothing unusual stood out, but then she didn't know how a silversmith's workshop should look. Ceramic pots and bottles were lined up behind an organized spread of assorted tools, pincers, small hammers, huge hammers, scraper-like instruments, and wooden handles with metal blades attached. A shelf connected to the wall held different-sized clay molds, and an enormous container filled with wet clay stood in the corner. An anvil stood alone, with a variety of leather gloves hanging on hooks on the wall behind it.

The workshop opened into a tiny, enclosed courtyard, barely large enough to hold a small brick kiln, its firebox now cold. One courtyard wall bordered the street, allowing the smoke, heat, and fumes of the smelting process to drift into the open air. But not all the exhaust escaped. The smoke that had stung her nose yesterday rose from here, pervading the second floor. She had felt sorry for Benjamin in the cramped darkness of his room, listening to the constant din of the hammer. Now she felt worse.

There were several silver pieces laid out on the table, beautifully crafted, but none more exceptional or different than the statuettes and medallions she had seen displayed in the shop. Many boxes had locks, but they were open, and when Sabina looked inside, she didn't recognize the contents, nuggets of a greenish color, a fine gray powder, and another box with white granules larger than salt.

On Davos's workbench, she found a box, closed but not locked. She lifted the lid. It held a number of small silver nuggets. Nearby a glass bottle contained a shiny silver liquid.

Sabina opened the corked end of the bottle and tipped a tiny drop out onto the table. It instantly beaded up, racing ahead of Sabina's touch as she tried to return it to the container. This substance she recognized. At a dinner party, everyone had laughed when the hostess brought out this oily entertainment. Droplets rolled around in the guest's palms and slid through their fingers as they competed in vain to keep it captive in their hands. This spilled droplet rolled off the table and burst into hundreds of tiny mercurial silver balls. Mercury. She replaced the cork.

Had she not been searching the room, she could have missed the medium-sized wooden box tucked into a corner, with a leather apron thrown over it—a locked wooden box. This lock was new and much sturdier than the door lock. Davos had multiple tools that could be used to break open the lock, but it would take a series of blows to break it, and that would create a loud disturbance. She pulled a thin metal hairpin from her coiffure.

Surprised at the unexpected recall of Zarmig's lock picking instructions after so many years, she thrust the pin, then twisted it slightly, working through the device's resistance with increasingly more delicate maneuvers. The metal wire wormed its way into the lock's inner mechanisms, pushing against the pins that held the small bolt in place.

She could almost hear the concealing snores of her tutor so long ago. Instead of a wooden box, she had plied her tutor's book cabinet. Its lock clicked as it rotated and opened under her nimble fingers. Zarmig had waited outside the door. She had grinned as she exchanged the pilfered scroll for a bracelet with colored bits of glass, and she had glowed under Zarmig's praise. A second successful venture returned the *borrowed* scroll to its cabinet.

This, unlike her tutor's rusted lock, proved more difficult than expected. Had her skills rusted? Her frustration grew with each fruitless click. She lost track of time. How long could Yechiel continue distracting Davonia? When was Davos due back? Her fingers, gripping the thin wire pin, began to shake. She heard a noise and froze. It came from the street beyond the courtyard outside. Her fingers began cramping. She couldn't hold the pin steady. She gave up and dislodged the pin. The lock clicked open.

She stared inside the box. She picked one up and counted eight goddesses that were identical to Benjamin's, except for their dull gray color. Confused, it took her a minute to comprehend why valuable silver nuggets lay openly on Davos's workbench, and this ordinary lead remained secured inside a locked box. Except this wasn't plain old lead.

An angry male voice boomed from the other side of the door. "Davoniaaaa! Where's my key?" Davos had returned.

Sabina dropped the lead votive. What had she done with the key? She couldn't remember. A muffled female voice shouted from farther away, but Sabina couldn't distinguish the words.

She didn't look for a hiding place. Her search had revealed an efficient and compact workshop. No wasted or empty spaces existed.

Sabina's cramping fingers fumbled picking up the votive. She threw it into the box and slammed the lid closed. Her teeth chattered; her fingers shook. Davos could not know she had found the lead goddesses. She snapped the lock shut and threw the leather apron over the box. She ran past the workbench. Beside the bottle of mercury lay the key. She snatched it up. She pressed her ear to the door. All she heard were her teeth chattering. She clenched her jaw tight and still.

Yechiel's voice, raised in irritation, echoed from down the hall. She lifted the latch and braced for a confrontation with Davos, waiting in the hallway outside. No one pushed their way in. She cracked open the door, risking a peek through the narrow slit. Her heart pounded in her ears. Her hands felt numb. The hall was empty.

The discussion boomed louder with the door ajar. Davos's brash voice, irritated and quarrelsome, reverberated from inside the shop across the hall. Sabina slipped out the door, quickly closing it, then dropped the key by the door. Her blood pounded in her ears. She turned, took two steps into the hall, and looked up just in time to avoid bumping into the burly man she had seen leaving the shop earlier, Davos.

She froze. A chill ran down her back and across her arms. She couldn't move. Davos grunted and glared at her, then at the workshop door.

"Sabina, there you are," Yechiel pushed forward, positioning himself between Davos and Sabina. She stared wild-eyed at Yechiel. "Sabina, your insistence on using the latrine has wasted all of our time."

A flustered Davonia stood off to the side.

185

"I found several pieces you would like," Yechiel continued as if he didn't have a fire-breathing dragon at his back, "but we will have to return another time. Thank you for your excellent service, Davonia." Yechiel motioned Sabina toward the front door. She walked, stiff-legged, past a glowering Davos.

"The key. It is here. By the door." Davonia pointed and dropped to her hands and knees on the floor. "Look, it must have fallen from the nail."

Sabina didn't look. Before Davos had time to discover the unlocked workshop door or before he had time to wonder at the timing of the missing key, Sabina and Yechiel escaped down the hall and out the front door.

They hurried down the block. Sabina expected Davos to come barking after them at any moment. They turned the corner. Sabina stumbled. Yechiel did not reach out to catch or steady her but pointed to a stone bench alongside a house. She collapsed onto it, her knees and hands shaking, her face white.

"You look as if you have seen a dead body? Or did one of your raised-from-the-dead prophets scare you?"

Sabina stared at him. Her throat constricted with fear. She didn't speak.

"I am sorry. I made a poor attempt at a joke." He sat down at the other end of the bench. "I wouldn't have let Davos hurt you. You were in no danger."

Sabina's breathing slowed; her hands relaxed. She said nothing.

Yechiel waited. When color returned to her face, he asked, "Did you find anything?"

"I found that Davos is a lying hypocrite," she said in a squeaky voice. She cleared her throat, determined to regain her composure.

"You determined that from his workshop?"

"He made Marcella abandon her faith in Jesus because she would offend the goddess, and Artemis would punish them and destroy their livelihood." Her voice was returning to normal.

"We knew that already."

"But we did not know he does not fear the wrath of the goddess any more than he fears the wrath of Jesus. He is making a mockery of the worship at the temple and the offerings and gifts given to Artemis to garner her favor. His votives are worthless."

"I disagree. Davos is a highly talented silversmith. I should know, I examined each of his designs, painstakingly, every goddess votive in there, with rapt attention, to every detail, while you were visiting the latrine."

"Not every goddess."

"Davonia said he had more impressive creations in the workshop. You saw them?"

"I saw them, but I don't think lead statuettes would count as more impressive."

"Lead?"

"I think he is making votives out of the lead."

"No one would pay for a lead votive. As Davonia warned, who wants to anger the gods?"

"He is somehow passing them off and selling them as silver. He is a liar and a hypocrite."

"He is a counterfeiter."

"If Benjamin discovered Davos's scheme, it would be a perfect motive for murder," Sabina said. "Davos would have been arrested and executed."

Yechiel took Benjamin's votive out and turned it over. "There is a reason it does not have Davos's mark on it. Davos would not want it traced back to him. He would be ruined if his customers or his guild found out."

"May I see it?"

Yechiel placed the votive into Sabina's outstretched hand. She removed the same pin from her braided hair and jabbed the point into the statuette and dug along its shiny surface. A thin piece of gleaming silver flaked off into her palm, revealing a dull gray underneath.

Sabina and Yechiel looked at each other. Neither said a word.

FIFTEEN

Sabina, dressed in a slave's tunic, stood behind a seated Yechiel in the scriptorium's waiting room. She scratched at the tunic's rough wool chafing her skin. Worse was the unfamiliar teasing of air against her naked calves. But a bit of smugness soothed the infuriating timidity of playing a slave. She had successfully fooled the astute door-slave-turned-watchdog for Master Valerius. Pistus ignored her as if she were any slave attending her owner and waiting to be of use.

She also took satisfaction at keeping the hardest part of her promise, she had not spoken a word, and they'd been there at least ten minutes.

The view from the waiting room opened into the first atrium and across to an office and its library. The racks of pigeon-holed slots in the office held perhaps a hundred rolls. Title tags hung from the ends of each roll. Guessing at the total worth of the library made Valerius a wealthy man.

Apollos had assured them Valerius followed Christ, and the scriptorium provided Benjamin the perfect cover, meeting the growing demand for Christian scriptures. Sabina assumed none of the displayed scrolls were Christian, much too prominent, much too dangerous to keep out in the open.

Looking to the left of the first atrium, Sabina observed its twin atrium, where she had watched the woman and the child playing yesterday. Its view was now blocked by long billowing curtains pulled across, impeding the cool breeze that accompanied the drizzly day. The draperies parted, and Valerius strolled toward them.

Yechiel bounded up at Valerius's sudden appearance.

"The curtains are my feeble attempt to keep the crassness of commerce from intruding upon my family's activities." Valerius bowed to Yechiel. "Most of our commercial work is accomplished in the stalls and markets of the agoras and the basilica, sales receipts, land contracts, tax recordings, transfer of slave ownership, administrative dictates, etcetera, etcetera. I offer customers the convenience of my home office only when requested," Valerius said.

"Benjamin spoke highly of your reliable service."

"He did not discuss his family much, but then our time of getting to know each other was cut short. I am honored that I can accommodate your needs. Perhaps the changing of a will, a secret adoption, or a lucrative marriage proposal?" Valerius walked toward the office housing the scrolls. Yechiel followed. Sabina trailed behind. "My scribes and slaves are bound by oaths of fidelity and silence. The privacy of my home alleviates any concerns for clients requiring anonymity."

"Could transcribing a document requiring anonymity make a scribe a target for revenge?" Yechiel asked.

"I don't understand your question." Valerius stopped and faced Yechiel.

"What if someone found out they were going to be written out of a will or unexpectedly divorced? Would that person want the scribe who wrote the document dead?"

"Ahh, I see now. I have heard the rumors of Benjamin's unnatural death. Our work is not as exciting as you imply. Our days are quite tedious; nevertheless, Benjamin's talents were not squandered on drafting divorce decrees and altering wills. He copied literature."

"Such as?" Yechiel asked.

"Jewish literature. The sacred books of your people. Benjamin's rigorous education by your Jewish scribes gave him a rare distinction among my employees."

"Our scribes are called by God to their profession early in life, Benjamin at age thirteen."

"Yes, Benjamin considered himself a guardian of scripture. Including the ceremonial washing of hands before and after touching God's word," Valerius said. "His unique talents and knowledge of five languages were put to profitable use."

"Profitable? He copied Jewish scripture for you to sell?" Yechiel asked with unconcealed displeasure. "A Jew would not purchase scripture unless certified by the rabbis."

Valerius said slowly and with a note of caution. "Others are willing to pay for the ancient wisdom and prophecies of the Jewish God. Especially when Benjamin's copies met the rabbi's exacting standards." Valerius stopped leading them toward his office.

Sabina couldn't stop herself. "You mean the Christians?"

Yechiel glared at her. Valerius's voice took on a guarded edge. "I do not interrogate my customers. If some are Christians, they do not announce it to me."

Sabina bit her lip. She understood Valerius's hesitation. Disseminating Jewish literature remained legal, but if Valerius believed Yechiel sought to expose him as a Christian, Valerius would never answer their questions. Valerius had nothing to fear from them, but she had agreed with Yechiel to keep her relationship with Apollos and the church a secret until they cleared the scriptorium's employees of any connection to Benjamin's murder.

"I do not need ancient scripture. Just a letter written in proper Latin. That demands better writing skills than I possess, I am afraid."

Valerius smiled and bowed his head. "I am at your service." His eyes remained wary as they watched Yechiel. Valerius turned toward his office.

Sabina exhaled a pent-up sigh.

"Benjamin boasted of you as an excellent scribe and instructor." Yechiel walked beside Valerius. Sabina stayed several feet behind.

"Thank you." Valerius appeared to relax under Yechiel's praise. "Benjamin completed his training here rapidly. I had nothing else to teach him."

Pistus, the house slave, approached and whispered into Valerius's ear.

Valerius nodded. "If you would excuse me for a moment, I have a small matter to attend. You had asked to see where your brother worked. I must warn you. It is quite dull."

"I would very much like to see where he spent his final days."

"Pistus can show you to the workroom. I will join you shortly. Rufus, my freedman and personal secretary, will help you choose the material for your letter. I will, of course, personally write it, as promised." Valerius bowed and brushed aside the hanging curtains and left through the second atrium, disappearing from sight.

"This way." Pistus gestured away from the library and atriums.

Yechiel followed Pistus through the open archway, between the pair of painted palm trees, and up a stone stairway. Sabina followed, staying an appropriate several steps behind. They arrived at a second-story balcony. They walked under the covered walkway, protected from the drizzle of the day, looking down into the garden Sabina had seen on their first visit. One slave removed green algae with a net from one of the garden ponds.

Laughter floated up from among the shrubs and flowering trees. Valerius was chuckling at the giggles of a child. The laughter faded as Pistus led them along the length of the upper walkway. They passed numerous closed doors and reached the end.

They entered through a propped open door, and the mist-shrouded outdoors disappeared.

Sabina felt as if they had walked back in time, out of today's clouds and into yesterday's glaring sunlight. To their right, five iron stands holding two glistening brass lamps each were spaced along a row of five chairs. The chairs, each with a book stand near it, were positioned along the south wall, under large open windows that drew in stray light escaping from the gloom outside. Lit braziers sat on the floor in between each of the chairs, dispelling the day's damp chill. Shutters flanked the windows, and the iron bars used to secure each, rested on the floor.

Scattered sheets of parchment lay strewn across the floor, their ink drying. A ten-foot section of papyrus, glued together from smaller segments, stretched out on a narrow table dotted with pens, glue pots, and ink wells. Five chairs positioned in a line faced the windows. The first three were empty. The last two chairs were occupied by men bent over, writing on papyrus sheets they balanced on their knees.

One of the men looked up briefly then returned to copying a scroll held in place within the frame of a book stand. A small table situated between the two chairs held an inkpot and an assortment of reed pens and a knife for sharpening.

Sabina jumped at the noise to their left. A third man poured ink from a jug into a small ceramic inkpot.

"Rufus," Pistus called out to the scribe seated in the farthest chair. The writer gave no sign he had heard the slave, scribbling intently with his pen as they approached.

The scribe appeared a bit older than Benjamin. Beyond a prominent forehead, now bent inches from his lap, flopping lengths of brown hair he continually brushed behind his ears concealed his face.

"Rufus." Pistus cleared his throat.

Rufus dipped his pen, blotted the excess ink, penned a few letters, and pushed his hair behind his ears. Yechiel wondered if the man was deaf.

After a few seconds, Pistus screeched, "Rufus, Benjamin's brother is here."

Rufus leaped up, knocking his chair over; the papyrus rolled off his lap. He scrambled, grabbing the papyrus scroll with one hand and setting the chair upright with his other. He bumped into the small table beside him. It tottered, nearly spilling the ink as it wobbled before righting itself. "Must you sneak up on me like that," Rufus snapped at the slave.

Pistus rolled his eyes and puffed out a huge sigh. "Master Valerius requires your services."

Rufus ignored the slave. He laid the rescued scroll on his chair and bowed to Yechiel. "I am Rufus Quintus. Chief scribe and secretary to Master Valerius."

Pistus snorted. "Principal scribe?"

"Soon to be appointed principal scribe." Rufus's gaze moved to Sabina, lingered, then skittered back to Yechiel. "I apologize. Once I begin work, the outside world disappears."

"I am Yechiel ben Jonah."

Rufus shook his head. "Benjamin's brother. I was saddened to hear of his death. Such an illustrious future ahead of him."

"You knew of his future plans?" Yechiel asked.

"No," Rufus stuttered. "I mean, he didn't tell me...I assumed. Naturally, Benjamin's skills ensured a successful future."

"Then you were not friends?"

"Friends? We were co-workers, having sat beside each other for two years. He began his apprenticeship shortly after me."

"And Benjamin completed his," Pistus sniffed.

"Have you finished your apprenticeship as well?" Yechiel asked.

Pistus smirked at Rufus.

Rufus glared back. "I have two more years under Master Valerius. I am not as gifted as Benjamin."

Pistus squeaked in assent.

Rufus, red-faced, turned on the slave. "Enough from you. I will have you beaten."

Yechiel and Sabina exchanged glances. Pistus had attacked, homing in on Rufus's abilities, or lack thereof. Did Rufus's threat to beat Pistus reveal an insecurity Benjamin's talent had exacerbated?

A small bell attached to a cord by the doorway tinkled. "I am summoned," Pistus said. "Master Valerius directed you to show Yechiel where Benjamin worked." Pistus retreated, with Rufus glowering at the slave's back.

He shook his head, flipping his hair away from his face. "His space has not been assigned to anyone else. No one else is good enough for it," Rufus muttered, then blinked and looked at Yechiel. "I am so sorry. He was your brother. So unforgivably rude of me."

"You did not like Benjamin?"

"No, no! A bit jealous is all. He's an understandable favorite of Master Valerius."

"Was Benjamin resented by others as well?" Yechiel asked. Rufus did not refute Yechiel's assertion.

"I cannot answer for the other men. But I must explain that I did not resent Benjamin. Our craft is very exacting. It must be. Demanding perfection and intolerant of any lack of precision. We were admonished for being idle, or using too much ink, or wasting papyrus, or making small, inconsequential errors, censured for small spatters of ink on a page no one would notice."

"Master Valerius sounds very exacting."

"Oh, not Master Valerius. Benjamin criticized us."

"Benjamin?" Sabina blurted in surprise.

Both men turned toward her. She bit her lip. Yechiel shot her a warning glance and looked away. Rufus directed his response to her. "I hope you do not think I sound petty. Benjamin believed he helped us when he pointed out our errors. He didn't understand why others were not as passionate about the quality. He was…"

"Too helpful?" Yechiel suggested. Rufus reluctantly returned his attention to Yechiel.

"Exactly." Rufus thumbed his hair behind his ears, nodded, and it fell back into his eyes. "He didn't understand the position he put the rest of us in."

"I don't understand," Yechiel said.

"Benjamin would not stop to eat or take a break to rest his back. It made the rest of us look as if we didn't care about our work, just because we got hungry."

"He could be challenging when he set his mind to something," Yechiel said.

"It is not that we didn't like Benjamin." Rufus looked around and lowered his voice. "When he finished with his assignments, he would stay and help the rest of us finish our work."

"After his own work?" Yechiel asked.

"He transcribed incredibly fast. I would dictate and barely have to slow my reading."

"Which is why you put up with Benjamin's criticisms?"

Rufus nodded his gaze, avoiding Yechiel. "He helped me the night before he died."

"And Master Valerius approved of his helping?" prodded Yechiel.

"Oh no," Rufus paled. "And I pray you not tell him. Our work is assigned exclusively by Master Valerius. That is one of his rules. I could be fired, and the others sold. I told you only, so you did not think I held any animosity toward Benjamin. I am truly sorry he died."

Especially if you now must do your own work. Sabina scrutinized the scribe.

"Show me where my brother accomplished this incredible work."

Rufus led Yechiel to one of the empty chairs. Nothing lay on his book stand. "This is…was Benjamin's. He had just completed his last assignment for Master Valerius on expensive parchment. Commissioned by a wealthy patron."

"Do you know the final assignment he worked on?" Sabina asked.

Yechiel glared and raised his eyebrow in warning. She pinched her lips together.

"He had just completed the book of the Jewish prophet Isaiah. Benjamin said nothing, but you could tell he was very proud of his accomplishment." Rufus stole a furtive look at Sabina. She smiled at him, and he abruptly turned away.

Benjamin's workspace looked no different than any of the others; a clay container of reed pens, an inkpot, and a blotter sat on a small table under the window. His book stand rested in front of his chair. No parchment or papyrus remained on it, nothing to compare to the burnt pieces from Benjamin's room.

Yechiel bent and ran his hand along the back of the chair. He lifted a pen from the table, examined it, and returned it. "Were there times when Benjamin took his work home?"

The horrified look on Rufus's face answered Yechiel's question. "No work leaves the scriptorium unfinished or without Master Valerius's seal. All work must be completed on time and stays at the scriptorium until then."

"Another rule that is occasionally relaxed," Yechiel said.

Rufus blushed. "That rule is never broken."

"Master Valerius is writing a letter for me. He suggested I choose my writing material. Can you show me my options?" Yechiel asked. "Does Valerius transcribe up here as well?"

"He meets clients in his office downstairs. His other work is done over there." Rufus pointed to the area on the other side of the door, where the man pouring ink had left. He guided Yechiel to a spacious alcove set apart from the main room. In the space stood two book stands. A padded chair faced the stands, with its back to two large windows brightening the corner space. A scroll lay on each of the book stands. Except for the padded chair cushion, it looked no different than the other five workspaces.

Rufus glanced at Sabina. She stared back at him. Rufus turned a bright red and spun around, bumping into Yechiel.

Yechiel shot Sabina a warning look. "She can be irritatingly bold at times."

"She?" Rufus feigned a misunderstanding before looking over at Sabina in earnest. "I hadn't noticed." Rufus turned toward a library cabinet opposite the windows in the alcove. "This serves as storage for our supplies. The top half of the cabinet's receptacles contain our finished scrolls, and the bottom shelving stores work in progress."

Sabina's eyelashes fluttered. It had been years since she had practiced any feminine arts. She was enjoying it more because it appeared to be irritating Yechiel.

"You may choose from our extensive selection of quality inks," Rufus's words tumbled over each other either in embarrassment or an attempt to impress.

Sabina smiled in response.

Rufus pulled out a piece of parchment and handed it to Yechiel to examine. "Exceptionally smooth papyrus and exotic parchments, not just common sheep and calfskin." Rufus smiled at Sabina.

"Is Valerius worried about theft?" Yechiel asked, rubbing a thumb over the smooth surface of the animal skin.

"I should think so," Rufus said. "His collection of books has been gathered from around the world. Some of our inks are extremely rare."

"I see Rufus is boring you with an inventory of our supply closet." Valerius swept into the room, startling Sabina. The man had a talent for appearing with no warning.

"I apologize for leaving you alone," Valerius said. "My young son has a gift for knowing when I am engaged and picking that moment to interrupt." Valerius smiled, displaying his fatherly pride. "You can see why I meet my clients downstairs. It would not do to have my reputation ruined by working from a storeroom. Did Rufus help you select your material?"

"We were just getting to it." Yechiel snapped his fingers, summoning Sabina. Sabina's body tightened. He held out his hand.

If Valerius noticed the stiffness with which she reached into her pouch and handed Yechiel the small square of charred parchment, he did not show it.

"Perhaps you have parchment of this type?" Yechiel offered the sample to Valerius.

Valerius glanced at it briefly and handed it back. "I am not familiar with this…but if the parchment is your preference, might I suggest this one." He walked toward the cabinet.

"Master Valerius, if I might," Rufus interjected.

Valerius turned. "Rufus, you're still here. I believe you have work to do."

Rufus looked flustered at the abrupt dismissal but bowed, and under lowered eyelids, departed with a lingering glance at Sabina.

Yechiel watched him leave, then turned to Sabina. "Some privacy, please." He waved her away, and Sabina, dutifully silent, left the two men.

Valerius and Yechiel's conversation faded to a drone as she padded after the retreating Rufus.

"What are you writing?"

Rufus jumped at hearing Sabina's voice and caught his chair before knocking it over again. His scroll dropped to the floor. He picked it up and placed the work face down on the book stand, hiding the open section of the scroll he had been copying. "You startled me." He clutched his pen.

"Sorry." Sabina looked at the back of the scroll. "What are you working on? Is it a secret?"

"No."

"Why are you covering it up?"

"I'm not…I mean, I don't need to. It's a copy of Ovid's poetry. Unsuitable for a woman." He did not uncover the scroll.

"I have read Ovid's poems."

"You can read?" he asked skeptically.

Sabina bit her tongue. "Not all slaves are illiterate. Is that what you usually copy…unsuitable books?"

"Ovid is extremely popular," Rufus asserted loudly.

"Unsuitable things usually are." Could this have been the source of Benjamin's burnt parchment? The wording *lust of the eyes* would match Ovid's lascivious scenarios. "Did Benjamin copy Ovid's poetry?" Or read it?

"No. Master Valerius informed us Benjamin's skills weren't to be wasted reproducing unconstrained lusts of the flesh." Rufus pinched his lips tightly together.

"Your skills aren't wasted on Ovid's…unconstrained lusts?" Sabina lowered her eyes and blushed, not needing to act. This heated banter crossed beyond her limited and comfortably safe interactions with men.

Her embarrassment appeared to hearten Rufus. "I have learned to live above the discomforts and lusts of the flesh."

If his furtive looks earlier were any indication, he had not risen as far above *the lusts of the flesh* as he asserted. Pistus's goading had also provoked in Rufus the very human response of retaliation. Had Benjamin's success, pointed out by Pistus, frustrated Rufus's ambitions. Had Rufus's insecurity matured into jealousy? To hatred? Or murder?

"It must have been hard to watch Benjamin's prospects rising on the dignified and honored writings of history?" Sabina probed, hoping to gain an insight into their working relationship. "Whereas your advancement depended on mediocre love poems."

"You are mistaken. It is I who copy the ancient knowledge of the—" Rufus stopped abruptly, clamping his jaw shut and tucking a loose hank of hair behind his ear.

"Ancient knowledge?" She had heard those same words when Apollos had described the religion of the Gnostics. *They teach salvation based on ancient wisdom that is revealed to a chosen few.*

"I copy the knowledge of our philosophers Plato, Aristotle, as well as poetry. Benjamin had expertise in the language, origin, and structure of the Hebrew sacred texts. It made sense Master Valerius would assign him those works. As Master Valerius's personal secretary, my assignments—"

"Were copying Ovid." As personal secretary, how much did Rufus know about the scriptorium's clandestine transcribing? Did he know Benjamin and Valerius were Christians?

"As you say." Rufus put his head down in a gesture of humility; his hair flopped over. It did not hide the white of his compressed lips.

"I have heard Christians also believe the Jewish texts are scripture."

"Copying and selling Jewish texts is not illegal."

"Benjamin said he copied books and letters written by Christian believers."

Like an inexperienced performer in a play, Rufus's eyes flew open in mock surprise. "If he did, he acted on his own."

"You sat by him. Surely you knew if Benjamin transcribed Christian documents?"

"Valerius would allow nothing to endanger his family and his business." Nervously, he turned from Sabina. His eyes sought out Valerius at the far end of the room, perhaps afraid he had revealed too much. He switched subjects. "I assure you my master is a devoted Roman subject. What did Benjamin tell you?"

She came here to get information, not to give it. But if she was to find out what Rufus knew about Benjamin's work, she needed a reason that would explain how she knew about Benjamin's labor at the scriptorium. A revelation would ease Rufus's suspicions at the same time. She had to take a chance. "Benjamin converted me to Christianity."

Rufus's eyes widened, this time in genuine surprise. "You're a Christian!"

"Not so loudly, please." Sabina nodded toward Yechiel. "Benjamin had just begun teaching me. Now he is dead, and the books and instruction he promised are lost to me. I had hoped by coming here with my master, I would find…" Sabina trailed off, hoping her storyline sounded convincing.

"You desire to learn?"

"Yes, but my master, Yechiel, will not allow any within his household to worship Christ." That part of her story rang true. "Benjamin taught me the sayings and love of Jesus. He transformed my life. With him gone now..."

"Perhaps the books are not lost to you."

"Benjamin was my only link to this wisdom."

"There are many ways to attain knowledge. My master owns the writings of many great prophets. Master Valerius does not censor the commissions he accepts."

"Then you have Christian writings?"

Rufus paused. Once more, his lips pursed, his brow wrinkled.

"I am no danger to you. I risk all by asking you."

"We do. I apologize for my earlier evasion. My master is protected by powerful people in the city, people who rely on his discretion. But even Master Valerius cannot flaunt his Christian activities in Rome's face. We are vigilant to conceal our Christian beliefs."

"Your beliefs?" Sabina caught her breath.

"Like Benjamin, I too am Christian," Rufus whispered.

"You can help me," she let her breath out in a rush.

Rufus smiled. His first genuine reaction. "I admire your thirst for truth. The writings you seek are the beginning, the gate to the way, the truth, and the life."

"Benjamin said Jesus was the way, the truth, and the life."

"You are new to the faith and its lifelong journey...a search for wisdom not written on scrolls that decay or stone tablets that crumble."

Where was this going? Sabina shook her head, puzzled at his cryptic references to truth and wisdom. "Where are these Christian writings? I have money."

"Man values money, but this physical world is not important," he said. "The path you seek is not for the simple-minded."

"Do you think me simple-minded?" Sabina forced a smile, biting back the simple-minded urge to smack him.

"You misunderstand me. The spiritual path to understanding is a path of reason and difficult to learn…but not impossible for women, who are bound by their emotions to the physical world."

"I understood you perfectly." She did not know why he angered her. Rufus's belief, this prejudice, had ruled her entire life. But her female emotions would not advance her cause. "Benjamin said we all have unique and special gifts given by God to use in His service."

"Yes, yes, I can see why he chose you. I sense in you the ability to understand, to open your mind to your special gifts. A spiritual guide could lead you on the path of higher understanding." Rufus reached out and lightly touched her hand. He blushed.

She resisted the urge to pull away. How had they veered away from the topic of Benjamin? "Was Benjamin on this path to a higher understanding?"

Rufus's confidential attitude changed. He pulled his hand back. "Benjamin had the potential to attain the highest levels of knowledge."

"But he died before he had the chance?"

Rufus didn't answer.

Across the room, Valerius and Yechiel emerged from the alcove. Yechiel held a rolled letter.

Rufus looked nervously toward the alcove. "I must go."

Her heart sank. She had more questions now than when she started talking to Rufus. She needed to speak with him. "If you don't help me, I don't know where else to go," she pleaded.

He bowed his head, his hair flopping forward. He turned his pen over and over in his fingers. He raised his head and planted his hair firmly behind his ears. He shuffled his feet and faced her. "Special women can gain enlightenment."

"Rufus." She placed her hand lightly on his arm. She felt him tense, felt the heat of his skin, but he did not pull away. "Help me understand." She watched as the flush traveled up his neck, coloring his face.

"If you truly seek answers…come tonight, after sunset, to the grotto of the goddess Hekate, outside the city, past the Temple of Artemis." He stammered and peered nervously over at Yechiel. "Alone." He pulled his arm away and fled.

For a second, Sabina watched him rush off, then turned to the writing stand. She lifted the edge of the scroll. Tipping her head, she read.

In the balmy meads, the female lows after the bull; the female is always neighing after the horny-hoofed horse. Passion in us is more enduring, and not so violent; among men, the flame has reasonable bounds. Ovid

Lusts of the flesh, indeed.

SIXTEEN

Sabina pushed one of her hairpins farther into the coils piled atop her head. She chose a pair of small silver hoop earrings from her jewelry box, earrings that had belonged to her mother. They lay next to a tiny circlet of braided thread. She picked up the colored cotton strands, faded and worn, gifted to her as a newborn. Its intricate pattern a legacy passed down through generations of Amisi's female ancestors. She had woven ancient Egyptian incantations into each of the colored threads, the green strand for prosperity, yellow for beauty, the red health and longevity, and the black strand granted fertility.

Fertility? Eight years ago, her dreams of children had died with her husband, Xeno. In one day, she had risen to the dignity of a married woman, then plummeted to the destitution of a widow, dependent once again on her father's purse-strings. Marcus's prospective proposal tonight offered another chance at a new life with meaning and purpose.

Sabina rubbed the frayed fibers with her thumb, dropped the band back inside the box, and closed the lid.

She paused to adjust the drape of her white linen over-tunic one last time. Amisi had chosen the color to emphasize Sabina's purity, integrity, and innocence. Sabina wasn't sure Marcus was looking for a representation of a vestal virgin, but there was no arguing with Amisi. And it was a lovely tunic. Amisi had spent an hour braiding and fussing with her hair. Normally there would have been plenty of time for soaking in a tub of rose water, painting her nails, and applying oils to her skin. Her entire day should have been devoted to preparing for her dinner guest. Amisi's excitement had turned to nervous lecturing. "Where had Sabina been all day? Did she entertain men for dinner every day?" Sabina was looking forward to a glass of wine to calm her nerves.

Her preparations had been further rushed by Marcus, who had requested an early dinner. He had business scheduled later in the evening. Thankfully, his early leave-taking would allow her time to change clothing and meet Rufus at Hekate's Grove. She plotted. She would have to give Amisi a quick briefing of the evening, then say she was exhausted and needed sleep. She would have to sneak out without alerting Amisi, the door attendant, or household slaves. A shiver of fear prickled the hairs along her scalp. This idea was appearing more and more ridiculous as the evening neared.

She took a deep breath and headed to greet Marcus waiting in the reception room.

"Welcome, Marcus." The stocky, well-muscled man stood only one inch taller than Sabina. His face, in the Roman style, was smoothly shaved. His light brown hair was cut short and glistened with raindrops. His tunic's leather belt was studded with small gems. "I see Amisi has taken care of your drink." Sabina thought of Amisi's love potions, then batted the thought away. "Our dinner is ready." She led Marcus into the small dining room located off the atrium. Four slaves holding trays of food and jugs of wine stood in a line along the wall. Two dining couches had been arranged at a right angle. Sabina sat on one, then lay on her side, lounging. She motioned for Marcus to recline on the other. Their heads didn't quite touch, enabling easy conversation.

Amisi and the cook had outdone themselves. The table was set with the family silver. Extra slaves stood ready with the first course of wine, trays of cheeses, pickled vegetables, and fresh lettuces to ease the stomach.

"I have looked forward to this evening." Marcus inclined his head and picked several radishes and leeks to add to the goat cheese on his plate. "Thank you for inviting me."

"I could hardly ignore your request to meet, although I am curious as to your reason." The attending slave poured wine into Sabina's goblet. She sipped. The wine tasted stronger than usual. Amisi? "I have been warned not to scare you away with querulous debates."

"Your wit is one of the reasons I wished to see you again. But I admit that makes it difficult to impress you with my own extraordinary cleverness." He smiled.

"My nurse would say intelligence is a defect in a woman." Sabina nibbled a piece of lettuce to calm her nerves. It had been years since she'd been courted.

"Intellect is never a flaw." Marcus paused, tipping his head as he watched her. "But you are an enigma, and your formidable viewpoints would give weak men pause."

"You make me sound like Medusa." Sabina laughed uneasily. She signaled for the second course. Two slaves brought platters of hard-boiled pheasant and quail eggs and a container of honey wine.

"More like Psyche. Whose beauty sparked Aphrodite's jealousy."

Sabina blushed. She shifted uncomfortably and switched topics. "You speak of giving men pause. You have heard of my curse?"

"Ah, yes, the curse. The gods are fickle. My voyages are a gamble, fortunes good and dire befall me. Judging by my experiences, I would bet my life those three deaths were bad luck, not a god or goddess's curse. That doesn't mean I am not a religious man. I support the temples, observe the festivals, and honor my ancestors."

"The gods, ancestor worship, luck." Sabina frowned. Everything she and her father disagreed about. Could she begin a new life fighting against the same obstacles to her faith?

The smile fell from Marcus's face. He dropped a half-eaten egg onto his plate. "You mystify me. I expected a smile. Instead, you appear displeased."

"I'm sorry. Memories of the deaths are unsettling."

"I bring up my beliefs only to assure you I am open-minded." Marcus's brows drew together. A look she already understood as he weighed his next response. He picked up his napkin, twisted it then threw it down on the table. "I have a confession." He stood up.

207

She had only seen Marcus confident, sure of himself, and a bit cocky. "Should I be worried?"

Marcus coughed and shifted from one foot to another. "I am betrothed," he blurted out.

"Oh." Sabina's heart skipped rapidly, then slowed. She should have known. She didn't want to admit to the level of disappointment now closing her throat. Her next thought was how upset Amisi would be. All of Sabina's contemplating and weighing Marcus's assets versus negatives had been a waste of time, and she hadn't yet come to a conclusion. Was she one of those women who didn't want something until she couldn't have it? "Why are you here telling me this?"

"She is fifteen…my fiancée. I have met her only once. My mother arranged it. She is adept at increasing our family fortunes."

"I see." Sabina didn't see. She wanted to tell him to go away before she started to cry. "Your fiancée is rich."

"She comes from a powerful and wealthy family. You may have heard of the family. Gaius Vestorius Artemas.

"Marcus, I am confused, and I think you should leave."

"Of course, you are confused and upset. I have started badly. Let me explain." He paused, licked his lips, and sighed. "As you know, I am rarely in Rome. I travel most of the year. I have had no time to court a wife. This union…my betrothal was presented as a most advantageous marriage."

"By your mother. I got that."

"And my father." He shifted again, his eyes roaming the room. "The arrangement appeared a logical solution. She was beautiful and rich."

Sabina's self-confidence was dropping by the minute. "Marcus, I have no idea what this is all about, but if I hear about how wonderful your fiancée is one more time, I will throw you out myself." Her voice trembled. Why had Marcus made her think he'd want to marry her? Or had it only been Amisi's yearnings working their way into Sabina's thoughts? She rose in an attempt to regain her equilibrium. Her emotions were careening wildly. She turned her back to him, keeping her tears at bay.

He walked around and stood facing her. "Please hear me out."

"Do I have a choice?" Her hands clasped tightly.

"My family gave me an ultimatum. I am thirty-eight. It was time to get married. I had to think of the family legacy. Who my wife was meant little to me at the time. I know that sounds callous. I was focused on business, my work, my trading. Money was as good a reason to marry as any."

"And the reason most marriages are made." Sabina thought of her dowry and the arrangement between her father and a bankrupt Xeno. She avoided his gaze. She was no longer hungry.

"My family is ambitious. My oldest brother will soon be a senator. We have climbed our way into the highest echelons of society. My parents intend for us to stay there and reap the benefits."

"If you're explaining why my family can't compete with the family of Gaius Vestorius Artemas because my father isn't a senator, you can stop. You've made your point." She didn't try to stop the snide tone of her remark. It helped cover the trembling in her voice trying to regain some of her composure and self-worth.

"That's what I've been trying to say, most inadequately. I don't need your father's title or money. I want to marry you, Sabina."

She stopped, blinked, and plopped down on the couch. If she were the fainting kind, she would have continued dropping to the floor. "If this is a proposal, I can't imagine a worse one."

"You have captured my imagination. I am not immature enough to believe in love at first sight or third sight, as in our case. But I feel an intense attraction to you. Something I had not thought possible in such a short period of acquaintance."

"But you are betrothed."

"I agreed to the marriage to end my mother's relentless matchmaking. No one has been able to compete with my love of travel, adventure, the excitement of making deals. I have found someone who intrigues me. My family will be happy for me."

"Intrigue? But not love." At least the man honest, if not particularly polished.

"You will find me pragmatic. Love is built over a lifetime together."

For the first time, she considered his offer a possibility.

"With one promise from you, I will break the engagement."

"Promise?"

"That you will wait for my return six months from now. It will take that long to conclude my business transactions. My business will always come first. I would not deceive you into thinking otherwise. But you can also count on me. When I promise, I deliver. Ask my customers."

"You sound like you are selling me on a transaction."

"In a way, I am. You will share in my success. You will always be cared for."

"After your other business transactions."

"It is my business that allows me to make this offer. Will you join me?"

"Your proposal is...unusual."

"Do not worry. My family makes up for me. They are extremely traditional. They will welcome you."

To be welcomed into a family. The thought sent shivers throughout her body. It also scared her. She had focused on a life with Marcus, how her life would change. She had given little thought to his family. A family meant closeness, emotions, and expectations. There was so much he didn't know about her. So much for him to disapprove.

"I, too, have a confession," she said.

His face froze. "You love another? The man accompanying you the other day?"

Sabina stopped her eyeroll in mid-roll. Yechiel, as a competing suitor, was more than her brain could process. "No. We are working together." She saw the perplexed look in his eyes. "He's married." Marcus's jaw tightened his expression, turning grim. "Honorably married. It is complicated. But in two days, our *work*," she stumbled over the word, "will be over." And Apollos will be free from jail or dead.

His jaw relaxed, but his expression remained skeptical. "You fascinate me more each time we talk."

"I had enjoyed our conversations until your betrothal revelation."

"But you will forgive me because you find me highly attractive?"

She laughed, "Yes, bu—"

"If you speak the truth and find me desirable, then no other confession matters."

"This confession matters." Her breathing sped up. He had been honest with her about his marriage. She should grant him the same. Hers was a simple confession—I am a Christian. He would leave the house appalled and that would be the end of the evening. She opened her mouth, but nothing came out.

He was staring at her.

"I am a…I have a…" She started to sweat; her breath came in uneven pants. She couldn't tell him. "I have desired a home of my own and independence from my father. Your offer would allow me to…"

"Leave Ephesus."

She exhaled a heavy sigh. "Yes."

Marcus smiled but without humor. "Not all women would be happy to leave their friends, family, and the home they grew up in, to travel across the sea to Rome. Your independence and self-confidence are traits I admire."

"I wouldn't say I'm self-confident."

"I travel. My wife must be content to be alone…all the while longing desperately for my return."

"I would miss your humor."

"Then I have a chance. I leave in two nights when the tides are favorable. I will, with your permission, come for your answer to my proposal."

"You have not proposed."

"Only because I am a clumsy suitor." He grabbed and held her hand. "Sabina, will you be my wife?"

All the air left her. Tears filled her eyes as she stared at their hands clasped together. She wanted to revel in the possibilities of a life she had never thought possible after Xeno's death.

"You look worried. If you are afraid of your father, he has given his permission."

"When did you see my father?" Her father had said nothing about speaking to Marcus. Or had he? The day in his office, when she had convinced him to allow her to question Apollos, he had warned her about taking actions that could negatively affect a future marriage offer. "I offered this proposal to him last week."

"I am not worried." She shook her head and forced a smile but pulled her hands from his. "I'm sure my father is thrilled." Overjoyed to hand her and her troublesome Christianity over to someone else.

She should tell Marcus. Now. Give him the chance to change his mind. But what if she decided not to marry him? Shouldn't she decide if she was going to accept his proposal first? She didn't have to confess this minute. Coward.

Marcus squeezed her hands, his eyes twinkled, his muscles bulged as he lifted her into his arms, and in one breath-taking moment, he kissed her.

Her heart fluttered. It seemed as if the warmth from his mouth melted its way down into her breast. She had not expected the kiss nor her delightful reaction. She pulled back, pressing her lips together to keep from grinning. "Shall we continue dinner?"

"Indeed, let's celebrate my eloquent proposal." Marcus grabbed his goblet of wine. "To six months from now."

Sabina laughed, her lips quivering. "Bring the main course." She signaled the servers.

Sabina relaxed on her couch. Marcus adjusted his tunic, and they reclined, heads together. The third course arrived on a platter loaded with grilled wild boar, baked sparrow, clams, and boiled eel seasoned with tuna sauce.

"I have to wake early tomorrow. My days are busy with numerous transactions, which precludes late evenings," Marcus said, spearing several pieces of meat with his knife. "I must complete them before I leave for home. I apologize for this abbreviated evening. May I return two nights from now for your answer." He surprised her, captured her fingers, and kissed them.

Sabina swallowed, choking on a tiny bone from her last bite of the sparrow. "Two nights." How could she possibly decide in two nights?

"I know it is much to ask." His hand ran up her arm and back down, entrapping her hand, massaging it. Rough calluses grated along her skin. Not the soft hands of a merchant, but the weathered hands of a working trader.

Her lids lowered briefly. She did not pull away but daringly stroked his palm in return. She looked into his eyes, feeling the pull of his masculinity. So, this was seduction. But who was seducing whom? She didn't know. "I will thoughtfully and seriously consider your offer," she said breathlessly, batting her eyelashes as Amisi had recommended.

"Is something wrong with your eyes?" Marcus pulled back, his brows furrowed in concern.

"No, no, I was just thinking." About wringing Amisi's interfering neck.

"It is all I can ask." With one more caress, he released her hands.

She pulled away and looked at the server as the dessert arrived. Marcus declined and watched Sabina eat. She barely tasted the honey-coated figs and dried apples mixed with almonds.

When she had finished her fruit, he rose. "Stay." He motioned to her as a servant entered with a different variety of wine. "Enjoy your wine. We shall see each other soon." He bowed to her. A huge grin showed off his white teeth. He appeared to puff out his chest, and with a lingering glance back at her, he bounded from the room.

She looked at her hands, still tingling from his touch. Other parts of her body were tingling as well. She blushed.

Amisi will be ecstatic.

"Amisi!" Sabina shot up from the couch. The wine, the romance, and the rich food had lulled her into a relaxed and sensual forgetfulness. Rufus awaited. With Marcus leaving early, the household could settle into an early night, allowing her to slip away from Amisi unseen.

SEVENTEEN

The earlier drizzle had stopped, but its residue infiltrated the last rays of the day. A fog slinking in from the Aegean Sea shrouded the tombs outside the city walls in a blue-gray haze. The burnt crackle of heat lightning lit up the distant sea. Soon it would be completely dark. Sabina gripped her torch. The rising howl from the sea boded a storm, but the breeze messing her hair lacked energy, and the skittering clouds proved empty of rain, like phantoms without substance.

However, the person trailing her was real. She had first noticed him at the Koressos Gate when she exited the city. The shadow moved in step with her, not attempting to blend into the dwindling foot traffic of the evening. A woman carrying a shopping basket bolted past her. Sabina dodged a boisterous group of drunken men strolling toward the city.

Rufus had invited her while at the scriptorium. That was hours ago. Would he have sent someone to make sure she came? Why? Had someone at the scriptorium learned she planned to meet Rufus outside the city walls after dark? Had Rufus betrayed her?

The Temple of Artemis was a sanctuary for run-a-way slaves, thieves, brigands, and generally not friendly people. A dangerous meeting place for anyone at night. She stepped up her pace. Had Amisi noticed she had left and alerted her father. Had he sent Zarmig to bring her home? Zarmig's security sounded very comforting.

215

Sabina fumbled in her mantle, her fingers brushing against the small knife Zarmig had given her years ago. She plucked it from its pouch. She also remembered his warning during the lessons on how to use it. "It might scare away inexperienced thugs, or make a letch think twice before assaulting you. Otherwise, it is useless. Better to know what to stay away from." Maybe not the best decision to come alone.

Sabina gripped the elegant bone handle and steadied her hand holding the torch. She passed a few scattered houses of the sprawling suburbium. The fog distorted any of their stray candlelight, and the torch created prowling apparitions out of every tree and bush she passed. Lightning cracked the deepening indigo sky like shattering glass. Sabina jumped, dropping the knife. She bent down and picked it up. The man was closing in. In the distance, she saw the glow of the Artemesium's torches.

She sped up. The man sped up. Sabina ran.

Even through the fog, the hundreds of temple torches lit the surrounding area, shining between the tall cypress trees and scrub brush. The light beckoned safety. Sabina reached the entrance to the temple grounds, panting loudly. Pain gripped her side. She bent over, then straightened and peered over her shoulder. A swirling patchwork of light illuminated the road. The man was gone. She took a deep breath. "Ahh," she gasped at the pinch in her side and took shallower breaths.

She swung her torch to the right then the left. If someone had been following her, she had evaded him, or he had turned back. Or, she squinted through the foggy monochrome of ash gray, her imagination had conjured a villain out of an ordinary man returning home. The hand gripping the knife clenched. She uncurled her fingers and released a stinging flow of blood. She inhaled two deep breaths and relaxed.

A branch snapped.

She spun around, smacking into a solid hunk of flesh. She screamed, jumped back, and struck a tree. The torch dropped and went out. Her eyes darted back and forth as she wielded the knife in her shaking hand. She had panicked. Zarmig's lectures raced through her mind. *Panic, and you die.* Calm down. She gripped the knife tighter and brandished the slender blade at the dark silhouette. Then she turned swiftly. She twisted to the left. Her right hand swept the knife up.

The man's arm jerked up, blocking the blade.

"Guaranteed to poke a pin-sized hole in any criminal hiding in this grove."

Yechiel's sarcastic voice broke her focused concentration. Her lip quivered as she clenched the knife in her shaking hand, an inch from his pulsing neck artery. "You're lucky I didn't poke a hole in your throat, sneaking up behind me like that."

He glanced at the knife and frowned. "Sneaking? I have been openly following you since you left your house. You can put the knife away."

She lowered her arm, but her fingers refused to relax their grip on the knife. Breathe. "From my house?" She tried to hide the tremor in her voice. "Why?"

"After I told you Valerius was hiding something. I was suspicious."

"About Valerius? He was hiding his Christian activities."

"It was you I was suspicious of. You took my word for it. Definitely out of character."

"What is wrong with my character?" She lifted her chin. Her grip on the knife relaxed.

"Initially, I appreciated not being subjected to your badgering…"

"You told me not to ask questions." Sabina's voice raised. She slipped the knife into its hidden pouch.

"That hasn't stopped you before."

"You followed me because of that?" She started walking

"And when I asked you about Rufus, you were evasive. You told me he was a Christian and ended the conversation. That was not a casual admission, yet you did not explain why he would trust you with that information. You were hiding something."

"Rufus asked me to come here…alone."

"To the sacred grove at dusk? Since when do Christians pay visits to the goddess."

"We don't." The location had baffled her.

"It was your idea to share our discoveries," Yechiel prodded.

"We are, but I don't know why he asked me here. Not yet. I came to find out. While Valerius was writing your letter, Rufus spoke of ancient wisdom, a secret knowledge Benjamin could have attained."

"That sounds like your bishop describing—"

"Gnostic believers. When I asked about Benjamin, Rufus told me to come here tonight for answers. Perhaps Benjamin came to Hekate's Grotto. Did Rufus poison him when he refused to worship the goddess?" Or had Benjamin refused?

"And you didn't stop and think why he might want you alone after he admitted being jealous of Benjamin? He had a motive for the murder."

"He doesn't know we are searching for the killer. That is not a reason to harm me."

"Men have other reasons to hurt women. And there are safer ways to investigate."

"Not if Rufus trusts me."

"You think he is going to confess to poisoning Benjamin?"

"No, but Rufus knows something. There's a reason he asked me to come."

"You are in danger here. I am appalled your father has given you this freedom."

"This is Artemis's sanctuary. Anyone attacking me would be expelled from the temple's protection."

"Which is why you carry a knife?"

Sabina bit the inside of her lip and put the knife back in her pocket.

"One problem with the sanctuary. Lawbreakers claiming asylum tend to lack a certain reverence for the law, the goddess, and her temple."

"The temple priests live nearby."

"The temple priests guard the monies and treasures of Artemis from the thieves living in their gardens."

"I am here, so there is no point in arguing," Sabina said.

"Since I am here, I will accompany you."

"You can't. I told Rufus you are anti-Christian."

"Away from the Artemesium's torches, it will be darker. I will stay in the shadows."

She sighed, hoping the relief washing over her at the offer of the company wasn't apparent. Perhaps Yechiel was correct. Rufus had spoken of suppressing sinful passions. If Rufus's intentions were dishonorable, they could include her.

And the worship of Hekate, the goddess of dark magic and spells, went entirely against Christian beliefs. His confession that he, too, believed in Christ came after Sabina revealed her conversion. Had her strategy backfired? Perhaps instead of gleaning information from Rufus, he had lied and lured her here. But for what purpose?

The statue of Artemis Benjamin hid could be a sign he had converted to Rufus's path of a higher wisdom. What had Magnus told her? *Benjamin was not faithful.* Had Magnus suspected more than an affair? Had he murdered Benjamin out of a distorted sense of Christian duty? She needed to find answers to these questions.

"The Artemesium is this way," Yechiel pointed to a broad paved path heading toward the distant glow of the Temple of Artemis. Her eternal torches were setting ablaze the 127 white marble columns soaring sixty feet into the heavens. Their brilliance extinguished the thickening fog of the low swampland surrounding it.

"I am to meet him at Hekate's Grotto. The shrine is in the sanctuary but nearer to the river."

"The sister goddess of Artemis. I have heard her pagan rites are practiced during the darkness of a new moon," Yechiel said with confidence.

Sabina looked up at the gleaming full moon. "We follow the path of white stones."

"You have been here?" Surprise evident in his voice.

"My nurse, Amisi, worships Hekate. I have heard her talk about the grotto and small bone-white stones."

The chilling moisture from the bordering river dampened their clothing as they followed the maze-like path twisting deeper into the thick pine and cypress forest of the grove. The moonlight grew fainter and fainter, but the stones reflected any light slipping through the canopy overhead.

"The route is well marked. I have never seen stones like this. Your nurse could find her way even in the dark of a new moon."

"Not just Amisi, most of the population of Ephesus has stolen down this *hidden* path to petition Hekate to ward off the curse of an evil spirit, or to put their curse on a rival, ex-lover, employer, master, landlord, cheating merchant, cheating wife."

"I understand."

The croaking of frogs grew louder as they made their way closer to the river. A tiny glow in the distance filtered through the scattering of thinning trees. Sabina heard voices ahead. The breeze rustled the leaves higher in the trees, but on the ground, the fog clung to the damp earth, knee-high and deathly still as she led the way. She thought she heard Yechiel say something and turned around. Yechiel had disappeared.

At the crunching of feet on gravel ahead of her, she twisted back. Rufus stood at her side. She screamed. Her nerves jolted in alarm. "Rufus!"

"Did I scare you?" He smiled. "I knew you would come. I have been waiting." A dark hooded robe nearly hid his face. A shank of hair slipped from the hood. He pushed it back. "Do not fear." He stretched out his hand to her. She wanted to slap it away. Instead, she stepped out of his reach. He frowned.

"You said I would learn more of the one true God, of my Christian faith." Perturbed, she hurled the accusation. "Hekate is pagan. My nurse prays to Hekate, asking for magic powers for the spells and charms she sells."

His frown turned to an expression of understanding. "You think I deceived you? We do not worship Hekate. We are all believers in Christ, the Savior."

"Then why are we here?"

"Spirits can draw us closer to Christ. Hekate is one of those spirits, a dark angel to be sure, but she can lead us into the presence of the eternal Father God."

"And my nurse?"

"Hekate's pagan devotees sense her power. Their worship is instinctive. Your nurse is incapable of experiencing the divine beyond her emotions."

"Unlike you?"

Rufus bowed his head in assent. "Hekate has no magical power to fulfill the base desires your nurse intreats. Hekate is only a spirit, a conduit to a higher plane of awareness." Rufus took her arm and hurried her farther down the path. "We don't want to be late." She allowed him to lead her deeper into the grove.

She slowed once and tugged her arm free. She looked behind, hoping to see Yechiel. She didn't. "I am confused." This was not the Christian message she knew. Against all sensibilities, the night, with its screeching crickets and skittering creatures, was taking on an otherworldliness that raised the hairs on her arms. The brightness of the moon exposed the path to the grotto but did nothing to ease her apprehension. She stopped walking. "I think I should go back."

He turned to her. "I believe you were guided by the Holy Spirit to come here tonight. For a purpose," he said.

"A purpose?" She asked nervously. To find out if you and your higher plane of awareness murdered Benjamin. She thought of Apollos. She couldn't leave until she knew more.

She watched as Rufus unslung a pack he had been carrying and began rummaging within. He removed a dark robe and held it out. "This is for you. Tonight, you leave your confusion and darkness behind and enter the eternal light."

"Jesus offered His life and message as the light to lighten mankind's darkness," she said.

Rufus stopped and faced her, grasping and squeezing her hands tightly between his. His voice took on a passion. "Jesus's disciples journeyed with Him while He dwelt on the earth. Those primitive fishermen recount the everyday life they shared with Jesus, what they saw, what they heard. What they could understand, but their knowledge is incomplete. Jesus the Christ reveals a new salvation to those of us who live in these latter days."

Sabina pulled her hand free. She slipped the robe over her tunic. It fell to the ground. Rufus handed her a roped belt. She cinched the draped covering with the belt. "Jesus is revealing this salvation to you?" Sabina asked, trying to hide her skepticism.

They continued walking. "Not to me, but the Holy Spirit communes with great men of learning. In visions, the divine Savior Jesus Christ revealed this sacred mystery to our prophet."

They stopped at the edge of a clearing. Stars sparkled overhead, and moonlight flooded the shrine of the goddess Hekate. An open-air temple stood in the center of the clearing. Six black granite columns supported a rectangular roof, six-foot by twelve-foot. Each column held a flaming torch, mimicking the Temple of Artemis. The play of moonlight and the sputtering of the flames made the columns appear to shift in shape and solidity. She noticed about a dozen people in dark robes roaming around the perimeter of the temple. Some with hoods pulled up, their faces indiscernible in the shadows.

"There." Rufus pointed across the clearing. A gaping black hole rose from the earth. This backdrop, visible through the temple's pillars, blotted out the low eastern horizon. "The entrance to the cave; Hekate's sacred Grotto."

Closest to them and pillowed in fog, stood an altar. Its chiseled blocks matched the rough, unpolished granite of the temple's pillars. The blocks were piled in a five-foot-high cube. Tiny specks of mineral sparkled within each fitted block.

Rufus's voice took on a nervous giddiness. "At the scriptorium, I sensed the eternal spark of enlightenment within you. It is rare in women. The Savior does not defile the mysteries of the eternal Father God by revealing them to simple minds. The eternal truths are sacred."

"Benjamin was a scholar. Did he have the eternal spark?"

"I believe he did. He had great potential. Benjamin's pursuit of knowledge was his greatest strength. It was also his greatest struggle."

"He struggled with his Christian beliefs?"

Rufus did not answer at first. "Our chosen path is not easy. Christ, the great teacher, is no longer with us. Obtaining salvation requires a new teacher, a prophet, to guide us. Most people trust in their own wisdom; they scorn the sacred." Rufus grimaced and waved toward the altar.

Broken bits of wheat cake littered its top. A hunk of wormy cheese moved among the crumbs as if alive, and the putrid smell of a dog carcass, left all day in the sun, polluted the surrounding air. "The remains of the day's gifts offered in expectation of Hekate's favors," Rufus said, then seized Sabina's arm.

A man appeared out of the temple. He wore the same dark robe, with the hood pulled up. He looked identical to everyone else except for a silver mask covering the top half of his face. He carried a long wooden staff. All eyes turned to him.

"The prophet," said Rufus with a breath of awe. He shuffled forward as if pulled by a magnet and tugged Sabina with him.

More people seemed to materialize from the surrounding trees. The dispersed group closed in around the man in the silver mask.

The prophet raised the staff and called in a commanding voice. "Hekate, on this night when light overcomes darkness, open the path of knowledge and free us from the evil bondage of this world."

His cape swirled, enveloping him as if swathed in a whirlwind. He strode to the altar.

"Eternal Father God, we reject the primitive blood sacrifices of this world. They are desecrations. Instead, we offer the elevated purity of our minds as holy sacrifices," the prophet proclaimed. He lifted and shook the staff. Its upper end exploded into flames. The crowd gasped. The light flashed off the silver of his mask. A faint glimmer reflected behind him in the darkness of the cave.

He swept the flaming end of the staff across the altar top, clearing it and sparking tiny embers as the tainted offerings dropped sizzling to the ground. The dog's fur ignited briefly, set on fire by smoldering bits of straw falling from the end of the prophet's staff.

"Ahhhh," the crowd exhaled as one. The prophet turned to the grotto and raised both arms toward the sky. Torches burst into flame inside the cave. A sheen of water could be seen, dripping down the walls and into the inky black waters of a still pool. The spectators were stunned into silence.

The prophet continued, "Hekate, expand our consciousness, open our minds to the mysteries revealed by the divine teacher Christ the Savior."

Sabina was so intent on watching the man with the silver mask, she had not noticed a chalice being passed through the crowd of initiates until Rufus jostled her elbow. He handed her the ornate silver chalice. Entwined snakes circled its stem and bowl. She held the cup, and the snakes' glass eyes glinted in the torchlight.

"Take this cup and drink from it all of you," the prophet instructed. "This cup is the new covenant which is poured out for the salvation from your sins. Do this in remembrance of Jesus, the divine messenger whom death never touched, who lives eternally." She lifted the cup and sniffed the liquid; it was odorless, not wine as she had expected, water perhaps. She turned to pass the vessel to the man next to her.

Rufus seized her wrist before she surrendered the chalice. "Join us." He signaled her to drink.

Visibly shaking under Rufus's scrutiny, she squeezed her eyes shut and held her breath, bringing the cup to her mouth to take a small sip. Rufus took hold and tipped the cup, filling her mouth with the liquid. She choked, coughed, and swallowed. Her eyes widened. She grimaced, puckering at the bitterness of the brew, and pushed the cup away. Her tongue and lips burned.

Rufus smiled and pulled the cup from her shaking hands. He passed it to the man next to her.

She bent to spit the vile potion from her mouth, but there was nothing left.

"Sabina?" Rufus said, turning toward her.

She jerked up, coughing, trying to catch her breath.

Rufus nodded, his eyes large and dilated.

She couldn't feel her tongue; the burning had numbed her mouth. Surely, Rufus hadn't poisoned her. He drank from the cup. A wave of dizziness came and went. She needed to leave. But black robes surrounded her, and Rufus remained close to her side. She could hear the thudding of her heart pounding in her ears, but her hands had quit shaking. She prayed her legs weren't going numb.

"Hekate." The prophet enthralled, compelled, and drew the people closer. "The eternal Father God is calling us. Open the path of light."

People crowded together, inching toward the prophet. Sabina felt a push from the person behind her.

Rufus motioned Sabina to follow him. She nodded but let the person behind her slide by.

"We meet at Hekate's Grotto, entrance to the underworld. Enter these waters, putting to death your old self and putting on the righteousness of knowledge." His voice rose and fell, its cadence hypnotic. "Wash away the evils of this material world."

Sabina took a step back.

"Come." The prophet's arms flew open. He pointed his staff to the mouth of the grotto. "Be baptized into the spirit of saving knowledge." There was a shiver of movement and shuffling feet. Murmurs emanated from the group. No one came forward.

"You are right to be cautious; the path of true knowledge is difficult. Rest assured, I will be with you always," the prophet comforted. "My destiny is to share the vision of divine light the blessed angel revealed to me. Your destiny is to rise to the heights of God himself." The prophet turned and, without looking back, walked toward the opening of the torchlit cave. Its silent pool beckoned.

A woman broke from the group and followed the prophet, her dark robe a swaying silhouette before the cave's fire.

"Begin your transformation, unite your spirits with that of the eternal God." The prophet's message echoed from the recesses of the grotto.

Rufus stepped forward, responding. "Open our minds, angel of light."

A man followed the woman. Gradually the crowd advanced toward the pool. Sabina let them pass by. She looked over and saw Rufus striding toward the water. She lost him in the converging mass of dark robes. His budding convert was forgotten.

"Open our minds, angel of light." The reply was louder this time as more people joined in chanting the incantation.

Several initiates walked to the mouth of the cave and stood around the edge of the pool. The woman went first. The prophet did not enter the pool. He supervised as two acolytes appeared and guided the woman down a set of steps and into the deep water. Cradling her in their arms, the two acolytes laid her back, dipping her under the water three times.

"In the name of the Father God, His messenger Jesus, and the Holy Spirit," the prophet chanted.

The two men raised the woman, sputtering and coughing, from the water. She stumbled, restricted by the heavy water-soaked robe. The two men removed her long covering. With the weighty burden gone, she rose from the water and glided up the stairs, an apparition in her clinging white tunic.

A man stepped forward, grasped the hands of the two assistants, and stepped into the pool. The response swelled. "Open our minds, angel of light."

Sabina stood alone by the altar. She slipped quietly behind a yew tree, removed the dark robe, and dropped it on the grass. She turned and ran. The chanting of the worshipers faded as she fled the clearing. The fog had dissipated in the chill of the evening. The shining brilliance of the full moon turned the path's white rocks into a star-strewn escape from Hekate's sacred Grotto.

Footsteps followed her through the grove.

She sped up. A white rock slid into her sandal, cutting her foot with each stride. She tried to shake it out as she ran. Her heart thumped. She sucked in a ragged breath. One thought controlled her mind: escape!

"Sabina, stop," Yechiel yelled.

She sucked in ragged panting breaths. She slowed but didn't stop.

Yechiel huffed up beside her. "Are you all right? I lost sight of you when everyone circled the priest."

"Imm ffffn," she mumbled.

"Please stop. I can't understand you."

She halted and stared at Yechiel. Her eyes widened. Her mouth moved. Like sparks of life flowing into a numbed limb, every word stung the reviving nerves of her lips and tongue. "I'm mumm." She pointed to her mouth, tears streaming down her face.

"You're hurt! Rufus hurt you?"

226

"Ooo." She shook her head and started jogging away from the grotto. "I'm mumm."

"Are you going to be all right?" Yechiel followed. His voice was concerned.

She shrugged her shoulders and tried to calm her panic. The burning stings were subsiding into tiny prickling.

"We should stop."

"Ooo." She sped up.

"The priest? Did you learn anything?"

She shrugged her shoulders again. She had learned a lot. But what it meant, she didn't know. Tonight incited unsettling questions, not answers. Rufus said he thought Benjamin had the *divine spark*. Did that mean Rufus had converted Benjamin from the Christian faith to this? What was *this*? The prophet spoke of Jesus Christ and salvation, but it wasn't the Christ the apostle John taught, and it wasn't the salvation Jesus had preached.

"Were they Christian?" Yechiel asked.

She vehemently shook her head. "Oooo."

He reached and grabbed her stola, pulling her to a stop. "Who were they? Hekate's worshippers? Rufus told you—"

She threw her arms in the air motioning him to silence.

A cryptic grin tugged at the corner of his lips. "*You* are telling *me* to stop asking questions?"

She closed her eyes in exasperation, then spun around and kept walking. Even if she could talk right now, it would not be to him.

They walked side-by-side, guided by the fullness of the moon and the dazzling brilliance of the Artemisium. Neither spoke. Yechiel brandished his knife, one much larger than hers, and escorted her home.

EIGHTEEN

The throbbing in her head woke her from the nightmare fog of Hekate's Grotto with a vision of Benjamin face down in a black pool of water. She sat up. Dozens of shadowy demons swirled around her in the gray of dawn, their ashen robes flapping. She ducked, and a spike of pain shot through her head. Another swept by. She screamed, but only a ragged breath croaked from her raw throat. A staccato of light and dark barraged her as the creatures flew between her and the sun's early rays.

A shadow swooped toward her. She threw up her arm and gasped, sucking in the familiar odor of guano, bird excrement, and molting feathers. She blinked, clearing her vision, and took another sniff.

Cleopatra fluttered and alighted on her lap, cooing softly. Sabina's cry of relief came out a strangled gurgle. She clutched the pigeon, cupping it to her cheek. Cleopatra returned the nuzzle, melting Sabina's heart. Amisi's cure to banish devil spirits was the smoke of frankincense. For Sabina, it was the incense of the pigeon loft.

She didn't remember climbing these stairs after Yechiel had escorted her home. She didn't remember collapsing in exhaustion on the straw littering the cold tiles. But her stiff, aching bones told the story. Antony butted in, cooing, joining his mate on Sabina's lap. She stroked the birds, soaking in their warmth and affection. For as long as she could remember, she sought God's voice and solace here, trading the commotion of humans for the soothing ruffle of her birds.

Cleo and Antony pecked under her mantle, searching for treats. She tried clucking bird language, but her swollen tongue felt cemented to the top of her mouth. Dry sand coated her mouth; a dull throb of a headache made her close her eyes. At least the numbness had disappeared.

She sat, eyes closed. A bitter rush of failure assaulted her. Like the burnt parchment, she had new pieces to the puzzle but didn't know how they fit. She hugged her pigeons, feeling the rhythmic pumping of their hearts. Tomorrow, Apollos would be unofficially executed. Jesus's teachings flooded her mind. *Therefore do not worry about tomorrow, for tomorrow will worry about its own things.* Her swirling anxiety settled into resignation. *Sufficient for the day is its own trouble.* Help guide me. God had given her one more day. Perhaps, for the last time, she would speak to Apollos.

First, she had to get downstairs, preferably before anyone found her here. She opened her eyes, triggering a chiseling pain. She clamped her eyes shut and marveled at the potency of one swallow of the initiate's bitter drink. She kissed each bird, shooing it gently from her lap. Slowly, as if she'd drunk too much wine, she wobbled on unsteady legs out of the loft, squinting and closing the door on the loft full of fussing, fluttering pigeons waking up.

Arriving at her bedroom, she said a silent prayer for not tumbling down the stairs. She slipped out of her clothing, dropping it in a pile on the floor. Her mattress beckoned sleep. She sat on the bed, letting the throbbing in her head pass.

Amisi flounced in, throwing open the shuttered doors. Light streamed in. "Out again. You don't care that I don't sleep. That my hairs are turning gray." Her lecture abruptly stopped.

Sabina opened one eye but didn't move.

Amisi stood, her mouth pinched, her eyelids narrowed. Sunlight flooded the bed.

Sabina opened both eyes. Pain flared then eased back to dull drumming. "I need one of your headache draughts," she croaked.

"A headache?" Amisi keenly picked up Sabina's mantle, plucked a piece of straw from it, and held it to her nose. Grunting, she shook pigeon droppings onto the floor. Instead of folding it, she draped it over her arm. She stopped. She hefted the fabric, noting the solid weight of the knife. She pulled it from its hidden pocket. "This," she directed the knifepoint at the incapacitated Sabina, "is Zarmig's doing?"

"Zarmig has nothing to do with this. He's as concerned for my safety as you are." Her throat hurt, her head hurt, her hair even hurt. "Please." Sabina braced for an argument.

Amisi didn't argue. She nodded, her concern and love evident as she shook her head and left the room.

Sabina leaned back carefully and closed her eyes. Amisi did care for her, loved her, and had protected her from birth. But she didn't need protection from secrets concerning her mother and Apollos the night she died. And Sabina was no longer a child. It was her choice to make. Did she trust her mother's reasons for swearing Amisi and Apollos to silence?

Sabina's thoughts circled to Rufus and the secrecy surrounding the ceremony and the rites of last night. She shivered, remembering the masked prophet, a mortal man promising the robed seekers eternal life—an eternal life depending on the prophet's new revelations. He invoked the name of Jesus Christ, yet he preached a different message, a message of secret knowledge. A gnostic belief Apollos had warned her about, and a message the devotees believed was their way to heaven. Knowledge and adherence to the prophet overrode the special relationship God offered to Sabina and anyone else who accepted His love. Had she infiltrated a sect the church leaders had united in condemning?

What ignited Rufus's devotion to this prophet? Had the prophet performed miracles like Peter and Paul? Had all his predictions and prophecies come true? Was he commissioned to speak God's words? Apollos, Timothy, and John returned over and over to the infallible words of Christ, their eternal measuring rod to determine the truth. What did the followers of this masked prophet use to test his inspired vision? A vision they were entrusting for their eternal salvation.

If Rufus had introduced Benjamin to this gnostic alternative, did Benjamin's response lead to his murder? She needed more information. Did answers to both mysteries lie with Apollos? Her father had allowed her a final meeting this afternoon, until then, Apollos continued locked away and inaccessible. But she had other sheep in her flock. She had Portia.

Amisi returned with a steaming bowl, one that did not have mystic snakes entwined around it. "I warned your father. Zarmig trained you to run loose like a ruffian."

"He trained me to protect myself. Please, Amisi, I don't need a lecture. I need a potion." She couldn't tell Amisi where she had been last night. If Amisi found out, she would worry, stew, fuss, and blackmail Sabina. Her father would never allow her outside the city walls if he found out. And Amisi would hoard this bit of information like one of her rare herbs, applying it as leverage with Sabina's father. All for Sabina's good, of course.

"Drink it all." Amisi gently helped her sit up. She handed Sabina the hot bowl.

Sabina sniffed. The draught smelled almost as vile as last night's brew tasted. When she paused, she saw a small smile flicker across Amisi's concerned face. Sabina had witnessed the same smile as a child when learning the consequences of a poor decision. She held her breath and gulped the medicine, gagging on the last swallow. The potion burned its way down her throat, hitting her stomach with a radiating warmth. "Yuck." The lesson learned last night? Don't go out drinking with strange men.

By the time Amisi had helped Sabina dress and coil her hair, the headache was gone. Its residue lingered in a tender spot on her left temple. Sabina respected Amisi's medicinal skill with herbal balms and potions even if she didn't welcome the spells and charms that usually accompanied the healing.

This would be Sabina's last chance to find the truth about that night and why Apollos had been furtively summoned to her mother's bedroom. Nearly twenty-one years had passed since her mother's death. What kind of a secret was worth keeping that long? A terrible, painful, wounding secret? Would it destroy the only memories and images she had left of her mother? She was beginning to think that if her mother was hiding a sin, she didn't want to know. Whatever Apollos could tell her, it was best taken to the grave. And if she stopped his execution, he would return to being the beloved bishop she had always trusted. She would not ask him to break his promised silence…or shatter the loving and loyal memories of her mother. She had made her decision. She would trust her mother.

Sabina had no stomach for breakfast this morning. After a few bites of cheese, she pushed it aside to plan her day. She usually helped prepare and deliver the weekly food ration to the twelve widows in the church. Five were disabled, and two had small children. All had no family to support them, unlike Livia.

She could ask if Portia knew anything about Rufus and Benjamin's association and share that she had found Livia. Portia had been converted by Timothy after Paul had assigned him as the first bishop and overseer of the growing Ephesian congregation. She continued to study Scripture with him. Perhaps she had learned about the gnostic practices and could give some insights on the rituals Sabina had experienced last night. Portia might even know Rufus.

Sabina hurried to Portia's, weighing how much time she could allocate to the kitchen, not much. Portia ran to her the minute she entered. Portia grabbed her hands and pulled her into an embrace, cutting off Sabina's deliberation.

Portia dragged her to a bench. "I hoped you would come today. Did you talk to Apollos? How is he? Can I visit him? Where is he? Does he need—"

"I spoke to him and delivered a meal," Sabina said.

Portia closed her eyes. She took a deep breath and opened her eyes. "Thanks be to God. How is he?"

"He thanked us for our prayers."

"And?"

"And he is still in jail."

"Where? I can bring food to him this afternoon." She stood up. "Feya is cooking today. Come, we will put a food basket together."

"He is not allowed visitors."

"But he needs food and fresh clothing."

"I will inquire when I bring him your basket." Sabina hurried ahead, not wanting to explain Apollos's unusual isolation. "I normally help in the kitchens today, but…"

Portia followed her. "You are caring for Apollos. God has put you in a place no one else can access. Please keep him safe."

She was sure Portia did not mean to increase the pressure she already felt, but the crushing guilt for being partially responsible for his imprisonment nearly made her break down. "There's little I can change."

"You are doing your part; God will do His; and I will do mine. I have hired a lawyer, Vibius Basus. His clever discourses surpass even Cicero. Once the lawyer talks to Apollos and hears the facts, he will convince the governor Apollos is innocent."

"A lawyer?" Sabina stopped and faced her. Hiring a defender would be the expected course of action if it did not involve the church and her father. Her father couldn't afford to let a trial take place. He would prevent any questioning of Apollos in front of the governor. "The greatest orator in the world can't free a man who has confessed to murder."

"He only confessed to free us. And it worked." Portia breezed past her. "Your father let us go. Now Apollos can change his plea."

"A trial will expose Apollos's Christian faith. Flavius Fortunus is the presiding magistrate. He will demand Apollos burn incense at the altar of our emperor, a living god," Sabina said.

"I am aware of the difficulties," Portia snapped at her, showing her frayed nerves. "I am sorry."

Sabina had never seen the elegant and composed Portia so distraught. Even on the night Apollos was arrested, Portia led the group by her courage and serenity.

"Many Christians do it to save their lives," Portia said.

"Apollos will not." But Apollos will never have the choice. There would be no trial exposing her connection to the church. But she could not tell Portia that. She would live with it in guilty silence unless she discovered who poisoned Benjamin. "Portia, what do you know of Benjamin's coming to faith?"

"What do you mean? He was a Christian."

"And Jewish. What do you know of his conversion?" They entered the kitchen, and the noise of bantering and food preparations drowned out any reply.

"Did he speak of a different kind of chosen people?" Sabina probed. Had Benjamin gone from welcoming all into God's family to limiting salvation to a select few?

"Benjamin believed as we do, that God has accepted Messiah-believing Gentiles into God's chosen people. His family disagreed."

The smell of the baking bread joined the savory steam hissing out of a huge pot. Sabina's mouth watered. Her stomach grumbled, the bites of her breakfast cheese long gone.

Feya stood over the boiling stew pot, wiping her forehead with the back of her hand and blinking rapidly. Three female slaves looked up from their scrubbing, peeling, and chopping vegetables.

"Sabina is going to see Apollos today," Portia said, back to her focused and efficient self.

Feya wiped her hands on an apron and reached for a basket. "Have you found the murderer then?" All five women stared at her. "God knows we need Apollos back home. What with his arrest, half the congregation has gone into hiding. But them poor babes beggin' in the streets are still hungry and showing up at the door."

Sabina looked at Portia. "I haven't found the murderer."

"Tell Apollos we are praying for his release every minute of the day and night, and for you, Sabina," Feya said.

"I told you are not alone," Portia said. "Everyone is supporting you with prayer."

"I attended a worship service at Hekate's Grotto last night."

"Attended?" Portia's eyebrow arched.

"I participated in it."

The women gasped. Portia stared hard at her. "Do we need to increase our prayers for your safety?"

"No. Maybe," Sabina stammered, remembering her fear as she bolted from the haunting scene. "Their religion teaches a new interpretation of God's Word. With a mystery salvation gained by working through levels of veiled learning."

"That sounds like gnostic drivel," Feya said. Sabina blinked, surprised by the older woman's understanding.

"You've heard of the Gnostics?" Sabina asked.

"They're the reason our beloved Timothy went thundering off to confer with the other bishops," Feya said.

"And that's what nearly caused us to lose John to heart failure," Portia said. "I thought he had mellowed since his return from Patmos, but his protests at being left behind sent him into a gasping fit clutching his chest for air. It took nearly dying for him to realize he wasn't in any shape to travel."

"When he finally calmed down, I heard him lecturing Timothy on the key points the bishops needed to refute at the council." Feya chuckled, slamming her knife into a carrot. "He made sure he had the last word."

"The prophet last night preached the pathway to salvation was revealed by Jesus, the great teacher."

"That is a dangerous distortion," Portia said. "The Gnostics don't believe Jesus is God. They think He was a spiritual messenger from heaven. But what do they have to do with Benjamin?"

"I think Benjamin may have belonged to this group," Sabina said.

Feya snorted her derision. "Benjamin was too smart to fall for manipulating Scripture like that." She waved her knife in the air. One of the slave girls hopped back from the flailing blade.

Sabina pressed. "Being intelligent doesn't mean you can't be deceived."

"It does with Benjamin. He knew his Jewish faith, like me." Feya scooped up the turnips, carrots, and leeks, adding them to her pile of onions, and dumped them into the boiling pot hanging over the fire. "He grew up with ancient prophecies promising a Messiah who saves all humanity from the evils of sin. Portia, can you hand me more onions?"

Portia retrieved four large onions from the storage cupboard. "The Gnostics mix Christ's sacrifice with the mysteries of the pagan cults. I am not surprised they meet at Hekate's Grotto."

"There was a man there...Rufus. Have you heard of him?" Sabina asked.

I know several Rufuses." Feya reached for a bowl from a shelf.

"He would be a Christian. He worked with Benjamin."

Portia looked at Feya. "I don't remember Benjamin mentioning a Rufus. Do you?" Both women shook their heads. "But then Benjamin did not spend much time chatting."

Sabina recalled the faceless shadows of last night's worshipers. "Could other Gnostics be worshiping in our church?" Sabina asked. "If it had been daylight, I might have recognized some of the participants."

The young slave squeaked. Her knife slipped and fell to the floor. She bent to retrieve it. After a long minute, she rose, no longer looking at Sabina. She stared at her turnip.

"I haven't heard," Portia said. "Timothy said the movement is spreading. People are spellbound by new religions, traveling preachers, and even magicians."

"This prophet said his knowledge came from an angel in a vision," Sabina said.

"Benjamin was guided by the Scriptures." Feya stabbed her knife into the wooden cutting board and bent over to retrieve some leeks. "He didn't need an angel, Gnostic, Jewish, or Christian."

"Benjamin taught our children to trust in God's Word." Portia shook her head. "Why would he teach one thing and believe another?"

These women seemed confident Benjamin's grounding in God's Word protected him from the prophet's message. Sabina wasn't convinced. "What if Benjamin wasn't deceived? Perhaps the prophet promised him power."

"Pig-spit," Feya slapped the hand of one of the women taking a bite of a carrot.

"Power! Benjamin?" Portia rolled her eyes. "Is that why he spent his time teaching children Scripture verses?"

"I heard Magnus humming one of Benjamin's Scripture songs, but don't tell Magnus I told you. He'd stop singing just out of spite, for—" Feya stopped.

"Spite for Benjamin?"

"I didn't mean that." Feya shook her head.

"Apollos said they were both nominated to fill the deacon opening," Sabina said. "With Benjamin out of the way, Magnus would be assured the position."

"Magnus has large sails to fill," Portia answered. "His grandfather was converted to the faith by Paul himself, and his father was one of our first deacons. I can see him intimidating Benjamin, but murdering him? No."

"You agree Magnus wanted a position of honor, of authority," Sabina pointed out. "And he had access to Benjamin's food and wine."

Feya guffawed. "Not much glory in cooking, chopping, and making sure the babes get fed."

Portia waved her hand dismissively. "Magnus can be quarrelsome and belligerent, but underneath he is a decent man."

"I need to find out what the argument was about between Magnus and Benjamin."

"Go ask him. He's in the alley," Feya gestured with her knife to the back door propped open to expel the heat. "It's not his turn, but he offered to fill in wherever we needed the help."

"That's how he'll earn my respect," Portia said. "I've been arguing for another deaconess to help with the kitchen work and with instructing the growing number of women."

"But the elders always pick a man," Feya smirked.

"Here, you can lend a hand by dumping these." Feya thrust a bowl of garbage peelings and onion skins into Sabina's arms on the way out the door.

"Speaking of men, you didn't ask about last night?" Sabina pulled Portia off to the side of the kitchen, out of Feya's hearing.

"You just told us."

"I mean about Marcus."

"Oh, Sabina, I'm sorry. I would have remembered your dinner if you hadn't scared me to death describing the incident in Hekate's grove."

"Before I went to the grove, Marcus asked me to marry him."

"After you told him about your faith? I'm happy for you."

"I didn't get a chance to explain my beliefs yet."

"Yet?"

"I will tell him everything tomorrow night before he leaves for Rome. If he can accept that I will not worship his gods, his emperor, or his ancestors, he has six months to change his mind. He said he was open-minded. I wanted the chance to decide."

Portia paused, then said with concern, "What kind of a decision is it if he cannot accept who you are, what you believe? Will you be any better off than you are with your father?"

"That's not fair. You already have a husband and children. I married Xeno thinking he was my last chance. God is granting me everything I thought was no longer possible." Sabina's hands gripped each other.

"You are right. I have been blessed. And I would not keep that joy from you. Have you decided what your answer will be?" Portia took Sabina's hands in hers.

Sabina nodded. "I will accept Marcus's offer."

"Then, congratulations." Portia hugged Sabina.

"Marcus may not want me after my revelation."

"Either way, pray God's will be done. Now, see what Magnus has to say about his poor behavior, while I put a basket together for Apollos."

NINETEEN

Sabina strode through the back door she had snuck out three days earlier, fleeing Flavius Fortunus's guards. She felt as if she knew less about Benjamin's murder now than she did then. She knew Magnus, Davos and Marcella, and Livia had been at the church the night he died. So did Apollos. To prove Apollos didn't poison Benjamin, she had to demonstrate someone else did. And that looked increasingly impossible the more she learned about Benjamin's life.

And where did Rufus fit? Rufus had told her he was a Christian. Yet, the worshipers last night were not worshiping Jesus Christ. Were they Gnostics? Portia and Feya believed so. Had Rufus proposed a gnostic alternative to Benjamin? What if, instead of joining, Benjamin had threatened to reveal Rufus's nighttime worship to Valerius? Would Rufus have killed to protect his career? His livelihood?

The formidable spiked garden wall greeted her, but today the sturdy gate stood unlocked and open. Under a tangle of branches and shorn leaves, Magnus reclined on his side, leaning on an elbow, in animated conversation with Livia.

Sabina hesitated at the door and stared at the pair. "Livia? Magnus?"

Both heads shot up. "Sabina!" They said in unison. Magnus rolled upright and scooted away from Livia.

Observing them together confused her. Their image bobbed in and out through the investigative facts she had accumulated so far. She found no logical reason for Magnus and Livia to be together.

"Magnus was showing me how to debone a fish." Livia pointed to a basket of uncut fish at her feet. Her face flushed red.

"I just finished demonstrating." Magnus grabbed a knife resting on a board in front of him.

"I've never cleaned fish," Livia said, making a face and shrugging her shoulders. "Magnus said it's dangerous if you do it wrong."

"A dull knife is more dangerous than a sharp one." Magnus ran his finger along the curve of the blade." He reached into the basket, picked up a fish, and slapped it down on the board. He inserted the knife at the tail end of the fish and ripped it through to the head.

"Feya asked me to come." Livia looked to Magnus for affirmation.

He nodded, slipping his fingers into the fish's belly and scooping out the entrails.

Livia grimaced and looked away. "I am helping feed the orphans. We are, I mean, they are hungry."

"I'm sure she is grateful for your help," said Sabina. Could it be as simple as that? Were her suspicions tainting innocent activities? "Magnus, I didn't get to thank you for your assistance the other day. Were you hurt by the guards?"

"Nah, not even a bruise." Magnus shrugged, glancing sideways at Livia.

"I am glad to hear that." Sabina remembered the thudding of the guard's boots connecting with flesh. Perhaps more than one bruise.

"I got work to do." He grabbed another fish.

"I'd like to ask both of you a few questions?" Such as what are you doing here together? Livia said she hated Magnus. Magnus had cast aspersions on Livia, under duress, she had to admit.

"What about?" Magnus jammed the knifepoint into the board, taking on a disagreeable expression. "Feya's waiting for the fish."

"Just to clear up a few things. We didn't get to finish our last conversation." Sabina kept her tone even and tried not to stare at the knife.

"Oh, you mean the meeting at the latrine, with a knife slicing my throat." Magnus ran his thumb across his throat.

242

"Ooh," Livia stared at Sabina.

"I had nothing to do with that. I pleaded with Yechiel to let you go."

"I don't got anything to say to you or this Yechiel." He picked up a second fish and aggressively slit it down the middle.

"Magnus, you said you didn't kill Benjamin."

"That's right."

"Then help me find out who did."

Magnus's eyes shifted over to Livia. "I don't know nothin' about his murder." He pinched his lips together and stared Sabina down, looking like a defiant two-year-old.

"You were the last person seen eating with a man who was poisoned. And then you ran away. It is not just Yechiel who thinks that looks suspicious. You either talk to me or to the Roman authorities," Sabina bluffed. She hoped he wouldn't think too carefully about why the authorities weren't questioning him now.

"Poisoned! You've been listening to the hags gossiping in the kitchen. I agree with Apollos. Benjamin choked on an olive." Magnus challenged her with his defiant glare.

She wanted to grab his nose and pinch it. Surely, he couldn't be that dull? Exasperated, Sabina stepped forward and bent down, her eyes even with Magnus. "Apparently, you haven't been listening. Apollos is not sitting in jail, waiting to be executed because of an olive." She straightened up.

"She could've poisoned Benjamin just as much as me." Magnus waved the knife toward Livia, his voice wheedling.

"Me!" Livia squeaked. "I loved him." Livia crossed her arms across her chest and puffed up. "Besides, people were walking around and visiting and passing by his table the whole time. Anyone could have dumped poison in his food." She pointed out the far-reaching list of suspects Sabina didn't have time to question.

"I'm not accusing either of you," Sabina tried to mollify Magnus's defiance and Livia's wariness. "If you think about that night, you might remember something important."

"I got there late. I didn't pay no attention to Benjamin," Magnus growled.

"People saw you arguing with him." Sabina pointed out, her voice rising. "I saw you!"

"A little tussle over a cup of wine," Magnus shouted defensively, then lowered his voice. "That's all."

"Benjamin wrestled over your cup of wine?" Sabina asked skeptically.

"Yeah, all right." He looked at Sabina a bit sheepishly. "I grabbed his cup. I just wanted to rile him up a bit by drinking his wine." He glanced toward Livia. "I'm not going to murder someone over spilled wine. He'd drunk most of it anyway. Like I said, he acted drunk."

Sabina remembered her father's conclusion that the poison had been concealed in the wine. If his assertion was correct, Magnus's revelation might have just provided him with an unintended alibi. "The murderer dumped the arsenic in Benjamin's wine. If you had drunk it, you'd be dead."

Magnus blanched and mumbled under his breath. "I best get these cleaned."

"If you had laced his wine with arsenic, I doubt you'd have been struggling to drink from his cup. Benjamin saved your life. And cleared you of his murder at the same time."

The kitchen door opened. Feya stomped out and stared at the two gutted fish and the nearly full basket sitting untouched. She planted her hands firmly on her hips. "The vegetables are boiling into mush while we're waiting on you two."

"Faster if I clean um myself," said a pale and subdued Magnus.

"Come inside, and I'll help you." Feya held the door open. He heaved himself up, grabbing the basket in one hand and the knife in the other, and scrambled toward Feya as if rescued by an angel.

Livia sprinted up and started to follow.

"Feya, if you could spare Livia a minute more, I'd like to talk to her," Sabina said.

"I thought that's what you've been doing." Feya closed the door behind Magnus.

Livia crossed her arms. "I'm not telling you anything cause I didn't poison him. I knew Magnus didn't kill Benjamin either."

"How did you know?"

"Because I know who killed him. Marcella poisoned him or maybe her husband."

"If you remembered something, why didn't you tell me?"

"I've been thinking about what you said about everyone being at the church. Marcella started to talk to Benjamin. I would have been jealous, but Marcella is old and ugly, and Benjamin didn't like her." Livia paused, then added, "That's why she poisoned him."

"Did Benjamin tell you he didn't like her?"

"He didn't have to tell me. When a woman is in love, she knows these kinds of things. And when Marcella's husband stomped into the church looking for her, he probably put more poison in Benjamin's cup." Livia's enthusiasm for her topic was growing.

"You saw Marcella near Benjamin's table?"

"There were so many people. No one would have noticed if Marcella poured a whole bucket of poison in his cup."

"Then you didn't see her?"

"If I try hard, I'm sure I can remember Marcella poisoning Benjamin."

"No." Sabina gave up. "Livia, when did you arrive at the church that night?"

"I wanted to get there early. Benjamin didn't want me to miss the reading from the book he finished writing. He had the whole scroll memorized. He had memorized a lot of the Scripture."

"I didn't know that."

"He said all Jewish boys have to memorize books of Scripture. He made all the orphan children memorize. He didn't make me, but I did, anyway. I wanted to surprise him."

"That must have been a wonderful surprise."

"I never got to show him. I worked hard all week for nothing."

"Would you like to recite it for me?"

"It's not very long." Livia's eyes lit up

"I would love to hear it." Sabina imagined Benjamin coaching the children and Livia sitting and listening.

Livia smiled and raised her chin. "'I am the LORD, and there is no other. I did not speak in secret, in a land of darkness; I did not say to the offspring of Jacob, "Seek me in chaos." I the LORD speak the truth, I declare what is right."'

"That is beautiful. Benjamin would be proud of you."

Livia beamed. "He would have. I practiced the words in my head all day and fell asleep. When I woke up, I cried because I had missed the celebration and all the food and hearing the scroll read. I ran the whole way to Portia's house, and no one was there except Benjamin." She squealed and clapped her hands. "I was early. I just started to recite my verse when the man brought the scroll. Then we ran out of time."

"Benjamin didn't bring the scroll?"

"The man from the scriptorium delivered it because the ink needed time to dry."

"Did Benjamin say the man's name?"

Livia scrunched her face in thought. "Yes, but I don't remember it."

"Did he say the name Rufus?"

"Maybe. I recognize that name."

"Did anyone else see the man?"

"Probably. The slaves were setting out the food and wine by then."

"Livia, this is important. Think very hard. Do you remember seeing Rufus go near Simon's table or touch his wine cup?"

Livia paused, taking her time and biting her bottom lip as if deliberating the essence of the universe. "Well, I remember them both coming inside and standing by the table and talking about the scroll. Then the man Rufus," Livia looked for confirmation from Sabina, "handed Benjamin the scroll, and Benjamin walked across the room, and put the scroll on the altar. Then he walked back to his table, and they talked some more and said goodbye. And then other people started showing up." Livia let out a huge sigh.

Rufus had lied. He said he had no contact with Benjamin the day he died. More importantly, Livia witnessed his proximity to Benjamin's wine cup. "Were you watching the man by the table the whole time?"

"No, I just watched Benjamin."

Sabina sighed. "You have been a tremendous help."

"Would you help me with something?" Livia folded her hand in her lap demurely. "Remember when I told you we couldn't get married because Benjamin didn't have money."

"I do."

"I lied. Benjamin told me we couldn't get married. I cried. I told him Theo's mother said no one would want anyone as worthless as me. That's when Benjamin gave me the coin, the one like he gave you. He said only someone trusted by God could guard a coin this special. He said God has a special purpose for all His children."

"Yes, He does." Sabina remembered a verse from the book of Jeremiah. *'For I know the plans that I have for you,' declares the LORD, 'plans for well-being, and not for calamity, in order to give you a future and a hope.* This was a promise Sabina was desperately holding onto. "You have the coin to buy your passage home to Corinth."

"It's not mine. I can't spend it. Benjamin said it was a special coin that had to be protected and kept secret. But since he gave you one, I don't have to keep it a secret from you."

A twinge of guilt pricked Sabina's conscience. Livia had assumed Benjamin had given her the second coin. She didn't correct her. Could these coins hold a clue to Benjamin's murder and Apollos's release?

"I need to give the coin back," Livia said.

Sabina stared dumbfounded. "To whom?"

"I don't know. But I know where. I need to go there after I'm done helping Feya. Feeding the orphans is a very important job. Feya needs my help." Livia puffed out her thin chest, pride lighting her face. "Will you come with me?"

Sabina looked at the sun. She guessed she had an hour before the agreed-upon meeting with her father and Yechiel. She smiled at Livia. "You have a crucial job. If I help, we can get it done quicker." She understood why Benjamin had trusted this young woman.

Livia directed their way up to Marble Street. The two women walked side-by-side, each hefting one side of a heavy food basket, juggling it

between them. Portia and Feya had not skimped on their contribution.
"When did Benjamin show you this place?"

Livia fidgeted with her basket handle. "I just found it."

"You found it?"

Livia's face flushed pink. "Benjamin didn't know, but sometimes I would follow him. One day I followed him here."

"Do you remember him talking about Gnostics?"

She shook her head. "What's that?"

"It is a group of people who say they are Christians, but they don't believe Jesus Christ died and rose from the dead. I think Rufus is a Gnostic."

"Maybe he's like me and believes all those people saw Jesus's ghost."

Sabina remembered the prophet's words, seconds before she drank from the silver chalice. *The divine messenger whom death did not touch.* "They don't believe Jesus died," Sabina said.

"Oh yeah, he died. John said if Jesus didn't rise from the dead, then our faith is worthless."

"Was that in John's letter?" Sabina's heart started racing. Could this be the mysterious letter she found burnt to ashes in Benjamin's room?

"I don't think so. After they quit talking about spirits, I didn't pay much attention to what Benjamin was reading."

"Did Benjamin keep the letter?"

"No, he gave it back."

Sabina tried not to let her disappointment show. Another dead end. She and Livia walked on in silence.

Sabina had witnessed God's power in His healings, His miracles, and His visions. John's words had authority. Yet John had not convinced Livia. Benjamin had the benefit of the teachings of John and the apostles. Was he skeptical? Had he embraced the prophet's message instead?

They traveled through a wealthy neighborhood and passed by the wine shop advertising a new wine from Italy. Livia stopped at the next block. Sabina looked around in recognition. To her left, a nondescript alleyway branched off, one of the hundreds in the city, unremarkable except for the fact this was the third time in three days she had been here. They had just walked past the corner where Yechiel had requested she meet him for their two visits to the scriptorium.

"It's down the alley." They entered the narrow deserted side street, an ordinary back alleyway between old buildings, dark and dirty. The plaster had broken off the walls during one of the many earthquakes that had rocked the town, revealing the brick underneath. Earthquakes were widespread, repairs not so much, especially on seldom-traveled side streets.

Livia stopped by a section of exposed brick and dropped her end of the basket with a clank. "Sorry."

Sabina lowered her end of the basket. Was this the clue she needed to free Apollos? Would she find another gold coin?

Livia pointed to the side of a building, "It's up there."

Sabina squinted in the dim light but saw only broken plaster and exposed bricks. "I don't see anything."

"There's a loose brick." Livia jumped and then jumped again, pointing to a large section of the wall with the foundational brickwork exposed. "Benjamin left a coin there. I can't reach it."

Sabina had to stand on tiptoe to reach the brick Livia indicated. She gripped the edges around the deteriorated mortar, and the brick slid into her hand.

She dropped down and handed the brick to Livia.

"Search inside," Livia ordered.

Excited, Sabina rose again on her toes. Her fingers sifted through the crumbles of mortar and grainy bottom of the hollowed-out cavity. Empty. Disappointed, she felt one last time. Her fingers brushed against a tiny piece of papyrus caught against the rough side of the hole. She pulled it out and held it up to the light filtering into the alley from overhead. There were no words, only a blank corner of papyrus probably torn from a more extensive section that had been pulled from the hole.

"Nothing else?" Livia watched Sabina examine the papyrus slip.

"There is no writing, but this papyrus is new. Someone put it there recently." Sabina replaced the torn fragment.

Livia unwrapped her makeshift bag of coins. This time a gold coin glinted among the copper ones. She took the coin and handed it to Sabina. "Put it there."

Sabina examined the coin. The same chalice and inscription as hers. "You want me to leave your gold coin here?"

"It's not mine."

The coin that had fallen from Benjamin's robe the night of his death didn't belong to Sabina either. She put Livia's gold disk in the hollow and replaced the brick. She needed to return her coin. But not to this hole. To Yechiel.

She wondered if the person who searched Benjamin's room had been looking for these? Had Benjamin given Livia one, not as a token of his trust, but to hide it in an unlikely place? But then why keep the other one? And if the vandals weren't looking for gold, what were they looking for? The votive of Artemis? The burnt letter? Something else? Sabina's head swirled. She wasn't any closer to finding out who had poisoned Benjamin, and tomorrow Apollos would die.

Her father had Apollos's confession in writing. She knew her father and had no doubt that if she did not find out who murdered Benjamin, Apollos's death would eliminate a dangerous threat. Her father would not risk Apollos falling into the hands of Flavius Fortunus or any other city official.

She knew, if she had not pleaded for time to find the real killer, Apollos would already be dead. So far, her labors had not changed that end.

TWENTY

S abina's unplanned alley detour with Livia had taken longer than anticipated. She prayed for God's guidance, and here she stood at the prison door, no closer to freeing Apollos than when she had started.

She stumbled forward, hampered by the growing weight of the Feya's food basket. The wicker handle cut into one palm and then the other as she transferred the weight. Portia and Feya had packed enough for a healthy man to eat for a week. Apollos didn't have a week.

Sabina thought back to the beginning of her investigation. Had it only been three days ago? She had been desperate to find the truth about her mother. To learn more about the night she died. Would Apollos have revealed his involvement if Zarmig hadn't intruded during her last prison visit?

The longer she waited to learn the truth, the less enthused she became. Would the few surviving memories of her mother prove to be a lie? A fabrication weaved to comfort and soothe a confused eight-year-old child. Would Apollos's revelation bring joy or more pain? In these intervening days, she was fast deciding she didn't want to cause that child more hurting or sadness.

Had God used her mother's secret to compel her to begin this path of inquiry to help Apollos? Had God prodded her overactive curiosity, or had she willfully gone her own way, starting with confronting her father? She didn't know. But she did know she couldn't go anyway but forward.

What had made her think she could solve a murder? Was she trying to impress her father? Instead of gaining his admiration or love, she had pushed him farther away and risked both of their lives. All to what purpose? Her footsteps stopped outside the door. She closed her eyes. "Dear God, don't let me be the cause of more pain or hurt. Not to Apollos, my father, myself."

She opened her eyes and looked up. Yechiel had appeared several feet away, watching her.

"I spoke to Livia and Magnus," she said.

"And?" His brows rose in a question.

"I don't believe either killed Benjamin."

"Is that what they told you?" His cynical skepticism accented every word.

Sabina related the conversation with Magnus and his admission to tussling with Benjamin to drink the poisoned wine. "I witnessed the incident."

"I agree his blundering idiocy makes him an unlikely suspect. What of the girl? Could she be Magnus's lover?"

"Livia insists she loved Benjamin."

"I doubt—"

"She also just returned a valuable gold coin Benjamin had given her for safekeeping."

"What?" Yechiel reached to grab her arm, then pulled back.

Her eyebrows raised in surprise. "Livia had little motive or knowledge to poison him. She returned the coin to a—"

"Stop," Yechiel cut her off with a warning slice of his hand. Zarmig stepped beside them.

Sabina wanted to confess she, too, had a coin. Did Yechiel always have to be so rude and abrupt? She would return his coin, but now that could wait.

As soon as they were inside, Zarmig took the basket of food from her and checked the contents. "No knives."

"They're difficult to eat soup with," Sabina said.

Zarmig grunted as he led them past the guards and into the jail. He set the basket outside Apollos's cell while he unlocked the door. A lit oil lamp had been placed in a niche in the wall.

"You may take the lamp in," he nodded to Yechiel.

Yechiel picked up the lamp, Sabina took the basket, and they entered the cell. She recoiled at the nauseating smell of the room, striking her nostrils. She blinked, her eyes adjusting to the darkness, and all sensitivity to smell disappeared when she saw Apollos.

She dropped the basket and ran past Yechiel. She knelt by the crumpled form of Apollos. He slumped against the slick black of the mold-coated walls, chained. In three days, the damp chill and poor air had spawned a deep cough that racked his wiry frame. His beard was matted and crawled with tiny insects. Zarmig entered but left the door open, doing little to air out the stifling stench of the room.

"Sabina." Apollos blinked and pushed himself up slowly.

"Apollos, I have brought food. Hot fish stew from Feya and Portia."

"God's angels." Apollos's clammy gray pallor frightened her. She could barely hear his voice. He braced against the wall as another shuddering cough shook his body.

Sabina placed her hand on his forehead. "You are hot." She felt the aching cold of the stone floor seep into her knees, the damp from the mildew soaking through her tunic.

Yechiel set the basket with the meal down near her.

She bit her lip as another racking cough rattled Apollos's chest. "I gave Amisi directions to bring blankets." She glared at Zarmig. "This cell is freezing!"

"Your father is allowing no one in to see him."

"It's blankets. Compassion will not jeopardize our family."

"It could," Zarmig said.

"Look at him. If your treatment continues, Apollos will not last until I find the murderer." Sabina narrowed her eyes. "Or was that our magistrate's plan all along?"

Zarmig tipped his head but stopped at shrugging his shoulders. "There are consequences for murder."

"Where are the blankets?" Her own body shook. Her anger magnified her sense of frustration and fear. Apollos coughed again, and a shudder convulsed his body. She adjusted the chains so he could stretch his legs.

Zarmig went to the door and yelled. "Guard, bring me the blankets delivered yesterday."

Sabina lifted Apollos's shoulders. She turned toward Zarmig. "Can't you get them?" Leave us, her mind screamed. I need time alone. She watched any chance of questioning Apollos in private disappear.

Zarmig shook his head. "It is not allowed."

"He is chained! He can barely sit up. Do you think he is going to break free?" Zarmig, Yechiel, and Sabina stared at the older man propped against the wall, his eyes closed, his breathing labored.

Zarmig smiled grimly. "No. Be thankful your father's generosity has allowed you this final visit."

"His generosity?" Sabina rolled her eyes and pulled away from Apollos, not hiding her anger. "If we find the murderer, it will benefit him just as much." As a child, she had learned to ignore Zarmig's smug allegiance to her father when her nerves weren't frayed.

Had she expected Zarmig to leave? No. But she couldn't communicate her actions of the previous night to her father's chief spy. Once Zarmig learned of the incident to Hekate's Grotto and relayed the exploit to her father, her freedom and the investigation would end. Her actions at the grotto provided another reason for her father to forbid her from going out alone or even from leaving the house.

Sabina lifted the cover from the basket. She took out the bowl of stew and a spoon. "Can you eat it?"

Apollos's glassy eyes sank into dark circles. Red patches highlighted his cheeks.

Apollos nodded and took the bowl. A coughing fit rattled the dish. Soup sloshed onto his lap. Sabina took the bowl and held it to his lips. He sipped slowly between deep, rasping breaths.

How long would Zarmig allow them to remain? More importantly, how long could Apollos withstand questioning? She had no choice but to question Apollos in front of Zarmig. As much as she desired information about her mother, questions about the murder had to be asked first. And that meant revealing her late-night escapade.

A guard knocked on the door and passed two blankets to Zarmig.

Sabina got up and took them, laying one over Apollos's lap and wrapping the other around his shoulders.

After the warmth and nourishment from the soup, Apollos sat up straighter, and his coughing subsided. Sabina offered the leather skin of watered wine and tore off a chunk from the loaf of bread. Apollos labored to chew slowly, taking one small bite and washing it down with a sip of wine.

Sabina held out the loaf again, and he shook his head as another cough overtook him.

"Apollos, we went to the scriptorium, as you suggested. We asked about the parchment from the burnt letter. Valerius did not recognize it."

"I had hoped he could help you," Apollos leaned his head back against the wall.

"Do you know Rufus, one of Valerius's scribes?

"Only by name." Apollos turned his head and coughed. "Benjamin would mention him occasionally when reporting on his training or a shared work task. Benjamin told me Rufus is also a Christian in secret, of course."

"I do not think Rufus is Christian," Sabina said.

Apollos raised his chin and straightened his back, leaning forward. "If that is true and Benjamin found out about Rufus's duplicity, he could have threatened to expose Rufus to Valerius." His chains rattled.

"I am not sure Benjamin was a Christian either," Sabina said.

Yechiel's expression suddenly stiffened, and his eyes bore into Sabina.

Apollos shook his head, bracing himself with his arms. "That is not possible."

"Last night, I found out Rufus is a member of a secret cult," she frowned, disapproval in her tone.

"The Christian movement is growing?" Zarmig's eyebrows raised. "I would think you would admire such devotion."

"They weren't Christian," Sabina said.

Zarmig relaxed against the wall and shrugged. "You take your faith too seriously. What difference does it make? Bend a knee to Caesar, offer incense to Artemis, eat the meat sacrificed to Apollo. All religious paths are equal. Your Messiah's death doesn't make him the only way."

"Truth is by logic, singular," Apollos's voice rose energetically. "There cannot be two. For one to be true, the other must be false. You profess truth or lie, not both." He ended with a wheeze.

Sabina patted his shoulder, quieting him. "Rufus said his path is a newly revealed Christianity. He invited me to their worship service last night."

Zarmig straightened. "You turned him down naturally."

"Benjamin didn't turn Rufus down…either." Sabina did not look at Zarmig as she related the ceremony at Hekate's Grotto. She explained the ritual, the altar, the sharing of the communal cup, and the baptism in the dark waters of Hekate's cave.

The red spots on Apollos's face grew brighter against his gray skin. He trembled. "Your allegation of Benjamin's unfaithfulness disturbed me. Now I am appalled at your lack of judgment. Sabina, what were you thinking?"

"That is the same question I asked." Yechiel nodded, his brows drew together.

Sabina looked at the three men's formidable stares, no, formidable glares. Zarmig said nothing. He appeared calmer than the other two men. Not a good sign. He had heard her out, his face composed, his hands still, his eyes blazing.

She bolstered on. "Where would we be if I hadn't gone with Rufus? We would know nothing about Rufus's religion. I had no choice."

"You always have a choice," Zarmig growled.

"You must stop this search. I will not be responsible for your death," Apollos's voice faltered. He wheezed, stopping to catch his breath. "You have no idea who these people are. Alone with strangers at night. A masked prophet!" Apollos coughed, then gasped for air.

Sabina put the wineskin to his lips. He managed to swallow another sip. He coughed then closed his eyes.

"There could have been anything in that cup…poison." Zarmig's face lost its composure and flushed blood red with anger.

Her face fluctuated through several emotions before she blurted out, "I admit there were unexpected events I had not thought through, but Rufus welcomed me to a worship service, to proselytize. His cult is trying to entice people to their religion, not kill them."

"He may have killed Benjamin," Yechiel said.

"And how will we find out if we don't take a few small risks?" Sabina reasoned and realized her chin was quivering. Reliving last night brought those frightening risks back to reality.

Zarmig's hands opened and closed as if seizing and strangling the air. "This is the end of your investigation." Zarmig went to the cell door. "I will report this to your father. He may kill both of us, you for endangering your life and me for allowing it."

"Father gave his permission to hunt for the murderer. I will report to him today when I bring the evidence to prove Apollos's innocence."

"You have no evidence." Zarmig pointed out.

"The proof lies with Rufus. He said Benjamin had the eternal spark and that he had great potential. He said Benjamin was struggling."

"Potential for what?" asked Yechiel.

"Struggling with what?" asked Apollos.

"He nearly divulged Benjamin had been chosen," Sabina said. "If the prophet told you an angel in a vision had selected you, you would be tempted."

"Pagan philosophers have taught this flattering arrogance for thousands of years." Yechiel's jaw clenched. "Benjamin would see through the falsehoods."

Apollos struggled to sit up straighter, then fell back against the wall. "It is a gnostic deception."

"He wouldn't join these Gnostics," Yechiel said.

"Portia and Feya agree with you," Sabina said. "Rufus confessed their prophet's revelation was needed to complete the apostolic record. The Gospels aren't wrong, just insufficient. He could have convinced Benjamin that Gnosticism didn't conflict with Christianity. If Benjamin discovered the lie after beginning his journey into the new knowledge, perhaps he was too embarrassed or frightened to leave them," Sabina suggested.

Apollos exhaled and closed his eyes. His head dropped. "False prophets, which come to you in sheep's clothing, but inwardly they are ravening wolves."

"Rufus said Benjamin was struggling. What if he was questioning his faith, questioning God's perfect message?" she asked.

"Everyone questions. But Benjamin knew where to search for answers," Apollos said. "The Scriptures."

"What if he decided the Scriptures were insufficient?" Sabina asked.

"He would be in quicksand. Scripture would then be unreliable, untrustworthy. You cannot have two truths." Apollos's breathing stopped. When he drew his next breath, his chest heaved in labored rattling. His eyes fluttered open, then closed again.

"This is ludicrous," Yechiel snapped. "Benjamin based his life on Scripture, unchanging truths given by God and protected by God," Yechiel said. "God's Word doesn't change."

Apollos opened his eyes. His voice was barely discernible. "The enemy does not have to change what is written. All Satan has to do is sow a seed of doubt as to its origin, just as he did with Eve, asking her to question God's word 'Did God really say?' and as soon as Eve doubted, she began sinking in quicksand, her firm foundation gone."

"No one would trust in one man's vision?" Yechiel challenged.

"A grotto full of people would disagree with you," Sabina said. She bit her lip. Am I floundering in quicksand? She had prayed for God's word to reign over her life. But she hadn't meant it. When she chose Xeno, she had doubted God's message of love for her, felt His message insufficient.

Apollos started to reply. A violent coughing spasm stopped him. When it passed, he breathed in a shuddered rasp. Sabina lifted the soup bowl to his lips. "Eat." She tucked the blanket tighter around him. The talk was exhausting him.

Sabina tilted her head to the side, frowning as she mused. "I think something enticed Benjamin."

"Enticed?" Yechiel asked.

Sabina offered the wineskin.

Apollos shook his head. "No," his voice, a muffled echo in his throat. "No one could lead Benjamin astray. He knew, better than all of us, that Christianity stands or falls on the trustworthiness of God's written Word." Apollos coughed again. His head fell forward,

Sabina shifted her body, settling closer to Apollos, and gripped his arm with quivering fingers. "Rest. We can talk later," she said with more conviction than she felt.

Apollos lifted his head. His whisper was barely inaudible. "The powerful Spirit that raised Jesus from the dead lives in me." He nodded and tried to continue. His throat emitted a croak and then silence. Apollos closed his eyes. His head lolled against the wall, exhausted. Asleep?

"Looks like your interview with the powerful one is over," Zarmig said, uncrossing his arms and reaching for the lamp.

Sabina laid Apollos on his side on one of the blankets, keeping the other wrapped over his shoulder and torso. His body shook, then a deep sigh escaped, and his eyes fluttered before he lay still. Sabina dropped her chin and took a slow breath as she watched the answers she yearned for about her mother drift away into Apollos's dreams.

Was this God's answer? Apollos unable to tell her about the night her mother died. He couldn't talk. He didn't stir. "I will send Amisi with her concoction of honey and mint tea." She glared at Zarmig. "And a tincture for lice. Make sure he gets it."

Zarmig signaled for them to leave. Yechiel picked up the lamp.

Sabina reluctantly took a last look at the sleeping man. She stood up and followed Zarmig out of the room. She listened to Apollos's rattled breathing and another spasm of coughing as the door closed. Please don't die. I will be back tomorrow. I promise.

"We need to question Rufus," Sabina said breathlessly. "Livia saw Rufus at the church the night Benjamin died."

"Rufus admitted he was jealous of Benjamin's position in the scriptorium as Valerius's favorite," Yechiel said.

"Jealousy does not make him a murderer," Zarmig said. "But Christians gathering illegally at night are dangerous…you should warn your father." He chuckled at his joke.

Sabina glared at him.

"We will get his authorization and question this scribe Rufus," Zarmig said. "I am curious."

"Sir," Sabina burst into her house, her voice hoarse from racing ahead of Zarmig and Yechiel. They had crossed town and traveled up the hill to her house. The doorman pointed her to the dining room. Her father reclined alone at an early dinner. She stopped to catch her breath and panted. "I know who poisoned Benjamin."

"Do you?" Her father asked, picking up a piece of chicken and slicing a piece of meat from its bones. Not raising his eyes, he speared it with the knife and dipped it in a dark brown sauce. He chewed leisurely.

"Apollos isn't guilty." Her breathing slowed down.

"You found proof?" he asked, swallowing, and tearing off the last piece with his fingers, dipping it, eating, and wiping his fingers on his napkin.

"Yes…not yet. We need to question Rufus, a scribe who worked with Benjamin."

"Rufus?" Her father pushed the chicken aside. "We will not need to bother. I have located the guilty person. Is Zarmig with you?"

"Another suspect?" Sabina shook her head, stunned. "Who? How? Do you have proof?"

"I do." He picked up the wine goblet and guzzled the remainder of the wine. Banging the goblet down, he regarded her for the first time. "Rest assured it is not your lowly scribe."

A slave entered and placed a bowl of water on the table. Her father dipped his sticky brown fingers in the dish and dried them with his napkin. He swung his legs off the dining couch.

Zarmig entered, followed by Yechiel.

"You took your time returning. I found our witness." Her father stood and adjusted the folds of his tunic.

"To Benjamin's murder?" Sabina asked, bafflement in her voice.

"Bring him in." He signaled to the slave who had delivered the water.

One of her father's guards returned, hauling a sniffling skinny street boy about eight or nine. His tears created white stripes down his grimy cheeks. His body was shaking so hard Sabina thought he might be having a fit. "Sirrrr."

The guard slapped him across the face. "Shut up."

The boy whimpered, then was silent. His eyes round, his lip quivering.

"The street boy, sir." The guard saluted.

"What street boy?" Sabina whipped her head between her father and the quaking child.

"We have the messenger Zarmig intercepted delivering the note meant for Flavius Fortunus detailing your illegal Christian assembly that night," her father repeated.

"I told you I don't know anything about Christians, 'cept their vermin, sir." The boy's voice shook.

The guard struck the boy hard across the mouth. "I warned you once."

Sabina flinched. The child didn't move or back away. "There are hundreds of street orphans. How did you find him?"

"Three days of persistence and a little luck." Her father frowned at the boy. "He has been questioned."

"Questioned or beaten?" Sabina's heart constricted. She looked at the boy, searching for injuries. "What could you learn by harming a—"

"Stop your pitying." Her father's irritation cut her off. "His stuttering barely made sense as it was. We didn't need pain erasing any information he managed to remember. And he remembered well." Her father withdrew a sestertius from a wooden leather pouch tied to his belt and gave it to the boy.

The boy's eyes darted between her father and the brass coin in his hand.

"Remember, we pay our informers well. You're free to go."

With one darting look at the soldier nearby, the boy bolted from the room.

"His answers led us to the go-between who paid him."

"And the man who killed my brother?"

"The go-between steered us to the man who wrote the note to Flavius Fortunus and the man who probably murdered your brother." Her father looked over at Yechiel. "We don't yet know the motive."

"Who?" Sabina asked.

"A man who is not adept at concealing his actions," Zarmig said.

"A man named Davos," her father said. "He's a member of the silversmith's guild."

"Davos! Davos killed Benjamin?" Sabina attempted to fit this information into various scenarios.

"We know of him," Yechiel said.

"We questioned his wife, Marcella. He was angry that she is…was a member of the church."

"Then he had a motive to destroy the church. Why would he kill Benjamin?" her father asked.

"I know of one reason." Yechiel pulled the small votive from his purse and handed it to her father. "This is the votive you found on Benjamin's body. It is a forgery. Benjamin must have found out Davos was counterfeiting."

"Then our suspect has more than one crime to answer for." Her father examined the statue and handed it to Zarmig.

Zarmig's fingernail picked at a loose piece of silver flake. It fell to the floor.

"Will you arrest him? And let Apollos go?" Sabina asked.

"Zarmig will arrest Davos. I will question him. If he admits to the murder, I will free Apollos tonight."

Zarmig held the votive out to Yechiel.

Yechiel shook his head. "It has served its purpose."

TWENTY-ONE

T he warm temperature from earlier in the morning cooled as wispy tendrils of clouds wove into gray curtains and filtered the afternoon rays. Sabina wrapped her mantle tighter around her shoulders.

Sabina and Yechiel led Zarmig and two of her father's guard detail to the side street near the silversmith. They stopped at the bench on the corner where she had collapsed after evading Davos. Could that have been only yesterday? The terror of fleeing the workshop blurred the day's events. A frightening apparition clouded her thoughts.

But today was a new day. The burly Davos would not intimidate Zarmig, and he couldn't deny the evidence against him. After Davos confesses, her father will arrest him, and Apollos will be set free. A tickle of satisfaction ran like ants over her skin. She pointed around the corner. "The workshop and house are to the right. In the center of the block."

Yechiel smirked. "You cannot miss the sign above the door. It couldn't be more obvious if he were advertising a brothel."

"Wait here." Zarmig held his hand up to stop Sabina. "I will first determine the connection between the silversmith and our magistrate of religious observances and ascertain what Flavius Fortunus now knows of Sabina's involvement in the church." He motioned the two guards to follow him into the street.

She sidled after them and peeked around the corner.

"Fires of Zeus," she heard Zarmig blurt a second before he smacked into her in an apparent about-face.

"Ayeee." She flew, landing on her backside. "Ouch."

Zarmig rushed to help her up. "I told you to stay here."

She rubbed her backside, dusted the dirt from her clothing, and let out a groan. "I did."

"What happened?" Yechiel asked, stepping up beside her.

"You tell me." Zarmig stepped aside, and Sabina and Yechiel peered around the corner of the building.

Guards and slaves swarmed Davos's shop. The door leading into the house swung loosely from one broken hinge. Men entered empty-handed and exited with boxes, furniture, statuary, and a small kiln Sabina recognized. Slaves loaded the boxes and household items into carts and wagons lining up outside the home and workshop.

Sabina stepped away from the corner building for a closer view. "What's happening?"

"Looks like we're late to the festivities." Zarmig nodded. "Those are Magistrate Flavius Fortunus's men. I recognize several of them."

"Is Davos with them?" Yechiel asked, alarm showing on his face as he stepped past Sabina and around the corner. She followed him.

Zarmig grabbed the back of her mantle and pulled her back. "Don't go prancing into the open. Stay by the building," Zarmig warned.

Sabina shook free from Zarmig but only peeked around the corner.

Yechiel stepped back and addressed the small group. "The guards are ransacking the workshop. They've arrested Davos. He's chained to the first wagon. He's bleeding and cradling his arm."

"But...but how did they find out before we did that he killed Benjamin?" Sabina shook her head in disbelief. She sidled around the corner, keeping her back pressed against the plaster of the building. "Where is Marcella? I don't see Davonia." Sabina searched through the tumult of slaves and guards, searching for the mother and daughter.

"On the bench." Yechiel appeared beside her and pointed, his view higher than hers.

Sabina saw the women sitting in front of the shop next door, away from the melee. They clung to each other. With one free hand, Davonia held a torn shoulder seam together, partially covering an exposed breast. Both were chained.

"Guards were grabbing some entertainment," Zarmig said.

"They're not unguarded," Yechiel said.

A solitary guard stood ten feet away, his back to the women, watching other guards load carts with plunder from the house and shop.

"Looks like Flavius did our job for us." Zarmig stepped beside them. "We're done here."

"No." Sabina grabbed Zarmig's arm. "My father said he wouldn't release Apollos until Davos confesses."

"If Davos killed Benjamin, I need to hear the pig confess." Yechiel set his teeth, almost into a snarl.

"You have to arrest him," Sabina pleaded.

Zarmig lowered his chin and stared at her. He pointed to the chaos. "There's not a bird dropping of a chance that's going to happen."

"Zarmig, Davos is a danger to us." Sabina's grip tightened. "We don't know what he told Flavius about the church. What if Davos or Marcella told Flavius about me?"

"We need information," Yechiel agreed.

Zarmig paused. "The feud between Flavius and your father complicates this. If the guards recognize me, they won't let me near Davos."

"I could go," Sabina said pleadingly. "Marcella and Davonia—"

"Please do." Zarmig gestured with a flourish toward the shivering figures of the two huddling women. "And make sure you confess to whatever information Flavius didn't beat out of Davos and his family. Don't forget to mention your relationship with the murdered Christian. That should make their day." He crossed his arms. "There is one guard I don't recognize. If he's new, there's a chance he doesn't know your father or me. Stay here." Zarmig pinned Sabina with his glare. He strode toward Davos.

Before Zarmig got near Davos's wagon, the young guard approached him, posturing with his hand on the hilt of a short dagger hanging at his side. "This street is closed. Magistrate Flavius Fortunus's orders."

Zarmig stopped. "I heard a Jew was murdered three nights ago."

"A Jew." The guard spat on the ground.

Zarmig nodded toward Davos. "Your man may have been involved."

"Won't matter. Magistrate Fortunus caught this scum dipping lead in silver."

"Counterfeiting coins?"

"No, the temple priests located fake silver votives in their piles of loot. Captured a tourist who dedicated a lead offering for his sick wife. It took a bit of sleuthing, but we traced the fake to this blasphemous dog."

"Nice bit of law enforcement. Fakes are hard to detect." Zarmig thought of the flaking silver from Benjamin's votive.

"Naw, it's vigilant temple wardens and priestesses. Like hawks, they make sure they get their compensation. The wardens knew as soon as they melted the votives. Just a dull puddle of grimy lead." The guard laughed. "Artemis don't spend silver and gold, but the temple wardens and priestesses sure do."

Zarmig laughed at the guard's joke. "Lead buys cheap wine."

"I wouldn't risk it." The guard shook his head. "The warden's outrage demanded *damnatio ad bestias*, death by beasts. The governor ordered Magistrate Flavius Fortunus to track down the blasphemer, in whatever city he lived."

"Protecting our goddess's honor," Zarmig said.

"Magistrate Fortunus found him a few miles from the temple. He's strong, with lots of metal-smithing muscles. It should be enjoyable entertainment when the beasts tear him to shreds at the goddess's festival," the guard said. "Piece of irony there."

"I'm not interested in the counterfeiting."

"Course you're not," the guard smirked. "Who wants to get their grubby paws on all that silver."

"I have one question for your prisoner," Zarmig said.

"You can go piss down your leg." The guard pulled the dagger from his belt. "Magistrate Flavius would shove a metal poker up my butt if he caught me allowing access to our prisoner. You being Magistrate Catius's right-hand man and all."

Zarmig returned to Sabina and Yechiel. "We are done here." Zarmig signaled her father's two guards. "You heard the guard; their concern is Davos's counterfeiting."

"We still don't know if he's the murderer," Sabina said.

"What difference does it make? Justice is served."

"Not for Apollos. Father won't release him without a confession to Benjamin's murder. Is there anything we can do?"

"Nothing," Zarmig said. "The guards know me."

Zarmig was right. They were too late. Apollos's only chance at freedom was bound to a wagon of death.

Sabina looked at the two women huddled together. "Will Marcella and Davonia be set free?"

"The guards hadn't heard about the murder." Zarmig looked at the guard posted near them. "But Flavius Fortunus will question them about their roll in the counterfeiting."

A cold chill spread throughout Sabina. She pulled her mantle in around her, but it offered no warmth or comfort. She would pray Roman mercy was granted to these women, innocent or not.

Marcella had appeared incredulous when she heard of Apollos's arrest. She could not save her husband, but would she be willing to confess to save Apollos from the fate awaiting her husband?

"I could question Marcella." Sabina's heart beat faster. "She may know why Davos poisoned Benjamin. Father would accept her testimony."

"We are leaving. It is over," Zarmig said.

"The guards don't know me. I will be just a concerned neighbor."

"Once the guards finish sacking the house, we have lost any chance to find out what happened," Yechiel said.

Sabina swallowed hard. "I am a woman. To the guards, insignificant."

Zarmig surveyed the area. "There is only one man posted. If that guard so much as twitches in your direction…"

"I will leave immediately," Sabina said.

"Your father is going to kill me." Zarmig frowned.

"Be careful," Yechiel said.

His comment caught her off guard. Did Yechiel just show concern?

She shook her head. Only because he needed Marcella's confession as much as she did. "I have no intention of ending up the guard's evening entertainment."

Sabina pulled her mantle hood over her head, hiding her hair and half her face. She hurried into the street, then stopped and acted shocked as if seeing the uproar for the first time. She did not need to fabricate the roiling of her stomach, the nervous sweat under her armpits, and the wide eyes of fear as she approached the pair of disheveled women. The lone guard stiffened to attention as soon as he caught sight of her. "These are prisoners."

She took a deep breath and continued to walk in his direction. "She is my friend." She pointed to Marcella.

The guard's gaze assessed Sabina from head to sandals. "In that case, you're welcome to join us." He leered.

She stopped and tried to sound assertive. "I came to see if they are unharmed." She noted welts and cuts on both women.

"I can vouch we've taken good care of 'em, especially the young juicy plum." He smirked, ogling Sabina again. "Ah, go ahead. Be quick about it. The house goods are nearly loaded." He nodded for her to proceed.

A loud crash sounded from the area of the wagons. The guard turned his attention to the drama taking place at the house, where another guard began kicking a slave who frantically scuttled around grabbing broken pieces of pottery. Their guard laughed. He forgot Sabina.

"Marcella?" Sabina knelt beside the women.

Marcella's eyes, puffed and bloodshot, barely opened from crying. She stared at Sabina with no acknowledgment. Davonia sat beside her mother silently and pale. She did not raise her head to look at Sabina. A long minute passed, and Sabina wondered if Marcella's injuries left her senseless. Her tunic wasn't torn, but the red marks on her face and arms would turn a nasty black and blue by tomorrow. "You're hurt." Sabina placed a trembling hand on Marcella's arm.

Marcella's eyes widened in recognition. "Sabina. You should not be here. It is dangerous."

"I know. I am allowed to speak to you." Sabina spoke calmly, steadying the alarm that left her voice quaking.

Marcella's fingers, entwined with her daughter's, tightened. "There is nothing to say."

Davonia looked up, one eye swollen shut, the other darting nervously between the guard and her mother. She appeared heedless of her disarray, matted hair, and the red scratches up and down her arms. Davonia's ripped tunic gaped, exposing a breast. She noticed Sabina's glance and pulled her hand free from her mother's, and tugged at the torn fabric, partially concealing what she could of her bare skin.

Sabina watched Davonia shiver, oblivious to the chill blowing in from the sea. No, not unaware, in shock. Sabina picked up a shawl crumpled on the ground and wrapped it around Davonia's shoulders. Davonia shut her one unswollen eye, but tears streamed from both.

Sabina adjusted her mantle and sat beside the huddled women. She put a hand on Marcella's back. Marcella flinched.

"I can help. If you are a Roman—"

"We are not Roman citizens." Marcella began quietly crying again. "But it would make no difference. Our crimes are serious. The authorities discovered Davos was selling false silver votives, cheating Artemis of her tribute, and stealing her rightful offerings. He dishonored his profession, his guild."

"Surely, no charges can be made against you and Davonia?"

"We are cursed and will all be punished." Marcella lifted her wrists, exposing the chains. "Our home and business are confiscated by order of the Magistrate of Religious Observances. There is nothing anyone can do." Marcella's red eyes looked pleadingly into Sabina's. "I have destroyed our lives." She bent over, her head on her lap.

"You have done nothing wrong, Mother," Davonia pleaded, looking at Sabina and wiping her tears but showing no other emotion, her flirting sales pitch replaced with a dull, barely audible drone. "Artemis punished my father. She struck him ill after he dishonored her."

"By making lead offerings? "Sabina asked.

Davonia nodded.

"And Benjamin?"

"His sickness came because of his unbelief. She will not punish us for what my father has done." Davonia's once confident smile now lost in raw and swollen lips. Gone was the saucy banter used to entice customers into buying the silver votives, jewelry, and souvenir medallions. Sabina guessed those had been the first items confiscated by the guards.

Marcella raised her head and looked at Sabina. "It did not matter that I returned to worship the goddess; it did not matter that I paid her homage. She is taking her revenge."

"We did not know he was counterfeiting." Davonia's chin rose, and her voice hardened in a brief note of defiance before lowering her head. "She knows we are innocent," she mumbled.

"You are innocent," Marcella said. "I knew what he was doing."

"You could not have known." Davonia looked at her mother. "He kept his deception hidden, the door to his workshop always locked. No one knew."

Marcella looked up, misery etched in every line of her face. "I knew. I went into his workshop and took a votive. It was crude, not his most beautiful work. I chose it because I thought he would not miss it. I did not know at the time it was counterfeit."

"Why?" Davonia asked.

"I did it to cure your father's illness," Marcella said.

"Livia said Benjamin got sick shortly after he moved to your house. How long has your husband been ill?" Sabina asked.

"His headaches started soon after Benjamin moved in. The rental room had been vacant, and we were desperate for money. I remember my relief when Benjamin paid his rent, but when I handed Davos the money, he yelled at me to get him a draught for his headache. I thought it an odd coincidence that Benjamin had just told me he intended to lie down because of a headache."

"That doesn't explain why you stole the votive," Davonia repeated.

"Davos said Benjamin's refusal to worship Artemis was to blame for his headaches and stomach cramps. He said I should never have rented the room to Benjamin. I thought if Benjamin honored the goddess by carrying her statue, Artemis would bless our house and cure your father. I know now it was the irreverent lead statues." Marcella looked at her daughter. "Forgive me."

"Father always blames others. That is his way." Davonia showed her first spark of life, bitter resentment. "Why didn't you ignore him?"

"It is not so simple when the accusations come from your husband. He blamed me for our financial troubles, not enough sales, people not appreciating his craftsmanship, my Christian worship, his complaints never ended."

"When did you take the votive?" Sabina asked.

"The day before Benjamin died. I was tired of fighting Davos. I told Benjamin I was returning to Artemis and the old gods of my ancestors. Benjamin belittled Artemis, equating her to nothing more than a carved rock, a false idol with no power. I ran, confused and angry at Benjamin and Davos. I unlocked the workshop and went inside. I found the crude votive discarded in a corner."

"And that is the votive Benjamin carried?" Sabina asked, watching the guards loading bed frames into a cart. How much time did they have left?

"Yes, I thought Davos had rejected it because of its poor quality. The night I went to the church, I slipped the votive into a small pouch Benjamin wore tied to his robe. I found out later it was Davos's first attempt at counterfeiting."

"Benjamin did not know about the votive?" Sabina guessed.

"No, he would have been horrified. I thought if Artemis cured him, I would be vindicated."

"She reigns superior over Jesus." A small spark of the spirited Davonia resurfaced to defend her goddess.

Marcella nodded and turned to Sabina. "The next day, you visited and told me Benjamin had died. I nearly collapsed. I believed I had killed him. That Artemis punished him for mocking her in his unbelief."

"I promise you that an angry goddess did not use arsenic on Benjamin," Sabina said. "Does Davos use arsenic in his metalsmithing?"

"No." Marcella's facial muscles tightened. "Is this why you came? Because you think my husband a murderer?"

"I did not know of your adversity until just now. I am sorry."

"I don't care why you're here. The gods have decided our fate."

"I hope to save Apollos. He faces death for the murder."

"I am in no position to help," Marcella said. "Davos does not use arsenic in his silver craft. He used lead and mercury to fashion his counterfeit votives. We have no poisons."

"Did Benjamin know about your husband's forgeries?"

"No." Marcella lowered her head and didn't look at Sabina. "But Davos believed Benjamin had found out. He was enraged when he came to the church that night. He pushed Benjamin and accused him of stealing the votive. I didn't understand why Davos was so upset over an insignificant votive."

"What did Father do when he found out you stole the votive?" Davonia asked.

"He doesn't know."

"You didn't tell him?"

"I was going to, and then he admitted to the counterfeiting. He warned me Benjamin could use the stolen votive as blackmail to ruin us. I was terrified to confess I had given the votive to Benjamin. Then Benjamin died. What did it matter if a dead man took the blame?"

"When did you find out about his counterfeiting?" Sabina asked.

"After you and Yechiel left my house. I went to Davos, upset over the damage to the room. I demanded we inform the night watchmen. But Davos said no. When I told him I would report it, he admitted he had demolished the room looking for the votive Benjamin had stolen. I could not understand why he destroyed the room, searching for a cheap votive."

"When did he destroy the room?" Sabina asked.

"Before he came to the church that night. We fought. I yelled that it would take more money to repair the damage than what the votive was worth."

"And he confessed to the counterfeiting?" Sabina asked.

Marcella nodded. "The Festival of Artemesia is coming up. Thousands of devotees and tourists will inundate the city. It is our chance to sell hundreds of votives, but it takes money for Davos to purchase the silver."

"Money, we don't have," Davonia bit her lip and clutched the shawl.

"This way, he could produce hundreds of votives in time for the festival. He promised it would only be this one time. He had already made money selling a few. He said no one would find out."

"And you believed him." Davonia let out a sob. Tears rolled down her cheeks. "Oh, Mother."

Marcella nodded, her tears falling.

The noises from the house changed. The running footfalls slacked off, the barking of orders quieted. The wagons creaked under their loads.

"If he thought Benjamin had stolen the votive," Sabina said. "He had a motive to kill Benjamin."

"Davos is not innocent, nor am I. I stole the votive and betrayed my husband by not telling him. I brought this upon us." She waved her arm toward the guards carrying out their tables, vases, chairs. "But regarding Benjamin's death, Davos and I had nothing to do with it."

"Davos sent a note to Flavius Fortunus before Benjamin died."

"I know nothing of such a note."

"It summoned the authorities to the church the night of the murder," Sabina said.

"My husband was furious at Benjamin and me, but I was with Davos at the church. He had no opportunity to administer the poison."

Two guards approached and spoke to the guard watching the women. All three turned and stalked toward the women.

"I do not care what happens to Davos or myself...my unbearable sorrow is for my daughter."

Dull drumming of thunder rattled the distant sky. Sabina looked up; the gray curtains closed in as if night were approaching instead of late afternoon. The wind picked up, rustling the mother's and daughter's clothing as they stood.

"This is not your fault," Sabina said. "Your husband's forgeries were going to be discovered and traced back to him. He gambled your lives that it wouldn't be this soon."

273

One guard jerked Davonia to her feet. "You're coming with us."
Davonia looked up blankly, offering no resistance.

Marcella screamed.

Another guard pushed Sabina away. She stumbled. Hopelessness tightened her throat, and tears flowed for the second time this week.

Sabina felt another kind of emptiness. Marcella had shared her faith with Davos, and he had been open-minded, allowing her belief in Jesus Christ until her belief threatened to destroy their way of life. What would Marcus do if confronted with that pressure? She didn't know, and uncertainty left a hollowness in her gut.

She had told Portia she wanted what Portia had. But Sabina needed more than a husband. She wanted someone to share her faith. Someone to communicate the love and hope given to her by Jesus. Portia and her husband, Horace, prayed to the same God, growing in the Spirit of Jehovah, and worshiped together. They taught their beliefs to their children, generously supported others who struggled. They loved, hoped, and forgave as Jesus did. Could Marcus be that husband? She needed to find out.

Marcella's and Davonia's hands were chained together. One guard spent extra time securing Davonia. She winced when he ran his hands over her and closed her eyes while he secured a metal collar around her neck.

"Pray to your God for her, Sabina. The goddess has closed her ears and her heart."

Sabina cleared the lump from her throat. "I will pray for your family every hour."

They were tethered to the back of a cart loaded with their possessions. An old nag would soon pull the cart down the street, away from their home, away from their freedom.

❧

Sabina, Yechiel, her father's two guards, and Zarmig watched as the small caravan of guards, slaves, and prisoners fell into a confused formation. "Marcella denied having arsenic. She knew nothing of the note and insisted Davos did not poison Benjamin," she reported.

"Doesn't sound like a confession," Zarmig said.

"And with each passing minute, we lose our chance to get one," Yechiel stared at the swirling lineup of wagons, locking his gaze on Davos. A guard jerked him to his feet. "We have come this far only to watch the murderer slip out of our hands with no confession."

"It appears Flavius Fortunus has not pursued the murder since his search of Portia's home," Zarmig looked at Yechiel. "That is good for Sabina and the church."

"It is not my intention to implicate Christians." Yechiel looked at Sabina. "But we have no evidence to stop this Flavius Fortunus from resuming his search after our only proof lies mauled and half eaten on the arena floor. They did not object to Sabina talking to the prisoners."

"She is not interviewing Davos." Zarmig crossed his arms.

"I am no threat to them. A solitary Jew."

"You must not say anything that would prompt the guards to focus on the murder."

"I will be discreet."

"As you said, with each passing minute," Zarmig said with a flourish of his arm.

Davos stood shackled behind a wagon and flanked by two guards clad in leather jerkins. His left arm dangled at an unnatural angle at his side. Sabina heard the swagger in the voice of the guard who answered Yechiel's request. The guard, whether overly confident or overly lax, permitted Yechiel a few minutes with the prisoner. Sabina let out a long breath when the guard motioned him forward.

Both guards remained at Davos's side. "We leave in a minute. Be quick."

Bleeding, bruised, and sniffling, Davos frowned at Yechiel. "You? I recognize you from my shop yesterday." The swelling and split in Davos's lip slurred his speech. He tensed, his eyes narrowed. "Are you a part of this?"

"I'm here because of my brother, Benjamin."

"Benjamin's your brother? I hope he's rotting in the bowels of his Christian hell. This is his fault," Davos said, looking at his ransacked home, then over to his wife and daughter. Sabina strained to hear his mumbled words. "I didn't kill him."

"That is your defense?" Yechiel's glare bore into Davos, the venom clear to her even across the street.

"He was a thief. He stole from me."

"You informed the authorities about the chur—" Yechiel stopped and looked at the guards listening to the conversation. "His location the night he died."

"Let's say I alerted the authorities. I'd be an idiot to alert them I would be poisoning Benjamin. Come on over and arrest me."

"We traced the letter to you."

"And imagine my shock when I found out my wife sneaked back there right after a *concerned* citizen sent a message to Magistrate Flavius Fortunus requesting the whole heathen lot of 'em be arrested."

"But you went there. You threatened and assaulted Benjamin. We have witnesses."

"Who? My imbecile wife swore to me she'd quit that rotting flesh-eating cult. I wanted Benjamin out of the way. I don't deny that, but I didn't need to risk murdering him when all I had to do was send a letter and the magistrate would do it for me. I'm no killer."

"But being a devoted husband, when you went to the church to save your wife, you could have conveniently poisoned Benjamin."

"Did my wife also tell you I wasn't there long enough to piss in his wine, let alone poison him? I dragged her skinny hide out of there as fast as I could."

"Before Magistrate Flavius arrived?"

"You got that right. I wanted every one of 'em tortured, and if I was lucky, executed." Davos's split and puffy lip made his sneer lopsided. "The only flaw in the plan was the gladiators. Benjamin would die too quickly." Davos's chortle ended in a croak.

"And your plan included tearing his room apart, burning Benjamin's letter, and smashing a hole in the wall?"

"I got a bit upset. Nearly broke my hand. I didn't burn any letter if you're referring to that tidy pile of ashes in the brazier. Why would I take the time? I can't even read."

"You're done." The leather-clad guard jerked Davos's chain. "If you're lucky, the gladiator will finish you off quickly. But you don't seem like a lucky man to me." He laughed and shoved Yechiel away. Yechiel stumbled back as more guards arrived, and the wagon started forward.

TWENTY-TWO

Sabina watched the wagons fall into line and parade away. Davos cradled his arm and repeatedly stumbled, the links of his shackles dragging on the ground. The wagon Marcella and Davonia were chained to lurched forward, jerking Marcella to her knees. Davonia stumbled to reach her mother, pulling her upright. The women appeared in shock, not noticing Sabina as they shuffled past, staring at their feet. Davonia's ripped tunic flapped loose in the wind. Sabina looked skyward to the storm billowing in.

"Is he guilty?" Zarmig asked when the wagons of seized plunder and prisoners had passed, and Yechiel rejoined them. "I missed a bit of what Davos said."

Sabina suspected Zarmig had heard nothing of the conversation between Yechiel and Davos. She had had to strain to hear the exchange, and she had two functioning ears.

"He admitted hating Benjamin but insisted he didn't poison him," Yechiel said. "He admitted to sending the letter to Flavius."

"Divulging the location and time of our worship service," Sabina said.

"Which we already knew," Zarmig shrugged.

"I agree it doesn't make sense. Why would he summon the authorities to the church if he planned to be there poisoning Benjamin?" Yechiel said.

"Marcella admitted she stole back to the church without Davos knowing," Sabina said.

"He says he rushed to the church to save his wife?" Zarmig said. "Do you believe him?

"I don't know," Yechiel shook his head, and Sabina could hear the frustration in his voice.

"Well." Zarmig slapped both hands on his thighs, then turned and dismissed the two men accompanying him. "It's been an entertaining afternoon, but I can't think on an empty stomach. We passed a popina on our way here. It looked clean enough." Thunder rumbled overhead, and the promised rain began to patter against the stones and Sabina's head. She pulled her mantle over her head.

She hadn't eaten since breakfast, but thoughts of Marcella and Davonia being led away chained behind a wagon, shaking uncontrollably in the cold of drenching rain, left a massive knot in her stomach. She wasn't hungry.

They ran from one dripping awning to the next as the pattering turned to pommeling. When they reached the popina, Sabina's mantle had gained several pounds.

A shower cascading off the popina's awning flushed the litter from the sidewalk of the small eating establishment's paving and into the street; eddies swirled with gnawed fish bones, a sea of olive pits, and rotted vegetable peelings. Sabina wondered about Zarmig's definition of clean. They ducked inside and jostled their way to the counter. The rain and wind increased, spattering in through the open arched doorway. She attempted to wring the surplus water from her mantle, then gave up and took it off.

They weren't the only people taking shelter from the storm. Men with gleaming faces slipped in after their workout and bath at the neighborhood gymnasium. Two women were purchasing supper and laborers needing an end-of-the-day beer filled the standing-room-only establishment.

"I'll have a bowl of your stew and a mug of spiced wine," Zarmig yelled over the din and the head of a shorter man demanding the attention of the cook, who scrambled to dish up the specialty of the day, cold fish head stew.

"Hey, I was here first." The short man whipped around. His belligerent scowl faded to acquiescence as he stared into the broad leather and iron-studded chest of Zarmig. Silently he turned around.

The cook plopped Zarmig's meal on the counter. "How can you eat that?" Sabina sniffed at the bowl of slimy lumps swimming in broth, grimaced, and pinched her nose shut.

"I'm hungry, and it's raining harder than Poseidon pissing on an oyster shell," Zarmig garbled, and a dribble of broth ran down his chin. "Try it." Zarmig held out a spoonful with tiny floating eyeballs.

"Not if I were starving." She shuddered.

Yechiel shouldered in beside them, shaking his head at the offer of food.

Zarmig crunched on the spoonful and wiped his mouth with his arm. "We already knew Davos sent the letter. Nothing new there. If he poisoned Benjamin, he's gutsier than I am. He would have no idea when Flavius and his guards would arrive."

"I agree he got caught up in his scheme," Yechiel said.

"Which explains his grabbing Marcella and his panicked departure." Sabina continued. "I don't think he had time to locate Benjamin's cup and, unnoticed, slip arsenic into it."

"Did you get Davos to confess to anything besides sending the letter?" Zarmig asked.

"Destroying Benjamin's room, but he denied burning the parchment," Yechiel reported.

"Marcella said Davos vandalized the room looking for the votive," Sabina said. "He's going to be executed. I don't understand why he would deny burning the letter."

"Unless he didn't do it," Zarmig said.

"I don't see him controlling a fit of anger, then sitting down to start a fire just to burn a letter," Yechiel said.

"Then you believe him? He didn't kill Benjamin?" Zarmig finished off his wine, belched, and ordered another.

"He admitted wanting Benjamin dead. He's a man who would brag had he succeeded in poisoning him," Yechiel said.

"If you are right, that means the murderer…" Sabina's thoughts sobered. Tomorrow her father would rid himself of Apollos and the danger he posed. And the murderer would never be found. Sabina turned away. "Our last clues were Livia seeing Rufus delivering Benjamin's scroll and the burnt scraps from his room. If it wasn't Davos who burnt the parchment, why didn't someone just take it?" Sabina asked.

"Maybe whoever burnt it was afraid to be caught with it," Yechiel surmised.

"Afraid of what?" Sabina said. "A blackmailing love letter with the words '*how can he love*' and '*is a liar.*' There weren't enough pieces for us to know."

"There's your problem. You don't know dirt from diamonds," Zarmig said.

"The parchment and the scroll both point to the scriptorium," Sabina said.

Zarmig wiped the grease from his mouth with the back of his hand and stood up. "I agree we need that conversation with Rufus." Zarmig turned away from the counter. "Where is this scriptorium?"

Sabina grabbed her mantle. "Across town." She struggled to wrap the clinging sodden wool around her. She managed to drape it across her shoulders but did not pull up the sopping hood. The rain had slowed to a drizzle, but the wind blew stronger, buffeting them as they exited the popina. Sabina shivered. Lightning charged across the sky, signaling a bank of clouds closing in and plunging the early evening sky into instant darkness. Sabina stumbled in the shadows. The follow-up clap of thunder ushered in a whoosh as the clouds opened and dumped their reserve of bone-chilling rain. Sabina sneezed.

"I think we'll be having that conversation with Rufus…dry and early tomorrow morning."

"We don't have time to waste," Yechiel and Sabina said in unison, then looked at each other, blinking water out of their eyes.

"Neither do you have Magistrate Catius's authority to go barging in on a respected businessman. We'll meet at the scriptorium tomorrow morning."

A shudder of cold ran from Sabina's wet feet up the length of her body and ended with her chattering teeth. Hearing Zarmig's mandate, the emotion and exhaustion of the day crashed in on her. Adrenaline and determination had kept her energized. Now the thought of sleep, food, and thawing her shaking muscles in a hot bath drained whatever strength she had left. Wind-whipped raindrops stung her face, and she sighed, thinking of Davos's ambition and pride and the lives he had destroyed.

The following morning, rested, warm, and full of barley porridge, Sabina walked beside Zarmig, dreading the day. Or, more precisely, dreading how it would end. Last night's deluge had receded to a whimpering mist. Somehow overnight, Amisi had dried Sabina's rain-soaked covering, and she pulled its protective warmth around her as if shielding her from the failure that loomed with Apollos's imminent death.

She tried to focus on the positive. But her meeting with Marcus tonight added new worry. She needed to explain her faith, her belief that Jesus was the promised Messiah of the Jews and the Savior of humanity. God came to Earth to suffer and die, to redeem the world from its sin, death, and sorrow. If Marcus didn't run away, she would accept his offer of marriage. Her future now rested in the open-mindedness of Marcus.

Yechiel waited for them under the shelter of the scriptorium's portico. Sabina shook the water from her mantle wrapped to protect her hair.

Davos, if he was guilty, was now beyond their reach. And Magnus's blanching reaction when he realized he had nearly poisoned himself by drinking from Benjamin's wine cup declared him innocent. Yesterday had turned the investigation to Rufus. Her night at Hekate's Grotto had muddled Rufus's relationship with Benjamin. Questions piled one on another, and she needed clarity. She needed answers.

"Let's see what we can muck up in this sewer-torium," Zarmig growled.

"If Rufus is a Gnostic, I'm not sure he'll admit it after I ran away from the grotto." Sabina bit her bottom lip as Zarmig raised his hand to the duck door knocker.

"If Rufus is a Gnostic, it may have nothing to do with Benjamin or his death," Yechiel said.

The door suddenly swung open, followed by a crash. Pistus stared out at them, a dropped cloth-wrapped bundle at his feet. "The scriptorium is closed." Pistus bent over. The limp bundle clanked as he poked at it. He glared at them. "We open again in two weeks."

"Two weeks? Valerius did not mention closing to me," Yechiel said.

"Who are you again?" Pistus smirked and picked up the bag. The broken pieces tumbled together.

"A sudden change in plans?" Zarmig stepped forward.

Three household slaves scurried in the background, packing wicker baskets.

"A long-scheduled holiday for the family. And well deserved, I might add," Pistus said, juggling the bundle to close the door.

Zarmig braced his hand against the door, stopping it from shutting. "We are not here for your master. We need to speak to Rufus."

"Rufus? Whatever for?" Pistus asked, quite puzzled.

"Is he here?" Muscling Pistus aside, Zarmig stepped around the slave and pushed the door open. He started down the hall. Yechiel and Sabina followed.

Pistus dropped the bundle a second time, ran ahead, jostled Sabina, and planted himself in front of Zarmig, blocking the door to the stairway alcove leading up to the scriptorium. "You cannot go up there. You must have permission from Master Valerius."

"We already have permission from Magistrate Catius Sabinus," Sabina said.

Pistus did not move. "Rufus is at his home packing. He is to accompany the master to the family villa."

Zarmig turned and strode toward Valerius's office. Pistus started to follow Zarmig's retreating figure, stopped, and stared nervously at Sabina and Yechiel. He chewed first one side of his bottom lip, then the other.

"Is he taking his entire library with him?" Zarmig's voice boomed from inside Valerius's office.

Pistus bolted toward the office. Sabina heard him say, "I will gladly escort you up to the scriptorium, but I must first inform Master—"

"No, I will inform Master Valerius," Zarmig said.

"I will get him," Pistus said, his tone of haughty annoyance loud enough for Sabina and Yechiel to hear.

"Then stop standing around," Zarmig yelled at Pistus while staring at Sabina.

Sabina and Yechiel leaped up the stairs and hurried down the hall to the scriptorium.

"Sabina!" Rufus stood up, and the scroll he was writing on fell from his lap and plopped on the floor. He leaned over and picked it up. "I knew you would be back."

"Are you accompanying Master Valerius on his holiday?" she asked.

"Yes, yes, but there is much work to finish here before we can leave." His hair fell across his face, and he pinned the strands behind his ears with one hand while placing the scroll on a book stand with his other. "When I found your discarded robe, I thought you had wavered, but here you are." He beamed.

"I have more questions," Sabina said.

"Of course, you do. Of course, you do. You are a seeker of truth."

"The night at Hekate's Grotto—" Sabina began.

"You felt the power of the prophet, the glorious exhilaration." Rufus's eyes gleamed, his smile widened.

"Rufus, you didn't answer when I asked if you had invited Benjamin to worship there," Sabina said.

"Benjamin?" Rufus's smile faded, and his eyebrows drew together. He looked first at Sabina and then stared at Yechiel. "Are you not here to join us?"

"No." Sabina and Yechiel answered at the same time.

"Then why?" Rufus turned to Sabina.

"To find Benjamin's murderer," Sabina said.

"I see. And your first visit here, with your master," Rufus nodded to Yechiel, "was because of Benjamin?"

"Yechiel is not my master," Sabina said. "I am a free citizen."

Rufus sniffed and shook his head. "Your deceptions grow. I would gladly have answered questions without the falsehoods."

"You have not answered my questions," she said. "Did Benjamin worship at Hekate's grove? Was he baptized in the dark pool?"

"Benjamin was blessed to be chosen as one of the first converts," Rufus said.

"You lie." Yechiel stepped toward Rufus. "Benjamin would never defile himself by entering a pagan temple."

Rufus held up his hands and backed away. "Not pagan. The ceremony Sabina witnessed is the restoration of true Christianity. Our beliefs are spreading among all Christian communities."

"They are not the teaching of Jesus," Sabina said.

"You do not know the newly revealed teachings of Jesus," Rufus said. "Beliefs must change with the times."

Sabina shook her head. "The prophecies of the Jewish prophets in the Tanakh, the Hebrew Scriptures, concerning the Messiah, never change," Sabina said.

"You are wrong. The great Father God has sent a prophet to expand the old prophecies."

"There is no need for another prophet. Jesus fulfilled the prophecies." Sabina knew she argued in vain but couldn't stop. "Jesus vested the apostles with His authority. The foundation of Christianity is the message entrusted to the apostles. Those who receive the message of the apostles receive the message of Jesus."

"You sound like Benjamin," Rufus said. "He was the perfect convert, his life of service, his devotion to God, his search for truth. He would have risen, perhaps to the heights of a god himself."

"If you had not murdered him," Yechiel said.

"If he had joined us." Rufus looked nervously at Yechiel. "Benjamin rejected the new revelations."

"And was killed because of it," Yechiel accused.

"No. That is not the way of the enlightened." Rufus bowed his head. "Benjamin, like Sabina, denied the knowledge of the truth, the gnosis. There is spiritual death for unbelievers, not a physical one. Benjamin cut himself off from the truth."

Sabina wasn't satisfied that Rufus was telling the truth. "When did you last see Benjamin?"

"The night before he died. We were working late together."

"You mean he stayed to help you with one of your assignments?" Yechiel asked.

"Benjamin had put the final coat of preserver on his Isaiah scroll. It was taking longer than usual to dry in the humidity. And yes, he offered to help me finish copying a letter while he waited."

"What kind of letter?" Sabina asked.

"A boring one, I can tell you," Rufus said. "Someone was professing Jesus is the Christ, yet again."

"Do you remember what it said?" Sabina asked.

"Not really. I don't normally get assigned religious work. It's tedious. I do remember one sentence because Benjamin had me read it aloud to him three times."

"Did Benjamin do that often? Have you repeat?" Yechiel asked.

"Never. I read, he wrote. Done. Memory was his genius."

"Did he tell you why he wanted it reread?" Sabina asked.

"No. Benjamin just stopped writing and asked me to read the sentence over, as I said. Two more times. Then we continued until we finished the letter."

"Did anything you repeated sound unusual?" Sabina asked.

"Not unusual or even remarkable. The same picky arguments we hear from church leaders all the time."

"Then it was written by a leader of the church?" Sabina asked.

"I don't know. There wasn't a signature. Anonymity is wise for that type of letter."

"Can you tell us what you remember?" Yechiel asked.

"Only because I had to repeat it." Rufus recited, "'By this you know the Spirit of God: Every spirit that confesses that Jesus Christ has come in the spirit is of God, and every spirit that does not confess that Jesus Christ has come in the spirit is not of God."

Sabina's heart sank. None of what Rufus recited matched the words on the parchment fragments she had found: *"how can he love, who is true and we,* and *is a liar.* If they were from the same letter, it appeared impossible to prove. Yechiel was right. They were wasting time trying to match her puzzle pieces.

"Was the letter addressed to anyone?" Yechiel asked.

"No, but that's not unusual. No one wants their name attached to a potentially treasonous letter," Rufus said.

Yechiel was right. The burnt parchment had no tie to the scriptorium or Benjamin's murder. But as one of her last clues, she'd follow it to its end before she gave up. "Rufus, what were the letters written on?" Sabina asked, hoping one last time the ashes in Benjamin's room would lead to something useful.

Rufus paused and shifted from one foot to another. "Parchment."

"Expensive parchment?" Sabina asked, looking at Yechiel.

Rufus nodded. "The letters were important to someone."

Sabina held out the small piece of parchment they had shown Rufus and Valerius two days before. "You started to comment on this when I showed it to Valerius."

Rufus's eyes shifted rapidly away, avoiding her inquiry. "The pieces are so small." His fingers tucked hair behind his ears, hair already securely anchored in place. "I was mistaken."

"You're lying," Yechiel said.

Rufus pinched his lips tightly together.

"Please, Rufus, I found this fragment in Benjamin's room." Sabina handed him the burnt piece. "Have you seen this parchment before?"

Rufus ran his thumb over the fragile animal skin. "Maybe, but it cannot be from the letters. No work leaves here."

"Where did the letter and its copy go?" Yechiel asked.

Rufus pointed to his workspace. "When Master Valerius assigned this, he directed me to leave the original and the copy here on the book stand when I finished. That's what I did." Rufus paused as if thinking. "Benjamin stayed longer. He said he needed to check the Isaiah scroll."

"How much longer?" Sabina asked.

"You could ask Master Valerius. He was working downstairs in his office when I left. I didn't kill Benjamin. He was alive when I left. That was the last time I saw him, I swear."

"Rufus, a woman, saw Benjamin with you at the church the night you poisoned him," Sabina said.

"She is mistaken." Rufus's voice rose, pink spots appeared on his cheeks. "The last time I saw Benjamin was Friday night at the scriptorium."

"Benjamin told her you were bringing the Isaiah scroll to the church. She saw you deliver it," Sabina said.

"It is true I offered to bring the scroll. Benjamin doesn't work on Sundays, so I offered to deliver it to the church the next day. It would be dry by then," Rufus said.

"You admit to going to the church?" Yechiel said.

"I offered, but someone else took it to the church." Rufus shook his head, his locks falling loose from behind his ears.

"Someone else? How convenient," Yechiel said.

"The scroll's ink was dry when I came to work the next morning. I rolled it and secured the wax seals when Master Valerius entered. He asked about the scroll. And I told him I promised to deliver it to Benjamin at the church."

"Could Valerius have found out Benjamin helped you with the letter?" Sabina asked.

"Master Valerius asked. I admitted Benjamin had helped me with the letter. I believe he already suspected."

"Did Valerius get upset?" Yechiel asked.

"No. He offered to deliver the scroll to Benjamin in time for the reading."

Zarmig burst into the room. "Where is Valerius? Pistus told me he would meet us in the scriptorium."

"He is not here," Yechiel said.

"Rufus said Valerius delivered the Isaiah scroll to Benjamin the morning of the murder," Sabina said.

"I thought Livia pointed to this crook. Didn't Rufus bring the scroll to the church?" Zarmig said.

"I'm not a—"

"Shut your mouth," Zarmig growled. "Even the gods will not come to your aid you if you are lying."

Rufus's lips quivered.

"Livia didn't remember a name. It was I who mentioned Rufus." Sabina realized her mistake.

"Valerius had no reason to poison Benjamin," Yechiel said.

"We need to find out what Master Valerius knows about the letter Rufus and Benjamin copied," Sabina said.

"You," Zarmig growled at Rufus, "sit."

Rufus dropped into his chair.

"Stay," Zarmig warned. Rufus nodded, his eyes sparkling with tears. "We aren't done with you."

Yechiel and Sabina followed Zarmig as he rushed out of the room. They hurried down the stairs turning the corner at the bottom into the atrium. Zarmig barreled into Pistus, knocking the slave into the wall.

"Excuse you," Pistus rubbed his shoulder.

"Where is your master?" Zarmig asked.

"Unfortunately, Master Valerius is gone." Pistus raised his chin and pinched his lips shut.

"Where?" demanded Zarmig.

"I told you he is taking a holiday in his country villa." Sabina heard a quiver in the tone of this haughty slave. Pistus tried holding Zarmig's stare. He couldn't.

"No," said Zarmig, hooking his leg around Pistus's leg and knocking him to the floor. "You said he was here ten minutes ago." Pistus sprawled on his back and, like a crab, scuttled away, sliding on his rear-end. Zarmig backed Pistus against the atrium wall and planted a foot on the groveling slave's chest.

"I didn't realize he had already left, I swear it." Pistus wheezed. "I cannot breathe."

Zarmig removed his foot.

Pistus slowly picked himself up, keeping one eye on Zarmig as he brushed imagined dirt from his tunic. "You should go back and question the idiot Rufus."

"About what?" asked Yechiel.

"Whatever Rufus has done to get my master in trouble," Pistus said.

"Who said your master is in trouble?" Zarmig asked

"My master has nothing to do with Rufus's lies."

"What can you tell us about Rufus's letters?" Sabina asked.

Pistus turned toward her, his face blank.

"The letter Benjamin copied for Rufus," Sabina said.

"I saw baskets of scrolls when I entered Valerius's office earlier," Zarmig said. "Perhaps one contains letters. We'll take a look."

"Not the master's office?" squeaked Pistus. He ran ahead, as if leading them to the office, then stopped, extended his arms, and blocked the doorway.

"Not again," Zarmig said, cracking his knuckles.

Behind Pistus, Valerius entered the office through the archway leading to the gardens. He looked up, his expression dismayed. "Pistus, stop this inexcusable behavior immediately and apologize to our visitors and let them pass."

"Master, you are...back," Pistus said in a high-pitched squeak. He stepped aside, allowing Sabina, Yechiel, and Zarmig to enter. Pistus bowed. "Forgive my mistake."

Valerius clapped his hands, appearing delighted to welcome honored customers. "Be assured I shall punish Pistus severely for his reprehensible conduct. He is protective of my privacy. I apologize for not being here to greet you." He smiled at Zarmig. "Packing for a restful holiday is proving more arduous than working."

Three large woven baskets lay on the floor, filled with scrolls. Assorted piles of additional scrolls lay scattered around the room, leaving the library pigeonholes empty. One smaller leather hamper sat on the desktop piled with manuscripts. "It appears even your holiday will not be relaxing." Sabina motioned to the inks and pens boxed next to the leather hamper.

"Indeed, in my profession, not all confidential work can be relegated to slaves or novice scribes." Valerius picked up a scroll lying on the desk and tucked it in the leather basket. "Last one. Yechiel, what can I do for you? Did the letter I wrote prove unsatisfactory?"

"The letter was perfect," Yechiel said.

"We hope you could answer a few questions about a different letter," said Zarmig.

"Now I am confused." Valerius shook his head.

"We spoke to Rufus again," Sabina said.

"Rufus?" Valerius looked at Zarmig's uniform. "Has he done something wrong? Something illegal I should be aware of?"

"Rufus said he and Benjamin copied a letter," Sabina said.

Valerius smiled. "It is their job."

"They wrote it the night before Benjamin was murdered."

"Murdered? I have heard rumors a Christian bishop was arrested. I know him. It is difficult to imagine him committing such a crime," Valerius said.

"He is innocent." Sabina could not see the whole Benjamin puzzle, but Rufus's information had filled in a few blank pieces. Valerius could add the proof. "A Christian wrote the letter they copied."

Valerius avoided Zarmig's glare. "Occasionally, I accept controversial correspondence. You cannot fault Rufus for that. If I turned down everything the authorities banned, I would be out of business."

"You don't seem surprised Benjamin aided Rufus with his work that night," Yechiel said.

"Rufus is skilled at coaxing others to share his burden. That surprises no one," Valerius said.

"Rufus said you were unaware Benjamin helped the other scribes," Sabina said.

"Ridiculous. I knew from the day Benjamin arrived that he assisted the others…mostly Rufus. Benjamin's script is superior to the other scribes and noticeably distinct. The work got done, so I allowed it."

"Without telling the scribes you were aware of what was happening?" Sabina asked.

"I did not want to encourage Rufus and others to take advantage of Benjamin's dedication. If they thought it was forbidden, they limited the practice. Now," Valerius picked up the leather basket, "I have been more than generous in delaying my departure. I see no reason to indulge what appears to be a pointless curiosity. If you will excuse me, Pistus will show you out."

Zarmig pulled a chair over and leisurely sat down. "We have the authority of Magistrate Catius Sabinus to investigate the murder of Benjamin ben Jonah. You will answer our questions here or at a formal court hearing," Zarmig bluffed.

Valerius set the basket on the table but didn't release the handles. His jaw flexed, and he glared at Yechiel. "I see. Needing a letter written was a ploy."

"My grandmother will enjoy reading your legible script more than mine." Yechiel shrugged.

"Your duplicity baffles me." Valerius's fingers turned white, gripping the handles of the basket. "I am more than willing to clear up whatever concerns you have. Please hurry, however. My wife and son are waiting for me."

"When did you discover Benjamin had helped Rufus copy the letter?" Sabina asked.

"When I went upstairs to lock the scriptorium," Valerius answered, his tone flat with anger, no longer the pleasant host. He glared at Sabina.

She knew there would be little he would willingly share from now on. She needed to drill through his pretense and expose what was worth murdering for in the letters. "Was Benjamin there?" Sabina asked.

"No."

"And he had taken the letters he and Rufus were working on?" Sabina asked.

"Nothing leaves the scriptorium without my permission—"

"So, when the letters were missing, you must have been angry," Yechiel interrupted. "Did you confront my brother and demand he return the letters?"

"Did you not hear me? No work leaves the scriptorium. The letters were on the stand where Rufus had left them." Valerius's pursed his lips.

His voice came out strained as if working to keep his voice civil. "What possible reason would Benjamin have to take insignificant letters?"

"That was my next question," Sabina said. "Rufus said the letters contained statements of Christian beliefs."

"Rufus cannot remember to tie the thongs of his sandals. But, yes, the letters contained common Christian beliefs shared with friends."

"Who wrote the original letter?" Yechiel asked.

"I cannot reveal that." Valerius looked directly at Zarmig. "In the hands of hateful zealots, those testimonials signify a death sentence."

"We don't need the name of the author," Sabina rummaged in her pouch containing the burnt and washed-out scraps. "You can prove Benjamin didn't steal your letter by showing us the two letters to confirm what Rufus remembers reading."

"And you may sail off on your holiday," Zarmig said.

Valerius took his time looking around the room. "In fact, I have not had time to dispatch the letters. They are here somewhere." Valerius said, turning his back to them as he rummaged through the leather basket.

Sabina's heart constricted. If Benjamin didn't steal the letter, then Rufus or Valerius had no reason to poison Benjamin. She bit her lip and tipped her head back to keep her tears from spilling. She had been wrong. She had imagined a link between the letters and Benjamin's scraps of parchment. No connection existed. She watched as Valerius took out several scrolls, examined their end tags, and set them aside on the desk. Her stomach churned. She would leave here without discovering who poisoned Benjamin or why. Apollos would die.

With shaking hands, Sabina pulled a piece of parchment from her pouch. She would never know what it said or why someone destroyed it. She rubbed her finger over the scrap. The burnt edges flaked away, but the fragment's distinct thickness, texture, and color remained unaltered.

Valerius slowly pulled out two unsealed scrolls. He turned to face Yechiel. He handed one to Yechiel and one to Zarmig. "The two letters."

"We need time to read them. These scrolls are thick," Sabina said.

"Keep them as long as you like. Give the letters to Magistrate Sabinus if you like. I don't have time to indulge your curiosity." Valerius reached out and clutched the leather basket.

Yechiel and Sabina looked at the basket then at each other. Yechiel unrolled his scroll.

Sabina blinked back tears as she started to return the fragment to the pouch, stopped, and slowly began to unroll the scroll. She placed the tiny scrap on Valerius' letter. She stared at the scroll, then at her fragment, then back again, her confusion growing. The parchments matched perfectly. "You said you did not have this kind of parchment when we showed you the fragment."

"I said I didn't recognize it. I can't remember every variety I sell," Valerius said.

Yechiel looked at her, frown lines deep between his eyebrows. Their eyes locked. He, too, remembered Valerius's denial when shown the fragment. Valerius was lying. Why? He had provided an alibi by producing the two letters. But if Benjamin didn't steal the letters, where had the matching parchment come from? And how did it get in Benjamin's room? "You said the author wrote these to like-minded friends. How many friends?" Sabina asked.

"Two letters, two friends. Just an old man's blathering," Valerius waved dismissively.

"Then you won't mind if I confirm that." Yechiel put his letter down and reached across the table for the leather basket.

Valerius pulled the basket away, but Yechiel quickly grabbed the top edge of the basket.

"These are private papers," Valerius said between clenched teeth.

"Or Christian subversive literature?" Zarmig stood up.

Valerius held tightly to one of the basket's wooden handles.

Yechiel tugged. Valerius pulled harder.

Yechiel let go.

Valerius stumbled backward, upsetting the basket. It toppled over on the table. Scrolls rolled out and dropped off the table cascading in a waterfall of unfurling black and white that carpeted the floor. Zarmig stomped on a run-away scroll.

Valerius's eyes blazed in anger as he reached for the basket.

In slow motion, the basket rolled out of his reach, precariously balanced on the table's edge, then thudded upside down on the floor at Sabina's feet.

"You clumsy ape," Valerius screeched, leaping for the basket. "Those scrolls are valuable. Don't touch them."

"Let me help." Yechiel came around the table and shouldered Valerius away from the basket.

"Get away from me, or I'll—" Valerius reached for the basket, but Sabina was already righting it.

She lifted the basket and held it frozen in midair. "Ooh." She stared at the spilled contents on the floor. A silver mask lay shimmering brightly in the room's hazy light, cushioned by the bed of scrolls where it had fallen. She set the basket on the table and bent to pick up the mask. A familiar silver mask.

Sabina looked up in confusion. "Valerius?" The imperious smirk on Valerius's face answered her question. It made sense. Rufus had been led into the gnostic religion by someone he believed and trusted. Why not the learned and wealthy Master Valerius?

Valerius grabbed at the mask, tearing it from her hand, and ran. Sabina caught at the hem of his tunic, but Valerius's momentum ripped the fabric from her fingers. She fell, knocking over a second basket of packed scrolls.

"What the?" Zarmig jumped back. The chair crashing to the floor.

"It's the mask from the prophet at the grotto," Sabina said.

Yechiel kicked loose scrolls aside, slipped on one, and regained his balance. Zarmig jumped past him over the slippery carpet of parchment. Yechiel followed, passing Sabina, who watched as Valerius disappeared between the two painted palms and into the alcove at the bottom of the scriptorium stairway.

Chasing a few steps behind, Zarmig jerked to a halt at the reverberation of a slamming stairway door. Zarmig reached the door a second after Valerius. Yechiel and Sabina trailed behind. Zarmig grabbed the latch just as a bolt thudded into place on the opposite side of the door.

Valerius's echoing footsteps bolted up the stairs. Cursing, Zarmig rattled the door latch and rammed his shoulder into the door once, then again. The door did not even creak. "A rear door!" They turned and ran back to the office to the quivering, wide-eyed figure of Pistus, who had backed himself into a corner.

"Where are the back stairs? Now!" bellowed Zarmig bearing down on the small man.

Pistus, completely translucent, stuttered. "In th…th…the garden."

Sabina followed the men running through the office and into the garden. They looked up and saw Valerius running along the second-story portico, racing toward the scriptorium. They saw no second stairway.

Zarmig pointed to the collonade bordering the garden. They split up, with Zarmig barreling around the pool. Yechiel ran to the garden's left collonade, and Sabina turned to the right, each sprinting toward a different covered walkway.

Within a minute, Zarmig called out he had found a second stairway. Yechiel ran toward him. Sabina tripped on her robe. She stopped to untangle it, looked up, and saw Valerius stealing along the upper hallway back toward the locked stairway door. In no time, he would be down the stairway, unlocking the door and fleeing into the street.

She shouted, "Zarmig! Yechiel! Valerius turned back." She could wait, hoping they heard her, or she could cut Valerius off, giving Zarmig time to discover Valerius had backtracked.

She retraced her path across the garden, darting through the office and into the atrium, reaching the stairway just as the door bolt slid back.

Valerius's gasp of surprise when he saw her turned to anger. His body lurched back as if to run up the stairs. Instead, he spun around, facing her.

Sabina hoped Zarmig and Yechiel had followed her. But when she saw Valerius glance behind her and smile, his eyes lighting up, she knew they had not heard her yell. She faced a murderer alone.

"Go home to your cooking pots, woman. You are playacting in a drama far beyond your capabilities."

The insult stung because she knew it to be true. But she was not alone. "You poisoned Benjamin? Why?" Zarmig? Yechiel, where are you?

Valerius swaggered slowly toward her. "You dare question me? You know nothing."

"I know you're a murderer." Keep him talking. Find out what is going on.

"Benjamin was ill. He died. No one can prove otherwise."

"Was it because of the letters?"

"Sabina?" Yechiel's voice rang from the top of the stairs.

"Valerius is down here," she shouted back.

Valerius charged, shoving past her. Her head crashed into the wall, and a sudden shooting pain speared her skull. A circle of lights spun around her head. The lights shrunk to pinpoints then vanished. She slid to the floor, her eyes seeing nothing but black as she listened to Valerius's footsteps running out the front door.

TWENTY-THREE

Sabina sat on the floor, her eyes closed. Her head pounded to the rhythm of Valerius's footsteps growing louder. Louder? Was Valerius returning? The steps stopped. Her stomach lurched as a wave of fear washed over her. She opened her eyes, confused to see Yechiel standing over her. Zarmig catapulted into view at the bottom of the stairs.

"He escaped," she whispered.

Zarmig knelt beside her. "He attacked you? Are you hurt?"

"Dizzy, I hit my head."

"Stay by her," Zarmig ordered Yechiel. "Where did he go?"

"I think out the front door. I did not see him." The small alcove spun around. She closed her eyes.

Zarmig rose and ran out of the door, cursing.

"You are injured?" Yechiel asked.

"A little." She nodded, not opening her eyes. Did she detect sympathy in his voice? "I will sit here until the floor stays in one place."

Zarmig returned. "He is gone. We will assemble our guards and hunt him down. He will be in our custody within the hour. Where is Pistus, that lying sniveling dog of a slave who helped him escape?" Zarmig strode back toward the office.

Sabina opened her eyes. Her head hurt. She struggled to stand, pushing herself partway up then sliding back to the floor. It rocked as if she were trying to stand up in a small fishing boat.

"Who has fled?" a voice called from the top of the stairs.

She had forgotten about Rufus.

"I couldn't stay in the scriptorium when I heard shouting." Rufus bounded down the stairs.

"Valerius ran when confronted with evidence against him," Yechiel said.

Rufus shook his head vehemently. "You have made a mistake. Master Valerius is incapable of the sins of this world. He is—"

"Escaping," Sabina said, looking at Rufus's bewildered face.

"He is touched by the divine revelation of the eternal Father, God. Your murderer is someone else," Rufus said.

"I believe you are the suspect next in line," Yechiel said.

"Oww." Sabina rubbed the back of her head and squinted up from the floor at both men.

Yechiel pointed to Sabina. "Your divine master did this. Are you able to stand?"

"Take my hand," Rufus reached out and assisted her unsteady rise.

Grasping Rufus's outstretched hand, she rose and braced her back against the wall, testing the floor, the walls. They remained anchored in place. Her dizziness receded. "Valerius was evasive about the letters. They connect him to the events surrounding Benjamin's death."

Zarmig strode into the atrium. A simpering Pistus gripped by his tunic collar scrambled to keep his feet under him as Zarmig hauled him toward the alcove. "I found him hiding like the rat he is. This one is going to pay for every worthless minute I lost searching."

"You are choking me," Pistus coughed.

Zarmig lifted the slave higher. Pistus' toes danced inches off the floor. Zarmig dropped him. Pistus stumbled, clutching at the wall to regain his balance.

"We shall leave immediately to report Valerius's escape to Magistrate Catius and arm for the search."

"We need to read the letters," Sabina said.

"Then Benjamin didn't steal the letters?" Rufus asked.

Sabina turned to Rufus. "You can confirm if the two letters Valerius gave us are the ones you and Benjamin copied."

"And prove my master's innocence. Thanks be to the eternal Father. Where are the letters?"

"In Valerius's office," Yechiel said.

"Stay if you want, Sabina, but these two accomplices come with me." Zarmig pointed at Rufus, who had slunk behind Sabina.

"Rufus is our only witness to the letters," Sabina pleaded. "The only clues we have."

"You can't trust Rufus," Pistus said, straining to breathe. Zarmig struck him across the face. Pistus staggered back, his eyes filling with tears.

"I agree with the slave," Zarmig scowled at Rufus. "The scribe is suspect."

"We need him," Sabina pleaded.

"I waste time arguing. Keep the scribe, but watch your back," Zarmig said, hoisting Pistus up and dragging him toward the door. He pushed Pistus outside and slammed the door.

Yechiel looked at Rufus peeking out from behind Sabina. "Tell me, scribe, if the letters are innocuous, why did Valerius run from us?"

"There is no reason. I copied nothing but boring doctrines." Rufus blushed. "Master Valerius would not have chosen me to copy valuable correspondence."

"There has to be something in them." Sabina sighed, trying not to lose hope. "He didn't want the fragments we found in Benjamin's room connected to the scriptorium. Why?" Still unsteady on her feet, Sabina hobbled into Valerius's office. Yechiel and Rufus followed.

They sorted and organized the jumble of dumped scrolls, rolling them up and placing them into groups. Five thin codex books had also fallen from the basket. Curious, Sabina picked one up. She had seen only two of these new inventions. The codices had individual pages cut into squares and bound together between a front and a back cover. The codices were smaller to transport, and churches had begun using them to share the books of Scripture between congregations and towns. Sabina placed each codex in a pile off to the side.

"There are about fifty scrolls. Most are papyrus." Sabina separated the papyrus scrolls into the second basket. The remaining eighteen parchment scrolls she collected and laid on the table.

"Here are the letters Valerius gave us." Yechiel held up two scrolls.

"Rufus." Sabina handed him one of the manuscripts. "Would you please read aloud?"

Rufus took the scroll. He sat on the floor and unrolled the two-foot-long letter from one end, rolling it up at the other as he read. Sabina and Yechiel stood behind him, leaning down and following along over his shoulders.

Sabina listened intently for the words from Benjamin's fragments. She read *'is a liar'* just as Rufus recited it. A shiver of excitement ran down her neck.

When Rufus read, *how can he love,* Sabina's pulse raced. Then together, she and Rufus read the final fragment aloud within their sentence. *That we may know him, that is true and we are in him who is true.*

"Benjamin had a copy of this letter in his room. It has the same wording as the fragments I found."

"These are words from the letter I remember copying." Rufus re-rolled the scroll.

"Which means there were more than two letters." Yechiel handed his scroll to Rufus. "Here's the second letter Valerius gave us."

Rufus unrolled it several inches, then stopped. He ran his fingers over the parchment then turned to Sabina. "This is strange. May I see the first scroll again?" Sabina passed him the first scroll. He unrolled each scroll partially and laid them side by side. "You said Master Valerius gave you these and told you they were the letters Benjamin and I transcribed?"

"Yes."

"Whoever wrote the first letter also wrote this second one. Look at the script." Rufus pointed to several words. "Look at the spacing, the even flow of the ink. It is an expert script. I thought it was Benjamin's except—"

"Benjamin only copied one letter the night before he died," Sabina said.

Rufus nodded. "Benjamin didn't write these letters, nor did I. Someone else wrote or copied these letters."

"Valerius showed us two letters," Sabina said. "If we include Benjamin's, there were three."

"Perhaps more," Yechiel said.

Sabina gathered the pile of parchment scrolls. "It makes sense that the letters were all written on the same parchment. We should only have to examine these eighteen." She divided the scrolls between them.

After reading a few verses, Sabina put her scroll down. She felt the heat of a blush rush up her face turning it as red as Rufus's face the first time they met.

Yechiel looked up. "Is it the letter?"

"No," she said.

"How much did you read?" Yechiel questioned.

"Enough," she said.

"Are you sure?" Yechiel pressed.

"I'm sure!" Exasperated with his questions, she blurted out, "Christian verses don't contain 'they could not meet each other's eyes but lay relaxed in pleasure, shy, fearful, breathing hard.'" Embarrassed by her outburst, she looked at her feet.

Yechiel's mouth puckered in a smile. "It sounds much like Jewish verses from Solomon's love poem, the Song of Solomon."

Surprised, she heard a teasing in his voice. When her face cooled, she looked up. Yechiel was concentrating on reading his scroll.

Rufus tossed his head, flipping his hair out of his eyes. "That is a passage from *Xenophon of Ephesus*. It's the trials and adventures of the lovers Anthia and Habrocomes," Rufus said. "For every copy of Plato's *Republic* sold, Master Valerius sells ten of *Xenophon of Ephesus*."

Sabina chose another scroll. After several minutes of reading, she set that scroll aside as well. The third scroll took longer. It contained Christian text similar to what Rufus remembered. She read for almost twenty minutes. She finished and re-rolled the scroll without finding any of the verses Rufus had recited.

Yechiel threw his scroll on the floor. "With great forbearance and skepticism, I have read several letters extolling the miracles of your prophesied Messiah, Jesus. None have your verses."

"There are only eight more scrolls." Rufus counted down.

Eight more! The letters were taking longer than Sabina had anticipated. She had several hours before sunset, before meeting with Marcus. She had time, but they must hurry.

The next scroll Sabina opened began with the words Rufus had read in the first two letters. *That which was from the beginning, which we have heard, which we have seen with our eyes, which we have looked upon, and our hands have handled, of the Word of life.* Sabina searched for the author but found no reference to who wrote the scroll. She kept reading, and with half of the manuscript unrolled, the wording corresponded precisely.

"I found another copy." She and Yechiel said simultaneously. Each looked at the other, then held their scrolls open for the other to see. The verses Rufus remembered were in each of their scrolls.

"Read your letter aloud," Sabina directed. "I will follow along in mine." Yechiel began reading.

When he recited the verses Rufus had read three times to Benjamin, Sabina stopped him. "You misread the last sentence."

"I read it perfectly," Yechiel said.

"That's what I remember repeating," Rufus agreed.

"No, mine says 'Every spirit that confesses that Jesus Christ is come in the flesh is of God.' You read that Jesus Christ *is come in the spirit.*"

"Read it yourself." Yechiel held out his scroll and showed her the words he had read. "This says *in the spirit*, not *in the flesh.*"

She looked to Rufus for an answer.

He shrugged, taking her scroll and reading the verses. "The next line in your copy is different also. Where yours says *spirit* mine says *flesh.* Look."

Rufus held out her scroll for Yechiel to see. "'And every spirit that confesses not that Jesus Christ is come in the flesh is not of God.' I can't see that it matters."

Sabina's eyes grew wide, and she stared at him. "It completely changes the meaning. The mixed-up words are opposites," Sabina said. How could Rufus, a trained scribe, have missed the significance of the different phrasing? No wonder Rufus didn't copy critical work. She shook her head and examined the letter again. She wondered if a scribe as careless and unobservant as Rufus had made the errors?

"If so, which version is correct? We have found five letters using *the spirit* and one letter saying *the flesh*?" Yechiel ask.

Yechiel read aloud to the end of his letter concluding with "'This is the true God, and eternal life. Little children, keep yourselves from idols. Amen.'"

"Everything else matches word for word." Sabina rolled up her scroll.

"There is more." Rufus pointed at the two different scrolls. "Look closely at the script. The ink in the one single letter flows unsteadily, thick to thin."

Sabina followed Rufus's finger as he traced words with small splotches of ink and uneven spacing. Why hadn't she noticed it?

"The script of the five *spirit* scrolls is uniform with an even, smooth flow, perfectly spaced. The letter Valerius gave me to copy was like these five and written by a master scribe. Someone different wrote the single letter.

"Obviously, the first copyist made an error and it was repeated into the other copies. Mistakes do happen." Rufus blinked rapidly and flipped the lock of hair out of his eyes.

"In the Jewish traditions, mistakes do not happen. Scribes edit and catch each other's errors," Yechiel said.

Rufus shrugged his shoulders. "Why would anyone proofread a personal letter. The customer dictates what we write. He signs the letter, and we collect our fee. Nothing suggests the letters are anything but what Master Valerius said, copies of a letter between Christian friends, with a few minor mistakes."

"Flesh…spirit, spirit…flesh, thin ink…thick ink." Yechiel threw a scroll across the table. "None of this proves Valerius poisoned Benjamin. Or that Apollos didn't."

"No," Sabina said quietly. "But it means something, or Benjamin wouldn't be dead."

"It makes no difference...Valerius has escaped." The flat tone of Yechiel's voice echoed her exhaustion.

"My father will capture Valerius. Of that, I am certain," Sabina said. "Valerius is probably in custody this very minute."

"If Valerius is Benjamin's murderer, we are no closer to proving his motive than we were three days ago...we are out of time."

"It is late. We can wait for word of Valerius's arrest at my house." Sabina gathered the six scrolls and placed them in one of the smaller baskets that had held some of Valerius's writing tools.

"What about these." Rufus pointed to the discarded basket of papyrus scrolls.

"We do not have time..." Sabina trailed off.

"I can read them," Rufus said.

Sabina raised her eyebrows. "Zarmig will be furious if we leave you."

"You can trust me. I, too, am searching for answers. I am confused about Master Valerius. My feelings tell me he is innocent."

"Your feelings?" Sabina asked. "What about the Word of God? You dismiss thousands of years of fulfilled prophecy and Jesus's miracles to rely on your feelings?"

"I cannot explain my experiences. Master Valerius is a prophet of the mysteries. When he prayed with me, I felt the presence of the divine spark for the first time in my life. It touched me." Rufus looked at the floor. His hair fell into his eyes. He did not push it back.

"I am sure your experience seemed heartfelt, but feelings are highly untrustworthy," Sabina said. "Emotions are easily manipulated. A false foundation leads to false—"

"I prayed. I know what I feel is true." Rufus raised his head.

"Prayed to whom?" Sabina asked.

"How can I explain it to one who does not seek the path to eternal truth?" Rufus pursed his lips.

"Our eternal truths are conspicuously different," Sabina said.

"The teachings of the prophet do not permit murder," Rufus said. "Let me stay and read the remainder of the scrolls. I swear on the eternal Father God and Christ His holy messenger if I have unwittingly played a role in Benjamin's death, I will accept the consequences. I wish to help."

"And if you find proof of your prophet's crime?" Yechiel asked accusingly.

"What we have found proves my master committed no crime, and I did not commit this sin." His shoulders drooped, and his hands lay limp at his side. He said no more.

Sabina did not trust Rufus, but her options were limited. She could waste time arguing with him…time she didn't have if she was to meet Marcus. It would be dark in less than four hours. The tides wouldn't wait. "I will inform my father of your help," Sabina said.

Yechiel stomped away from the scrolls scowling at Rufus. "And we tell your father the murderer poisoned Benjamin as punishment for miscopying an obscure Christian belief?"

"Benjamin didn't copy any of these scrolls." Sabina grabbed the small basket of parchment scrolls. "Valerius lied about the parchment and hid the letters. We have to find out why."

"It's a fool's quest," Yechiel grumbled under his breath and followed her.

TWENTY-FOUR

When they arrived at Sabina's home, they encountered Magistrate Catius Sabinus as he slammed out of the front door. He strode to a waiting horse. The guard who had delivered the animal from the stables sat astride a second horse.

"Did you capture Valerius?" Sabina asked.

"He is in my custody."

Sabina gave a knowing nod to Yechiel.

"He fled directly to my office, demanding protection from Zarmig and your inquisition." Her father took the reins and hoisted himself into the saddle.

"What?" Sabina's mouth opened in disbelief.

"I am meeting him and Zarmig at my office." Her father mounted his horse with the strength and flexibility of a man ten years younger than his fifty-eight years. The horse spun around. Her father reined in the bit.

"Then Apollos will be set free?" Sabina asked.

"Zarmig said Valerius swears he is innocent." Catius looped his rein around his hand and turned his horse to face Sabina. The horse pranced.

"Valerius poisoned Benjamin," Sabina said.

"Then present your evidence against him tonight. We will deliver him to the prison holding your priest, Apollos. One of them will go free." He pulled the reins, turning the horse, and galloped toward

Curetes Street and his office at the State Agora.

"The evidence?" Sabina looked at the bag containing six scrolls.

The only facts she could testify to were that someone had changed a couple of words in a private letter and that Valerius was the prophet of an illegal cult. And Valerius had taken the only physical evidence of his involvement…the mask. She was trying to free the bishop of a banned religion by accusing Valerius of being the leader of a banned religion. If the situation were not so dire, she would have laughed. But it was Apollos who was innocent and under arrest and Valerius who was guilty and free. There had to be something in the letters. Benjamin risked stealing and dying for something.

"We will wait at the prison." Yechiel began walking. Not knowing what else to do, Sabina followed.

The same guard blocked the prison door. "The prison is closed to visitors. No one is allowed in at night."

"It's not night yet." Sabina was acutely aware of exactly when the sun would set tonight. The shadows were lengthening as the sun hovered above the horizon, but fading daylight persisted. She estimated two hours before nightfall. God would not make her choose between a future with Marcus or Apollos's life.

"Magistrate Catius Sabinus and Zarmig directed us to meet them here today. We need to speak to the prisoner."

"Zarmig?" he looked behind Sabina. "I have had no new orders."

"The Magistrate, my father, is this minute, hunting a murderer. The prisoner has information that will aid in apprehending the villain." Sabina emphasized the words *my father* using the authority she knew guards were accustomed to hearing. Please, God set Apollos free tonight, Sabina prayed fervently. "We will see the prisoner. Now."

"I cannot allow anyone in without Zarmig's permission."

She knew the command her father held over his soldiers. A commander's authority, combined with their loyalty, meant only their leader's directives were law. These municipal guards were slaves and, unlike trained soldiers, were used to obeying orders from any superior. How far could she push her privileged status? "Are you saying I would lie about an order from my father, an official magistrate, the Eirenarch of Ephesus?"

Sabina watched the guard's gaze skitter from Sabina to the prison door, then back, indecision at his two losing options. "No one is allowed to speak to the prisoner."

"Do you think that is what my father meant when he ordered me to meet him here today? That I would be turned away and kept waiting outside in the cold…by a slave?"

"No, I…I," he stuttered.

Sabina pounced. "We have spoken to the prisoner here multiple times. Magistrate Catius Sabinus will not be pleased."

"If you are concerned about him escaping," Yechiel held his hands up in a harmless gesture, "you could lock us in with him until Magistrate Catius arrives."

Sabina visualized the family water clock drip, drip, drip. How much time before the tide went out? Marcus hovered in the back of her mind. He would wait at her house until the last possible minute. Amisi would see to that.

The guard shuffled from foot to foot. His head turned toward the street as if hoping to see her father riding to his rescue. The street stood empty. He pulled his keys from his belt. "Your bag is not allowed. And no weapons."

Yechiel removed a knife he had strapped to his belt and handed it to the guard.

"I carry nothing but scrolls," Sabina hurried to open the bag. The guard rummaged through the pack and passed it back.

Sabina and Yechiel waited while the guard, taking his time, unlocked the door and let them inside. "These visitors are here on orders from Magistrate Catius Sabinus." He addressed the jailer with an arrogance Sabina guessed was hiding his doubts. "They are here to interrogate the prisoner." He turned them over to the jailer with a frown and left.

Sabina pulled her mantel up to hide her smile.

The jailer locked the door to the outside. They followed him as he took a torch from the wall and led them down the hewn hall and deeper into the jail. Sabina recognized the metal banded door blockading Apollos's cell. He opened the door and motioned them into the black hole.

"You will leave the torch," Sabina said, imitating her father's tone. The guard nodded, placing the torch in a wall bracket. He closed the door, locking them inside.

Again the smell assaulted her before her eyes were able to adjust to the dimness. A shiver of foreboding ran up her arms.

Apollos leaned against the wall, wheezing in his sleep, a blanket drooped off his shoulders.

"Apollos, it is Sabina." She knelt beside him, relieved he was alive.

He woke, blinking rapidly at the sudden light in the blackness of his cell. He looked much the same. The blankets' warmth and the food had kept him alive…for his beheading. She pushed that thought away.

"An angel of good news?" Apollos coughed, but his voice sounded stronger.

"I hope so. I bring a mystery scroll. Are you well enough to look at it?" Sabina knelt and felt his forehead. Damp with fever before, it now felt cool to her touch. She held his hands, cold fingers, but he squeezed back, not the limp grip of before.

"I feel stronger. The stew, the blankets were a blessing. They provided hope." He coughed again, but the coughing did not persist nor rack his body. And his eyes lit up with interest when he asked, "A mystery scroll?"

"Scrolls." Yechiel crouched down and took one scroll at a time from the basket and laid them at the feet of Apollos.

Apollos sat up straighter and adjusted the chains around his ankles. "Six," he counted.

"Do you remember the scraps of burnt parchment I showed you?" Sabina asked. "The ashes in Benjamin's room match the parchment and the wording of these scrolls. I believe Benjamin stole one, or more, of these letters from the scriptorium."

"Stealing is a grave sin. What would possess Benjamin to steal?" Apollos reached for one of the scrolls.

"We are hoping you can answer that," she said.

"When we visited the scriptorium and asked for Valerius's help, he lied to us," Yechiel said.

"The highest leaders of the church trust Valerius. He has risked his life for Christ and his church."

Sabina shook her head. "Valerius has been lying to the church leaders. He is the head of a gnostic fellowship. He conducted the ceremony I attended. He led the rituals."

"The prophet at Hekate's Grotto?" Apollos gasped.

Sabina nodded. "I found a mask among Valerius's private papers. It was the mask the prophet wore at the grotto."

"A mask could hide the face of anyone." Apollos's voice was losing conviction, and his face paled.

"It was in his office. He took it and fled," Sabina said. "I believe he is hiding information concerning Benjamin's death. Valerius may have poisoned Benjamin."

"That is impossible." Apollos's chains rattled as he spoke.

"You poisoning Benjamin is impossible," Sabina said. "Valerius fled, leaving these scrolls. Five are identical. One scroll differs by a few words."

"Scribes make mistakes," Apollos said, raising his hands. His chains stopped his gesture.

"And a different person wrote it," Sabina added. "I believe Benjamin died because of the scrolls, and if he did, they are proof of your innocence."

"You would accuse Valerius of murder based on a few incorrect words? I will not be a part of this."

"There is other evidence." Sabina related the sequence of events the night Benjamin and Rufus copied the letter. "Benjamin found something disturbing in the letter. Rufus said Benjamin had one section read aloud multiple times. Rufus alleged Valerius delivered the Isaiah scroll to the church shortly before Benjamin died. Valerius had the opportunity to poison Benjamin. I believe something written in these letters prompted his murder. I just don't know what."

"I did not kill Benjamin." Apollos pushed the scrolls away from him. "But I will not have an innocent man take my place."

"Read the letters. If there is nothing in them…" You will die, she thought. "Valerius will come to no harm."

"I am tired. Valerius is a trusted follower."

"Please, it won't take long," Sabina pleaded.

Apollos took the scroll she handed to him.

"Thank you," she said.

Apollos unrolled the scroll part way. He squinted, put it down, and rubbed his eyes. He picked it up again and held it, almost touching his nose. "I cannot see to read."

"The torch." Sabina gestured toward the wall.

Yechiel brought it to Apollos.

He covered his eyes and shook his head. "I have been too long in the dark."

"I will read it." Sabina took the scroll from Apollos. "This scroll differs from the others." She read the lines Rufus had repeated to Benjamin. "Every spirit that confesses that Jesus Christ is come in the flesh is of God."

Apollos frowned. "Valerius wrote these?"

"Valerius told us the writer was a Christian who wanted copies made for two friends," she said.

"But we found six letters, not two," Yechiel said.

Sabina pointed to the parchments. "I believe Benjamin took the letter he copied and perhaps the one Rufus was reading and burnt them. That would make eight letters."

Apollos stared at the letters. "Whoever wrote this has a sophisticated understanding of Christianity."

"Valerius said it was a simple man," Yechiel said.

"Simple words, perhaps," Apollos said. "But it depicts a concept found in the Gospels and the letters of the apostles: a Christian concept we profess but which defies human comprehension, the nature of Jesus Christ as fully God and fully human."

"Beyond human comprehension…and reason," Yechiel added.

"It is the core of our Christian belief, our faith, our trust," Sabina said.

Yechiel took one of the other scrolls. "Here is one of the five that differs." He read the same verses. "'By this you know the Spirit of God: Every spirit that confesses that Jesus Christ is come in the spirit is of God.' The scribe wrote *spirit* in place of *flesh*."

Apollos sat quietly. He did not move for several minutes as he reread the scroll. "I do not think the scribe made a random mistake. Flesh and spirit are opposites," Apollos said.

"Rufus said the wording didn't matter," Sabina said.

"Someone carefully chose those two words." Apollos lifted one letter. "This first letter affirms Christian beliefs. The second states a gnostic heresy that is spreading and seeks to destroy the foundation of our faith. I would say the two words matter very much."

"Valerius is a Gnostic," Sabina said.

"So is Rufus," Yechiel pointed out.

Apollos shook his head. "The letter Yechiel read teaches the gnostic belief that Jesus did not come to our world as a man in human flesh but only appeared to us as a spirit. If Jesus has no physical body, he could not die."

"And if he did not die, taking the punishment for the sins of man, we are condemned by God's perfect judgment. Our faith is worthless," Sabina said.

Yechiel looked puzzled. "Would Benjamin have known the letter he was copying was a gnostic belief?"

"He would have known it was not Christian," Apollos said. "There are many gnostic philosophies."

"Five copies were the gnostic letter," Yechiel said.

"Benjamin may not have known there were more copies," Sabina said. "Perhaps he thought he had destroyed them all."

Apollos shrugged his shoulders. "One or five, there are hundreds of false doctrines circulating. He could not set fire to them all. The only solution is to trust our original Gospels."

"If Benjamin stole the letters, it still doesn't tell us why someone poisoned him," Yechiel said. "Valerius had other letters."

Muffled noises from the outside corridor interrupted the conversation. A guard's voice grew louder.

"I do not believe Valerius is guilty." Apollos stifled a cough. "In a few hours, I may be dead."

"Do not say that." Sabina clutched his hands.

"It is a probability that I must face. Something has weighed on my heart for too long."

Sabina looked worried.

"It is my turn to request your attention. On your first visit to the prison, you asked about your mother. Zarmig interrupted us. Your mother warned me of his loyalty to your father."

"I know what you are going to say, and I don't need your answer. If my mother swore Amisi to silence and you cannot speak of it, her secret is best left in the past."

"I believed that too until I sat in this prison preparing to die. I don't think your mother would want this information to die with me."

"I loved my mother; her memory is all I have left."

"I too loved your mother—"

"Stop!" Sabina stood up. "Thank you for being willing to share your relationship, but I don't want to know."

"Your mother and I were friends, very dear friends. But I was not going to tell you about our relationship. Please."

Reluctantly Sabina sat.

"I was there the night of her last miscarriage, but the story goes beyond one night."

"Apollos, you don't have to…"

"You were told your mother had three miscarriages after your birth."

She nodded, wondering what that had to do with Apollos and her mother. "All daughters. My father made his displeasure known. He wanted a son."

"We men are accustomed to getting our way."

"Instead," she whispered, "my mother died from loss of blood."

"She did die from blood loss, but not from a miscarriage. The baby was born alive. In the years after you were born, your mother delivered three healthy girls."

Sabina sat mute, incapable of comment, movement, or denial. A spasm contracted her throat. She couldn't breathe. If his tale were not so wrong, Sabina would have gotten up and left. Apollos didn't or couldn't know such contradictory details of her family. She wanted to go, flee, but she sat, the spasm radiating throughout her body. Her legs were shaking upon hearing his lie.

"After the last birth, Amisi and the midwife could not stop the flow of blood. I watched as life drained from her; they tried everything they could. Your father, like the two births before, refused to acknowledge a female child."

Sabina sucked in a lifeline. She choked out. "That's not true. He accepted me." She had been correct to leave the past alone, but it was too late.

"Yes, God's blessings for that." He leaned forward and reached out, grasping her hands with weak fingers. "You are in shock. I understand."

"My mother would never have abandoned her…" Sabina couldn't finish. The thought seared her heart; she knew, without a doubt, her mother would never willingly give up her children.

And then another thought even more appalling crossed her mind. Sabina narrowed her eyes in accusation and jerked her hands from Apollos. "Husbands reject bastards every day, children they suspect are not their own. Was the baby illegitimate?" Her mental protests offered no relief as her life was dismantled before her eyes.

Apollos's eyes flew open wide enough for Sabina to see the whites registering shock. "Illegitimate? No, no!" In a belated understanding, he blushed, his dark skin deepening in color. Sabina did not think his eyes could grow any rounder. "Your mother's loyalty and love for your father was beyond question. She desired no one else."

Sabina wanted to believe him, but then she would have to acknowledge the choice her mother made. "No one told me."

"Your father feigned the deaths of the first two babies. He ordered Amisi to take the babies away as soon as they were born."

"My mother?"

"Your mother didn't know. He told her they were stillborn and swore Amisi to secrecy."

Sabina felt her heart drop into her stomach, taking with it her ability to think. She silently stared at Apollos as she attempted to absorb information that changed everything. Everything she knew about herself, her family, her life.

"Take them where?"

"I assume outside the city walls. Where unwanted babies die of exposure."

"Only the poor, families unable to feed another mouth do that," Sabina argued.

"It is not only the destitute who have unwanted and embarrassing pregnancies."

"But these were wanted."

"Yes, your mother wanted her children."

It had been her father. She closed her eyes, trying to absorb the revelation, trying to comprehend his actions. She could not. He had worked hard to build and protect the family and their fortunes. Was this his way to consolidate his wealth? "And Amisi?" Sabina could hardly speak.

"She took the first child and watched until someone claimed her."

"Oh, thank God." Sabina covered her mouth as a sob escaped. Tears flowed down her cheeks.

"Your mother mourned the death of the first baby. Amisi didn't add to her misery. However, after the second birth, your mother heard crying. She questioned Amisi until Amisi broke her promise and confessed that the child had lived. She had taken the second baby and given it away to a family she knew."

"I don't understand. How could Father have done this to his own children?"

"You have been taught to value human life, Sabina. It is not so for everyone. Amisi told your mother the first girl carried a red mark spreading from her cheek down her neck and the second had a deformed foot."

Sabina nodded. "Father would never accept deformity in one of his offspring. He is a vain man. When did you learn of these births?"

"I did not know until I witnessed the last birth and your mother's death. I know only what Amisi shared with me of the others."

"My mother asked you to attend her?"

"No, your father summoned me when your mother was dying."

"My father? I don't understand. I thought you—"

"I believed he summoned me to provide spiritual comfort for a Christian friend. When I arrived, she lay in a bed of blood, nearly unconscious. The baby was born shortly after. I had to deduce much as your father did not speak during the birth or after, except to warn me to tell no one about the child. His obvious agony at your mother's death shattered him."

"His love for my mother does not absolve him."

"He did not expose the baby," Apollos said. "It would not be uncommon for a female infant born to a dying wife."

"He made his decisions based on pride."

"Or grief. Your father remained by your mother's side for hours after she died. When Amisi placed the child in my arms, she directed me to leave her with a Christian family."

"He promised my mother I would be allowed to practice my faith. She must have extracted the same promise for the baby. Amisi said mother died of a broken heart."

"She carried a deep sorrow in her heart, but despair didn't control her. She had a daughter to raise and stayed strong for you and her love for your father," Apollos said.

"Amisi had no choice. She is a slave. But I will never forgive my father."

"He let you live. Your mother loved him for that. Her love for you overcame her grief. Perhaps your father reciprocated her love by allowing your sister to live."

Sabina said in a tone of wonder. "I have a sister."

"Three if they survived."

Sabina pressed her lips together until they turned white. She couldn't absolve her father so quickly. "This Christian family, who are they? Do they live in Ephesus? Do you know my...sister?" The word sounded foreign.

"One of the reasons I did not share this information with you is because I have nothing helpful to disclose. The family was traveling from Syria to Rome. They stopped in Ephesus for a short time. I thought it safer for Leah to be away from your father. I would have no idea if they reached their destination."

"Leah?"

"Her baptized name."

"I would like to find her. Help me."

Apollos reached out and took her hands in his. "Your father swore Amisi and me to silence. He did not want the child. If he found out you were searching, it could endanger Leah or turn your father against you. That is not a risk your mother would want you to take. Forgive me. I have placed my burden on you."

"Burden? How could siblings be a burden to an only child?" The idea of having sisters jumbled her thoughts and her emotions. It changed everything. The burden would be living with her father. How did you forgive after a betrayal so intimate? How had her mother found the strength? She pushed thoughts of her father from her consciousness and walled off the emotions about to overwhelm her, her hate, her confusion, her anger. Next, she had many, many questions for Amisi.

Sabina tensed, hearing the bolt slide free and the lock to the cell click.

"Thank you for telling me." Sabina rose.

Zarmig swung the door open and entered. "Magistrate Catius has arrived."

"My father will see justice done." Sabina bent and squeezed Apollos's hand. But after Apollos's news, she was no longer confident her father knew what justice was. She stood and crossed the cell to Zarmig. "Has Valerius been captured?"

"In a manner of speaking." Zarmig held the door open for her and Yechiel.

"What do you mean?" Sabina stopped.

"After Valerius escaped and ran to your father, he asserted his innocence. He is suing you for defamation, saying his arrest was entrapment."

"A trap?" Sabina raised her eyebrows, not believing what she was hearing.

"He is shrewd," Yechiel said.

"Surely, my father does not believe him." Sabina shook her head, trying to make sense of the turn of events.

"If Valerius brings this before the governor, it won't matter what your father believes. Valerius is passionate that you are the guilty one. Come with me." Zarmig gestured to her and Yechiel.

"And Apollos?" She asked.

"Apollos stays," Zarmig said.

Sabina turned to look at the chained man. "He was to be released tonight."

"Go." Apollos gestured toward the door. "Do not fear for me."

She turned back to Apollos and knelt. She clutched his hands. "Valerius will not get away with his lies." She opened her mouth, wanting to add words of encouragement, but her lips closed in silence.

"Have faith, Sabina. Believe what the author of the Christian letter wrote, it is the Spirit that bears witness, because the Spirit is truth." Apollos said. "We bow to the will of God."

Sabina stood and dragged her feet as if the floor were a sea of sand.

Yechiel gathered the scrolls, put them in the basket.

She stared at the scrolls and ignored Zarmig's impatient tapping on the door. She mumbled, "The author of the letter." She spun and ran back to Apollos. She knelt. "Valerius refused to tell us who wrote the letter…the words *it is the Spirit that bears witness, because the Spirit is truth.*"

Apollos patted her hand. "Take comfort in those words."

"Sabina, your father is waiting," Zarmig said.

Sabina leaned toward Apollos, gripping his hands tightly in hers, and whispered in his ear.

Apollos's eyes widened, and he replied. "At Nathan the potter's house, near the market agora."

"I can prove you did not kill Benjamin. My father will free you tonight." Sabina stood rapidly and hastened out of the cell.

Yechiel handed the basket of scrolls to Sabina. Zarmig looked on suspiciously as she took the one scroll Apollos had indicated was Christian and gave it to Yechiel.

Zarmig grabbed the torch, slammed the door, and slid the bolt home. He escorted them down the short hallway. "Amisi gave me a rather ominous message to deliver."

"I think I know." Sabina bit her lip.

"You must return home immediately before it is too late. A litter is waiting outside the door."

"I have time," Sabina said with certainty. She knew Apollos would be released as soon as she spoke to her father. Sabina stopped Yechiel outside the door. "Show your scroll to the potter Nathan near the market agora. I pray I am right, and you return immediately."

Yechiel's brows lifted in question, but before he had a chance to speak, they entered the prison's outer office. Sabina closed her eyes in the sudden glare of lamplight. When she opened them, she gave a startled jerk, standing between two of her father's guards were Valerius and Pistus.

TWENTY-FIVE

A solitary jailer ushered Sabina and Yechiel into the small outer office and stared into the mocking smile of Valerius. Zarmig wedged himself in between the jailer and the door guard. None of the men moved aside as Sabina and Yechiel squeezed into the room. Sabina pushed past Zarmig to stand opposite the two men guarding the door. The only open space surrounded her father, who sat buffered behind the jailer's table.

Valerius glanced at her. He sniffed disdainfully, put a napkin to his nose, fending off the odors of sweat, urine, and blood escaping from the prison cells, then looked away.

Pistus looked at her, cleared his throat, then mimicked his master, sniffing and turning away.

Sabina scrutinized Valerius. She assumed he had received the same treatment by the guards as Davos. She expected to see the same bruises and welts found on Apollos, but Valerius carried no scarlet bruising. His hair fell neatly in place, his robe spotless.

"I demand this matter be cleared up immediately," Valerius's voice rose in an imperious tone. "I have magisterial friends who—"

"You demand?" Catius rose from his chair.

Valerius countered. "I am bringing indictments of defamation and harassment against an innocent Roman citizen."

Pushing aside the conflict raging inside her, Sabina watched her father. Processing her family revelation would have to wait. Apollos needed her now. Her father assessed Valerius, his eyes turning dark at Valerius's brazen threat. "This is not a trial," Magistrate Catius addressed Valerius. "I am in charge and will determine if there is cause to issue a formal accusation against anyone in this room."

"I believe that exceeds the responsibilities of your position as a magistrate," Valerius countered.

Valerius's boldness in challenging her father either was a daring bluff or Valerius had influential friends. Sabina's brows drew together in nervous thought. Either scenario posed a danger. Charges of defamation would expose Valerius as well as Sabina. If Valerius was willing to carry out his threat, her father must strategize against the possibility of offending the scriptorium owner's powerful allies.

"Worthy Valerius. Our governor does not permit murderers running free within the city," her father said. Sabina pictured two leopards circling each other, assessing each other's prowess, cunning, and survival skills.

"Nor do I. I promise to do everything in my power to assure the man you have arrested is tried and executed for Benjamin's murder," Valerius said.

And eliminate all suspicion from yourself. Sabina hoped her father saw through this ruse.

Her father bowed to Valerius. "I request only a few minutes of your time to clear up this misunderstanding."

Sabina looked from her father to Valerius. "Misunderstanding! Valerius killed a man. He ran from us when we confronted him with the evidence."

Her father glared at her but said nothing. He sat at the table. "I will hear evidence from both sides."

Sabina looked at Yechiel then back to her father. She read Yechiel's thoughts, not difficult since he had voiced them a hundred times. They had no evidence to present. "Sir," Sabina stepped forward, bumping into the guard on her left and Yechiel on her right. "Is it necessary for everyone to remain here? Yechiel's statement will be identical to mine and Zarmig's. It's late. He needn't stay."

Her father's eyes narrowed into a cunning glare. He tipped his head and addressed Yechiel sternly. "Does the Jew wish to revoke his right to testify in the murder of his brother? You will not have another chance."

Yechiel's jaw tightened. He fingered the cord of the scroll and hesitated. Looking over at Sabina, he shrugged and lowered the rolled parchment to his side. "I agree to accept the testimony of your freeman, Zarmig. We witnessed the same events."

Her father frowned and stroked his chin, nodding to Zarmig.

Zarmig's face played through several quizzical expressions before he turned to Sabina's father. "The facts are straightforward. I will make a statement."

Sabina looked at her feet. Zarmig knew her too well. Could he read her expression now? Had she made a terrible miscalculation by asking Yechiel to leave? What if she needed Yechiel to bolster her case against Valerius? Without his errand, she had no case. She bit her lip and winced. She had already chewed it raw. If Yechiel failed, Apollos would die.

"If that is your wish, you may go." Her father waved him off. The two guards near the door parted.

Yechiel pushed the door ajar. Twilight filtered in from outside.

Her father pointed to the jailer's table he was sitting behind. "Yechiel will leave the scroll. I understand it is evidence."

Yechiel dropped his hand from the door latch, paused, and looked over at Sabina, who met his eyes. He walked back and deposited the scroll on the table, then turned and left without looking at anyone.

Sabina bit her bottom lip until it bled. Her hands shook. She wanted to cry but would not give Valerius or her father the satisfaction.

"Sabina," her father motioned to her. "You are free to join him. Stop this now. Consider the consequences of this misunderstanding."

He was giving her a way out, a way to go home. Her father knew. Of course, he knew. About the marriage proposal, Marcus sailing to Rome, dusk's deadline. Was there a note of entreating, of concern for her future? She scanned the room, stopping at the jailer's door, behind which Apollos lay chained. Or was this the easiest way for this problem to go away? Their eyes locked. "It's not a misunderstanding," she whispered. "I'll stay."

For the first time in her life, her father looked away first, then nodded. "Very well."

Valerius's snide voice snapped her to attention. "It is obvious you have nothing to hold me on. If you are letting people go, I demand my slave, and I be released immediately."

"Innocent men do not run," Sabina's voice quivered. She had to stall for time. She had to stay here all night if needed until Yechiel returned…if Yechiel returned.

"Persecuted men do." Valerius pointed a long-manicured finger at Sabina. "You ransacked my home. I fled because of some absurd plot this deranged woman dreamt up." Valerius's voice dripped with rebuke. A look of loathing flashed across his face, replaced with the cold air of dismissing a poorly behaved pet. "Now that we have nothing more to deliberate. I have an appointment in the country." Valerius moved toward the door. The two guards flanking him shifted, blocking the entrance. Valerius spun, facing Catius.

"I will hear the testimony of all the witnesses assembled here." Catius looked over at Sabina. "State your grievance."

Sabina stood silent. Her thoughts were whirling away like dandelion puffs in the wind. All she could think of was Yechiel returning to his home and Apollos being sentenced to death because she had failed to find anything to convict Valerius. She hefted the basket full of scrolls. Arguing theological doctrines would mean nothing to her father. Portia said when God asks us to do the impossible, He will provide. Dear God, make Your grace sufficient for me, and Your power perfected in my weakness.

"There, you see? Nothing." Valerius waved his arms. "I refuse to be humiliated by this woman's vengeful imaginings. I am innocent, and unless she can prove—"

"We have proof," Sabina stammered. "We found your mask."

"What significance is this mask?" her father asked.

"The mask is a sacred symbol of my religion," Valerius said. "It in no way interferes with my allegiance to our esteemed lord and emperor. I dutifully offer sacrifices of incense at the Temple of the Sabestoi. My beliefs do not prohibit such earthly tributes."

Her father nodded his approval.

Sabina wanted to say, of course, if you killed a man, what would stop you from sacrificing to Rome's gods? "You killed Benjamin because he stole something from you." Sabina's hands shook as she untied her leather pouch and dumped the burnt parchment pieces on the table in front of her father. "I found this letter in Benjamin's room."

Valerius laughed. Pistus sniggered. Even the guards chuckled.

"Sabina?" Her father's voice reverberated with a warning.

"These scraps of garbage prove nothing." Valerius narrowed his gaze accusingly and pointed his finger at her. "You could have planted them in Benjamin's room."

"Me? That is ridiculous." How had she ended up defending herself against Valerius's twisted lies?

"No more ridiculous than the accusation I murdered Benjamin for stealing a letter. Magistrate Catius, I demand you return my property immediately."

"He can't have the letters." Sabina whipped around and faced her father. She could not let Valerius take the scrolls. "They are not his."

"I have already admitted the mask is mine, and Zarmig can verify the letters were in the same basket at my home."

"Zarmig?" her father nodded to him.

"We found the letters at Valerius's home. In the same basket as the mask."

Valerius stepped toward Sabina and reached for the container holding the scrolls. "Now, my wife has had a very long day."

"If that is all you have, Sabina, Valerius may go. Give him his scrolls."

Sabina looked desperately at her father. "Benjamin knew—"

"That is enough, Sabina. Give the man the scrolls." Her father raised his voice.

Sabina dropped the basket but grabbed the Christian scroll from the desk. "You can't have this one."

"Sabina!" Her father's voice deepened into a threat.

"It's not his," she pleaded.

"Prove it." Valerius held out his hand as he advanced toward Sabina. "I copied all the letters."

She clutched the scroll behind her back, crushing it in her fist.

"Give him the scroll, or I will have you thrown into the same cell as your beloved priest," her father said, bearing down on her. Valerius advanced from the opposite side.

The jail's front door slammed into the back of one of the guards standing in front of it. Surprised, everyone in the room spun around, their heads swiveling to stare at Yechiel, poking his head around the partially opened door. Outside was bathed in total darkness. "May I come in?"

"I said I could prove the scroll doesn't belong to Valerius." Sabina nearly burst into tears.

She watched her father glaring at Yechiel, but he directed his question to her. His display of gritted white teeth showed the measure of control it took to contain his temper and the situation. "What antics are you playing at, woman?"

"Please, let him in." Sabina turned to Yechiel. "Were you successful?"

"Yes," Yechiel gasped, sucking in deep breaths. Sabina noted his sweat-soaked bangs were curling off his forehead.

"Please." Sabina swallowed hard. "Valerius demanded proof. I have it. Yechiel has it."

Her father glowered at her. "Yechiel forfeited his right to confront Valerius."

"There is a new witness," Sabina said.

Her father ignored her plea and gestured for the guards to block Yechiel from entering.

Valerius flashed a sneer of triumph at Sabina. "I am leaving." He flicked his wrist at Pistus, giving the order to follow. "Out of my way." The guards didn't move.

Sabina watched her father's lips curl away from his teeth. "You asked for proof," he said, firmly establishing who was in control. "You'll want to stay to hear it."

"A testimony of truth this time," Sabina said.

"Admit Yechiel. Everyone else outside," her father gestured toward the door. "Not you two." He pointed toward Valerius and Sabina, then nodded toward Pistus. "Zarmig, keep a close watch on that one." Her father's two guards, the jailer, the door guard, and Zarmig, dragged a whining Pistus from the jailer's chamber.

Valerius stood motionless, his eyes gleaming and his chin raised. "I will end your career, Catius Sabinus."

The three turned at the sound of the door latch. Zarmig opened the door. "Yechiel has the evidence."

"Let's finish this." Her father nodded his assent.

Zarmig flourished Yechiel in, followed by a wheezing and gasping, hunched over figure concealed beneath a dark cloak. "Let me help." Sabina went and lifted the covering off a wizened and frail older man.

"This is your evidence?" her father spat, obviously irritated.

Sabina addressed her father. "Sir, may I introduce the apostle John. You may have heard of him. Our emperor repealed his banishment from Patmos recently. John, this is Magistrate Catius Sabinus."

"Magistrate." John bowed his head, then bent over and inhaled deeply. "I apologize…a minute to catch my breath."

"May he sit down?" Sabina asked.

Her father waved dismissively to a stool and frowned. "I have heard of you." His stoic scowl did not match the glint of curiosity in his eyes as he looked down at the stooped man. "You continue to defy the invincible Roman Empire, insisting your Rabbi Jesus rose from the dead. My daughter worships him as a God."

They waited until John's wheezing slowed, and he looked up and smiled. "We worship the one invincible God." Yechiel slid one of the guard's stools under him. For the first time, Sabina noticed John carrying a scroll. He set it on his lap. "Greetings, Valerius."

Valerius's eyes narrowed, but he said nothing.

Her father stared hard, looking from John to Sabina. "If this theatric is not pertinent to—"

Sabina held up the scroll she had been clutching. "This letter is John's. He dictated it to his scribe, Prochorus."

"And what is the scroll you have in your lap?" her father asked John.

John held up the scroll. "This," he took a deep breath, "is my original letter. I gave a copy of it to Valerius."

Sabina clutched the crunched scroll.

"When my scribe became ill, he wasn't able to transcribe the additional six copies I required, so I took one letter to my friend, Valerius, and hired him to finish the task. I thought I had entrusted it to a fellow believer in Jesus the Christ."

Sabina noted the word *thought*. Yechiel must have explained the necessity of John's witness. "While in his possession, Valerius falsified its contents and forged the other letters," Sabina said.

"Forgery! Will this woman's fiction never end?" Valerius said, his voice pitched higher than before. "I copied the letters as directed."

"You just claimed them as yours," her father said.

"It is my work I claimed," Valerius screeched.

"I will examine the letters." Sabina's father gestured. Yechiel took John's letter and laid it beside the letter Sabina unrolled on the table.

"Identical ink, parchment, and uneven script," Yechiel pointed out.

"Do you admit the letters are John's?" Her father glared at Valerius.

Valerius's face had drained of color. He remained silent.

"I have seen enough. It is obvious the letters belong to John," her father said. "You have laid out your case for Valerius stealing John's letter. And now we have two thieves. Valerius took this letter from John. And Benjamin allegedly stole letters from Valerius. I see nothing proving murder," her father said.

Color flooded back into Valerius's face, and he nodded vigorously. "As I said. The letters prove nothing."

"They prove you lied." Her father pointed to John's scrolls. "You swore you wrote all the scrolls."

"A minor misunderstanding." Valerius shrugged. "I did not steal the letters. I was packing the finished letters to return to John when this woman disrupted the transfer, and this entire farce began."

"You did not think it was minor when Benjamin found out you were altering John's letter by changing the text to your gnostic beliefs." Sabina felt the tension gathering in her shoulders. Valerius would not escape again.

"The council of seven prominent bishops were each to receive a letter," John said. "Their churches would have reproduced hundreds of copies and distributed them throughout the Empire. Each letter believed to be composed by me, endorsed with my apostolic authority… and spreading a fatal inaccuracy."

"Hardly fatal. Mistakes happen," Valerius said.

"Is that a confession?" her father asked.

"I confess the letters may have inadvertent errors. It has nothing to do with Benjamin's death."

"That is not true," Sabina said. "Benjamin had visited John a few days before his murder. John shared his letter. The very letter Benjamin found himself copying the night before he died…except it wasn't the same. He knew what John had written originally, and he knew someone had changed it. Did Benjamin confront you when you came to the church?"

"I was never there," Valerius sputtered.

"A witness saw you delivering the Isaiah scroll," Sabina said. "And they will testify you had access to Benjamin's wine."

Valerius lost his façade of composure. His gaze skittered between Sabina and her father as if weighing his odds. Then he raised his chin defiantly. "I didn't know why Benjamin took the letters. When I went to the church to deliver the Isaiah scroll, he admitted he was the thief. I demanded them back."

"You knew Benjamin would report it to someone, Apollos or John," Sabina said.

"Where are the stolen letters?" her father asked.

"Benjamin told me he had destroyed them…burnt them," Valerius rubbed his hands together and glanced at the pile of fragments on the desk.

"Everyone would have missed the changes, except my brother," Yechiel said. "He had the gift to memorize after one reading. He could have recited John's letter down to the last word. It's why he was a renowned scribe. When he destroyed the proof of your betrayal, he signed his death warrant."

"Don't be ridiculous." Valerius shook his head. "I thanked him for his diligence in discovering the imperfections. Benjamin agreed that ended it. I was shocked by his death." He wiped away an invisible tear.

John's body shook. "It was I who shook in despair and shock. Benjamin had sent an urgent message requesting to see me before the worship service," John's voice grew vibrant, strengthening beyond the reedy timbre of an elderly man. "I told him to wait until the next day. When I found out why Benjamin didn't show up, I knew he wanted to tell me something important."

"Benjamin had all the pieces to destroy you," Sabina said. "He had put them together and understood the forged letters were not the end of it, but the beginning. The foundation of your new religion."

"Jesus's resurrection is the evidence He is who He claimed to be and what He taught is true." John explained. "Benjamin understood the doubts your false words would sow." He pointed to Valerius. "The letters were a written testimony by me, the last apostle given authority to speak the words of Jesus Christ. You sought to twist God's truths through treachery and deceit and murder."

"Who says what truth is?" Valerius bared his teeth. "You? A wheezing senile, nearly blind cripple whose strange visions no one understands. Who made you the authority?"

"The Holy Spirit of the living God," John answered.

Valerius laughed. "Your God is pathetic. Who wants a grieving, crucified servant for their God?"

John spoke as if to a child. "The needy, the abused, the sick, and dying who know God understands their suffering and sin. Those who seek love and forgiveness."

"Your words will die with you, old man," Valerius smirked.

"My words, yes," John said. "But God promises 'The grass withers, the flower fades: but the word of our God shall stand forever.'"

Her father stood up and faced Valerius. "You are under arrest for the murder of Benjamin ben Jonah."

The smirking smile fell from Valerius's face. Zarmig reached for Valerius's arm, but he lurched back, straightening his shoulders, and with a tone of superiority, announced, "This is not over. You will all soon understand what suffering is." He strode toward the door, jerking to a halt in front of Sabina, and hissed, "Benjamin's attempt to stop destiny failed, as will yours." He bolted out the door. Zarmig followed at his heels, pulling Pistus behind him.

The stars were firmly fixed in the night sky when Sabina left the prison. She offered the litter Amisi had ordered to Apollos and John. The men gratefully accepted. John tottered as one of the litter carriers helped him inside. Apollos clambered in bruised, coughing, and weak, and John tucked him under his cloak.

"I am quite pleased with myself," John yawned.

"For solving Benjamin's murder?" Sabina asked.

"No, that victory belongs to God and you, Sabina." For a second, John's eyes lit up like a young boy. "When Yechiel insisted I run through town, I told him he asked the impossible. But God gave me the stamina to fulfill His purpose, although I didn't understand what that purpose was." His eyes fluttered closed. "I feel quite youthful."

Sabina smiled. "When God requires the impossible, He provides the means."

Apollos leaned out of the litter. "Sabina, how did you know the letter was John's?"

John opened his eyes and nodded. "There was no signature, nor had I affixed my seal to it." He lifted his hand, showing the ring with his unique symbol that, when pressed into wax, guaranteed the message was his.

"I recognized the words," Sabina said. "Apollos reminded me of the verse 'it is the Spirit that bears witness, because the Spirit is truth.'"

"But no one knew about my letter except my scribe, Valerius, and Benjamin," John said.

"The day Benjamin visited you. He brought a friend with him, Livia."

"Ah, I remember that dear child. She had been badgering him with a list of questions. Benjamin was having a difficult time answering them all." John chuckled.

"Livia recited your verse to me when we were having a conversation about ghosts," Sabina said.

John smiled. "She included ghosts in her list. She did not seem convinced by the reasoning of an old man."

"I think she understood more than you realize. She and Benjamin had been memorizing verses. That one must have meant something to her because she quoted it exactly as you had written it in your letter," Sabina said. "Then, when Apollos read the verse, I realized that you were the author of the Christian letter."

"Benjamin was naïve," Yechiel said. "He did not believe someone he trusted could be such a deceitful serpent."

"And he thought that by destroying the two letters, he could stop the spread of Valerius's ideas," Apollos said.

"He recognized the evil too late. It is what the Spirit of God warned about at the end of the age." John quoted his letter. "Beloved, do not believe every spirit, but test the spirits to see whether they are from God. For many false prophets have gone out into the world. By this you know the Spirit of God: Every spirit that confesses that Jesus Christ is come in the flesh is of God."

"The only way to test the spirits is against God's Word," Sabina said. "Benjamin did that."

"Yes, he was obedient, even unto death. God has taken our gifted scribe home, and I still have six letters that need copied," John said.

"You need care and rest." Sabina pulled the curtains shut, and the carriers trotted off. "God's blessing to you."

TWENTY-SIX

Portia and Sabina held hands and strolled the short distance from Portia's house to the harbor, listening to the early morning cawing of the seabirds swooping and diving for their breakfast. Sabina sucked in a lungful of tangy sea air, salty seaweed, and tar. "I will miss spring's fresh air once summer's stifling heat sets in." Sabina lifted her face to the breeze.

A small fishing craft hoisted a square sail. It grabbed a damp gust, billowed, and lifted the boat, skimming across the waves. It maneuvered between two larger vessels, past the harbor walls and enclosure into the open sea.

She looked out blankly and thought of Marcus as the boat disappeared. A hollow emptiness lingered in her chest, even though Marcus had sailed days ago.

"From happy to sad so rapidly," Portia noted.

"Marcus sailed for Rome before I could give him my answer."

"While you were saving Apollos?"

Sabina nodded. A tear trickled down her cheek. She pulled her hand from Portia's and wiped it away. Her throat tightened. "I'm not sorry Apollos is free."

"Didn't Marcus say he'd be back in six months?"

"He sails home to an arranged marriage."

"Oh, Sabina," the older woman wrapped her arms around Sabina's shoulder. Sabina melted into Portia's comforting embrace.

"I'm glad Livia asked us to meet her here. I used to run around these docks as a child, snooping through the stalls selling wares from unknown lands and strange people. Amisi would be wild with worry. She isn't speaking to me." Sabina pulled away and sniffed.

"Life isn't all bad."

Portia chuckled, then sobered. "You have no idea why Livia wanted to see us?"

"She refused to tell me."

"That girl is full of surprises," Portia said.

Sabina laughed again. "She is indeed. I wonder if Valerius appreciates that it was she, a young woman who wouldn't have met his spiritual standards, who provided the evidence that condemned him."

"Valerius hired Vibius Basus, the same lawyer I had engaged in exonerating Apollos," Portia said.

"I'm glad Apollos didn't need him." Sabina stopped smiling, a sickening hollow gnawed at her gut. "You said Vibius Basus always wins for his clients."

Portia nodded. "You haven't heard? Valerius's influential patrons purchased his innocence. Valerius is a free man again."

"Then my family remains vulnerable. Valerius could charge my father with arresting him on false evidence. There is no one my father can call to testify against Valerius. Not John, who is in hiding, or Apollos, who is the leader of a Christian church, or me."

"Valerius denied all Christian loyalties. He protects himself," Portia said.

"And Livia's witness wouldn't hold up against Valerius, a male Roman citizen. He committed the perfect crime," Sabina lamented.

"Not perfect. You exposed Valerius."

"My father stopped Valerius's plot." Sabina tried to smile, but the mood of the day had changed.

"It wasn't just your father. Your deduction, curiosity, and perseverance, your God-given talents stopped Valerius."

"God-given talents?" Sabina leveled her gaze at Portia. "My father believes I'm only capable of managing his house, hosting dinner parties, and tending gardens."

Portia wrinkled her nose. "I do not understand your love of gardening. It doesn't make it any less a skill." Portia dusted imaginary soil from her chalk-white hands, today adorned with three gold rings and precisely manicured and painted nails. "Do not discount saving Apollos because your father hasn't praised you."

"Piecing together a burnt manuscript isn't a skill."

"Are you sure?"

"Benjamin's gift of transcribing was a calling; Apollos's calling is knowledge of God's Word. You host our church and run a business. Others have children, families."

"You asked God for a purpose."

"I asked for a husband, children, and a home of my own. When Marcus came to Ephesus, I knew God had answered my prayers."

Portia shook her head. "I often instruct God on what is best for me. And I usually regret it when He listens."

"Is a husband too much to ask for?" Sabina let go of Portia's hand.

Portia lifted an eyebrow and tilted her head. "Would you have taken the risks you did with a husband or babies at home?"

Sabina shook her head, picturing the horror of Benjamin's death. "A husband would not have allowed me. It's not easy."

"If you had taken the easy way, we'd be burying Apollos today."

Sabina shivered, not wanting to think of how close that possibility came. "How is he?"

"He is improving. I insisted he recuperate at my house. Feya tends to his cough and administers medicine daily. He isn't strong enough for long visits, but he wants to say thank you. Can you stop by before you go home?"

"I would love to see him." Sabina lifted her face, relishing the warmth of the sun against her skin. Apollos was free, and the peace she found in deciding to let go of the past, her mother's and Apollos's, and focusing on the present lessened the melancholy of Marcus leaving.

"Have you heard any more about Davos and Marcella?"

"My father said Davos awaits the arrival of our new proconsul. Rome considers counterfeiters one of its most heinous criminals. Punishment for embezzling from the temple must placate the protector goddess of our city."

"Artemis will seek retribution on all the citizens of Ephesus for permitting such dishonor," Portia said.

"Davos will be made an example to others. The authorities will arrange a gruesome death by the beasts during the next festival games. His life will be his final sacrifice to the goddess."

"And Marcella and Davonia?" Portia asked.

"Marcella pleaded for her daughter. She couldn't convince the courts of her innocence or that she was ignorant of Davo's counterfeiting. Both women were convicted. They will be auctioned at the slave market in Rome." Sabina wiped the tears from her cheeks. "I couldn't help them."

Portia put her arm around Sabina. "First, you're questioning if you should have become involved, and now, you're complaining you didn't help more." Portia waved to a girl standing next to a small vessel. "There's Livia."

Livia waved them over, jumping up and down. "I'm going home, back to Corinth." She pointed to the ship moored at a nearby dock.

Sabina forced her mouth to stay closed until she had recovered from her surprise. "I'm happy for you." Sabina calculated the paltry jumble of coins Livia had shown her.

Livia clasped her hands together. "I asked you here to say thank you."

Sabina shook her head in confusion.

"For paying my passage." Livia's brows knit in consternation.

Sabina glanced at the ship then back to Livia. "No, I didn't." Her mind ran through different scenarios and could find only one, improbable as it appeared. "Perhaps your mother-in-law paid for it?" Had she misjudged the older woman?

"Don't be a goose. I didn't dare tell her I was leaving. She'd lock me up." Livia rolled her eyes at Sabina. "I thought because I returned the coin that you bought the…it doesn't matter." Livia's dismay evaporated.

In the next second, she clapped her hands in childish delight and danced around in a circle. "I get to go home, and my parents will be sooo happy."

"And surprised," said Portia scrutinizing Sabina's perplexed expression.

"It's wonderful." Sabina hugged the young woman. "And I am glad we get to say goodbye." She had doubted Livia, yet time and again, Livia had proven her character. Benjamin had not trusted Livia out of blind faith but a relationship built on honesty and trust. This girl, this young woman, earned Benjamin's confidence, and Sabina suspected his love as well. "May God bless you and keep you."

"And may His face shine upon you," Livia responded as a sailor helped her onto the boat.

"A most unlikely heroine," Portia said, standing on the dock and waving until the small ship unfurled its sails and navigated west out of the harbor toward the Aegean Sea. Corinth waited on the other side.

Sabina turned as soon as the ship glided out of sight. "Didn't you tell me a vendor is selling a lily and myrrh perfume from Egypt?"

"I bought some last week. It is hypnotizing. You should purchase some, but I can't leave Apollos alone for long. He refuses to rest. He's almost as stubborn as John," Portia said in an exasperated huff.

Sabina caught a flash of a striped black, tan, and red robe out of the corner of her eye. It disappeared amongst the crowd trudging up the street in the direction of the theater. "Can I meet you at your house?"

Portia winked at her. "You see something you like?"

"Something I'd like to check out," Sabina craned her neck, trying to catch sight of the robe's owner.

"Don't forget to stop by." Portia waved as she turned toward her home.

Sabina dashed ahead, weaving through a group of sailors and a knot of young slaves returning home with their purchases of the musky-smelling daily catch. She sprinted, catching up to Yechiel, entirely out of breath. He did not slow down as she dropped into step beside him. "I…" She panted. "Just said goodbye to Livia."

Yechiel grunted indifferently.

"It was strange. Livia received a ticket for passage back to Corinth. I thought the only way for her to get home would be to use the gold coin Benjamin had given her."

"You told me she gave the coin away."

"She did. I hid it behind a brick in an alleyway."

"You hid a gold coin?" Yechiel shook his head and smirked. "That sounds like something you would do."

"Livia took me to the same alley I saw you enter the first time we went to the scriptorium."

"And your point is?"

"She told me Benjamin couldn't spend the coin because it didn't belong to him. I think the coin was yours." He glanced at her but said nothing. "I believe you retrieved the coin from behind the brick, and you bought Livia's passage home."

"Speculating as usual?"

"I have the second coin."

He stopped and spun around. "You had it the entire time." Anger radiated throughout his body.

"I meant to tell you the first day we met, and then you were rude, and…I've been meaning…"

Yechiel's hand outstretched. "It doesn't belong to you."

"I didn't intend to keep it." She pulled out her coin pouch, dumped a few coins into her palm, and picked out the gold coin. She put the others back. She ran her finger over the coin's pressed characters. "I was wondering what kind of coins they are. Why did Benjamin have them? And why did he tell Livia they couldn't spend the coins?" She squeezed the coin tightly in her fist.

"Do you ever stop asking questions?"

"Do you ever answer them? The coins were the solution to finding Valerius. Benjamin first trusted Livia with the coin, and this coin convinced Livia she could trust me. It's because of her we solved the murder." She looked at her closed fist. "Here." She opened her fingers and dropped the coin into his outstretched hand. "I'm sorry I didn't return it right away."

Yechiel harrumphed and put the coin in a bag and began walking again. "It is important I have recovered them."

"You are welcome."

Yechiel stopped. He took a deep breath, his shoulders rising and falling. He shuffled his feet but did not turn around. "Benjamin's banishment turned out fortuitous for me."

"What?"

"I am answering your questions…your intrusive questions. Benjamin's departure made him a useful intermediary between our segregated Jewish community and the outside world. I recruited Benjamin for a role in a select brotherhood."

"Select?"

Yechiel turned to face her, his eyes intent. "Clandestine. Our members are sworn to secrecy and to honor any demand accompanied by one of these coins."

"So, Livia knew her wish to go home would be granted if she returned the coin?"

"No, Benjamin wouldn't have told anyone that. I have no idea why Benjamin gave her the coin, but I know he expected it back. Livia returned the coin. And she received her reward."

"She could have purchased her passage with the coin."

"If Livia had done that, she would have found herself in one of Emperor Domitian's prisons."

"I thought you were answering my questions, not confusing me."

Yechiel leaned forward, his mouth pursed as if debating her trustworthiness. He retrieved the coin from the bag and held it up, pointing to the stamped image. "This is the three-pronged rod of Aaron, the high priest, and Moses's brother. It symbolizes the Jewish authority over Judea, the land promised to my people. The coin was minted in the Jerusalem temple during the rebellion, before Titus and his legions destroyed Jeruselum, twenty-six years ago. The surviving coins now symbolize the Jewish resistance against Rome. Our vow to retake our land. It is unsafe to own one."

"I thought Benjamin no longer practiced Judaism."

341

"Benjamin insisted that worshiping the Christ did not change his loyalties. He would always be Jewish. He believed your Christ will return when we rebuild the temple in Jerusalem."

"We eagerly pray for His return."

"Regaining Jerusalem is the first step to reestablish our sovereignty and an independent Israel free of Roman rule."

She lifted her chin slightly and took a slow breath. "I see. Betrayal, sedition, subversion, pick whatever word you like." She raised one eyebrow, biting the inside of her cheek, almost afraid to ask more, but her curiosity, always her Achilles heel, wouldn't relent. "And the coins?"

"If the Romans had found you or Livia possessing one, you would have been charged with treason and tortured to reveal your subversive associates."

A beat of startled silence passed between them. "Why are you telling me this?"

"You returned the coin. I am honoring your request and answering your questions. Benjamin and I used the hollowed-out space behind the brick to exchange communications."

"Between members of your brotherhood?"

"Yes, but mostly I delivered greetings from my heartbroken mother to her youngest son."

"And as long as Benjamin kept the coins a secret…"

"There was no risk to him. He merely passed on messages. When I found the destruction to his room and the coins missing, I thought somebody had discovered his involvement in the brotherhood," Yechiel said, his tone thick with underlying guilt. "I agonized, believing I had caused his death." His voice dropped a note lower, relief evident in it. "Thank you for finding Benjamin's killer."

"We found Valerius together," Sabina said quietly. "Did you hear the authorities released him from jail?" Her voice rose with unrestrained anger.

"I'm not surprised. Valerius has powerful friends." Yechiel nodded, his voice calm. "His profession gives him intimate access to the secrets and political intrigues of Ephesus. You don't collaborate on legal documents for wealthy officials without becoming indispensable to them."

"Christians are powerless to charge Valerius with the murder. You could demand justice for Benjamin's death." Sabina's forehead creased in frustration.

"We won't." He shrugged. "Our community avoided blame in the Jewish revolt against Rome, but a shadow of suspicion remains over all Jews. A murder trial drawing the attention of the governor would not be in our best interest."

Sabina looked at Yechiel's coin purse and the seditious gold coin. He said, *avoided blame.* He didn't say *they weren't involved* in the revolt. She thought of the brotherhood and their plans for overthrowing Roman rule. "After demanding Apollos's execution for Benjamin's murder, you don't seem upset that Valerius has escaped punishment."

"That question I am not obliged to answer. Shalom, Sabina, go with God's blessings." Yechiel spun around and strode away, his robe flapping in the breeze.

"God's peace to you." Sabina watched until he melded into the stream of pedestrians, vendor carts, and litters. After days of doggedly searching for Benjamin's killer, she was confused by his reaction. She was furious that Valerius had evaded justice.

She shook her head, turned, and retraced her steps to Portia's house to visit a recuperating Apollos.

Portia ushered Sabina into the garden. A young man she didn't recognize nodded a quiet goodbye to Apollos and exited opposite them. Apollos reclined on a couch with dozens of pillows supporting him and stacks of blankets piled on top. Sweat glistened on his face.

"Are you well?" Sabina asked, kissing him on each cheek.

"I am being smothered in love and blankets. My cough is nearly gone. Thank you for coming."

"And John?"

"I am told he is much better. He and Prochorus have moved to another location."

343

"Hidden from my father."

"Yes, well, Portia told me we have him to thank as well as you. You took great risks to free me. I thank you."

Sabina blushed, remembering her original motivation to speak to her father. In her quest to prove Apollos's innocence, she had chosen to leave those initial questions unanswered and buried in the past. She shook her head, changing the subject. "Valerius has been released from jail."

"I heard. Unfortunately for Valerius, his freedom did not last long."

"He has been arrested again?"

"He has been murdered. A messenger just informed me the authorities suspect poison but cannot prove it."

Sabina blinked rapidly, digesting the news. "When? Where? Who would want him dead?" The second she asked the last question, a list of suspects crowded her mind: her father, tying up a threatening loose end? Yechiel, obtaining justice? A disillusioned devotee, failing in their pursuit of godhood? A disgruntled beneficiary of one of Valerius's wills?

"I was told Rufus has taken Valerius's place as the next prophet and is reproducing Valerius's writings for a growing band of devotees."

"Benjamin dies, but Valerius's deceits continue."

"Valerius is not the first nor the last to propagate the oldest lie in the world." Apollos shifted under the coverings and threw off one of his blankets. "Valerius believed he could become a god. Satan promised Adam that as a reward for rebelling against God. Man would fall up into heaven, not down into hell. Humans will strive and die for that untruth until Christ returns as the one and only God."

"Is there no way to stop their followers?"

"John's letter combats their heresy. John had it copied and sent to the bishops and congregations in Asia, Italy, Syria, Greece, Africa, Egypt, and Judea."

"John is ninety years old. He cannot repudiate heresies forever."

"God delivered His eternal refute through John's letter."

"That will not stop false teachers like Valerius from creeping into the church," Sabina said.

344

"No, but it will stop false scripture from deceiving anyone willing to search God's standard of truth. The Lord has not spoken in secret nor riddles." Conviction filled Apollos's voice.

"Satan knows the power of God is in His Holy Word," Portia chimed in, carrying a tray of fruit and nuts and a pitcher. "He will attack it, adding to it, deleting parts, distorting it." She put the tray down and picked up Apollos's discarded blanket, tucking it in tightly around him.

Apollos smiled, indulging the pampering. "The council of bishops is collecting funds to commission hundreds of copies of the Gospels to get them into the seeking hands of our people. The church is growing, God builds, and His word spreads."

"'Heaven and earth shall pass away, but my words shall not pass away,'" Sabina quoted.

"Speaking of a growing church," Portia sat down at Apollos's feet, "have you convinced Sabina yet? Am I getting my female *diakonos?*"

"I was getting to that," Apollos said, shifting to shuffle out from under his mound. He looked at Portia's eyebrows raised in warning. He settled back under the blanket. "Our list of deacons has shortened to zero."

"Magnus?" Sabina asked.

"After reflecting on the behavior required of a deacon, Magnus withdrew his name…for the time being."

Portia poured a beverage from the pitcher and handed it to Apollos. "Drink. You need liquids." She turned to Sabina. "I would like to nominate you for deaconess. I need help."

"I have no experience caregiving or comforting or soothing or any of the things you do."

"And you are not allowed to follow the same path God laid out for me. You would step on my toes." Portia didn't bother hiding her grin.

"We are all blessed with different gifts." Apollos put down his empty cup.

"I just had this conversation with Portia." Sabina waved him off.

"Are you arguing you didn't help me?" Apollos said. "I cannot think of another woman who has the courage, the intelligence, and the willingness to take the risks you did to save me."

"Those aren't very—"

"Common. I agree," Apollos cut her off with a wave of his hand. "Immerse yourself in Scripture. Let God counsel you."

"But be prepared for an unexpected answer." Portia pursed her lips and winked.

Sabina smiled. "Speaking of unexpected, I am going to try and find my sisters."

"What sisters?" Portia squealed.

Apollos was racked by a fit of coughing.

"You need to rest." Portia pointed to Apollos. "And that's from someone who has the gift of caregiving; it is time for your nap."

"I have one more item to discuss with Sabina," he said. "I almost forgot." Apollos fumbled under the blankets.

"You promised not to wear yourself out if I invited her here," Portia lectured.

"I can come back tomorrow." Sabina rose.

"No, please sit. John hopes to offer his gratitude in person. But until then, and in appreciation, he wanted you to have this." Apollos handed her a small box. No, not a box. The hard leather cover bound fragile sheets of papyrus together.

"A codex?" She fingered the pages in wonder.

"John's new scribe said it is much more practical than a scroll. I'm not sure people will agree."

Sabina opened the codex and read the words. "'That which was from the beginning, which we have heard, which we have seen with our eyes, which we have looked upon, and our hands have handled, of the Word of life; For the life was manifested, and we have seen it, and bear witness.'" It was John's letter.

Apollos patted her hand. "A copy of the letter Benjamin died for. The letter you helped save."

"I am overcome with joy." Sabina smiled wanly. She stood up and kissed Apollos goodbye, anxious to get home. She had much to think about, so many questions, and now a way to answer them. Grinning, she clutched the codex. She always loved a good book.

BIBLIOGRAPHY

All historical novels have pitfalls when attempting to recreate a world from surviving poetry, myth, diaries, inscriptions, graffiti, coins, maps, art, and foundations of cities two thousand years old and older. We piece together ancient family life, beliefs, social structure, justice, and injustices, through the colored glass of our culture. Research is essential and imperfect. My non-fiction research library and list of experts are growing. For those who'd like to delve into this fascinating era, I include a few of the resources used to ground this novel in current accurate and reliable details. Personal travel, the Bible, sermons, *Biblical Archeology Review*, *The Great Courses* video series, travel videos, and numerous websites contributed.

If you have a favorite first-century resource you would like to share, please contact me at liisaeyerly.com or liisaeyerly@gmail.com.

WORKS CITED

Apicius, and Joseph Dommers Vehling. *Cookery and Dining in Imperial Rome: A Bibliography, Critical Review, and Translation of the Ancient Book Known as Apicius de Re Coquinaria: Now for the First Time Rendered into English*. New York: Dover Publications, 1977.

De Franciscis, Alfonso and I. Bragantini. *Guide with Reconstructions: Pompeii, Herculaneum, and Capri, Past and Present*, 5th ed. Roma, Vision, 2016.

Erdemgil, Selahattin. *Ephesus.* Istanbul: Net Books, 1991.

Eusebius of Caesarea Bishop of Caesarea, and Paul L Maier. *Eusebius, the Church History: A New Translation with Commentary.* Grand Rapids, MI: Kregel Publications, 1999.

Fox, Robin Lane. *Pagans and Christians.* New York: Harper Collins, 1986.

Gryson, Roger. *The Ministry of Women in the Early Church.* Collegeville, MN: The Liturgical Press, 1980.

Koester, Helmut. *Ephesos, Metropolis of Asia: An Interdisciplinary Approach to Its Archaeology, Religion, and Culture.* Cambridge: Harvard Divinity School, 2004.

Josephus, Flavius, and Paul L Maier. *Josephus, the Essential Works: A Condensation of Jewish Antiquities and the Jewish War.* Grand Rapids, MI: Kregel Publications, 1994.

Shelton, Jo-Ann. *As the Romans Did: A Source Book in Roman Social History,* 2nd ed. New York: Oxford University Press, 1998.

Trebilco, Paul. *The Early Christians in Ephesus from Paul to Ignatius.* Grand Rapids, MI: William B. Eerdmans Publishing Company, 2008.

Additional background information and book discussion questions can be found at liisaeyerly.com/books/

ABOUT THE AUTHOR

Liisa Eyerly is the author of two Christian mystery novels set in ancient Ephesus. She is a retired elementary teacher and school librarian but will never retire from inciting the thrill of reading in all ages.

She has lived in some of the most beautiful areas of the US. The passion for exploring new places and connecting with people began there and inspired her writing. Her publishing career started after getting married, teaching, raising three children, opening a small business, closing her small business, and finally getting serious about writing. She is a relentless questioner (a trait not appreciated by her husband) and a novice student of Christian apologetics. Her writing goals are to be entertaining, thought-provoking, and surprising.

Book discussion questions can be found at liisaeyerly.com/books.

ROOTS REAWAKENED

Will the reignition of an old flame, bring Justine to the brink of hope or destruction?

More great books from...
CrossRiverMedia.com

Swept into Destiny

Maggie Gatlan may be a Southern belle on the outside, but is a rebel on the inside. Ben McConnell is enchanted by Maggie's beauty and fiery spirit, but for him the South represents the injustice and deprivation he left behind in Ireland. As the country divides and Ben joins the Union, Maggie and Ben are forced to call each other enemies. Will their love survive or die on the battlefield of South against North?

Surviving Carmelita

It was Josie's hands on the wheel, her foot on the pedal. Her fault. Now, sweet Carmelita will never see her fifth birthday. Where do you run when your world implodes and you can't function? Josie leaves her Chicago suburban home to stay with a cousin in Key West, unaware her journey is guided by an unseen hand and that a trailer park pastor, a battered horse, a pregnant teen, and a mysterious beachcomber might set her on the path toward redemption.

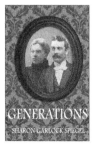

Generations

When Edward Garlock was sober, he was a kind, generous, hard-working farmer, providing for his wife and growing family. But when he drank, he transformed into a unpredictable bully, capable of absolute cruelty. When he stepped into a revival tent in the early 1900s the Holy Spirit got ahold of him, changing not only his life, but the future of thousands of others through Edward.

Claiming Her Inheritance

A shooting, a stampede and
a snakebite.... will she survive?

Available in bookstores and from online retailers.

Even more great books from...
CrossRiverMedia.com

LOTTIE'S GIFT

She's a little girl with a big gift. Lottie Braun has enjoyed a happy childhood in rural Iowa with her father and older sister. But the quiet, nearly idyllic life she enjoyed as a child ended with tragedy and a secret that tore the two sisters apart. Forty years later, Lottie is a world-class pianist with a celebrated career and an empty personal life. One sleepless night, she allows herself to remember and discovers that memories, once allowed, are difficult to suppress. Will she ever find her way home?

WILTED DANDELIONS

Rachael Rothburn just wants to be a missionary to the Native Americans out west, but the missionary alliance says she can't go unless she is married. When Dr. Jonathan Wheaton, another missionary hopeful, offers her a marriage of convenience, she quickly agrees. But she soon finds that his jealousy may be an even greater threat than the hostile Indians and raging rivers they face along the way.

ROAD TO DEER RUN

The year is 1777 and the war has already broken the heart of nineteen-year-old Mary Thomsen. Her brother was killed by the King's army, so when she stumbles across a wounded British soldier, she isn't sure if she should she help him or let him die, cold and alone. Severely wounded, Daniel Lowe wonders if the young woman looking down at him is an angel or the enemy. Need and compassion bring them together, but will the bitterness of war keep them apart?

Books that ignite your faith.

If you enjoyed this book, will you consider sharing it with others?

- Please mention the book on Facebook, Instagram, Pinterest, or another social media site.

- Recommend this book to your small group, book club, and workplace.

- Head over to Facebook.com/CrossRiverMedia, 'Like' the page and post a comment as to what you enjoyed the most.

- Pick up a copy for someone you know who would be challenged or encouraged by this message.

- Write a review on your favorite ebook platform.

- To learn about our latest releases subscribe to our newsletter at CrossRiverMedia.com.

Made in the USA
Monee, IL
06 March 2022

92391427R00197